THE WISHING STAR

THE WISHING STAR

THE STARLIGHT TRILOGY
BOOK ONE

Marian Wells

BETHANY HOUSE PUBLISHERS
MINNEAPOLIS, MINNESOTA 55438
A Division of Bethany Fellowship, Inc.

Published by Bethany House Publishers
A Division of Bethany Fellowship, Inc.
6820 Auto Club Road, Minneapolis, Minnesota 55438

Printed in the United States of America

Library of Congress Cataloging in Publication Data

Wells, Marian, 1931-
   The wishing star.

   I. Title.
PS3573.E4927W57   1985   813'.54   85-21469
ISBN 0-87123-817-9 (pbk.)

MARIAN WELLS was born in the state of Utah, and attended Northwest Nazarene College. Though *The Wishing Star* is fictional, the author has thoroughly researched and documented the historical events surrounding the story. Two of her other books, *The Wedding Dress* and its sequel, *With This Ring*, are written in a similar style.

PREFACE

The War of 1812 was America's second war for independence, as if this young country must stamp its foot and remind the world once more that it had to be totally free. America would not, after all her struggles, endure fetters of any kind. When the first European foot touched American soil, it stepped forward in an enormous stride toward freedom. And freedom was the banner flung over all, forever.

But people can be trusted with freedom only when truth is coupled with liberty. Truth can best be discovered in freedom, but sometimes people unwittingly allow themselves to be enslaved in their search for truth.

After this second war, as America stirred and stretched, rumbles of freedom began in the churches. From 1814 to 1830, many of America's old mainline churches were split apart, each intent upon establishing its own freedom—and its own view of truth. And during this time, just before the outbreak of genuine revival, large numbers of new religions emerged.

America began to see herself possessing a unique position in God's sight, providing a pattern of freedom and holiness for all people, becoming a leader for the world. Just as people reached out for land during the westward expansion, they also reached for new experiences and new ideas. Rapt attention was given to the second coming of Christ, and nowhere did this doctrine stimulate more anticipation and frenzied excitement than in the new religions.

It was this independent society which becomes the setting for our story. The daughter of a poor family living in the eastern states, Jenny Timmons' earliest years were shaped by poverty and superstition. Her mother held an unformed but earnest awareness of God. Most often these beliefs puzzled and frightened Jenny, perhaps because even in her formative years she was allowing herself to be manipulated by another force. All about her she saw curious people pressing out into the unknown spirit world.

Just as Jenny was nearing her twelfth birthday in South Bainbridge, New York, she met a young man who held an uncanny fascination for her. Thus began her early dabblings in the occult, and thus, as well, her wanderings in one of the new religions.

Jenny's story is set in the framework of a historical novel—historical in the sense that main events, locations, and some characters actually appear in records of the period, and fictional in development and style. Jenny herself is representative of young women of that time who were caught up in the tide of interest in the supernatural and the new religions.

CHAPTER 1

Screaming with pain, Jenny dodged the razor strap that snapped at her legs. As her father reeled toward her, she dashed across the splintery floor, leaped through the open door, and with a cry of terror fled for the woods.

Still sobbing, heedless of danger, she ran between the broken plow and jagged pieces of firewood. Finally the searing pain in her side slowed her. Gasping, Jenny cast a fearful look behind her. The sagging gray shack across the field blurred before her eyes. She wiped away her tears and peered again.

The doorway was dark. If Pa were there, she would see the red of his dirty old shirt. If Ma were standing in that spot, there would be the light square of her apron. Jenny leaned against the maple that marked the edge of the Timmons' field. Nearly twelve years old, small and thin, she snuggled against the rough bark of the tree. She knew her size, the dark tumble of hair, and her eyes colored like the woodland creatures made her nearly invisible to those in the house.

When her ragged breathing had calmed, she looked around. The patch of broken ground lying between her and the littered farmyard was filled with rustling brown cornstalks and decaying pumpkins. She felt all brown and withery, too.

Her mother's sad face rose in her mind. Jenny's hands curled; she pressed them against her bony chest to keep the aching sobs from coming past her throat. How badly she wanted to throw herself into her mother's arms, to feel the warmth and the love that must be there. *I'll be good, Ma. I promise I'll be good!* The ache subsided, but nothing was changed, either inside or out.

She squared her shoulders and focused on the door where her father soon would be standing. Rubbing her tattered sleeve across her nose and then sniffing sharply, she jutted her lower lip out in a way she wouldn't dare if she were facing him. "Pa," she muttered, even now not daring to say the words above a whisper, "you're nothin' but a drunken old sot. If it weren't for Ma's naggin' and fetchin' in the ladies' babies, we'd all starve. And you doin' little 'sides tippin' the bottle and yellin' at Tom for not gettin' at the plowing."

She shivered as the October afternoon poked chilly fingers through her thin dress. Wrapping her skinny arms around herself, she shook back her heavy dark hair and shifted from one bare foot to the other. Her eyes moved constantly, checking the house, the door, wondering how long it would take Pa to leave and weave his way down the road to the tavern in town. "If he don't go pretty soon, I'm gonna freeze.—But better that than the strap again."

She spied a shadow approaching the house from down the road—her brother Tom. Jenny watched him leave the path and head for the door.

Conscious now of the welts on her legs, she hopped from one foot to the other. A gasping sigh ended in a hiccup. "Poor Tom, you'll get it now," she muttered. Tom was seventeen—old enough to be called a man. But the droop of his shoulders said it all: he would never be a man as long as Pa was there to swing that razor strap.

She shivered and looked down at her legs. The white welts had turned red and begun to bleed. Miserably she watched as Tom crossed the yard and leaped the high step into the shack. She could guess what would happen next.

With a sob, Jenny turned and limped into the darkening woods. "He'll be coming," she whispered. "Pa'll send him after me. Like as not, Tom'll regret fetchin' me as much as I'll regret goin'. Next thing, Pa'll be jawin' me again for takin' the book; after that I'll get strapped 'cause I run out on him. I'll get twice beat for nothin'."

Weariness seeped through every part of Jenny's body, but she forced herself into a spiritless stride, winding her way into the forest toward that quiet, shadowed glen known only to Tom and herself. As she walked her thoughts dulled. She knew only the moss underfoot and the occasional sharp prick of twigs and dried leaves against her bare feet.

At last she stopped on the rim of a bowl-shaped depression in the forest floor. She trembled, listening for footsteps. But the quietness satisfied her.

She stood peering into the shadows beneath her. Some said such holes were Indian diggings, but now it was moss-carpeted, crowded with young hickory and elm. It was a place to hide and, sometimes, to dream.

She wiped her damp face, but her breath still caught at her aching throat in ragged sobs. Somewhere a twig snapped. With a quick jump, Jenny launched herself into the middle of the hollow and burrowed into a pile of wind-tumbled leaves.

She held her breath, listening. Finally, cradled by the quietness and growing shadows, she dared relax against her pillow of acrid leaves. She knew those gray-brown leaves were nearly the shade of her eyes, and somehow that knowledge made her feel secure, like a creature of the forest.

Overhead one crack of dusky sky was visible through the arch of trees. It wasn't dark enough for stars yet, but no matter—it was worth a try. Jenny whispered, "Star light, star bright, first star I see tonight, wish I may, wish I might, have the wish I wish tonight." For a moment she waited wistfully. If only, just once, that distant star would wink in response, telling her she was heard. She needed to believe there were good things ahead. Since the day she had learned to read, the world of books had opened the door of hope, but sometimes the hope grew dim.

Jenny sighed, but before she had time to escape into a distant world of castles and thrones, bowing servants and halls filled with unending tables of food, she heard the crunch of Tom's boots. Only half hoping he wouldn't guess her here, she pushed leaves about her shoulders and waited.

"Jen," he called. His boots crunched to the rim of her hiding place. "I know you're there, so say so."

"So," she muttered and waited for him to slide down to her. "Pa sent you?"

He nodded. "Whatcha been up to now?" His voice was harsh and impatient, but the hand that reached for her hair was gentle. His calloused hand under her chin forced it upward.

While the aching misery seeped back into Jenny, she studied her brother's face. Beneath the rough cap of tow hair, his pale gray eyes shone like bright marbles in his rough-hewn, wind-burned face. She saw the gentleness in his eyes, and knew that part of that gentleness for her was because of Pa. Tom accepted their lot, at least on the outside, but she couldn't. She muttered, "You're not like Pa, never."

He sighed, "Ya poor little urchin, you're scrawny black and white like a baby skunk. Times I wish you were, then Pa'd leave you alone." He ran his hand across her shoulders and arms while he studied her face. "Pa's drunk. You're too little to remember him when he was different." His face brightened. "But, Jen, it's all gonna change. Not having money and a chance to get ahead has been makin' him this way."

"Tom, you're tetched," Jenny retorted. "Every penny he's had has gone to the tavern in South Bainbridge. You know every cent Ma's earned for fetchin' the babies into the world has gone there too. Now he's stormin' like it's her fault a real doctor's moved into town and does all the fetchin'."

She paused and studied his face suspiciously. His grin made her uneasy; he'd been involved in shenanigans in the past. Slowly she said, "I don't mind you fetchin' a stray chicken home, but I mind you gettin' caught and feeling the strap like I did." Her hand crept down to her bare leg and Tom pulled her up onto his knees.

His voice crooned comfort as he gently examined the welts. Jenny fought tears and squared her shoulders. "There weren't no call, either; I was just lookin' at his old book."

"The green one, the witching one. Jenny, you know he's smacked you for that before! Why do ya get into it? I can't even read it, and neither can you." His eyes were mildly curious. She moved impatiently. How could you explain it to one like Tom? She knew how he was prone to take whatever life pushed at him.

"I can so read, Tom. You quit treatin' me like a little baby. I'm nearly twelve, or will be come January. There's even littler ones pushin' me out of my place."

"Just two," he replied. Tom was cuddling her close in his warm, rough arms.

With a sigh of contentment she snuggled in. "Tell me about the Indians makin' these holes. About the treasure buried deep down. Tom, what does it take to get down to the money and such?"

Tom got to his feet, sliding Jenny to the ground. "I don't know, but I sure aim to find out. That's one of the good things I have in mind. Come along, or we'll both feel the strap."

"You didn't say what you're up to." Jenny stood up. Her legs were stinging; oozing blood had clotted on the welts. After taking one painful step she sat down again.

Tom studied her for a moment. "I'll have to carry you then," he warned. She shook her head and got up. When she was standing, Tom started to speak, then cocked his head to listen. "I hear something, and I'm guessin' it's Pa comin' after the two of us. Let's head down the trail and come out on the other side of town. 'Twill give him time to forget, or get drunk. Quick!" Grasping her hand, he hurried her deeper into the woods.

Jenny trotted after Tom, trying to ignore the pain in her legs. When the trail rounded a hill, Tom suddenly stopped. Jenny stumbled into him and gasped with alarm. In front of them a shadowy figure, crowned in white, crouched in the middle of the trail. "Ghost!" she gasped, reaching for Tom.

"Hallo," Tom called. "Fancy seein' you here." Jenny scooted closer to Tom as the large figure moved. A face emerged as he rose to his feet. He shook himself and came toward them.

Jenny tilted her head backward and studied the figure. "Why, you're just a young'un, but 'bout the biggest thing I've ever seen."

He blinked slowly as if just awakening, then courteously removed his white hat. His bright blonde hair seemed full of sunshine, and his blue eyes sparkled as he grinned at both of them.

"A prince," she murmured. "But where's your steed? And

what's that?" She jabbed at the tattered white object. The hat flew out of his hand, and when it struck the ground a stone rolled out from the crown.

Jenny poked at it with her bare foot. "I'd expect a toad or an elf, but an old rock—"

In a flash he grabbed the rock and shoved it into his pocket. He still smiled, but now his eyes were cold as he bent down to her level. "Little girl, you're as ugly as something found under a rock."

"She's my sister," Tom explained. The fellow turned at the recognition of Tom's voice, and Jenny watched the careless, happy grin again claim his face. "My friend!" he exclaimed. "Have you settled your mind to join us?"

Tom cast a quick look at Jenny and nodded. "I'd be a fool to do otherwise."

The stranger turned toward Jenny, warning, "Now, keep it quiet; there's no profit if we're including the whole village in the scheme." Jenny stopped studying the length and breadth of him and focused her attention on his face.

Eyeing the bright hair and sharply arching nose that dominated his pale face, she demanded, "Tom, who is he?"

Tom touched her shoulder, "I told you. Remember the silver? We're gonna be rich, then Pa—" She moved her shoulders impatiently. Tom turned back to the youth, saying carelessly over his shoulder, "This is Joe. That rock—he sees things and he knows where there's buried treasure that the Spaniards got tired of totin' and hid in these hills."

Jenny studied Joe curiously a moment more, and then looked at the ground. Stubbing her bare toes in the soft black soil, she thought about it all. Their dream of buried treasure didn't seem much different than the thoughts and pictures that filled her head when she was alone in the glen.

She tilted her head and looked up into the blue eyes watching her. "It's like havin' pictures in your mind and makin' them come true, isn't it?" She paused a moment. "Does sayin' it all out loud *make* it come true?"

Caution crept into Joe's expression. "Like putting a curse or a blessing on something? That's so, little girl. But you're far

too smart for the size of you." He turned abruptly to Tom and
said from the corner of his mouth, "I'll be talking to you later
when there's no threat of the news spreading." He ducked his
head and without so much as a glance at Jenny strode rapidly
out of sight.

"What was he doin' down there on the ground?"

"I'll be switched if I know." Tom's voice was perplexed. "But
I'm guessin' it has something to do with our huntin' for the
silver. Somehow that fella makes me believe he can find it."

"Just sayin' so makes it come true," Jenny mused thoughtfully. "Well, that bein' the case, I'm goin' to marry that Joe
when I grow up."

Tom threw his head back and laughed in astonishment. She
watched him silently and resentfully until he wiped his eyes.
"Now, why did you say that?" Tom was sober now, staring down
at his sister.

"It's just in my bones. And if sayin' makes it so, why, then
this'll be the way to find out."

"Jen, you're just a tyke—you've no idea what you're sayin'."
His voice was the grown-up one, the one that signaled the five
years between them, and she hated it. Giving voice to her
thoughts had cut him off from her. Her shoulders sagged.

Turning, she started down the trail. His long steps brought
him even with her, and in silence they trudged through the
woods to the far side of South Bainbridge. Avoiding the saloon
on the town's main street, they hurried on. As they neared
home from the opposite side, their steps became slow and cautious. Tom took Jenny's hand, and they walked down the lane
leading to the ramshackle farm.

As they crossed the yard the sun dropped behind the wooded
hills, and Jenny shivered. Her dreamy thoughts about the afternoon were gone; now she was conscious only of her thin dress
and throbbing legs. After a quick glance at her, Tom stepped
through the door of the cabin.

Jenny held her breath until she heard the relief in his voice.
"Pa's gone." She heard her mother's rocking chair creak, and
Jenny leaped through the door.

"Ma!" Jenny crowded as near as she dared without touching

her. Ma didn't much like being touched. "I didn't mean no harm." Deepening lines creased her mother's face and darkness shrouded her eyes. Jenny's own throat was aching. She shifted her feet, still hesitating, wanting desperately to say and hear the things she needed.

But she swallowed the painful tears and studied her mother, the weary droop to her thin shoulders, the streaks of gray in her hair.

Ma turned from Jenny to Tom, peering through the shadows of the room to fasten on him as if grasping a sturdy oak. Tom moved uneasily. "Pa?" he questioned.

"Followed you a piece and then headed for town." She sighed and lifted the lamp to the center of the table. "Come on, young'uns. There's bread and milk for supper. I want you bedded afore . . ." Her voice trailed away, but knowing her meaning, Tom and Jenny watched silently as she moved heavily about the room, placing the dishes and lifting the jug of milk.

Suddenly her face brightened. Jenny saw the change—as if Ma had returned from a far country. It was the signal Jenny wanted. She flung herself at her mother, clasping her waist and pressing her face against the warmth. "I'm sorry." Jenny felt the rough hand on her hair and the quick gentle tug and heard the heavy sigh.

"I don't know what to do with you, child. You and him always at loggerheads." She shook her head and turned to raise her voice. "You up there, come."

Overhead scuffled feet, and Jenny looked at the ladder leading to the loft. Her sister Nancy was peering down, her face a pale oval in the dusk.

Jenny didn't need light to remind her of Nancy's blonde prettiness and dainty ways which made Jenny feel grubby and awkward. More scuffles overhead, and two more tiny pale ovals appeared beside Nancy.

Jenny watched thirteen-year-old Nancy lift Matt and push at Dorcas. Jenny's throat tightened again and she scrubbed at her eyes with her fists, quickly, before Nancy saw her. That afternoon those terrified faces had watched as the strap lifted and snapped.

"I'm the one, ain't I? It's my fault Pa's the way he is!" Jenny demanded, her voice shaky.

Ma straightened from her task of dividing the bread and stared. "Child, what's got into you?"

"Tom said I don't remember how it was before, because I was too little."

Ma looked at Tom before answering. Then, her voice dreamy, she murmured, "It was different." She sighed and shook her head. "But, no, it isn't you." For a long time she was silent, and Jenny thought she had forgotten her. Then reluctantly she said, "Could be hard times just bring out something that was there the whole time, but hid."

Finally Jenny sat down to her bowl of bread and milk, but she was watching Dorcas and Matty. Nearly two years separated them, but by their sober round faces, they could have been twins.

As she lifted the spoon, her heart was still heavy. Her mother was watching. Gently she said, "You could leave his things alone."

"I only want to read and learn."

"There's school for that. I don't read well enough to know the book. But I've heard him talk about the magic and such. I wasn't raised that way—to believe in those things. They make—" She stopped and shifted her shoulders uneasily. There was a troubled frown on her face as she slowly started again, "Maybe he's better'n you credit him. Could be he wants you to grow up knowin' the important things, and findin' a man who'll give you a good life."

She sighed and looked around the dimly lighted room. "Seems if a body looks for the good, he's bound to find it." Her fingers picked listlessly at a frayed spot on her apron. Abruptly she raised her head. "If you're bent on readin', there's my Bible. I don't know enough to read it for myself. But I know it says things that we're supposed to honor."

Jenny frowned over her mother's words, then slipped from her stool and pressed her cheek against Ma's shoulder. " 'Night, Ma. And I'll try to remember that and be lookin' for the good. Maybe just thinkin' hard and sayin' it out loud will make it be."

With one foot on the ladder, Jenny paused, wondering about all her mother had said. Why did it do any good to honor a book instead of reading it? She turned her face to the figure slumped in the circle of pale light. The question rose to her lips, but Jenny remembered that most often her asking things left Ma frowning, with questions in her eyes. Slowly she climbed the ladder.

CHAPTER 2

The South Bainbridge school was set on the edge of town in a lonesome place. Sometimes it made Jenny feel as if she were in another world. Just enough timber had been hacked out of the woods to clear a spot for the school and to pile fuel high enough for the winter.

Jenny loved the fresh wood scent of the log building; in fact, she loved nearly everything about the school—the sharp clamor of the school bell, even the musty smell of old books and damp woolen mufflers. But at times the high-spirited students made her pull in against the side of the building. There, like a stray field mouse, she watched them vent their boundless energy, twenty pairs of restless feet wearing the grasses of the field to a nub.

This October afternoon was one of the days Jenny clung to the side of the school. Dust hung like a curtain over the playground, while a gust of wind swished through the trees, tearing at the tortured soil. The wind moaning in the trees caught Jenny's attention, lifting her away from the school and the playground and filling her with a sense of utter isolation.

That wind meant winter was drawing near. Listening and watching, Jenny clenched her fists, wishing she could spread sunshine and wild roses across the field.

The shouting of the students broke through her thoughts and brought her back to the playground. Shoving away from the warm logs, she crept close to the group.

"Go, go!" rooted the students in the circle. "Amos, are ye callin' it quits? Scaredy cat!" The dust settled to reveal the victor—the new student, Joe. Jenny saw the grin on his battered lips as he flexed his arms and shoved at his sleeves.

"Come on, who's next?" he shouted. The ring of fellows eyed him cautiously as he tossed his bright hair, but no one would accept the challenge.

Jenny chuckled silently. Joe didn't seem to be much of a student, but he sure could fight.

Since that autumn day when she and Tom had discovered the twenty-year-old lad hunkered beside the trail with his face buried in his battered white hat, she had been paying sharp attention to him.

Granted, he was an on-again, off-again student. Since the day Jenny had first seen his bulk crammed between six-year-old Emily and ten-year-old Nat, with that wild beak of a nose humbled two inches from his slate, she had watched him. At first he could barely push the pencil over his sums, and her awe of him changed to scorn, particularly when she listened to him read.

But later the scorn was salted with respect when she saw him lick every youth in town. And later still her feelings were spiced with a nameless fascination as she watched Nancy bat her eyes at him and Prudence follow him about the school yard like an absolute ninny.

At this moment, the thought of those silly girls carrying extra cookies to him and offering to do his sums for him made Jenny snort with impatience. As if Mrs. Stowell wasn't feeding him right and his head didn't need to learn his own sums.

Jenny applied her scorn to Prudence, the lass who had tossed her long blonde curls, batted her eyelashes, smoothed her flowered apron, and said, "Jennifer Timmons, you are jealous!" Her eyes shrewdly surveyed Jenny and she added spitefully, "*You've* plenty of call to be. Scrawny as a scarecrow and brown as a gypsy, you are." She flounced away, swinging her skirts until her petticoats showed.

It wouldn't have been so bad, Jenny decided, thinking about it later, but the fellow who was filling in for Mr. Searles, the regular teacher, had taken it upon himself to smooth her ruffled feathers.

Just remembering had Jenny muttering to herself. "Didn't hurt, her bein' so uppity and proud, 'til he had to come and fuss over me."

At the end of this October day, Jenny was still busy thinking as she and Tom walked toward home. She found herself stripping away the pretty pictures her mind had built and facing things as they really were.

It hurt to admit that Prudence was right. Even Joe had said she was ugly. Life was bad. And Tom—she looked up at her brother and tried to see him clearly.

Tom was one of those on-again and off-again students, too. Jenny suspected he was more on-again recently because of the new fellow. "That Joe," she muttered. "Seems both of you go because of the other. Either that or it's better'n diggin' stumps in Mr. Stowell's field all day."

She turned on him. "You'd better be listenin' to Ma about forgettin' the ideas circulating. She says there's no way on this earth a man's goin' to get rich except by workin' hard at life. Tom, you know she's tryin' her best for us, not wantin' us to turn out like Pa."

"Dreamin' on rainbows," Tom said shortly as he hunched his shoulders and shuffled his feet in the leaves along the path.

"Is that it?" For a moment Jenny stopped, kicking at the leaves thoughtfully. When she looked up at Tom, she was searching his face for confirmation. "There's some who believe they can change things just by thinkin' hard and willing it so, and by makin' charms and chantin'."

"They are the ones who think they have power."

"Do they?"

"Some do, some don't." He stopped to grasp her arm. But his eyes were looking beyond her, shining as if he knew secrets. "Jenny," he whispered, "there's power out there to be had by the ones who know how to get it. Joe knows some of those things, and I intend to find out."

"Ma says there's secret things, but they're bad. Tom, Ma shivered when she said that, and I could tell she was mighty scared."

Tom turned to look at Jenny, and his eyes were very serious.

"If that's so, why doesn't she make you stay away from that green book of Pa's? She says if you must read, read that black one. But then she turns her back when you get Pa's book. I say she's scared, but she knows where the power is." His eyes were big again, staring past her.

"Tom, you best be listenin' to Ma." But he wasn't listening, and she tugged at his shirt. "Ma says everybody thinks diggin' will get him rich if he can just find a mine or treasure, but she says people dig and dig and never find a thing. She says a body needs to quit foolin' himself and settle down to pluggin' away for a living." By the time Jenny had delivered her speech they had reached home, and Tom went grinning on his way.

Jenny suspected he was proud of himself because he'd let her run on like a scolding mother. Suddenly the weight of her heavy thoughts slid away, and she was filled with a bubbling-up, running-over affection for Tom. Sometimes he was more like a friend than a brother.

When Jenny entered the cabin her father was asleep, sprawled across the bed with his mouth open. This was real life. Sometimes she needed to be reminded that make-believe wasn't real. She turned her face away to hide the fearful feelings that churned inside her.

Ma was at the table, bending over a pile of bright, new cloth. She lifted her face. "I've a dress finished for Mrs. Harper. I want you to carry it to her; we're needin' the money." She snipped at the thread. "Mighty uppity she's gettin', needin' somebody to do her sewin' for her. Last summer she was just a peddler's wife, common like the rest of us. Now she's puttin' on airs.— But never mind, we're reapin' well from her folly."

"Folly?" Jenny repeated, wondering what the word meant and why Ma used it on Mrs. Harper.

"Just hush and take it. Wrap that torn sheet over it, so you don't soil it." As Jenny reached for the heap of flowered material, Ma turned and peered at her. "Just look at you," she scolded. "Hair a mess and grubby clear to the elbows. Why can't you be like Nancy? Seems I never have to fuss about her washin' her face."

Listening to her mother scold, Jenny thought of her sister

sitting at home with a bit of sewing while she hoed in the field or hired out to the Moores when they needed a hand to pitch fodder to the hogs. In the honesty of the afternoon she still had a clear picture in her mind: Prudence with blonde curls and fair skin standing beside Jenny, weather-chapped and browned.

"I'm of a mind to grow plump and be delicate like Nancy and Prudence," she stated, "but I can't clean Mr. Moore's hog pen and come out looking like a lady."

Ma nodded her head. "And kind he is to find ways to help you earn a few pennies," she said with a sigh, touching Jenny lightly on the cheek. "You earn your keep; like as not Nancy will too with her needle. And like as not one of these days, you'll cease chasing after chickens and boys and take up the needle." She turned back to her sewing. "Now, brush your hair afore you go. Don't forget to fetch the money home safe."

Jenny brushed her hair, wrapped the dress in a scrap of clean sheeting, and pulled her mother's shawl across her shoulders.

The day had been sharp with the hint of the winter to come, and now—all too soon, it seemed—the evening shadows were tagging the heels of late afternoon.

Jenny hurried down the lane. Any excuse to go into town was a treat. If she scooted about her task, there'd be time to mosey home, to stare in the shop windows and watch the people.

For the time being she hastened her steps, passing the saloon, the dry-goods store, the sheriff's office, and the tiny little log building they called the lawyer's office.

Just as she was passing that office, studying it curiously in her usual fashion, the door flew open. She sidestepped to avoid running into the young man who rushed out in front of her.

"Oh, beg your pardon, ma'am." He spun around, then with a laugh he corrected himself. "You're not ma'am, you're Jenny, aren't you? Remember me? I taught school one day for Lemuel."

Jenny nodded, "Mr. Cartwright. 'Twas the day Joe Smith wrestled all the big boys and you wouldn't take him on."

"That'd make the newspaper. 'Substitute teacher wrestles student!' Seemed wisest not. You think I couldn't handle him?" The man grinned down at Jenny, and she realized he wasn't much older than Tom.

Silently she shook her head. "What does that mean?" he demanded. "Could or couldn't?" But Jenny just shrugged. She saw only his shiny shoes and the white shirt knotted with a silk tie. Overcome with shyness, she dropped her head, hugged the bundle close, and quickened her steps.

He kept pace with her. After a moment of silence, he said, "Jenny, you have a good mind. The best reader in the bunch. I hope you get to stay in school."

She stopped in the middle of the path, "Oh, yes; but why ever wouldn't I? Is teacher leaving?"

"No—" The word was drawn out, hesitant, and Jenny watched his face. He frowned as he studied her. "Do you have books at home to read?"

"Only one. It's Pa's, and he ain't too keen on me readin' it. Sometimes when he's gone, I snitch it. Ma pretends she doesn't see; otherwise she'd be in trouble with me."

"If you're careful with it, he wouldn't object."

She was shaking her head. "You don't know Pa. I even wash first. Just as long as he doesn't smack Ma, I'm willin' to risk the strap."

They walked on in silence until finally he asked, "Where are you going?"

She raised the bundle. "Ma's been sewin' for Mrs. Harper. She says it's about like one hog scratchin' another's back, but she doesn't mind. It brings in money."

"What do you mean?"

"He's nothin' but a peddler. Mrs. Harper should be doin' her own duds, not wastin' money like a fancy lady gettin' someone else to do her sewin' for her—"

"Mark, you heading for the Harpers', too?" They both turned and watched the young man approach.

"Yes. Michael saw the sheriff leave in a hurry, so he sent me to snoop around. Trust an attorney to have a nose for news." Jenny hesitated shyly and then walked ahead of the two as they began to talk. Their voices dropped and Jenny quickened her steps.

"Jenny," Mr. Cartwright called. She turned and he stepped

forward, saying, "Ah—couldn't you deliver that dress tomorrow?"

She shook her head. "Ma'll skin me. I'm to get the money tonight."

He hesitated and shrugged. With an apologetic glance at his companion, he muttered. "Could be just gossip."

"Like as not."

The three of them had just turned up the lane leading to the Harpers' when a horse cantered toward them. The rider sawed on the reins and said in a low voice, "Go on up, she'll need all the help she can get, poor soul." They watched him dig his heels in the horse.

Cartwright looked after the man. Soberly he said, "My friend, I think your information is correct." He turned to Jenny, and as he paused a wail came from the vine-covered cottage in front of them.

Jenny hugged herself and shivered, but before the men could move, the door burst open and Mrs. Harper rushed out. Screaming, she ran toward them and threw herself into Cartwright's arms.

Jenny gulped and watched, while Cartwright was patting and murmuring. He was also looking uncomfortably from her to the youth at his side.

Stepping forward, Jenny thrust the bundle at Mrs. Harper. "Ma'am, Ma's finished your flowered dress. Here 'tis."

The woman raised her head from Cartwright's shoulder and stared at Jenny. "My husband is dead! You're bringin' me a flowered dress and my husband is dead!—they're totin' him in here, butchered like a hog . . ."

"Butchered like a hog." Through the days and weeks that followed, the words stayed with Jenny, often goaded into her mind by the memory of that long, shrouded bundle being carried up the path. She still shivered over the horror she felt as Jake Evans nearly dropped his end when he first glimpsed Mrs. Harper and tried to snatch his cap off his head.

Later more details came out, and the words Jenny heard continued to be passed around town. Peddler Harper, God rest his soul, had been found deep in the woods with his throat slashed from ear to ear.

For weeks the tiny village of South Bainbridge, New York, vibrated with fear. Doors that had never had a lock were barricaded with the heaviest pieces of furniture in the house. Children were scurried indoors before sunset.

Scarcely had the nerves begun to steady when the murderer was apprehended. Word was passed through the streets by clusters of neighbors who met to discuss the news. The question was, Why? Who could imagine a man like that Jason Treadwell murdering a poor old peddler? Even Jenny recalled his sad, pale face.

In a town as small as South Bainbridge, there were only two places people could congregate to discuss the local news— the general store and the tavern. In each place the slant of the news differed.

The tavern version came out at the Timmons' table. Jenny sat between her mother and father, while her head turned from one to the other. Her father's dark brooding eyes moved across Tom, then shifted to her. "Where's a man to be safe? When a no-'count like Harper is done in, who'll be next?"

While he lifted his spoon and the others waited, Jenny looked around the group. Little Matty and Dorcas were too young to be touched by it all, but their eyes were round as they silently watched.

Pa scowled, shoved his bowl back, and took up his conversation. "There's things out there. Spirits. I've had enough experience in my life to know ya can't mess around with 'em if'n you don't know how to handle 'em. Harper for sure didn't. He shouldn't have been diggin' in the first place, messin' around in their territory." From beneath the scowling shelf of his bushy eyebrows he watched Tom. Jenny saw her brother squirm uncomfortably. Pa had that expression on his face—the one he used when he whipped her for taking his green book.

Jenny studied Tom; was it possible he had been reading the book?

"There's nothin' wrong with a little diggin'," said Tom, interrupting Pa's silent stare.

" 'Tis a waste if'n you don't have the power," he said heavily. "You're not even willing to study it out. I'm sayin' you best leave it all alone. If you don't you'll get in a fix. Them spirits are stronger than you. Messin' in their territory will getcha trouble, and nothin' more." His hooded eyes stared at Jenny, and she knew he was warning her, too.

Jenny's thoughts were full of the questions she was aching to ask. Ma said them for her. Gently her voice chided, "Now, Pa, be careful or the young'uns will think you're encouraging them in the craft. Has it ever got you a thing?"

Jenny watched the anger twist his face. The muscles on his neck knotted into ropes. But quickly before he could speak, Ma continued, "You know we weren't raised that way. Good, God-fearing families we both came from. They say the Bible teaches against spells and such, against believin' in the power."

Jenny's jaw dropped. Never before had she heard Ma talk like that to her pa. Caught in astonishment, Jenny nearly lost Pa's reply.

Now he roared, "Woman, you don't know what you're a-sayin'! The craft's been around longer than your black Book. If I haven't succeeded, it's 'cause you're never willin' to take chances, run a risk. This town's too goody-goody. I tell you, I'm sick of it, and I intend to quit it!"

Ma dropped her spoon and raised a troubled face. "Where'd we go?"

He shrugged while she looked around the room lighted only by the glow of the fire. The trouble faded from her face and Jenny watched hope brighten her eyes. "If we moved to the city you'd get a job. Like in a factory. And there'd be good churches." For a moment there was a question in her eyes. "If we could just get back in where there's proper church, everything would be different. I hear tell of camp meetings, and I pine for . . ." her voice trailed to silence and she sighed.

"I'm thinkin' of west," he muttered. "Farther west there's a heap o' land nearly for the takin'. And there ain't no churches." Jenny studied his face, wondering at the satisfaction in his voice.

Jenny watched Nancy gracefully gather the dishes and stack

them in the dishpan. Ma was speaking now, and Jenny knew it was talk from the store.

"Mrs. Taylor says Harper's widder is recoverin' right well. I guess I'd better get those dresses to her. Judgin' from the looks of her, she's gonna be a merry widder. Don't know what's goin' on, but there's talk she's signed an agreement with some fellas and is in line to make a heap of money. Don't sound moral to me."

Tom sputtered and choked. "Ma, 'tis business. She's just a-carryin' on a business deal her old man started."

Pa turned on Tom. "How come you know?"

Tom opened his mouth, closed it, and shrugged. Ma was staring at him and Jenny watched the frown grow on her face, "There's talk at the store about that new lad in town. If I heard right his name's Joe. They say he's bringin' trouble," Ma stated.

Tom protested, "That's no fair. 'Tis a busybody linkin' him with Harper's death."

" 'Tweren't that, even though everybody knows they were in on the business deal together," Ma answered. "It's the talk about the diggin' goin' on. They're sayin' Stowell brung that young fella out here on some crazy notion he has about findin' money by diggin'."

Tom jumped to his feet, knocking his stool aside. "He's just a young'un. I can't understand why people don't accept him like they'd do another's relation."

"He's nobody's relation," Nancy put in. "Besides, a fella that good-looking either has people pulling or pushing." She dried a plate and put it on the table. Leaning across, she faced Tom. "Just like you," she quipped. "How come you're so hot for defending him?"

There was no answer from Tom. Jenny watched him stare at his bowl. When she looked at her sister, Jenny saw the changing expression on her face. The saucy questioning air disappeared and a slight frown creased her forehead.

"Seems," Nancy said slowly, "the fella affects a person. There's something about him that makes a body hate or love him."

Caught by the statement, Jenny stood watching Nancy turn

aside with a sigh. She heard her mother say, "Nancy, you're not fourteen yet. You're not even supposed to know there's fellas like that." An anxious note in her voice made Jenny wonder what she meant.

Jenny was still thinking about that statement the next afternoon when she and Tom met Joe on their way home from school. Jenny had suggested cutting through the edge of the forest, and there was Joe sitting beside the trail. It was cold and crisp, and snow rimmed the rocks and bushes, but he was sitting there as relaxed as if it were a day in June.

When Tom hailed him, he got to his feet and waited for them to reach him. Speaking in a whisper, he said, "You know, when there's been a death like old man Harper, there's a surge of energy released in the spirit world. I was feeling it. Sitting here I was wondering how best to take advantage of the power."

Jenny shivered and jumped around on the trail. She too spoke in a whisper. "Are you goin' to be diggin' for treasure? Will you teach me how to use the rod? Tom said you knew all about it. What are charms? Are you afraid of the spirits? Have you ever seen one?"

He hunkered down beside her and grinned unexpectedly. "Hey, are you that uppity little kid from school? How come you aren't asking these questions during recess?"

She studied him for a minute, still dancing on her toes with excitement. "Because Ma says this diggin' for treasure is all wrong. Nancy would tell on me. Will you show me how to draw circles so the demons won't get me?"

He got to his feet, laughing. Jenny was disappointed to see the mood of mystery had faded from him. Hands on hips, she stood in the path staring up at him. "No one will take me serious. I'm tryin' to learn. If you and Tom won't teach me, where's a body to learn?"

Still chuckling, he said, "Too bad my pa isn't here. He's the one I learned from." And Jenny had to be content with that. She and Tom dallied a moment longer before leaving. When they turned toward home, Tom was whistling happily.

CHAPTER 3

One October afternoon, Jenny lingered behind the rest of the students, reluctant to go home. The waning afternoon was still warm, and the bright autumn trees surrounding the schoolhouse enticed Jenny. Turning her back to the raucous group headed down the trail, she watched the wind flick the red maple leaves like brilliant flags.

While she hesitated, staring at the trail cutting into the trees, a movement in the deeper shadows of pine caught her attention. A pale patch flashed, and she caught a brief glimpse of bright hair before the dark shadows swallowed the tall figure.

Quickly Jenny turned and trotted down the path. Without a doubt it was Joe. But just before she reached the trees, she hesitated. She was disobeying Ma. How many times had she been scolded for tarrying after school, and for tagging after the fellows instead of staying close to Nancy?

Jenny's feet began to drag, but all of the questions she had been wanting to ask Joe tumbled into her mind. If she hurried, he might show her how to use the rod.

As Jenny moved down the trail, she began to hear the clink of shovel against stone.

He was in a clearing, standing on a mound of dirt, digging. Suddenly shy, she hung back in the trees, watching. When he threw down his shovel and pulled the stone out of his pocket, she forgot everything except her curiosity. As she ran toward him, he jumped to his feet and turned. The quick smile on his face changed to a frown when he saw her. "What are you doing here?"

"I saw you comin' this way. I want to help. What are you seein' with the stone? Would I be able to see, too?"

"Jen, go home," he muttered. "Better yet, go tell Tom I need him to help me. There's something down there, for certain."

"Tom's helpin' on the Goodman farm today. They're diggin' potatoes and he's gonna get some."

"Just my luck," Joe muttered. "There's spirits down there protecting the treasure, and I sure can't get it without some help."

"I'll help. I know enough about diggin' to draw a circle for you." He was still frowning. "Tom could come tomorrow. I'll tell him tonight. Joe—" her voice dropped to a whisper, "are there really spirits guarding it?"

He studied her for a moment, "On your life there are. Come here and I'll tell you what I'm seeing. This is where the Spaniards buried a heap of silver. There were two of them, but one killed the other. It's the murdered one who's doing the guarding. I can see his slit throat." Jenny shivered and moved closer. "You want to look in my stone? We'll see if you have the gift."

Jenny eyed the dark stone he held out. After a moment she slowly shook her head. "I'm afraid," she whispered. "What would I do if I saw a spirit or something? Joe, I'm afraid." She backed away from him.

"You're a silly little baby," he teased.

"I'm not. It's just—" She hesitated, then crept closer. Climbing on the log beside the diggings, she peered down into the hole and then turned to look Joseph in the eye. He was close, and his head was nearly on a level with hers. "You just don't understand young'uns," she said. "Or girls. Some people get scared easier."

The teasing disappeared. "We have a house full of 'em." He put the shovel down and sat beside her on the log. "It isn't fun being poor, is it? 'Specially when no one takes you serious because your pa's— well . . ."

"My pa drinks and then uses the strap on us. Tom and me. Nancy and the little ones don't get it."

He was nodding, talking slowly like he had forgotten she was around. "Seems we were moving all the time. People pushing for money and pushing just because they thought they could get by with it. Always moving. Poor, too many kids around. Ma running a ginger beer and cake shop, painting old oilcloth just to keep us eating. No matter where we go, seems luck has run off and left us."

Now he straightened and grinned at her. "But it won't be like that forever. I'm going to *be* somebody. I'm going to make people sit up and take notice. No more will they be saying, 'There goes that Smith kid looking for trouble again.'" Abruptly he turned and grasped Jenny's shoulder. "Tyke, I'll tell you something, and don't you forget it. There's power out there. If you learn to tap the forces, you can have anything you want out of life."

"How do you know?" Jenny whispered.

His voice lowered, and his eyes glittered. "There's spirits out there to do my bidding. If you learn how to control the forces of the spirit world and use the rod and the stone properly, there's riches and treasure for the taking. Jenny, it's the rich man, the one who's learned all these things, who's respected. And it's for the taking.

"Back home, there's this fella. He's a magician and he knows all about these things and he's teaching me. Now my pa knows a little bit about it, but he doesn't have the power. He's worked with the rod and the digging for years, and he knows there's evil spirits guarding the treasures, but he doesn't have the power to break through them. But I have confidence in this fella Walters. He'll show me how to get the money and treasures."

As Jenny headed for home, she thought of what Joe had said; more important than the words was the feeling that now they were friends. Now Joe would tell her the things she needed to know, things that were in the green book. What would he think if she were to tell him how much she wanted the same things he wanted? But even as the thoughts came into her mind, she knew he wouldn't listen. He thought she was too young— but someday she wouldn't be.

Later that week, Jenny came home from school to find her father at home. Gratefully she took the egg basket Ma offered and scurried out to the barn. When Pa was drinking this early, she knew better than to tarry.

In the barn she found Tom bridling his horse.

"Where ya goin'?" Jenny asked. Pulling her shawl close, she leaned against the horse's flanks.

Startled, Tom jerked his head and looked down at Jenny. "Didn't know you were around. What difference does it make? Your nose is red," he added. "Did you just get home from school?" She nodded and watched him adjust the bridle over the horse's ears. "Better get in the house," he urged, " 'tis close to snowing."

"Been in. Pa's home." He turned to look at her, and she supplied the information with a nod. "I'm stayin' out of there. Lemme go with you."

He shook his head. "No. It'll be dark and cold before I'm back."

Jenny tightened the shawl about her and sniffed. "I can't go in 'til he's asleep. You and Joe weren't in school today; where were you?"

Still watching her, he shrugged and asked, "You been readin' his book again?" Jenny chewed her thumb and considered the question. How badly she wanted to tell him about the book, about all the secrets in it! She'd tell how at night the pictures and the strange words rolled around in her mind. Just now, thinking about the book made her ache to know what it all meant.

But Ma had said the book was evil. And Tom had been there listening, nodding his head, agreeing with Ma. If Jenny were to admit reading the book again, Tom could get her into real trouble. She shook her head.

"Honest, Tom, I haven't had it since—I never said a word, he just started in on me, and Ma said to look for eggs. She knows those hens haven't laid any for a month now."

The temptation was too great to resist. "Tom, do you really believe all those things Ma said about the book? How magic and money diggin' and usin' charms is of the devil? Do you really think the devil's out there just waitin' to get children who don't mind their parents and go to church and leave the witchin' things alone, do you?"

He gave her a quick glance before replying, "I haven't ever seen a devil. It would be hard to convince me to be scared of something I haven't met. Now take this stuff we're doin'; it's not a hard and fast way to make money, but it's interesting and a little exciting, just hoping."

Jenny saw the softening on his face and pleaded, "Please, Tom. Let me hang on behind you; I won't be a bit of trouble."

He tightened the cinch and sat down on the log. "Wouldn't set so good if I bring my little sister."

"Are you going to dig at the mine the fellas found? I heard you and Joe talkin' about it. I'd be quiet and nice. I want to see the mine."

"For one thing, it's miles from here. For another, that's not where I'm headed. We gotta wait on that."

"Where do I go 'til Pa's asleep?" Tom's hands made a helpless, questioning arc and Jenny pressed, "I'd hide in the bushes and just wait for you." With a sigh, Tom reached for her, and she grinned with relief.

The horse was old and stiff and her gait threw Jenny from side to side, but she clung to Tom and gritted her teeth.

They left South Bainbridge and when they had nearly reached Colesville, Tom cut south. Here the trees were thick and the underbrush almost covered the trail.

When the horse slowed to a walk, Jenny ventured, "No timber's been pulled across this road recently."

"That's fine, just fine," Tom muttered. The excitement in his voice brought Jenny leaning far over to see his face. He turned his head and warned. "Now you remember, you hide. Don't let on you're there while we have our meeting."

"With Joe?"

"And some of the others who'll be a-workin' with us."

"Mrs. Harper be there?"

"She's not workin' the mine; she's just a partner," replied Tom.

"I thought partners worked too."

"Well—" Tom sounded like he was scratching his head and Jenny tried to see his face. "Not if they're, well, silent partners. Harper was the workin' partner; now he's gone, she's his inheritor." Tom paused and slowed the horse. "I think this is the place. That hill. Joe says there's money buried in the mound."

"How'd he know?"

"He's been lookin' with his stone. We were out here last week, but the enchantment was bad. Joe says we're goin' to have to break it if we have a hope of reachin' the money."

Jenny peered at Tom. "Honest! How'd he find out?"

"I'm not right sure, but he's been doin' this long enough to have a pretty good idea how to go about it. He and his pa's been diggin' for years now."

"They must be rich."

"Naw," Tom paused. "Seems to be a pretty tricky thing, this gettin' the money. Joe says things have to go just right or the spirits whisk the whole treasure away."

Jenny shivered and hugged Tom close. "If it's so, it's a mighty risky gamble. Seems a waste of time."

"On the other hand," Tom added, "one good find makes all the failures worth the trouble.—Okay, off the horse and into the bushes."

Jenny slid off the horse and ran across the clearing. The bushes Tom pointed out were growing above the spot where the men had dug. By hanging on to the branches and leaning forward she could peer into the hole. After a minute Tom rode back to her and tossed his heavy canvas bags to her, saying, "Might as well sit on these until we need them."

By the time Tom's shadowy figure rode into the clearing, it had started to snow. Jenny huddled deep into her shawl and pulled one of the bags over her head and shoulders. The sound of horses and distant voices carried clearly on the cold air. She knelt on a bag and leaned forward to part the bushes.

A rider was calling out orders as he came into the clearing. "Now get this brush cleaned out of here. Every bit of litter has to go." She could see the speaker and guessed from the size of him that it was Joe. She heard him say, "No wonder you couldn't fetch up the chest before. All this mess is begging for trouble."

"Joe, if you'd come with us instead of staying at Stowell's peering in that stone, we'd known to clear the brush."

Jenny heard his heavy voice turn to the fellow talking, "And if I'd been here, we'd never have known all those spirits were guarding the treasure. Doubtless, even then it was needing more than digging to fetch that chest up."

"Did you get something for a sacrifice?"

"Stowell's bringing it."

When Jenny heard the word *sacrifice,* her heart began to pound. She leaned forward and eagerly studied the group clustered on the edge of the hole. "Aw, shucks," she muttered when she saw the men. Tom and Joe were the only ones she recognized, but the rest were very ordinary. They looked like farmers from the area.

Jen, you got your hopes up, didn't ya? she thought in disgust, even as common sense reminded her that the vision of satin capes and plumed velvet hats didn't have a place in this snowy forest. They were found only in books —and in Jenny's dreams. But she couldn't help her disappointed sigh.

For just a moment she dared to hope all those secret and glorious things in her father's book were about to take place before her very eyes. Then pictures of demons, especially of the one with a head like a goat, rose in her mind, and she shuddered involuntarily. If the book weren't evil, as Pa had said, why did she become fearful thinking about the mysterious dark words?

But fascination overcame her fear. Almost immediately Jenny heard the bleat of a lamb. Then a voice, "All right, Smith, here 'tis." Surely that voice belonged to Mr. Stowell.

She parted the bushes and eased herself forward just far enough to see the clearing. The group worked in silence. Several of the men shoveled debris, while others chopped dead branches out of the way.

Joe was showing Tom how to cut long stakes. Someone handed Joe a shiny sword, which he used to mark a wide circle around the diggings. Jenny's breath came faster as he marked a second circle. It was just like Pa's book!

"Why ya doin' two of 'em?" asked the man beside him.

"Instructions," Joe said tersely. "Now, lemme have the stakes. They're to keep off the evil spirits while we do the digging. See, we weren't careful enough last time. The enchantment is more powerful than we thought. Must mean there's more money down there than we'd guessed." Jenny felt the excitement run through the group.

Joe stood back to watch the last stake being placed, then he turned and disappeared. While Jenny stirred restlessly on the canvas bags, she again heard the bleat of the lamb. Suddenly there was an anguished squeal, and Joe appeared carrying the lamb. She watched with mingled pity and horror as he moved into the inner circle and marched slowly around carrying the struggling, bleeding lamb.

The men were waiting silently. The only sound was the low murmuring Joe was doing as he finished marching around, dripping the blood. When the lamb was quiet and limp, he nodded his head.

Now the men jumped for their tools and moved to the center of the circle. The group was still silent; only the sound of shovels against the earth broke the quiet of the night. When one grated against stone, Jenny rubbed her face and licked her lips. Edging nearer, she leaned breathlessly over the incline.

A shovel clunked woodenly, and a voice cried, "There's somethin' there!"

"Oh!" Jenny's cry of alarm rose to a scream as the branch she had grabbed snapped and she flew down the slope.

Sliding to a stop, she cautiously opened her eyes. A ring of muddy boots surrounded her. A man loomed above her, arm uplifted. Jenny gasped. *The sword!* She stared in horror, not daring to move, but deep inside she knew Pa's book was coming alive before her eyes.

The group about her was silent, motionless. Now she heard a sigh of resignation close to her ear and felt Tom's arms lifting her. "You all right, Jen?" She nodded mutely, looking from Tom's sober face to Joe's scowling one.

"Well, I guess that just about fixed it but good; we'll never be able to get the thing now." He looked around the group. "Fellas, let's go home," he said shortly.

From the shelter of Tom's arms, Jenny watched the silent group gather their tools in disgust and disappear behind the curtain of falling snow. It seemed like a dream. Nearly. At that moment she caught another glimpse of the crumpled, blood-smeared lamb beside the line of stakes.

CHAPTER 4

November passed. With Christmas came winter. In addition, as heavy as the clouds and as chilling as the rain and snow, came uneasy talk that moved through South Bainbridge, New York.

Jenny knew it first at school when she approached Mr. Searles, asking, "Joe Smith ain't been to school for weeks. Why?"

He peered at her. "Don't say 'ain't,' say 'hasn't.' Jenny, you're getting to be a young lady, and ladies don't talk like farmers. If you've a desire to make people sit up and listen to you, then learn to talk like a lady."

She twisted her face, thinking about what he had said, and he added, "Don't twist your mouth like that either."

"Why do you care how I talk?" She couldn't keep the wistful note out of her voice.

"I don't rightly know," he said slowly as he studied her curiously. "Guess it mostly has to do with Cartwright's saying you've got potential. He ought to know, he's had more teaching than most of us. He's heading east to read law at some attorney friend's office. When he comes back here, he'll be a lawyer. Maybe a justice of the peace like that fellow, Albert Neely. South Bainbridge is growing up, and we need all the learning we can get around here."

Jenny let the words swirl about her while she stared up at Lemuel Searles. Her mind was filled with the vision of Prudence with her blonde curls and crisply starched petticoats. "Even Prue doesn't speak all that good."

For a moment he looked like he did when he'd lost his place

in the midst of reading the big book. "Jenny, it's you we're discussing."

"Joe Smith," she reminded. Confusion slid over his face. "Mr. Searles," Jenny insisted, "it's Joe I'm a-askin' after." He took a deep breath, and while she watched his chest swell, Arnold Thompson scooted up and stopped beside Jenny.

"You know something new about Joe?" he asked. "The town's a-buzzin'. Pa said he heard things, weird-like."

Mr. Searles picked up the school bell and handed it to Arnold. "It's time for class, Arnold. You may ring the bell."

Curiosity nipped at Jenny like a playful pup. It wasn't the first time gossip about Joe had come up; but always, like the autumn leaves in a swirling wind, it had scattered and spun away. This time, she vowed, the talk would not slip past her.

During the rest of the day Jenny kept watching Arnold, sometimes meeting his teasing eyes. Once when she mouthed the message to him, "Tell me after school," he only grinned.

When the final bell rang, Jenny fought her way through the crowded room. Arnold was already out the door and with one teasing shout thrown to the wind, he was off across the fields.

When she caught up with him, he was waiting to torment her, saying, "If you was as pretty as Prue, I'd make you give me a kiss for tellin'."

She glared at him, "Just as I thought, you got no news, you're just joshin'." She started to turn away.

He caught her arm, saying, "I do so. If you'll buy me a licorice, I'll tell ya."

"I haven't a penny."

"Then you snitch it while I keep Miz Lewis busy." She shook her head. "Ma'll have a fit if I do and get caught." Arnold was hopping backward down the lane, still grinning. She ran to catch up with him. "All right—anything to know." They turned and ran toward town.

The store was crowded. Jenny paused to sniff deeply of the mingled odors. The smell of sweet spices floated above the mouth-watering scents of smoked ham and pickled herring. Arnold poked her and they squirmed their way between the Mortons and old Mrs. Johnson.

After a few well-placed jabs, the line in front of the candy jars parted. Arnold muttered and pointed out his choice.

"Can't," Jenny whispered. "There's too many lookin'."

"Just wait," he muttered; "they'll all clear out soon."

They drifted back and forth through the store, examining everything at nose level.

Jenny was conscious of the eyes watching them. Jake Lewis's were suspicious and alert; the others were curious. As she waited she listened to the conversation passing back and forth among those who lingered around the potbellied stove.

"Uncommonly coincidental." The white-haired man leaned on his walking stick and puffed at his pipe. Jenny studied him. His hair curled neatly against his stiff white collar. His walking stick was of dark wood, carved and polished, and capped with shiny brass. The man's gaze flitted across Jenny and Arnold and fastened on the portly man beside him.

"Oliver Harper's death was strange enough, coming on the heels of the gossip about the diggings, but coupled with this new development, it is indeed strange."

Jenny's mind screamed, *What new development*? She studied the floor and edged nearer the stove.

The portly man asked the question. "Meaning?"

"The agreement those fellas have signed. Seems Mrs. Harper will be getting a sizable chunk of money from that mine, providing those Spaniards really deposited a pile of silver in that cave."

The other chuckled, "Conscience money?"

"There's too much belief in the miraculous connected to it. Joe's made no bones about using a seer stone to hunt for treasure. Anybody will tell you there's plenty of conjuring taking place. Anybody who'll talk, that is. Seems the town is uncommonly quiet right now except for the rumblings behind the scene. And the rumblings are growing louder." He puffed on his pipe before saying, "If nothing else, I'd be happy to have the fear of God put into the sorcerers. It bothers me mightily to see the country accepting witchcraft as a good thing. Granted, not all think that way, but there's enough accepting it." When he stopped talking, he raised his head and Jenny watched his eyes sweep the length and breadth of the store. Turning, she saw the cluster of people caught motionless, listening.

In the silence that seemed to cloak them all, Jake Lewis moved. His voice was suddenly loud in the quiet store. "Here you, Arnold and Jenny, there's a piece of licorice for you to split. You've been waitin' an hour for a piece to hop out at you. So take it and be gone. My patience and my eyes are wearing out." He broke the stick of candy and offered it to them. Jenny and Arnold reached and scooted out the door.

Over her mouthful, Jenny said, "You got your candy. Are you going to tell?"

He shook his head. "If you'd given me yours I mighta told you. This way I'll hold on to the news until I get hungry for another piece."

Jenny shrugged. "You couldn't top what that important-looking fella said, and I'll not be riskin' my neck to hear more of your stories."

When Jenny reached home Pa sat silent, glowering beside the fireplace. Tom was hunkered down on a log on the other side of the fire, his face sullen. Jenny watched him whittle a stick with quick, impatient jabs of his knife.

Ma was moving about the room, the carpet slippers she had made out of pa's old felt hat, patched together with odd bits of cloth, slapping softly against the uneven board floor.

Jenny sat down at the table. "When I get growed, I'm gonna learn to talk like a lady so's people will listen to me. I'm gonna get Ma some shoes, and we'll all be rich. I'm right tired of livin' like this."

"You could start your reforming by learning to keep your face clean and your hair combed," Nancy retorted. "Nobody in this town talks good, but even that dumb Prue keeps her face clean. What's on your face, anyway?"

"Licorice," Jenny said, applying her tongue to the remains of the candy.

"How'd you come by licorice?" Dorcas asked, pressing wistfully against Jenny. The look stabbed remorse through Jenny, and she added *candy for Dorcas* to her mental list.

"Arnold and me were in the store. For no account, Mr. Lewis

gave us a stick to share. I reckon if you'd be sweet like an angel the next time Ma takes you with her, he just might give you one."

"Not with the bill we owe," Ma said sharply. Pa heaved himself to his feet. Abruptly he kicked at Tom's muddy boot.

"If'n you'd be tryin' to bring home an honest buck instead of hangin' around that lazy Joe, we'd be gettin' caught up on the bills."

In January Jason Treadwell was executed for the murder of Oliver Harper, peddler and money digger.

For a time the rumbles in South Bainbridge subsided as if in honor of the dead. But feelings and words, like a mole tunneling through a field, must surface. As February rolled around and the weather softened enough for conversation but not enough for work in the fields, clusters of people juggled words and sifted gossip.

In the log cabin that served as a meeting place for the Presbyterian congregation, the people were warned against the devices of the evil one. And the devices named were hunting treasures in the earth and dabbling with the ancient arts of witchcraft.

Ma was nodding her head vigorously. While Jenny listened, she noticed that the leader, Josiah Stowell, who had stood right up front in the past, calling the worship and leading the songs, was absent. She wondered why. Mostly she wanted to see his face and hear what he would say when they talked about the digging and the dead lamb.

Jenny was silent as she walked homeward. Just ahead of her, Nancy and Ma were talking. Jenny studied Ma's faded dress with the tear in the hem. She was thinking of the bright flowered dresses her mother had made for Mrs. Harper. Abruptly she said, "Money diggin' and the like can't be too bad if a body is able to earn a livin' from it."

Nancy and Ma stopped suddenly and Jenny bumped into them. Ma stared down at Jenny, "Child, what's got into you? Sure, I know that money diggin' is going on and that instead of fearin' it as the device of the devil, people are a-scornin' it as an idiot's folly, but you've been raised better."

"Have I?" Jenny was staring up at the two of them. She noticed that Ma was dark like she was, while Nancy was fair like Tom. Bewildered by their expressions, she realized she didn't feel related to either of them.

Nancy was demanding, "Didn't you hear what the parson said? Jenny, I fear for your soul."

"Nancy, you've no call to be uppity. There's too many good folks around usin' the rod and diggin'." Jenny flounced past her sister and scooted down the path.

It wasn't long after, that another stranger came to town. Jenny had been passing down the street on her way to school when she first saw Peter Bridgman standing in front of the lawyer's office with Mark Cartwright. She lingered on the corner watching them. She loved seeing and hearing new things. She felt like the world was flooded with sunlight and every detail of the street was bright with it, though the sun wasn't even shining.

Later she learned the stranger, Peter Bridgman, was nephew to Miriam Stowell, and he was asking hard questions. With Peter Bridgman around, the town heaved a collective sigh of relief. Now someone would *do* something. Poor Mrs. Stowell. Her husband, good man that he was, was being led astray.

Josiah Stowell, they said, had been the one who had gotten the notion all on his own to go to Palmyra and fetch the young seer here to help him decide where to dig for treasure. He'd heard that young Joe had a talent for finding things in the earth.

So Josiah's silver lined the pockets of that tall, young, blonde fella. It was strange enough for a man like Stowell, a good, solid, hard-working farmer, to decide in his old age to listen to those stories about hidden treasure; but he was risking the inheritance of his wife and children on his foolishess, as well. So Peter Bridgman was in town asking his questions. What Stowell's wife, sons, and daughters dared not say, Peter must, if the family fortune were to be saved.

One day Jenny followed Tom out to the barn. While he milked

the cow, Jenny hung over the gate and whispered her questions. "Why does that Mr. Bridgman care about what Mr. Stowell's doin'? Seems if there's money to be made, it won't make no difference how he's doin' it."

Tom leaned his head against the cow's flank and studied Jenny's face. His Adam's apple slid up and down his neck; finally he replied, "Jen, can't you understand people frown on treasure huntin'?"

"Why?" He shrugged and Jenny persisted, "Seems a body's entitled to work in his own way." She paused to lick her lip. " 'Sides, all that money's goin' be found by someone, so might as well be the one that wants to do the diggin'."

"If there's really money to be found," Tom said shortly as he returned to his milking.

"You think there isn't?" Jenny asked, astonished.

"There's stories. People always are diggin' and diggin' and never findin' a thing." Tom's voice dragged out the words slowly as he studied the pail between his knees.

Jenny settled back to think of the book, of those promises it made—if a person just did it right. Slowly the old excitement burned through her, excitement mingled with fear. She opened her mouth to tell Tom about all she was feeling, about what Joe said.

The eerie pictures she had seen in Pa's book crowded into her mind, and she stopped. How could she ever put them into words and make them as real to Tom as they were becoming to her? Tom looked like he had quit hoping in anything as he leaned against the side of the cow, squirting milk into the pail. She turned away. "Ma'll get me if I don't find the eggs before dark."

Suddenly winter was finished with New York State. The ice broke on the Susquehanna. March softened the air with gentle winds, and green fringes appeared on all the snowbanks. Life seemed to stir afresh even in the streets of South Bainbridge.

Jenny was walking to school alone, thinking restless springtime thoughts, when Arnold caught up with her.

"How about some more licorice?"

She eyed him suspiciously. "That means you have news to trade. Well, I'm not about to snitch anything for the likes of you."

"Aw, Jenny," he tormented, "you're a poor sport!"

"Go do your kissin' on Prue; then I'll get the information for nothin'. She can't keep a secret."

"Would it make a difference if ya knew it was about Joe Smith?"

Jenny stood still. Of course it would, but she wasn't going to let Arnold know that. She eyed him, seeing the way his eyes sparkled with excitement. Then she ducked her head and continued to walk slowly.

Tim Morgan caught up with them. "Say, Jenny, I suppose Arnold here has told ya all about it, huh?" He elbowed his way between them. "I'd never have guessed old Bridgman was that serious. Arrested! Ya goin' to the trial? Pa says we can. Everybody's goin'."

"She don't know!" Arnold howled. "You're spoilin' it all!"

"Of course I'm goin'," Jenny trilled while staring defiantly at Arnold. "Only problem, I don't know when it is."

"Tomorrow. Wouldn't surprise me if Teach lets school. Since it's Joe, he'll be wantin' to go too."

Jenny clenched her teeth and tossed her head. Her stomach was churning with the agony of unasked questions, but she smiled sweetly at Arnold and hurried her feet along the path. "There's the bell. Gotta run!"

The school buzzed with the news. She listened, but saved her questions for Tom. A wrenching inside advised her that silence was best.

After school she flew across the yard, leaving the talk behind, and ran to find Tom. Halfway home she caught up with him. "There's talk," her shortened breath ended with a sob. "They're sayin' Joe's been arrested, and that there'll be a trial. Why?"

Tom lifted his head. "You're takin' on like it's the end of the world. Bridgman's claimin' Joe's up to no good with his lookin' for the mine. Stowells are puttin' it all on to him. They're not wantin' to risk a thing." He shook his head mournfully. "Only way you can make a buck is by a-riskin' something."

Now he turned to look at her, "Say," he said slowly, "you're actin' like Joe's kin. Don't be worryin' your head about the menfolks, Jen. We can take care of ourselves. 'Tweren't all that bad. Old Joe'll have his day in court and then we'll be back to diggin'. Wanna go hear it all? It's tomorrow."

She nodded, rubbing at the dampness in her eyes. "You make it sound like funnin'—nothin' serious."

"Aw, Joe's a good guy. With that smooth tongue he'll be able to talk himself outta anything."

CHAPTER 5

Jenny's mood lightened with dawn. She skipped beside Tom as they headed for town. "There's Mrs. Harper wearing her new dress," Jennie hissed. Others were in holiday garb, too. The two joined the crowd walking toward the only building in town large enough for the trial.

"Hurry!" Tom warned. "The seats'll be goin' fast. I hear they're gettin' in two justices of the peace besides Neely. They're callin' it a Court of Special Sessions."

"How come you know so much about it?" Jenny asked, quickening her steps.

"I was down here when he got examined by Neely to see if he had to have a trial. They even had him in jail overnight. That's because he didn't have bail money."

"Will the Stowells be here?"

"My guess, he'll be testifyin'," Tom answered shortly.

Tom and Jenny had just wedged themselves into place on one of the narrow benches when the court was brought to order. The judge pounded his gavel on the desk, and Jenny leaned forward, craning her neck to see.

Jenny watched the serious faces of the men clustered at the front of the room. She recognized the man with the white hair and the walking stick. The portly gentleman was there too, and the doctor, taking notes.

On the right side of the justices, the witnesses formed a straggly line on the bench. She recognized Mr. Stowell, but most of the others were strangers to her. She did see Mr. McMaster, and Thompson, who worked for Stowell. He had been one of the

47

men in the group the night Tom had taken her to the diggings.

As she settled back to wait, Jenny recalled that night. Even now she shuddered at the memory of opening her eyes to find that man standing over her with the sword.

The clerk called Joe forward, and Jenny slid out to the end of the bench to study the bright-haired youth as he took his place. The men grouped together, their voices low. Jenny asked Tom, "What are they doin' now?"

"Swearin' in Joe." Behind Tom came a hiss for silence.

They had asked him a question, and he was telling them about his stone: "Back home there's a girl who had a stone. She could look into it and see things nobody else could see. I went to visit her and she let me take a look in hers." Joe's voice had lost its waver and it rose, filling the room with confidence.

"All I could see was a stone, far away but coming close to me. Turned out it was *my* stone. It shone like a light." Again Jenny caught a glimpse of the same strange gleam in his eye she had first seen when she was with Joe in the woods. He paused to take a breath and his voice deepened and dropped. "I could not rest until I found it. I got myself a grub bag and set out. I worked my way, following what I knew to be the direction to the exact location. I knew I would find it, and I did. 'Twas buried under a tree. I dug it up, carried it down to the crick and washed it."

Joe paused, and with his voice deepening again, he said, "I put it in my hat, and lo, I discovered I possessed one of the attributes of deity, an all-seeing eye."

A murmur rose and swept the room. Jenny looked around at the people and then turned back to Joseph. Justice Neely was asking him something. With an eloquent sweep of his hand, Joe held up the small chocolate-colored stone, by now familiar to Jenny. Silence settled on the room as the people studied the object.

Close to Jenny came a whisper, "There's those who really do see things in a peep stone. Reckon he's one of them?"

"He'll have to prove the power."

Another whisper asked, "What's he being charged with?"

The reply came, "Being a vagrant, a disorderly person and an imposter."

" 'Tis a shame; he's nothing but a tad. Let him have a little fun."

"Must be something to it, if he's come to trial."

Then Jenny heard Joe speaking again. "Josiah Stowell came to Manchester after me, and I've been working for him, looking for a silver mine and working around the farm. In between times, I've been going to school."

There was a question and the answer came. "He came lookin' for me because he heard I had the gift of seership."

And then the question. "Did you find the mine?"

"No. I persuaded him to give up looking."

Joe Smith sat down, and Josiah Stowell took his place. In the murmur of questions, the voice rose. Justice Neely was speaking. His voice was solemn, but the room was filled with his thundering question. "Josiah Stowell, do you swear before God that you actually believe the defendant is able, with the use of his peep stone, to see objects buried in the ground just as clearly as you can see the objects on this table?"

The old man straightened and, with a determination that set his double chin to wagging, declared, "Your Honor, it isn't only a matter of belief; I positively know that Joseph Smith can see these marvelous things!"

In the uproar, the gavel smote the table and the next witness, Mr. Thompson, was called. "This here fella says to Mr. Stowell that many years ago a band of robbers buried a treasure. They placed a charm over it all by having a sacrifice done, so it couldn't be got at less'n he had what he called a talismanic influence. So they decided to go after it. Joe called for some praying and fasting, and then they set out and commenced to dig." He paused to swallow hard, then continued.

"They found the treasure all right; we heard the shovel hit the box. But the harder they dug, the more it slipped away from them. One fella even managed to get his hand on it before it slid clear away from him. Finally Joe called a council of war against this foe of darkness—spirit, he said it was. We knew it was a lack of faith or something wrong with our thinking, so Joe devised a plan."

There was a gulp and Thompson's voice rose with excitement. "We got a lamb. Stowell knelt down and prayed while Joe slit the lamb's throat and spread the blood around the hole. This was a propitiation to the spirit. But we never did get the money."

A sigh swept the room and Jenny squirmed and looked at Tom. " 'Tweren't the time you was there," he muttered.

As the day warmed, the crowded room grew stuffy. More witnesses were called, and Jenny moved restlessly on the bench. When the last witness had taken his seat, the heads of the justices tilted together.

Justice Neely then slowly got to his feet. His voice droned in the heavy air of the room. Although Jenny strained to understand, his words were meaningless to her until she heard, "We the court find the defendant—guilty as charged."

There was a second of silence, and in the breathless pause Jenny saw Joe leap to his feet and dash through the crowded room. But Jenny's eyes were riveted on the men at the front of the room.

Justice Neely was still standing, hands calm at his side. The other justices hunched over the table just as quietly, watching Joe run. He passed the constable who was sitting beside the door with his chair tilted back against the wall, his hat shading his eyes.

"He's gone," Tom breathed softly. "He's taken leg bail, and I've a notion they don't care a snitch. Reckon we'll never see the likes of him again." There was a twinge of regret in his voice.

Over the sudden babble of voices, Justice Neely shouted, "Court is closed for this session!"

The only sounds in the stifling room were the rustle of skirts and the clatter of heavy boots. Slowly Tom and Jenny got to their feet to follow the crowd out the door. Jenny peered around Tom and saw the justices clustered by the table talking. She measured the distance and studied their broad, black backs. With a quick movement, she turned and dashed to the front of the room. The man with the white hair and the walking stick was saying, "I just can't see crippling the chances of this young fellow. He looks like, given a proper chance, he'll make good. I hope my hunch isn't wrong. Otherwise I'll be regretting this the rest of my life."

"I hope so, too. He was pretty eager to take leg bail once it was suggested. Must have had a few fears—at least he sure could run." The black-coated men moved restlessly and Jenny scooted for the door.

When she caught up with Tom, the crowd was standing in the street, somber-faced and questioning. Tom and Jenny joined the others and watched as the building was locked. They were still waiting as the line of dark coats moved quietly down the street with the constable following along behind. Now his hat was squared on his head and his hunch-shouldered gait made him look like a gnarled guardian angel, a protective shield between the justices and the questioning citizens of South Bainbridge.

When the last man had disappeared from sight, the crowd stirred. "Why do you suppose they went to all that trouble and then just set there and let him run?"

"He weren't much more'n a tad," a sympathetic voice answered. "Those gentlemen are right fatherly. I hear they're feelin' he's a deprived youth who needs a good warnin' to straighten him up."

"I wonder if that's really the case," came a voice from the depths of the crowd. "Is that all he is? There's been a heap of riling up since he's been around. I'll not forget the way those fellas toted Peddler Harper down off the hill, stone-cold."

Jenny squirmed her way through the crowd to see the speaker's face, and the square-shouldered man standing beside him turned to look at her. It was Mark Cartwright. For a moment, Jenny's eyes caught his and she saw the questioning frown.

Now another spoke reluctantly, "I heard a fella say, and I'm not mentioning names, that he asked young Joe if he really could see money and all these wonderful treasures. He said Joe hesitated a bit and then said, 'Between the two of us, I can't see 'em any more than you or anybody else, but a body's gotta make a living.' "

Tom tugged at Jenny. "Let's get along for home." He turned

down the street, Jenny trotting to keep up with his long strides. When they had left the town behind, Tom slowed and Jenny caught up with him.

"Did you see that Mark Cartwright?" she asked breathlessly. "He was listenin' to it all, and I don't think he was agreein'."

"You mean about Joe takin' leg bail?" She nodded, and Tom said, " 'Tis always that way. The rich can't be sympathetic about the poor."

Jenny was pondering Tom's words when they turned up the lane toward the Timmons' shack. She looked at the yard, the litter, and the straggle of hens, and her impatience boiled over. Flying at the chickens roosting on the porch and plow and scattered firewood, she whipped her shawl from her shoulders and shouted, "Out, you silly things! You belong in the barn!"

When she returned to Tom, he was watching her with a puckered frown on his face. "What's got into you, girl? Take life as you find it, Jen. You're a woman. That means you make no fuss. Remember your place in life. If you're born to be poor, well then, be content with it."

"And be abidin' this for the rest of my life? Tom, when I see people such as those fellas were, the justices and that Mark Cartwright, it makes me boil up inside—'specially when you talk like they're way up high, beyond the reach of us common folk."

As March slipped into April, the mellowing of springtime moved through the southern part of New York State. Blossoms on the wild plum and apple, dandelions and tiny buttons of meadow flowers added their scent to the newness of grass in the pungent pastureland.

Calves, black and white miniatures, took their places beside their placid mothers. Winter-stained flocks of sheep budded out with new white lambs. Spring rains blackened the woody branches of the trees along the pasture wall, and their halo of green seemed to bind everything together.

Fingers of green moss outlined the northerly edges of the stone walls as if spring had an abundance of green to spare.

When Jenny closed her eyes like two tiny slits, it seemed that the green, like paint, was dabbed everywhere.

One by one the older boys had dropped out of school to take their places in the fields. Now the girls went to school with only the very young children. And during recess, Jenny had Mr. Searle all to herself. The request was always the same.

Most often he would nod and point to the line of books on the shelf behind his desk, saying, "If you can't sound them out, ask." Jenny would choose a book and carry it back to her bench.

By late afternoon Jenny would walk slowly homeward, her mind full of the words and pictures. For a short time the books had helped her forget the other troubles that nagged at her thoughts.

Spring had brought a dark threat closer, one the Timmons family had felt all winter—Pa's spring stirring, the yearly urge to move west. But the urge was stronger this year. And over all was the troubling knowledge that Ma would soon be birthing again.

On the homeward walk Nancy talked about the West and Jenny thought with regret of all the books she hadn't been able to read.

"I hear it all," she replied grudgingly to Nancy's excitement. "But you forget the West is full of wild Injuns, with no stores or schools or books." She stopped to slant a look at her older sister's neat hair and patched dress.

"I doubt you'll ever have your dream of gettin' rich and having new frocks."

Nancy stopped in the middle of the path. The expression on her face, Jenny thought, was like being hungry with nothing to fill the hunger. Slowly she turned. Jenny needn't look to know she was seeing the peaceful pasture filled with black and white cows, and the rows of newly turned soil beyond. For just a moment, Jenny felt her spirit soar unfettered. "Maybe it won't be so bad."

Then Nancy turned to her. "Jen, what do you want most of all?"

Jenny answered quickly, and her reply caught even her by surprise. "To learn." Her toes dug down into the loam, rich soil.

"Like this, I want to dig into everything just to see what makes it go. I want to know about all the 'whys.' "

"Is that why you won't leave Pa's book alone?" Jenny's head snapped up and, startled, she nodded. Nancy looked thoughtful for a moment, "You're growing up, Jen. Last year you'd have gone for a stick of candy."

Silently they walked home. Candy. The last time Jenny had thought of candy, Arnold had promised information about Joe. And she had told Tom that she would marry Joe. Her lips curled at her silly, childish proclamation. She still recalled the way Tom had looked at her. He thought she had suddenly gone wild.

"One thing's certain," Jenny spoke out of the silence, "we've seen the last of Joe. When he hightailed out of the courtroom, I doubt he stopped 'til he got back to his ma's."

Nancy turned her green eyes on Jenny. "That happened over three months ago. You're still thinking about him—why?"

Jenny shrugged, but as they walked slowly up the lane toward home, she thought again about Joe and about the green book, wondering if all the promises it made could come true.

She'd told Nancy she wanted to learn. She'd told Tom she didn't want to live like this for the rest of her life. She'd told Joe she wanted to find the secrets of Pa's book. Maybe all those desires were somehow connected—maybe they would all come true together someday. Maybe wishing hard enough and saying it out loud would make it happen.

"I'm still scared," she whispered to herself, "of that glitter in Joe's eye when he talks about the spirits, and of the pictures in Pa's green witchin' book. But—" she paused, taking a deep breath, "I'm not goin' to be a baby about it anymore. If there's power to be had, spirit power to change the way things are, then I'll find it—no matter what!"

CHAPTER 6

Summer leaves were turning yellow and drying around the edges when the Timmons' covered wagon creaked down the main street of Manchester, New York.

From the eldest to the youngest, they were silent and slack-jawed as the marvels of the town unfolded before them. When the wagon had nearly reached the end of the main street, Nancy recovered enough to say, "Jen, I don't know where you got your information about the West, but this town is *bonny*; I could stay here forever!"

" 'Tain't the West," Pa muttered, gawking about with the rest of them, "but it's gonna have to do for now. I'm 'bout tuckered out."

Jenny's attention snapped back to the wagon, and she looked from her bleary-eyed father to her mother leaning against the wagon seat. The sight of her drawn face and swollen stomach tightened the fearful knot in Jenny's throat. Just for a moment, as she glanced at her father, anger surged through her. Quickly she turned her face before he could see the feelings that were becoming harder to hide.

Nancy touched her mother's shoulder. "It's far enough for now. Ma's not feeling up to another mile."

Jenny spoke slowly, trying to control the hope in her voice. "There's a school, and that's some kind of a big mill ahead. Pa, if we were to stay here, we could all go to school—even Matty's old enough now. Maybe—" She couldn't say *job* and *work* and *money*, but the thoughts were there. He frowned, glancing at her mother, and hauled back on the reins.

Tom finally tipped the balance in favor of staying on in Manchester. Pa had stopped the wagon beside the livery stable to wait for him—herding the milk cow kept Tom lagging far behind the wagon.

When he finally caught up, the pleased smile on his face slowly turned into a frown of concern as he looked at his mother, but his words were for his father. "The fella down the street asked me if we were stayin'. He says there's a place over two streets for let. Man at the livery stable owns it. He's lookin' for a hand. Name's Harris. I'm of a mind to see what he'll offer."

Before nightfall, the Timmons were moved into the small log cabin on a shady street. The cow and the crate of chickens were settled in the makeshift barn. While Tom and Jenny unloaded the wagon, Nancy swept a season's litter of dead leaves and dust out the door.

Later Tom straightened the sagging stovepipe and started a fire in the little stove. Now Jenny watched Pa. He was hesitating in the doorway and she wondered what excuse he would find. He finally said, "I'm of a mind to mosey on down the street and see if I can find a piece of glass for that broken window." Ma bit her lip and turned away.

Before she could stop them, Jenny said the words Ma had given up on: "We can get along without glass for right now. Why don't you just get some bread at that baker's shop and stay clear of the tavern."

His mouth gaped with astonishment, and Jenny brushed past him. Her impulsive words had startled her beyond fear. Maybe they had startled him beyond response. Jenny, stiff with remembered pain, waited for the blow that didn't come.

When Pa disappeared down the street, Tom turned to Jenny. "Your smart talk ain't usin' good sense."

Ma added, "Jen, don't be rilin' him. It just makes it worse." Jenny stared up at her mother, still unable to admit ownership of the words that had burst from her lips. Nancy clutched the broom, and Tom frowned.

Slowly Ma sat down on the chair Tom placed for her, saying, "Jenny, your sass ain't makin' life easier for any of us. What's got into you, child?"

Very soon, while the golden days of autumn were still warm and before the crystal ice began lining the streams, Ma felt stronger and was out getting acquainted. Jenny and Nancy took turns going with her. Wrapped in her old black shawl to hide her bulging abdomen, though it was sometimes warm enough to bead perspiration on her lip, Ma slowly strolled down the streets and investigated every shop.

One day when it was Jenny's turn to walk with Ma, she noted her flushed face and said, "Ma, I'll carry the shawl."

Ma's face flushed even brighter. "Lands no, child. With a family this size, I don't want to be pitied afore I even know my neighbors."

Jenny remained quiet, thinking new thoughts about being poor and having a pa like they had. She looked curiously at Ma, trying to see her as the neighbors would see her, but she couldn't get past the rusty old shawl and the faded calico squeezed tight over her body. Tired eyes were always ready to beg the pardon of the nearest person. Today she wore a timid smile, half in hiding until called upon.

When they stopped at the first gate, Ma hesitated, waiting for the woman sweeping her steps to look up. She was studying the neat house, and the frock the woman wore. Jenny knew Ma was calculating her chances of finding sewing. She also knew Ma was getting ready to pick at the woman's thoughts. Jenny remembered from the past that Ma would come home with a pocketful of facts. Like Matt collecting his marbles, she examined each one and carefully guarded it.

While Ma leaned over the fence and talked, Jenny noted how the apple tree bent under the load of shiny red apples. Her quick eyes took in the row of marigolds along the garden path. With another part of her mind, Jenny was admiring the way Ma was picking her store of facts from the woman, neat and quick—*like apples off that tree*, Jenny noted.

The woman said, "Camp meeting? My, but we've had them. There's one scheduled before the end of the month." She turned to wave her hand. "Over yonder there's a clearing, just the other side of the meetinghouse. Already they're fixing up a brush arbor. Don't know the fella's name who's coming. Don't matter much. People will either come to hear them all or they won't come to hear a one."

She turned back, leaning on her broom. "Me, I like them all. Gives a body something to do. My family's grown so's there's not much to keep me busy." Jenny saw her eyes move over the bulging black shawl.

Jenny pushed closer to the fence and said, "I'm goin' to school this fall; they're talkin' at recess time about some of the going's on. A bunch went to Sodus Bay to see the Shakers. It sounded like a fun time, watchin' the dancin' around and such. The big girls were whisperin' and laughin', but they wouldn't tell me why."

Ma's face flushed as they walked toward the shops. "Jen," she remonstrated as they hurried on, "you don't go makin' fun of religion when you don't know how a body believes."

"Does it matter how a body believes?" Jenny asked. " 'Sides, I didn't know I was makin' fun. It was just strange. Lettie was talkin' about some of the other going's on. She says that last year the schoolteacher, his name's John Samuel Thompson, had a vision. He told folks he saw Christ and he talked to Him. Another fella said there's a man over in Amsterdam, New York, who'd talked with God and was told every denomination of Christians is corrupt, and two-thirds of all the people livin' on the earth are about to be destroyed."

Ma shivered, then said firmly, "One thing's certain. Now that we're livin' in a town where there's a sizable church and the circuit riders get around regular like, we're goin' to be gettin' ourselves into church." Her voice dropped nearly to a whisper as she said, "Your pa don't cotton to gettin' salvation, but he was raised to know better."

Jenny was still wondering about "getting salvation" two weeks later as the evening of the first revival meeting approached. It seemed everyone in town was going. They talked about it at school and even Pa and Tom had promised Ma they would go.

That first evening, the sun was dropping behind the trees when the people started across town to the clearing behind the church. The Timmons joined the crowd, carrying shawls and quilts to pad the rough benches.

As they took their places, Jenny saw a black-coated man wearing a somber expression. Another man carried a shiny horn. When the man began to play the horn and the people began to sing, Jenny poked her mother and asked, pointing, "What's that?"

"The mourners' bench; now hush and don't ask questions. You'll see all soon enough."

After the singing, Jenny watched the somber-faced man open the black book, brace his feet, and lean toward the audience. When quietness stretched to the edges of the clearing and the only sound was raspy breathing and the chirping of crickets, the man began to speak.

He was holding the book high, but he didn't look at it. The words rolled from his tongue like music. " 'For God so loved the world, that he gave his only begotten Son, that whosoever believeth in him should not perish, but have everlasting life.' 'For the wages of sin is death; but the gift of God is eternal life through Jesus Christ our Lord.' 'For by grace are ye saved through faith; and that not of yourselves: it is the gift of God: not of works, lest any man should boast.' "

Jenny leaned across her mother, "*Grace*, that's pretty, isn't it? If you get a little girl, please name her Grace."

"Shush!" Ma's hand covered Jenny's mouth and her eyes were stern. Jenny was soon lost in contemplation as her mind drifted from one unfamiliar word to another.

The images these new words evoked were ethereal and meaningless, but she noticed their impact on those around her.

When Ma first began to tremble and Pa shuffled restlessly, Jenny sensed the mood of the crowd and the mounting tension. Often enough she had heard Pa say "hell," but now the man up front was wrapping the word in smoke and fire while the audience stirred uneasily.

Day after day the camp meetings went on and the tension in the town continued to build. Emotions were unleashed that varied from fear to joy, sorrow to happiness. And while the man with the book built pictures in Jenny's mind and poured the word-music over her, she saw Pa tremble and eventually refuse to accompany them to the meetings. She saw Nancy walk down the path to the mourners' bench and watched the tight sullen expression on Tom's face.

Suddenly the meetings were over, the leaves dropped from the trees, and ice skimmed the water pail. Warm emotions disappeared like autumn, and life returned to being ice-rimmed and cold.

And while Jenny was still frowning over it and trying to understand all she had seen and heard, there was now a settling back into the same old patterns.

The neighbor down the way, Mrs. Barfield, explained it all. Her marigolds were now black nubs, and both apples and leaves had disappeared from the tree. She said, with a touch of discontent in her voice. "Just like always. Expectation greater than the goods delivered. Them men talk with a great deal of steam, like kneeling there in the sawdust is the greatest thing ever happened to a body. Seems those kneeling think so too— for about a week or so. Then life's back to normal except for a few who try to go around convertin' the rest of us, just like we didn't really get converted in the first place.

"It's too bad the excitement don't last. That's what we're wanting. Oh, well, long as we escape hell, I guess that's all that matters. The preachers come around often enough to take care of the seekers. Seems it would be nicer, though, if the excitement would just last the winter." She shivered. Hesitating before she turned back to her house, she added, "Now, take them Shakers and some of those strange religions springing up all over the country. I don't cotton to them. There's too much in the name of religion that isn't. But, somehow, they end up makin' the rest of us decent folks wish we could share some of what enthuses them . . . people. I guess we're never happy."

The little rented house behind the livery stable now had the new baby; then Pa landed a job.

In the evenings after school, Jenny rocked the cradle and reflected that it was just as well little James was fretful. It kept her busy and seemed to ease her own restlessness a little, besides allowing her to read from time to time. Life at home was easier, now that Pa was working at the blast furnace. He seemed to be more content with himself and didn't take his frustration out on her.

Jenny, Nancy, Dorcas, and Matt were going to school. Tom was working at the livery stable, and Ma was sewing for some of the ladies they had met at church.

As Nancy had said, Manchester was a goodly town. It boasted pleasant homes on tree-lined streets, shops, a school, and—to Jenny the most important thing of all—there was a library. The town also had a woolen mill, a flour mill, and a paper mill, as well as the blast furnace where Pa worked.

On Sundays, the people donned their best clothes and paraded through the village on their way to the Presbyterian church. That is, most did. Tom didn't, and Pa didn't. And Jenny rebelled. "Jenny," Tom asked, "what's got into you?"

She felt the same kind of discontent that Mrs. Barfield had talked about, but Jenny saw it differently than Ma did. "It's not fair," she protested, "the one day I have to read, Ma makes me go to church."

She could have said it was boring, but she kept her silence while Ma talked about reading the Bible and Pa nodded his head in agreement. Jenny was separated, standing apart in her mind, knowing they would never understand. Even Nancy and Dorcas were lined up with serious faces and puckered frowns. To Jenny, the glance Ma threw at them seemed like a pat of approval.

Later, Tom repeated his question with a furrowed brow. He was milking the cow, and Jenny was pitching straw down to the pigpen. "Jen, what's got into you?" Jenny turned to look at him. The thoughts from Pa's green book stirred in her, and his question made the words burst from her. "Tom, aren't you hankerin' for more than this?"

He lifted his head from the cow's flank, and Jenny met his startled expression with a bravely lifted chin. She watched his eyes change, admitting the secrets they shared, and she went on in a whisper, "It's like you get a taste and then this isn't enough."

"Then I'm not the only one," he said slowly. After a moment

he continued reluctantly, "Jen, you're such a young'un. How do you come to have such thoughts?" She could only shake her head, not quite daring to put it into words. The feelings the book aroused in her were frightening, but she was fascinated and attracted nevertheless.

"Are you thinkin' of what we were doin' last year?" He studied her intently. "With Joe, diggin' for money?" She nodded.

"You got a likin' for that in a hurry." Tom spoke thoughtfully. "It ain't usual for the womenfolk to be that interested. Leastwise, the only one I know of is Lucy Smith."

"The only Lucy Smith I know is that little old lady at church."

He nodded. "Joe's ma."

"Joe Smith's? You mean she goes diggin'?"

He shrugged, "Naw, just interested."

"I didn't know Joe came from around here," she said slowly as she plucked the straw from her hair. "Smith is a pretty common name."

Tom nodded. "He's from here. You probably go to school with most of the young'uns in the family. Best get acquainted."

The next afternoon, walking home from school by herself, Jenny mulled over the restlessness she recognized in Tom. Her feelings were colored by a special kinship to him. She knew he was feeling the tug, too. She yearned to talk to him about Pa's book, but there was always the chance he would let it slip to Pa.

Jenny trembled, recalling the last time she had dared sneak the book from the rafters. Pa had nearly caught her. *Seems a body'd share it,* she reflected, even as she puzzled over the strange excitement that ran through her when she read the book. The feelings were akin to the ones she felt when she and Tom had gone to the diggings.

Abruptly Jenny realized she was already in front of the dry-goods store. Even as she stood there, she knew where her half-formed thoughts were going to take her. Quickly she turned away from her home and ran down the country lane. Earlier, Tom had pointed the way to the Smiths' cottage.

Though it was late and nearly time for chores, Jenny cut across the plowed field and headed into the trees beyond. She ran as fast as she could. Every minute saved meant more time with the woman named Lucy Smith.

Rounding a curve in the dim corridor of trees, Jenny caught her toe on a root and plunged headlong into the bushes. As she struck the ground, the bushes erupted with a flurry of movement. Gasping for breath, she stared upward at the unexpected flash of light. Heavy boots landed in front of her face. Shoving at the earth, she managed to push herself upright. She stopped, terror-stricken: a sheath of metal gleamed just inches from her nose.

"You're Tom Timmons' sister, ain't you?" the man barked. Then settling back on his heels and putting the sword on the ground, he continued. "Why you nosin' around?"

Gasping for breath, she shook her head. The hard expression on his face softened. "Scared the livin' daylights out o' you, didn't I?" Jenny examined her torn stocking and bleeding knee and didn't dare answer. "I'm Hyrum Smith. Come on, I'll have Ma fix up that knee. What you doin' out in the middle of the woods, anyhow?" He grasped her hand and pulled her to her feet.

Jenny tried moving her leg as she looked around. Just beyond Hyrum's shoulder she saw freshly turned earth. Glancing at the sword he held, she asked, "Been diggin'?"

He shook his head. "Them's old diggin's. Come along to the house." He added, "There's lots more diggin's around here."

"Did you find any treasure in them?" He shook his head. Shoving the sword into the sheath strapped to his waist, he explained, "Since we first moved here, we've been diggin' in the vicinity. The whole place is covered with holes."

When they reached the cabin and she was settled beside the table, she looked at the ring of curious eyes that surrounded her, and Jenny realized her problem was solved. Running through the woods, she had been wondering how she would explain her visit. It wasn't necessary now.

Lucy Smith talked constantly as she swabbed the blood from Jenny's leg. By the time the soothing ointment was applied, Jenny felt she knew everything there was to know about the Smiths.

The room was full of Joe Smith's relations, his sisters and brothers. Beside the fire stood a tall, gaunt man watching her. Their eyes met, and Jenny realized she had seen him in South Bainbridge.

The man with the sword was Joseph's older brother. She eyed the sword, trying to hide her intrigue. Hyrum must have guessed her curiosity. He pulled up a chair and held out the sword for her to see. Jenny hugged herself with excitement as he began to explain the markings. It was just as the book had described. Soon Lucy Smith was adding her comments, telling Jenny about the markings on the sheath.

"See this?" she pointed. "It's all to do with breakin' the charms the spirits have placed. You really need the sword to drive away the demon spirits. There's lots out there to be learned before a body can hope to be successful."

"Successful," Jenny repeated slowly. "You mean gettin' power?"

Lucy turned to peer at Jenny. "Lands, child, you set me back! I didn't expect such a young one with the knowledge. Yes, power. There's lots of hard work involved in gettin' it. Right now we're feelin' the lack and wonderin' if it's worth our time to study out Masonry to get the faculty of Abrac."

Lucy Smith leaned close to Jenny. "We're not wantin' anyone to think we spend all our time at this. But 'tis hard work to get everything to come out right. I keep tellin' them they gotta concentrate on the faculty of Abrac."

Jenny leaned forward and whispered, "What's that?"

"Abrac is a magic word. Some folks call it a formula, a way to release power. Better and more powerful than a charm. You put it on an amulet in order to work magic. See, you must learn what's necessary to make the word work for you. I'm guessin' that's why it's so hard to come by. I been hearin' that the Masons know how to conceal the way to get the power, so we're goin' to have to get on the good side of them if we want the power. When we get it, there's no stoppin' us. Too bad the Masons won't let womenfolk into their secret society. Guess we'll just have to let the men handle the problem."

"Abrac, is that—" Jenny gulped, but she must ask the question. "Is that why Joe couldn't get the money the Spaniards hid up?"

Lucy was nodding and murmuring, "Very likely. See, the word is from others, from Abracadabra and Abraxis. There's a lot more we need to know if we're to have success."

As Jenny got to her feet to leave, Joe's father addressed her. "So you're from South Bainbridge, huh?" She nodded. "Did ya go to the trial?" Again she nodded. He studied her for a moment, then continued, "Then you heard him tell everybody about how he got his seer stone. When he told me, I wasn't right thrilled about it all. The whole thing left a bad taste in people's mouths. They got the wrong idea. See, it mortifies us that people don't get the right picture. What he has is a mighty gift from God. It's terrible to think that the only outlet for it right now is in the findin' of filthy lucre, or earthly treasures. I'm prayin' constantly that the heavenly Father'll show His will concerning the use of this gift. He needs to illuminate Joe's heart, make the boy see what He has in store for him."

He stopped and turned his piercing gaze on Jenny again. "Now, I don't know why I'm a-wastin' my time tellin' a slip of a girl like you all these things big people needs to be worryin' about. But there it is, and you be a-doin' as you see fit.—Kinda like the fella, huh?"

One of Joe's sisters snickered, "Aw, Pa. She's just a babe, and you'll be a-tellin' her that all the gals like Joe."

" 'Tis true." Mrs. Smith got to her feet. "Even if he's my son, I admit he's a good-lookin' boy and all the girls know it. Now, Jen, please come back to visit."

At the end of January, Tom came home from the livery stable with his news. "Jen, you'll never guess what." He slid into his place at the table. "Joe Smith's back in town, goin' to be workin' with his pa."

Tom paused to take a bite of bread and Jenny's heart leaped. He added, "He's come with a wife. Married Isaac Hale's daughter, Emma. You remember Hale from the trial? He's the one from Harmony that's known for his huntin'."

"I remember," Jenny answered slowly, stunned by the news.

"Only, I didn't think he liked Joe very much."

"Married!" Nancy exclaimed.

"Aw, come on," Tom retorted, "don't be tellin' me you're soft on him too!" He turned to his father, "I've never seen the like. Every girl in the place fancies herself in love with Joe Smith. You'd think he was the only good-lookin' fella in town."

"What's he goin' to be doin' with his pa?" Ma asked.

"I have an idea they'll be gettin' back into the money-diggin' business," Tom answered, " 'Tis the only business I've heard tell them doin'."

"He been doin' good at it?" Pa asked, leaning across the table to look at Tom.

Tom shrugged, "I don't know. Old man Smith says he's been doin' it for thirty years."

"Is that so," Pa said, chewing. " 'Spect he's knowledgeable. The readin' I've been doin' of late leads me to believe there's profit to be had along that line. Might be a good idea for me to get acquainted with the old man."

Ma's spoon clattered to the table. "Now, you know better than that." She was chiding again. "Have you ever in your life heard of a body gettin' anything except trouble from that kind of business?"

The following Sunday Jenny went to church, but she spent most of the service trying to see whether Joe and his new bride were sitting in the pew beside Mrs. Smith, Hyrum and Samuel. Nancy noticed her peeking and whispered, "If you're looking for the newlyweds, well, they're not here." She poked Jenny and leaned closer, "Little ones like you don't get soft on big strapping fellas like Joe."

" 'Soft' like you and Prudence and the rest at school in South Bainbridge? I've never seen a bunch of girls as silly as you were last year," Jenny whispered back scornfully.

"You're just jealous you weren't big enough for a fella to notice you."

"I'm just too smart to line up behind the barn and play silly kissin' games with those slobby boys just to get kissed by Joe," Jenny hissed back, and was mollified when Nancy blushed.

CHAPTER 7

With the coming of January 9, 1827, her thirteenth birthday, Jenny experienced a growing consciousness of newness in her life. Trying hard to understand the feeling, she labeled it happiness and hugged it to herself.

The feeling was especially intense one day as she walked home from school. Winter was still hard upon the country, bringing bone-chilling dampness and vicious ice storms. But this day, the weather couldn't diminish the bliss that enfolded her.

She lifted her head high and allowed her mother's old shawl to slip back on her shoulders. Looking around as she walked homeward, seeing the stores, the library, even the blast furnace where Pa worked, Jenny felt for a moment what it was like to have everything she wanted. She gloried in the feeling. The best part of her life was school and the library. But there was another element. Her family was happy. She knew it by looking into their faces, listening to Tom whistle. Even Pa seemed at peace with himself.

During the remainder of the winter, the birthday feeling stayed with Jenny. She was content with her world of school, library, and home.

About springtime, when Jenny put down the latest library book long enough to notice, she saw changes in her family. Nancy was as tall as Ma. She walked and talked like a lady. When Jenny compared her own grubbiness with Nancy's new appearance, she was conscious only that she no longer knew this Nancy.

Ma and Nancy were often seen with their heads together. The new scholars, Dorcas and Matty, were becoming happy companions. And the picture of Jenny rocking James's cradle with one hand while the other held a book was also very familiar.

Just before winter gave way to spring, Jenny saw, for the first time, the maple trees in the valley being tapped for their precious sap. Soon the aromatic woodsmoke flavored with maple wrapped like a scarf of sweetness around the town.

When the snow slipped back to reveal the meadows carpeted in gentle greens, Pa began to show his yearly urge to move on. As usual, his unrest riled the family. But this year, Jenny, still wrapped in winter's peace, apart and separated, did not respond to the unrest. She held her silence as she watched her mother's uneasy frown and Tom's eternal pacing. Even James, who had grown into a plump, placid baby, responded fretfully.

"Teethin'," Ma declared. Matty and Dorcas just stayed in their corner and Nancy kept herself busy with stitching.

When it was time for plowing, all Pa could talk about was the West with its promise of virgin soil. Over and over they heard the arguments, and knew they were true. "Look at old man Smith," he said. "He told me hisself that when he came here in 1816 he paid near 'bout six dollars for an acre. If he'd gone to Ohio he could have had land just as good for a dollar and a quarter an acre. 'Sides, you know yourselves, the whole East is in depression." Desire for those fertile fields lay heavy upon him, so heavy that this year there would be no turning him back.

From her sanctuary behind the dishpan, Jenny listened, and finally she awakened again to reality, and her heart began to ache. It was impossible to believe there would be another town like Manchester. Just closing her eyes made her see the long line of library books she had not yet read.

At night she would kneel beside the loft window and whisper, "Star light, star bright—" Then she would pause, unable to put that nameless wish into words.

Then one cool, breezy evening, Tom spoke, his voice wavering only slightly. "I'm not goin'. I'm growed, and it's time I found my own way. I'd rather work at the livery for a year or so, then I'll . . ."

Studying his face, Jenny could only guess at the things he dared not say. But secretly she was applauding him. For the first time, Tom had stood up to Pa. As she stared at him, he straightened his shoulders, and a hint of a smile gleamed in his eye. Jenny didn't need to grin at him; he knew how she felt. She turned away, sad for herself but glad for him.

Pa watched them all for a moment. Jenny felt his eyes upon her. He broke the silence. "So be it. I can't be a-hangin' on to you if you've made up your mind. The rest of us will be goin'." Thoughtfully he studied Tom and then added, "It'll be lonesome for you. You'll be needin' to find a place to board, and that'll cut into your wages." But Tom's jaw was set, and Pa said no more.

On the warmest day of the spring, with the door open wide to catch any passing breeze, Jenny worked in the stifling cabin. She was fretfully begrudging the errand which had taken Nancy to the store. As she wiped perspiration from her face, she was even begrudging her mother's tasks outdoors as she washed and hung laundry on the bushes.

But while Jenny was lifting pans from the high shelf, she found the book.

"Oh, there it is!" she exclaimed with satisfaction. Hugging the book like an old, dear friend, she settled down on a bench and stroked the dusty cover. "For sure I thought he'd chucked you for good."

She studied the cover. It wasn't like the dark, somber book that belonged to her mother; this one was bright green with the figure of a woman on it, outlined in gold. Jenny traced her finger over the shiny illustration, again wondering about it. She ached with longing to open it, to read those enticing passages. Jenny ran her fingers over the gold letters of the title, *The Greater Key of Solomon*.

She peeked once, then was immediately lost to her surroundings. "Raphael," she murmured to herself. "I wonder who he is?" Her finger followed the words down the page, fumbled and turned the next page, and the next. The title of one chapter caught her attention, and excitement coursed through her as she continued, "This chapter is about how to render yourself master of a treasure possessed by a spirit. That's what Joe was tryin' to do. I wonder if he's read this book."

As she continued to stare at the page before her, she recalled her father talking about reading the book. For a moment her heart contracted as a picture arose in her mind: Jenny and her father, miraculously changed, working together as friends with the book between them. Jenny and her father, together with Joe Smith, digging up treasure—gold, silver, more than her mind could conceive. Her eager eyes again sought the words.

When the page before her dimmed, she realized the afternoon was gone. Then to her horror she discovered that the darker shadow was Pa! By his silence she knew he had been watching for some time.

"Why you lick your lips like that when you read the words?" he asked. He had lifted the razor strap down from the wall beside the washbasin. Jenny's vision exploded like a bubble. She tried to focus on the battered tin bucket. "Answer me! Why can't you leave my book alone?" he shouted.

His first blow knocked the book across the room. It spun out of sight under the edge of the bed quilt. She tried to see it even as she willed it to stay hidden.

When the blows had ceased and the scent of his alcohol-laden breath filled the room, when the blood was warm and wet on her legs, Jenny knew she would be staying in Manchester when Pa and the others moved on.

When Tom saw Jenny's bleeding legs and listened to her, he turned and without a word left. When he returned, he had a promise of a position for Jenny with the Martin Harris family. Harris owned the livery stable where Tom worked. She took comfort in that. *It's a link to Tom,* she thought as he told her Mrs. Harris needed a girl.

June found Jenny settled in her new home. Some days she regretted her position as hired girl in the household, especially when she stirred the wrath of Martin Harris. While his stern words condemned the dust in the corner and the weeds in the garden, his wife patted Jenny's shoulder, saying, "Never mind a word he says. He knows we couldn't be gettin' along without you."

It was true. Mrs. Harris was lame this spring, and limped slowly about her house and garden. They expected Jenny to fill the gap.

When her family had left, Jenny had watched the wagon lurch away from the little house behind the livery stable, carrying them away from her. As she thought about that scene, even now, the tears blurred that final picture. If it hadn't been for the pain in her bruised body and Tom's restraining hand on her shoulder, she would have run after the wagon, begging for her old place beside Nancy. If the tears hadn't filled her eyes, would she have been able to find in Ma's face the tenderness she longed for?

She recalled the day Pa had used the razor strap on her. She could still see how Ma had turned away when she saw the blood. Tom had washed her legs and rubbed in the ointment. Not Ma, not Nancy. Had her sin been too much? She didn't need to be told they thought she deserved the hurts.

Nowadays it helped to have Tom and the hard tasks at her new home. They wiped out the miserable, lonesome thoughts.

Tom had been given a spot in the loft at the Harris home, and he took his board with them. During the evening hours, he split logs and stacked them under the eaves to pay for his keep.

As the summer passed, Jenny continued to nurse the one secret she hadn't dared share with even Tom. She promised herself that she would. But as time drifted by, she forgot how Ma had turned away and how Nancy had scorned her. The guilty secret didn't seem as frightening nor as important now.

Come evenings, Jenny took out Pa's green book and looked at it, no longer trembling with guilt for stealing it. She still promised herself once in a while that she would share her secret with Tom.

As autumn approached, the Sabbath day became a high spot in Jenny's week. After the breakfast dishes were done and the dinner roast shoved into the oven, Jenny was free to change her dress and go with Mrs. Harris to the Presbyterian church.

Not that church had become important—however, for this

one day Jenny would be beyond the disapproving eye of Mr. Harris.

On that first Sabbath, Mrs. Harris had seen Jenny's perplexed frown as Martin Harris settled down on the porch, still wearing his carpet slippers. In the wagon Lucy Harris snapped the reins along the backs of the team and tried to explain her husband's newest beliefs. Jenny's eyes grew round with wonder.

"Why does he keep joinin' so many churches?" she asked. "I've heard of the Quakers, but what's a Restorationist and a Universalist?"

Mrs. Harris shrugged and forced a weak smile, but Jenny could see the pain behind her eyes. "Child," she said, "some people just never seem to be satisfied with settlin' for the truth. My husband Martin, he's a good man, been raised with true religion. But he's so restless, he's never made a commitment of himself to the truth. So he keeps lookin' for something new— and he always seems to find it."

Jenny stared at her new mistress, dumbfounded. Her own mother had taught her to honor the Bible and to read it instead of Pa's green book. But no one had ever talked about truth in this way.

"You mean," she stammered, "there's just one truth, one power?"

They had reached the church, and Mrs. Harris turned and looked Jenny square in the eye. "Lots of powers, child—some good, some bad. Only one truth." Her eyes softened. "Maybe someday you'll understand." She turned and limped ahead to find her friends.

In church, Jenny was becoming conscious of the people around her. She heard the pastor read the black book, using words she still couldn't understand. But her neighbors and school friends, the grocer and the man who had worked with Pa at the foundry were all changed. On the Sabbath day laughing faces were sober, thoughtful. School-yard folly was forgotten. Dirty shirts were exchanged for clean, and tousled hair was neatly braided.

Somehow there was a tie between this place, the words that man was reading, the serious faces under smoothed hair, and the truth of which Mrs. Harris spoke. She saw responses from the parson's listeners, and the quiet atmosphere of the church became shivery with intense feeling. Although Jenny didn't quite recognize it, the feeling awed, even frightened her.

Sometimes she was nudged into thinking thoughts about sin, about evil, about her soul, about heaven and hell.

She pushed aside that sense of foreboding and thought of her desire for spirit power. There were lots of powers, Lucy Harris had said. Which power, she wondered, was the one she wanted?

For some reason she couldn't understand the parson's words about sin and evil. But it made Jenny think of the stolen green book, the pictures of spirits, and the words of power. Again she felt the mingled fear and fascination and remembered the strange glitter in Joe Smith's eyes. *He knows*, she thought, *of the gold of the treasures guarded by the power of the spirits*.

Often at night, when Jenny was in her room under the eaves, seeing the moonlight, listening to the crickets and feeling alone, she found she couldn't sleep. Wide-eyed she would lie in the drift of moonlight, missing the sounds of her family's soft breathing in the room, lonesome for the warmth of Dorcas beside her.

One night, when the moon was high and the Harrises had set the rafters to trembling with their snoring, Jenny heard the creak of the barn door. She crept to the window, heard the distant clank of shovel against stone, and saw dim shadows slip through the yard.

The next day she followed Tom to the barn. "Tom, you're diggin' nights. Why can't I go with you?"

He looked astonished, then glanced quickly around. "Hush. I don't want Mrs. Harris to know. Look, Jen, I gotta get it across to you; this isn't fun, it's serious business. We can't risk a young'un messin' it up again."

"You're still blamin' me for not findin' the treasure over at South Bainbridge, aren't you?"

"Well, let's put it this way," he said shortly. "There's enough chance you did it that none of us will risk it again."

She studied him curiously for a moment before she said,

"Look, I'm older now. Trust me. From the way you said that, there must be some in the bunch knowin' about last time. There's no one else around except the Smiths."

He nodded, "You're right." He closed his lips tightly and turned to lift a forkful of hay to the cows. Jenny studied his expression. Tom wasn't going to say more.

She tried to find a way to break past the barrier. "Tom, you're shuttin' me out on purpose. We're all the family there is now." She let the lonesome feelings tremble through her voice.

He rumpled her hair. "Aw, Jen. You're the best sis I could have, but you can't be out followin' the fellas."

"Do you really think you'll be findin' something this time?" He said nothing. In frustration she turned away.

The matter would probably have ended with Tom's stubborn silence if it hadn't been for the trip to Palmyra. It stirred afresh her desire to be in on the digging.

The Harris farm lay tucked between the two villages of Manchester and Palmyra, New York. Jenny knew Manchester well—it was a wonderful place with its shops and mills. But she had never been to Palmyra.

The day Martin Harris declared he was going to Palmyra, Lucy Harris elected to go with him. Mr. Harris sighed in resignation. "Might as well take Jenny. I'll not have the time to tote you around, so ye better have company."

Martin Harris was unusually talkative on the ride. Watching his face as he described the building of the Erie Canal, Jenny was surprised to see his dreamy, contented expression. It was unlike the employer she had come to fear.

When the wagon reached the Palmyra side of the bridge, he said, "This is a great country, this United States of America. Just watch. The nation will be great because our democracy is based on the laws of nature. We'll steadily become more perfect and our people will be purified. One day the whole world will come running after us to follow our example." He waved his whip at the canal. "This Erie Canal is part of the dream. Sure, it costs, but it makes progress possible on a grand scale. It costs in lives and money for us to be moving westward. It's brave men doing it. There's not a power on earth can stop the progress once the Lord wills it. Manifest Destiny, they are calling it. This canal's been open less'n two years, but look at the boats."

When they reached Palmyra Jenny gaped at the crowds, whispering, "It's so big! Bet it's bigger'n New York City."

Harris laughed. "Less'n four thousand people." But sobering, he said, "That's a goodly lot though, and it's a fair town. You ladies be at your shoppin' and get back to the stables. I wanna be outta here before midafternoon."

As they climbed out of the wagon, Jenny spotted one of the stores and exclaimed, "Look! That shop has just books!"

Mrs. Harris glanced around and said, "Oh my, it does. Funny I never noticed it before." She studied Jenny curiously and added, "I don't claim to be all that interested in reading. If there's time later, I'll let you have a look."

With her mind filled with that one thought, Jenny trailed around the shops with Mrs. Harris, trying to be patient.

Finally, Jenny's arms loaded with parcels and Mrs. Harris's bag bulging, the woman announced her shopping completed and they turned toward the stables. Halfway back, Mrs. Harris stopped to talk to a friend. When Jenny shifted from foot to foot, the woman said, "Be off to the book shop, and then go on to the wagon."

When Jenny stopped, breathless and flustered, in the doorway of the bookstore, she could only fidget and sniff deeply of the dust and leather and ink.

"Yes, young lady, what would you like to see?" Jenny looked past a very white shirt and black string tie to a round face as friendly as the parson's. She smiled at him.

"Oh, everything," Jenny whispered. "Do you mind if I look? I'll be careful." She rubbed her sweaty palms on her dress.

He chuckled. "You're not the usual kind. Help yourself," he pointed to the double rows of bookcases, and Jenny eased herself between them, wondering where to begin. There were leather books and cloth-bound ones, dark covers and bright. Some wore strange titles she didn't understand. She also saw familiar books, ones she had read at school and at the library in Manchester, the ones the librarian had called classics.

As Jenny moved slowly down the aisle, touching books with

a cautious finger, yet not daring to pull them from the shelf, a bright green cover caught her eye. Hardly believing what she saw, she tipped it out of the shelf. It was the same from green cover to the gold outlines on the front.

The shopkeeper was at her elbow now. "You wouldn't want the likes of that book," he said gently. "It's not for fine young ladies."

She turned. "Why not?" she asked, surprised. Her hand still held the book. "It's a bonny book, all green with the gold lady."

He cleared his throat and continued to smile kindly at her. Leaning closer, he whispered, "It's a book about magic, witch-craft, and the like. Now, if I were to have my say, such a book wouldn't even be in town, but there's some who set great store by such things. Nowadays we don't hear much said against such teachings, but frankly I believe it is wrong, terribly so. I think this treasure-digging and using seer stones to hunt for lost ar-ticles or for telling fortunes is of the devil. But the owner, Mr. Anderson, insists we must provide what the people want."

"The book's bad?" Jenny asked, still fingering it.

His smile was gentle, his eyes full of concern. "It's of the devil. Satan is behind the likes of such stuff."

"Satan," Jenny stated flatly. She pulled the book down and turned the pages. "It's talkin' about power, knowledge, how to get things you want. Isn't that good?"

He looked astonished. "Child," he said, "there's power, and there's power. Not all power is good." His sensitive eyes took her in, and he was about to continue when the door opened. He turned and moved toward the front of the shop.

Jenny slowly replaced the book. She frowned, thinking about the strange manner of the little man, hearing the echo of Mrs. Harris's words. The booming voice from the front of the store caught her attention. As she looked up she heard the man ask, "You have some Masonic books?"

"Right this way." Beneath the clomp of boots, Jenny heard the shopkeeper ask, "Why would you be needing them?"

After a pause the man said, "I'm joining the lodge."

Suddenly Jenny recognized the voice. She popped around the corner of the bookcase. "Hyrum!"

They left the shop together. Jenny was chattering, running to keep up with Hyrum, when they met Mrs. Smith and the Harrises talking together on the street corner.

Martin Harris looked up at Hyrum and said, "Your mother's tellin' me you're about to join the Masonic lodge."

Mrs. Smith reached for the package Hyrum carried. "You found a book?" Her fingers picked nervously at the paper before she tucked it into her bag. She met Jenny's gaze. "Hyrum's been tellin' me about how this Masonic book might be helpin' a mite. He says we'll understand more of how to get the faculty of Abrac."

When the Smiths had gone their way, Jenny and Lucy Harris trailed far behind Martin Harris as he headed for the livery stable. Mrs. Harris shook her head. "That Smith bunch! I've never seen the likes of them, always wantin' something they don't have. First they used the seer stone to tell fortunes, and now this. But I suppose I'd be worryin' myself too if I were ridin' as close to losin' my place as they are."

Jenny turned to look after the little woman and her tall son hurrying down the street. "That's sad," she said, painfully aware of want. "The faculty of Abrac; I wonder—"

Mrs. Harris interrupted with a snort, "Hogwash to them! You should hear the latest story the mister is puttin' out. I heard him myself. He was talkin' to that man Chase. Says several years ago his son, Joe, had an appearance. 'Twas a spirit come to Joseph, informing him there was gold plates hidden near his home. Young Joe tried to get them, he says, but there was a toad guardin' them. Well, this toad changed into a man and hit him a wallop on the side of the head.

"Old man Smith's sayin' that in September Joe's to be let have the plates—genuine gold, he says, and need some translatin'. There's supposed to be a story about the ancient people on this continent.—I'm thinkin' if Lucy gets hold of them, she'll be translatin' them into cold, hard cash."

They were nearly to the livery stable. Jenny saw Lucy's quick glance toward Martin Harris's sturdy back. She also saw the tear in the corner of her eye and the impatient hand that flicked it away. Straightening her shoulders, Lucy Harris marched toward her husband, Jenny tagging slowly along behind.

CHAPTER 8

Lucy Harris turned from the stove, "Jenny, run out to the barn and fetch me some eggs."

With a quick nod, Jenny dropped her dish towel and headed for the back door. As she crossed the yard, she saw Tom lean over the railing of the pigpen, tilting a pail. The air was filled with the shrill squealing of hungry pigs. Jenny paused to watch Mr. Harris poke at the pig sow.

"Get out o' there and let the little 'uns have a chance!" he roared, flailing at her shoulders.

Jenny went into the barn and climbed to the loft to search through the straw for eggs. The squealing in the pigpen subsided, and Mr. Harris's voice rose. "Well, I'll be a-goin' out with you tonight. Joe said Walters will be there. I can't miss that. 'Sides, the other members of the Gold Bible Company will be there." Jenny heard the low rumble of Tom's voice answering him. She folded the eggs into her apron and slipped back down the ladder.

As she walked toward the door of the barn, Harris spoke again. His voice was low and deliberate. "The boy's got a talent. There's something there, and I believe he's learnin' how to get it. It'll help a lot if Hyrum will learn how to get the extra power from the faculty of Abrac." His earnest voice stopped Jenny just inside the door. "He's pretty convinced that joinin' the Masons will do it.

"You know, I was out to his pa's place once. Joe was a talkin' and I was standin' there pickin' my teeth with a pin. I dropped the thing in some straw and couldn't find it. Well, old Joseph and Northrop Sweet were there and they couldn't find it either. Just jokin' I said, 'Joe, use your stone and find it.' I didn't even know he had it with him. He pulled it outta his pocket, and stuck his face in his hat. Pretty soon he was feelin' around on the ground—without lookin', mind you. Then he moved a stick and there was my pin. That boy has a talent, and I'll be waitin' around to see what he does with it."

Slowly Jenny walked to the pen. "You believe it too? Do you 'spect he'll be findin' a treasure?"

She watched the excitement light his eyes and felt her own heart thump. "Something big," he said. "There's things buried out there. And there's forces fightin' against you. A fella over Palmyra way said they were diggin' by the old schoolhouse and the whole place lit up. Scared them so the bunch of them took out o' there. Later they were diggin' again, close to a barn. They looked up and a fella was sittin' on top of the barn. They say he was eight or nine feet tall. He motioned them to get outta there. They kept on workin', but finally they got so scared they took off."

Tom leaned on his pitchfork. "Do you know anything about using the rods?"

"Naw, but old man Smith can tell you about them if you want to know. He's been usin' them for years."

"Findin' treasure?" Jenny asked eagerly.

He shrugged. "Maybe. Depends on who you talk to."

"Jenny!" Mrs. Harris called and Jenny scooted for the house.

Martin Harris watched her go and said, "For a little 'un, your sister's sure interested in diggin', isn't she?"

Tom nodded soberly and went back to pitching straw. "Yeah. She's so little it's hard to take her serious. Is it possible for young'uns to get caught up in the craft?"

"Willard Chase's sister did. She has a green glass seer stone she uses all the time." Harris paused and then added, "I wouldn't be a-discouragin' it. Never know, she might really get the power."

That evening after Jenny had finished the dishes, she went upstairs and dug the green book out of the cubbyhole where she had hidden it. Studying the cover, she stroked it thoughtfully. She pondered about the strange uneasiness she had been sensing in church. She needed something, and she must reach for it, but the reaching couldn't be done with her bare hands.

As she thumbed through the book, she began to wonder—could it have anything to do with the power Hyrum had talked about it? She recalled Martin Harris's excitement, talking about the Gold Bible Company. Surely that didn't have anything to do with the black Bible the solemn-faced man at church read before he started to talk.

She sighed deeply and rubbed her eyes. Questions—the world was full of unanswered ones. Did Pa's book hold the answers for any? Could this green book give her the mysterious power it seemed to promise?

Mrs. Harris was still downstairs by the fire—maybe she would know.

Jenny crept down the stairs cautiously, Pa's stolen green book in her hand. As she reached the landing, the last stair creaked, and Mrs. Harris's head, bent over her worn leather Bible, snapped up with a start.

"Jenny, child!" she laughed. "You nearly did this old heart in! I thought you'd been asleep by now."

"I—I knew you were still up," Jenny stammered. "And—well, there's something I want to ask you."

"Come, sit, child." Mrs. Harris patted the footstool near her rocker and motioned Jenny nearer the fire. "What you got there?" She reached for the book, and Jenny pulled back.

"It's—was—my pa's." Jenny faltered, then her desperate curiosity overcame her. "I been readin' in it some, and I don't understand it all, but it talks about gettin' power—like Mr. Harris and Joe Smith are tryin' to do—" She gasped for a breath, then went on before Mrs. Harris could interject a word. "An' like the parson talks about on Sundays, and—" Jenny stopped, astonished at her own boldness. "Mrs. Harris," she plunged, "this black Bible of yours and this book—do they say the same, about gettin' the power, I mean?"

Mrs. Harris reached for the green book and gently pried Jenny's fingers from the spine. She winced slightly as she looked at the cover, then fingered the gold design thoughtfully.

"Jenny," she began, "I ain't much of a reader, and I'll confess

I ain't read this book, but I know what's in it—least, I know what it's about." She handed the book back to Jenny. "An' I know something of that Joe Smith."

She paused. "Child," she sighed, "remember me tellin' you that there's only one truth, but there's lots of powers?"

Jenny nodded slowly.

"This here," she raised the black book that lay in her lap, "holds both—the truth and the power. That 'un," she pointed to the green book crushed against Jenny's chest, "that book may tell you about some power, but it won't tell you the truth."

Jenny pondered this before she spoke. "Mrs. Harris," she drew out her words slowly, deliberately, "what is the truth?"

Mrs. Harris smiled faintly. "Somebody else asked that same question, child, a long time ago. An' the answer he got is the same one you'll come to someday. Truth ain't an idea, or even a way to get power. It's a person—Jesus, who died on the cross to save us all."

"From sin?" Jenny interjected anxiously, remembering the parson's sermons, seeing the strange wild glint in Joe Smith's eyes, feeling the stolen book burning against her arms and chest.

"From sin," Mrs. Harris agreed, "and from yourself. From greed and the burnin' for wealth and power like Joe Smith's got; from the stubbornness of doin' things your own way like my Martin's got . . ."

"Power," whispered Jenny. She turned her full attention to the firelit face of the mistress. "Mrs. Harris, my ma said this book is evil, but she didn't say why. The little man at the book shop said the power in it is from the devil. Is power evil? Is it?"

Lucy Harris's eyes were hidden in the shadows as her hands fingered the worn pages of the Bible. When she looked again at Jenny, a single tear had left a trail down her cheek, glistening in the light of the dying fire.

"Jenny," she began, "the only lastin' power lies in the truth. There may be power in the spells told about in your pa's book, or in Joe's seer stone and divinin' rods. But the real power to be had don't come through such tricks. It comes through faith, through God."

Jenny went to bed restless, disturbed by her conversation with Mrs. Harris. Faith seemed an awfully slow, awfully uncertain way of getting the power. And it didn't seem to offer much in the way of benefit for the here and now. Pa's book and Joe's stone promised a more immediate fulfillment—and it was easier to come by, too. The right words, a sword, some blood from a goat or a lamb, and a person could have riches *and* power, served up by the spirits like the rich folks' Christmas goose!

But what if Mrs. Harris is right? Jenny shivered at the thought. *If it really does matter where the power comes from—*

Jenny's thoughts were interrupted by the creak of the stairs. She sat up in bed, straining to hear. Only one familiar snore was coming from down the hall. When the creaking stopped, she slipped from her bed and knelt beside the window.

Twin shadows left the barn and moved down the road. Bright moonlight clearly revealed the progress of the two until they disappeared over the hill. Jenny continued to kneel at the window, thinking of the section in the book about moonlit nights. There was unusual power on these nights.

She fidgeted, rubbed at her tumbled hair, then jumped to her feet. Shoving aside the scary nighttime feelings and the echoes of her discussion with Mrs. Harris, she pulled on her clothes and crept down the stairs.

At the door she paused, but not long enough to heed her fears, then flew down the road after the men.

In the darkness of the woods, the road disappeared and the moonlight vanished. Groping with her hands before her, Jenny crept forward. Now excitement had her heart pounding. She moved from tree to tree, stopping to listen at each one.

When she heard the clank of metal and saw the bobbing light, she moved off the trail and slipped behind the group.

The lantern revealed Tom, Mr. Harris, and a dark man wrapped in a long black cloak. There were others, but she had eyes only for the cloaked figure.

Spellbound, she watched, certain this must be the man they called Walters the Magician. He was reading from a book. She strained to hear, but his words were an indistinct rumble of sound. As she watched his black-draped arms arching through the air, punctuating his words, she shivered, and a strange thrill moved over her.

The lantern light flashed off a sword, and Jenny crept closer. It was Hyrum. Joseph stood by holding a flapping rooster.

Carefully easing into the bushes, Jenny watched. Hyrum drew the circle, making the familiar marks. Restlessly she rubbed her hands together. *If only, just once, they'd let me be part of the group.*

After Joe spread the blood from the rooster, they all began to dig. The chill of the late night made Jenny shiver, and she hugged herself. Would the rooster turn the trick this time?

Silently, through the long night, they dug, while Jenny watched with growing frustration. Finally Martin Harris threw down his shovel in disgust.

They turned and walked back the way they had come, and only then did Jenny realize the east was brightening. She forced her numb legs to carry her down the trail. Dazed and disappointed, she didn't need to remind herself there had been no shouts of triumph to interrupt the black night. As she ran, tears of frustration welled up in her eyes. "Joe," she whispered, "you taught me all this. Why don't you fellas let me try?"

I am certain of one thing, she thought. *I am going to read that book and find the power.*

But Jenny's feet slowed as she remembered Mrs. Harris and the words the parson had read at church. Suddenly she was filled with a certainty that she should not read the book anymore.

As Jenny hesitated in the path, the sun burst through the trees. She lifted her chin and shrugged. *It's just a book. And if it teaches me the power, what harm can there be?*

When she opened the door to the kitchen, she discovered Martin Harris shouting for his breakfast, his anger breaking through every word his wife uttered. One quick glance at the gloomy faces sealed Jenny's silence, and she crept unnoticed about the room.

In September the rumors started flying. For several days there had been whispers at school. But Jenny had heard whispers before. This time she ignored them.

At lunchtime one day, she carried her pail down to the creek to join the students under the trees. As she reached them, the conversation stopped. Jenny saw the shared looks and was ready to turn away when one of the older girls called, "Jenny, wait!"

The girl's apologetic look swept through the group and she said, "She's living at the Harrises and he's been friendly with the Smiths; maybe she can tell us about it." Turning back to Jenny she asked, "Have you seen the gold plates?"

Jenny settled to the ground and crossed her legs. "Gold plates," she said with a frown. She flipped her braids over her shoulders and pushed hair out of her eyes. "I don't know what you're talkin' about."

"I guess everybody thought you were in on it because of Harris. People know he's friendly with Joe."

Jenny recalled what Mrs. Harris had told them, and thought briefly of Lucy's response. "What about gold plates?" she asked slowly as she concentrated on prying the lid off her lunch pail.

Mary Beth, the oldest girl at school, settled down beside Jenny. "They're saying the Smiths have circulated a story about Joe finding a bunch of genuine gold plates with writing all over them."

"Well, why don't you ask one of Joe's sisters instead of me?" Jenny questioned with a frown.

"There hasn't been a one of the Smith bunch in school since the story started making the rounds."

Now Cindy, Mary Beth's best friend, scooted close to Jenny and added, "Joe is saying he found them in a stone box along with a sword and a breastplate and some spectacles to translate the writing on the plates. He's calling the spectacles the magic 'Urim and Thummim.' I guess like in the Bible. Least the parson talked about such."

"They say Joe's getting set to translate the plates. There's trouble brewing 'cause he won't let a soul see them. He's claiming folks'll die if they do," Elizabeth said.

"Some of the fellas are mad because he promised to share the money with them, and now they're saying he won't even let them see what he has. But he's sure got something," Cindy continued. "Even his family owns they've seen something all done up tight in a piece of cloth."

After school that afternoon, Jenny walked slowly home. There were chores waiting, but she was thinking hard. Not since she had heard about Joe getting married had she returned to the Smiths. A sore spot still twinged in her heart whenever she thought of him. Now she clenched her fists and muttered, "Joe, I hate you for marryin' that gal. Didn't you guess you were mine? And I hate you, prissy missy, for daring to run off with him."

Jenny's hands relaxed. Her curiosity was bigger than her hate. Quickly she turned and ran down the trail that ended at the Smith farm.

Despite her bravery, she was relieved to discover only Lucy Smith at home that afternoon. Once settled in the gloomy cabin, across the table from Lucy Smith, she studied the woman. From her knot of graying hair to her button-bright eyes and curving shoulders, excitement possessed her. Jenny said, "I hear Joe's found a gold book."

Lucy leaned close to Jenny. "Oh my, he has! We've known for a time that it was to be. Joe's been workin' the stone and the charms, tryin' to get past the spirits a-guardin' the whole lot. It's been hard work and he's suffered much in order to get them."

"Did you see them?"

"Oh, no. Joe said he was instructed that no man could see the plates with his naked eyes and live. That's part of the reason he was given these funny spectacles. They're diamonds set in glass held together with bows, like regular ones. They're to be used to translate words on the plates."

"Is it a story written on them?"

"No. Joe says it's a history of the ancient people who lived here many years ago." Now she chuckled and patted Jenny's knee. "Just be patient and wait. Sooner or later you'll all be seein' them. I aim to exhibit them when Joe's all through translatin'. I'll be chargin' a price to see them, but after all the work, that's only fair."

One afternoon in late autumn, Jenny came in from school to find Martin Harris pacing the kitchen floor. She stood just inside the door, looking from his excited face to Mrs. Harris at the table. Her hands lay idle in the apple peelings, as she studied the knife she held.

Jenny glanced at Mr. Harris as he said, "Here I was just a-walkin' down the street when he came up to me. Proud, kinglike he was. He says, 'Martin, the Lord told me to ask the first honest man I met for money to get me to Harmony to get along with the translatin' of the gold plates.' "

Lucy Harris looked up at him in dismay, and he circled back to her in his pacing. "Quit thinkin' about the fifty dollars! Wife, I fear for your soul if you can't trust when a man says the Lord's directin' him. You know I've been searchin' for the truth all my life."

Jenny watched Mrs. Harris open her mouth as if to speak. Then she got to her feet, slowly, as if she had been hoeing in the garden all day.

When Martin turned to Jenny, she found the courage to say, "At school they're talkin'. Said Joe Smith found a book."

"The gold plates," Mr. Harris said reverently. "All that diggin' paid off. Yonder up the hill he found 'em."

On Sunday at church, Lucy Smith was the center of attention. Jenny elbowed her way through the crowd and listened as someone asked, "Mrs. Smith, what do the plates look like?"

"Well, Joe's not showin' them yet, but he did let me see the things that came with 'em. There's magic spectacles like diamonds. They are just like three-cornered diamonds set in glass and the glass set in silver bows. They're for readin' the plates. With them was a breastplate, big enough to fit a good-sized man. The whole thing was worth at least five hundred dollars."

Amid appreciative murmurs, Lucy continued, "The plates, they're gold. Like leaves of a regular Bible they are, only gold. I 'spect we'll be a-makin' a pile of money off this find. Joe's goin' to translate the plates and then I'll be a-showin' them. Figure I can charge twenty-five cents for a peek."

Later when Jenny started home, she passed a group talking on the street corner. Peter Ingersoll was speaking, and she waited to hear him.

"Well, judge for yourself," he was saying. "I met Joe walkin' toward home one day, carryin' something all wrapped up in his jacket. Didn't think too much about it all until a couple of days later; then he told me he had carried home some pretty white sand. His folks were all a-sittin' round the dinner table, he said, and they were a-wantin' to know what he had. Said he happened to think about a story he'd heard of a fella in Canada who claimed he found a book containing the history of the original settlers. He called it a gold Bible. So Joe says when they asked him, the words jest popped out, 'gold Bible.' He was just funnin', but they took him serious.

"So when they wanted to see the thing, he said they could go ahead and look, but he'd had a commandment sayin' that no man could look at it with the naked eye and live. Not a one of them would look at it. Then Joe slapped his knee and told me he had them all fixed and he intended to be havin' some fun with them."

Peter paused and Jenny stared up into his face. He frowned and slowly said, "This whole affair might be going too far. Chase here had dealin's with him, too."

"Right," the man beside Peter spoke up. "Joe come to me and asked me to make a carryin' case for his plates. I told him I didn't have time. I heard later that he told one of the neighbors he didn't have any book of gold plates and that he never did have, but he was just tryin' to trick me into makin' him a chest."

When Jenny was back in the Harris's kitchen, Mr. Harris was saying, "I've never seen such jealousy. Every man in the place is wishin' he'd been the one to find the plates. Now they're all a-tryin' to make off with them. Seems some fellas are claimin' Joe made promises and that he owes them shares in the plates. He's been sweatin' it out tryin' to keep a step ahead of them."

"What do you mean?" Jenny stepped up to the table.

"Well, Willard Chase's sister used her little green stone to divine up where Joe had hid the plates. 'Twas across the street from the Smiths' in the cobbler's shop. During the night a bunch got in the place and tore it up lookin' for the plates. They found the chest and split it open, but there weren't nothin' in it. That Joe's a cool one. While the others were all hot about the plates being stole, he admitted he got up durin' the night and moved the plates. You'd better believe no one will outwit that fella!"

A week later Jenny came home from school to find Mrs. Harris sitting at the table, her eyes red from weeping.

Jenny hesitated just inside the door. As she studied the face of the one who had befriended her, she wanted to throw her arms around the woman and comfort her. But shadowy things lurked in Jenny's mind. She was not quite fourteen and just a hireling—that alone was a difficult position to be in.

And how could she admit she knew about those sounds in the night? The angry voices, the bumping, and the smack of flesh against flesh. Could she admit hearing those cries from Mrs. Harris and at the same time admit that she had crouched, fearful and trembling, not daring to go to the rescue? Just thinking about those sounds plunged her back into the memory of last year—the picture of her father's face looming over her, twisted with anger.

A fly filled the silence with its buzzing. Jenny's gaze, riveted on the flushed face of the woman, was caught by the noise. She dashed for a newspaper, attacked the offender, and then walked to the pail of water beside the door. Still mute, she filled the dipper and carried it to Mrs. Harris.

With a nod, Lucy Harris drained the dipper, wiped her mouth and spoke. "He's gone. Flew in here, grabbed up a few things and left. I'm certain he's followed that Joe Smith and his wife to Pennsylvania. Seems there was too much persecution goin' on around here for Joe to settle down and get his translatin' done." Bitterly she added, "Martin's got more money than anyone else in this town, and is more gullible. Give him a flight of fancy, and he's off. God only knows what will happen. The Smiths all have glib tongues. If it's like in the past, it wouldn't surprise me a bit to see Martin separated from his money. He's lookin' for truth, and truth for Martin is always what tickles his fancy at the time."

Jenny searched for words of comfort. Finally she straightened up and said, "Mrs. Harris, if this is from the Lord, we can't be hinderin' it."

"You're soundin' like that Smith woman," she returned. "Truth is, Martin's always gone huntin' after any new idea for makin' money. Dear Lord, if only he could see!"

CHAPTER 9

Martin didn't stay long in Pennsylvania. However, Jenny's curiosity about the whole affair scarcely had time to be satisfied before a visitor provided some distraction.

Just after Jenny's fourteenth birthday, January 1828, Abigail Harris, Martin's sister-in-law, stopped by. She was there when Jenny came back from school; Jenny studied her with awe.

From her regal tower of graying hair to her bright, all-seeing eyes and her rustling black taffeta frock, she seemed the embodiment of authority. Whether it were skeletons or spiders hidden in the closet, Abigail Harris would be the one to find them.

Just after dinner, Lucy Smith and her husband Joseph also paid a visit to the Harris farm. As Mrs. Harris opened the door to the Smiths, Jenny had finished washing the dishes, and she crept into the parlor. Watching and listening, she winced. Lucy Smith was talking freely and eagerly, her little sparrow head bobbing about. "We're calling it the Gold Bible Business."

She scarcely gave Abigail time to ask a question before the details were spun out. Jenny squirmed with chagrin as she watched the sharp-eyed woman measure Lucy Smith's flow of words. The astonishment and surprise that swept across Abigail's face made Jenny cringe. When that expression changed to speculation and Abigail leaned back in her chair with her arms folded across her bony front, Jenny began to listen to Lucy's words.

". . . It was a spirit of one of those saints already living on the continent back before Columbus discovered it. He revealed to Joe all about the plates and told him where to find them."

Abigail leaned forward, her eyes narrowed. "I haven't seen a spirit. What did he look like?"

"Well," Lucy said, wrinkling her brow, "I'm thinking he must have been a Quaker." Without even noticing the trap, she hurried on, "He was dressed very plain. At the time, he told Joe the plates he was to have first off were only an introduction to the gold Bible. All of the plates on which the Bible was written up were so heavy, it would take at least four stout men just to load them into the cart to haul them home."

She continued, "It's interesting that Joseph was able to discover through looking in the stone the exact vessel the gold was melted in. He also saw the machine that rolled out the plates. At the bottom of the vessel there were three balls of gold left over, each the size of his fist."

Abigail's skepticism was lost on Lucy in her enthusiastic recounting of the tale.

Early the next morning, Jenny was at work in the kitchen, mulling over the conversation which had kept them all up so late that the Smiths too had decided to stay overnight. Abigail soon joined her. As Jenny prepared breakfast, Lucy Smith entered the room.

Lucy closed the door quietly behind her and, standing close to Abigail, spoke in a low voice. "Have you four or five dollars you could spare until our business is producing?" She added, "The spirit has promised you'll receive fourfold."

Abigail clattered the cutlery to the table. "And why do you need it?"

"Joe is in Pennsylvania, and he wants to return to see how things are going with us all."

Abigail continued to set the table, her face expressionless. "If Joe needs to know, I would think he'd look in his stone and save his time and money."

Jenny watched a perplexed frown creep across Lucy's face. Without a word, she turned and left the room.

During the following days, Jenny was glad to escape to school. At best, life on the Harris farm had settled into monotony as the snows outside deepened.

In the evenings, Mrs. Harris and Jenny sewed and knitted, while Martin and Tom talked constantly. Struggling with the knitting needles and tangled yarn, Jenny's attention wandered toward their conversation. She noticed it always seemed to circle back to the mystery of Joe Smith.

As she listened to Martin talk, Jenny decided that just like the winds of winter, first calm, then swirling in indecisive fury, the winds of Martin's passions swept him freely about. She guessed his restless feet would soon carry him east and south to Harmony.

Eventually his reasoning surfaced, "I've put a whole lot of money into this so far, and I aim to protect my investment."

Mrs. Harris's reply was similarly predictable. "It's chasin' the wind, nothin' but a dream. You'd best forget the fifty dollars before it costs you more."

But he left in midwinter, and a month went by before he returned. Coming in from school, Jenny discovered him pacing excitedly around the kitchen table and immediately noticed a new undercurrent in his voice. He was telling his Lucy how wife Emma was acting as Joe's scribe, taking down the words as he gave them to her. Word by word, the plates were being translated.

"What did they say? Did you see the papers?"

While he described it all, Harris's eyes danced. Finally Mrs. Harris demanded. "I know there's something more you haven't said—what is it?"

"Well, all your doubtin' and fussin' made me struggle with my faith, and I finally decided to do something about it. Joe gave me a copy of some of the characters, and I took them to New York to see a Mr. Mitchell. I was thinkin' he could decipher some of this for me and tell me more about the characters. He didn't know nothin'. But he sent me on to a Professor Anthon. This fella was a mighty smart man, but he sure is an infidel. First he was real excited about it all until he found out where I got the information. Even if he wouldn't give me a written statement, he did admit lots, and it's all stored right up here." He chuckled and tapped his head.

Tom leaned forward and asked eagerly, "And what did he say? Did he think there was something to it?"

Martin chuckled contentedly, "Yes, sir! He said the characters were ancient, shorthand Egyptian. So Joe was right all along. He also admitted they were Chaldaic, Assyriac, and Arabic."

By April, Martin Harris could endure the suspense no longer. He announced his intentions after breakfast. "You, Tom, you can handle the plowin' and plantin' evenings. There's Jake and Amos to help, too. I'm goin' to Harmony."

And Lucy Harris announced hers. "If you're going down there for months, I'll be goin' with you. Jenny is able to keep up the little that needs to be done around here and see that her brother is fed." Martin looked dubious, but realizing there was no sense to arguing he shrugged, and they departed.

At school, since the brothers and sisters of Joe Smith were seldom present, it seemed to be Jenny's lot to endure alone the curious stares and questions.

But Jenny was as confused as the other students as she faced their speculations: "I hear tell it was a spirit giving out the place of the plates." "I hear they are saying a divine one handed out the plates." "Jenny, does Martin get to see the plates?" Jenny could only shake her head. One thing she did know: they assumed she knew secret things. Deeply conscious of the tide of feeling, Jenny recognized a chasm widening between herself and the other students. Their questions made clear that she was seen as part of the inner circle, along with Martin Harris and the Smiths. They expected her to *know*.

It troubled her, not because she was suddenly marked as belonging to the money-digging group, but because of the barrier caused by the questions. She sensed from those glances and the whispers that the line was impossible to cross. Jenny was very lonely.

She had only begun to relax into the dream of being mistress of the house for a few weeks when Lucy Harris returned. "Rode in on the stage," Lucy announced as she moved about the house putting her possessions in order. She eyed Jenny sharply. "He'll never get away with it."

"No, ma'am," Jenny replied meekly, wondering what she meant.

"I searched the place over and didn't find a thing to indicate to me there were gold plates or even copper ones around. Tore through every cupboard, looked under the beds, and even scratched around in the woods lookin' for a place where they might be hid." Mrs. Harris concluded wearily, "Martin's been duped again. How that man can fall for such a line . . ." She settled down in her rocker, and Jenny brought her a cup of tea from the boiling kettle.

As the woman sipped she studied Jenny thoughtfully. "My, a few weeks away from home, and I see the change in you. I've neglected my duty to your mother long enough. She was right insistent that I make a lady out of you. She hadn't the opportunities I've had of education, and I aim to see you learn a little more'n her."

Jenny nodded. Mrs. Harris was beginning to sound like Lemuel Searles, saying she should be talking right and learning. She didn't voice her next thought. Lucy, after all, didn't talk much better than anyone else in Manchester.

She looked around the room, eyeing the books, the fancywork, the china. Jenny sighed wistfully. Yes, there *was* much more to learn, but she wasn't sure Mrs. Harris was the one to teach her.

Later Lucy had more to tell. She talked about Emma, and Jenny was aware of strange stirrings inside as she listened. "Pregnant she is, and Joe's sayin' that the plates couldn't be opened under penalty of death by anyone except by his firstborn, and that his child will be a boy. Some say this little fella will be the one to translate the plates when he's two or three years old."

"When is Mr. Harris coming home?" Jenny asked.

"I don't know," she replied slowly. "He's takin' over the transcribin' from Emma. Mighty important he's feelin', writin' down the Lord's words as Joseph is seein' them in the stone, one by one. I don't know . . ." she repeated slowly, "I just don't know."

As she stared at Jenny, her eyes darkened. She looked around the room, sighing. "He's taken so, I'm wonderin' if he'll ever be back."

But he was. In June Martin returned in triumph. He wore his air of excitement and mystery well, but his secrets were only for his household.

Jenny was there when he took out the papers and spread them on the table. Mrs. Harris leaned over to read them, mouthing the words slowly. She lifted her head. "What is this?"

"You wouldn't believe me, so I talked Joe into lettin' me bring all we'd translated so's you could see and read for yourself."

She jerked her head. "You mean this is the translation from the gold plates?"

He nodded, "The words that Emma and I've been takin' down while Joe translated."

Slowly she sat down to the table and pulled the sheaf of papers toward her. Martin got to his feet. "I'll do the chores, and we'll talk about it later." He was chuckling to himself as he took up his hat and left the house. Jenny watched him walk to the barn. His shoulders were squared, and he strode along as if he owned the earth.

Turning back to the table, Jenny settled down across from Mrs. Harris and watched her read. The paper rustled and Mrs. Harris sighed with exasperation. Now her brow furrowed and her finger traced down the page. "It's all so—"

"Can I see?" Jenny asked. Mrs. Harris lifted her face, her eyes snapping. She stared at Jenny without seeing her. And then suddenly she jumped to her feet. With quick movements she rustled the papers together and dashed to the stove. Another quick movement and she had shoved the papers inside. Immediately the flames shot up, engulfing the pages.

At Jenny's horrified gasp, Mrs. Harris responded. "Jenny, false teachin' like this must be destroyed. If I'm wrong, if this is truly all divine, then it won't be a bit of trouble to get another copy. Now, let's you and me finish cleaning the kitchen and go to bed before he comes in. I'd rather he asked me about this in the mornin' when he's better tempered."

Eager to win his wife over and supposing Joe's translations were safe with her sewing supplies, Martin held off discussing the translation with her.

Now the July heat lay heavy upon Manchester, though not as heavy as the tension Jenny felt waiting for Martin to discover what his wife had done. In the garden it was especially hot. Jenny straightened her back and leaned against the hoe. Even on the willows bordering the stream that cut through Martin Harris's farm, the leaves hung limp and dusty.

Her gleanings—carrots, beets, and onions—were also beginning to wilt. Glad for the excuse to return to the house, she dropped the hoe and gathered up the vegetables.

Jenny saw a strange horse tethered under the trees. Jenny had just reached the porch steps when she heard Martin. The agony in his voice stopped her and she caught her breath at the cry, "I have lost my soul!"

Overlapping it came another voice, familiar even though wrung with anguish. "Oh, my God, all is lost! What shall I do?" Heavy boots struck the floor, making Jenny shiver with dread. "Are you certain? Go search once more."

Martin's voice came through again, "I've ripped pillows and beds. I've torn the place apart lookin'. If they was hidden, I'd have found them."

A chill swept through Jenny, for the visitor could be only one person. She hugged her arms to herself. It had been so long. Not since South Bainbridge and the trial had she been near him.

Curiosity overcame her dread of certain confrontation, and Jenny entered the house. Both men turned as she stopped in the doorway of the parlor, her apron sagging under the load of wilting vegetables. She realized she was gawking, but she must see if his hair was still bright as sunlight. Even as she studied his long arrogant nose and glowing blue eyes, she was reduced to shy trembling. With only the slightest nod to acknowledge her presence, Joe demanded, "Where is your mistress?"

Jenny shook her head numbly. "I don't know," she whispered, not having the voice to admit more. She glanced quickly at Mr. Harris and saw that his face was white. The roll of flesh under his chin trembled. Jenny ducked her head and backed toward the door. "Excuse me. These must go in water."

In the kitchen Jenny moved quickly about her tasks, but

she was straining to hear. The voices in the parlor continued their uneasy, troubled rumbling. Jenny's fingers trembled in the biscuit dough as she thought about the evening before them. If it were only possible to send thoughts warning Lucy Harris to stay away!

But when the back door opened and Lucy came in, Jenny watched in astonishment. Flying about the kitchen, frying the fresh pork, poking at the boiling greens, Lucy held them all spellbound as her words kept pace with her busy hands. She was totally in command.

The men had moved to the kitchen at the sound of Lucy's voice. As the conversation continued, Joseph was reduced to being an awkward boy once again. He told of the birth and death of his baby son. With his heart in his eyes, with sorrowful words, he was weaving a picture of familial devotion that left Jenny awed and envious.

She crept closer to listen even as she wondered at the emotion that dug into her like tearing hands. But throughout the story of Emma's confinement and near death, Lucy Harris remained in command.

Her words soothed and then reduced him. He admitted, "I'll confess; I'm not a worthy husband or father." His face brightened. "But I will be."

"How?" Lucy's voice was suspicious.

"Well," he paused and then lifted his face. "I'm reforming my ways. I'm seeing how all the little things add up in my wife's eyes. I'm aiming to please her." He noticed Lucy's suspicious expression and added, "I really mean it. Knowing the importance, 'specially to her, I joined the Methodist church there in Harmony."

"You did!" Even Lucy was surprised and a pleased look crossed her face. "Well, there's hopes for the likes of you yet. After gettin' acquainted with your wife while I was there, I'm guessin' she was terribly pleased."

A shadow crossed his face. Heavily he said, "I gotta admit, it didn't take."

"Your gettin' religion?"

He shook his head. "They brought up that old story about

money digging and using the stone, and they rejected me. I couldn't join, even after they'd already accepted me.—But I tried," he added ruefully. "I was a member for three days."

During the meal, Jenny lost interest in the conversation. After they had finished eating, she cleared the dishes from the table, while the others went into the parlor. Having finished her kitchen duties, she returned to the parlor to listen.

Settling herself in the corner, she watched Joe as he talked to Martin. Something about him puzzled her. She felt as if she knew him, yet she didn't. The youth she had known in South Bainbridge had been fun, careless—even thoughtless. Now he spoke deliberately as if weighing his words. His eyes constantly sought the others in the room. This wasn't the student, the young lad who had stood trial in South Bainbridge two years ago. With a shock, she accepted the truth. Young Joe had become a man.

Jenny looked down at her stained hands and wondered if she had changed. If she had, Joe Smith didn't know it. She might have been a stick of furniture, for all the attention she was catching.

Her thoughts continued to drift, moving with unseen currents as the conversation moved about her unheeded. She felt a growing need to do something, to say something. She closed her eyes. Could she will herself to become a different Jenny?

As if thought made her free, her mind rose to wander the airy heights of imagination. Jenny, tall and poised, and Joe Smith really seeing her, bending his bright head to kiss her hand.

"Jenny!" The back door banged shut. The vision vanished. Tom was back from the fields, wanting his supper.

Jenny stared at her stained hands. But now there was a difference. She remembered the book, and a fresh desire was born.

CHAPTER 10

Jenny came into the kitchen just as Mrs. Harris said, "All he has to do is get a 'word from the Lord' and he can get himself out of any problem he wants. Martin Harris, how can you fail to see through it all?"

Lucy Harris was swishing about the kitchen packing bread and meat into a pail. Jenny guessed that Harris was leaving. As she continued to listen, Mrs. Harris's talk made it clear he was headed for Harmony again.

Jenny shrugged slightly as she sat down. These days she found it hard to sympathize with either one. In the back of her mind she felt the fuss over Joe would soon quiet down and everyone would forget him, just as they had at South Bainbridge.

Martin was very quiet, but Jenny noticed the excitement burning in his eyes. "Thin as paper it is," Lucy was declaring. "He can't come up with what he's already dictated, so he solves it with a 'word from the Lord,' sayin' Satan will try to confuse the work by givin' out different words. Then what does he do? He gets the plates of Nephi with a little different version of the same stuff." She shook her head. "Clever man; Martin, is there nothin' I can say to keep you from bein' his slave and dupe? I'm at my wits' end." Jenny was absolutely amazed at the woman's presence in the face of what she had done. She seemed to give not a snap of the finger to the fact that Jenny had seen her burn the manuscript.

Martin got to his feet and Jenny watched him pace the floor. His quick, hard strides across the room and back caught Jenny's attention and she began to feel his excitement. Lucy Harris continued to chide him, but neither he nor Jenny was listening to her.

When he passed Jenny again and saw she was watching, he stopped and said in a low voice, "She's makin' it all sound crazy, but don't you heed it. The fella's humble spirit testifies to the holiness of the callin'."

"What do you mean?" Jenny asked, moving closer to Martin. Lucy stopped her muttering to listen.

With his palms flat on the table, Martin leaned toward them and whispered, "This book is the Lord talkin'. Joe's been mighty reluctant to divulge it all at once, but bit by bit it's all comin' out. This last visit I had with him kinda loosened him up when he come to see that I believe in him and have confidence in what he has to say. Now he knows I'll not be blabbin' it all over the country."

Lucy retorted, "Like this?"

Ignoring her, he continued, "It's all comin' out. This book Joe has is holy. There's the divine behind the translatin' and the writin' of it."

Lucy demanded, "How do you expect to prove that?"

"It's been proven. But even more than that, the Lord is beginnin' to reveal himself to Joseph in a much deeper way. He's communicatin' through what Joe calls revelations."

"What does He have to say?" Lucy's voice was suspicious.

Martin pulled a crumpled letter out of his pocket and spread it on the table. "He's given me a copy of the revelation." Jenny watched his hands reverently pressing the creases out before he held it up. "Mind you now, this is the Lord talkin'. Otherwise, I'd not pass along the words. First off, the Lord's tellin' Joe that His plans can't be frustrated." He paused to slant a sharp glance at his wife.

"I'd have read you this before, but you were so busy fussin' over the little bit I did tell you, I decided to wait. Now listen. He also tells Joe that he's been called to do the work of the Lord. He's sayin' there's just no way to shy away from the callin'. He must be faithful or he'll end up bein' just like other men, without gifts or calling. He made it pretty clear to Joe that He has appointed him to get the message of the gold Bible out to the Lamanites."

"The Indians." Lucy's words broke the spell surrounding Jenny, bumping her back to earth. Now *gold Bible*, *Lamanites*, and *revelations* were just words, not corridors of mystery.

Jenny turned to look out the window. The nighttime wind had blown the last of the leaves off the trees, and dark clouds made it look near to snowing. She shivered as she realized, *It's almost Halloween.*

When Lucy spoke now the strident note was gone from her voice and Jenny thought she sounded worried. "It'll be a hard trip to Harmony. Don't you want to take Tom with you? Amos can handle the livestock by himself."

Martin shook his head. "No, I need Tom here. I've no way of knowin' how long I'll be gone. There's much translatin' to be done."

"Well, be holdin' your tongue." Lucy added wifely advice. "Your boastin' about it all before the fact isn't winnin' you friends around Manchester. Pretty soon you'll have a reputation for braggin' that rivals the Smiths'."

"Now, just what are you referrin' to?" Martin asked, turning reddened cheeks toward his wife. "I'm not braggin', and you know it."

Lucy Harris stepped in front of her husband. With fists planted on her hips, she looked him in the eyes. "It's around town and well nigh the gossip of the church folks how you're sayin' you've had revelations given out by the Lord."

"I've said they're from the Lord, and they are." His defensive tone belied the statement.

"That you saw Jesus Christ in the form of a deer and that the devil appeared a jackass with hair like a mouse?" She shook her head. "My, what details! And they're saying you've prophesied that Palmyra would be destroyed in 1836, and by the year 1838, Joe Smith's church would be so large there wouldn't be any need for a president of the United States. You might as well have gone the whole way and said you'd be second in command over all these United States!"

Martin Harris rubbed at his jaw and scratched his ear. He

had just opened his mouth to speak when the door slammed.

Jenny forced her fascinated gaze from Mr. Harris to Tom entering. He said, "I hear tell the new schoolmaster is boarding with the Smiths." Washing his hands at the basin beside the door, he continued. "I also hear he's from back Vermont way and that his folks are known by the Smiths. I'll need to be getting acquainted with the fella."

His voice revealed so much satisfaction that Jenny couldn't help saying, "I don't think you'll like him. He's like a towel that's been overwashed."

"You're talkin' about your schoolteacher!" Mrs. Harris's eyebrows rose halfway up her forehead as she turned to Jenny.

"They say he's good with the rod," Jenny said quickly. No need to explain she meant "divining rod," not the rod of correction. Lucy Harris would not approve of the first, and she *would* approve of the second, especially the fact that Jenny was pointing it out. "He's tryin' to help out the Smiths. They sure do need the money." Tom gave her a quick nod of agreement.

They sat down around the table and Mrs. Harris began ladling the stew onto plates. Martin Harris reached for the bread. "Tom, too bad I can't spare you around here. You'd enjoy the going's on in Harmony. But then I 'spect in another year we'll be seein' that young rascal Joe Smith paradin' around the streets of Manchester, a-wearin' his gold breastplate and carryin' a sword, with the gold Bible tucked under his arm."

"Mrs. Smith says," Jenny volunteered, gulping and wiping her hands on her apron, "that they are going to be makin' a heap of money off the gold plates. Joe's pa is tellin' people they're gonna use the money to pay for their money-digging business."

After supper was over, while Jenny cleared the dishes from the table, Martin Harris came into the room buttoning a clean shirt. Pulling on his coat and taking up his hat, he muttered, "I'll be out most of the evenin'. Don't wait up for me."

Jenny saw the troubled expression on Mrs. Harris's face as she turned to pick up her knitting. But as Jenny poured hot water into the dishpan, she was thinking not of Lucy Harris's expression but of Martin Harris's prophecies.

Swishing the dishcloth through the suds, watching the bubbles burst, Jenny began to sense the bubbles bursting in her heart. The sadness surprised her. Why had it suddenly become important to believe like Martin did?

Speaking through the silence from her rocking chair beside the fire, Lucy said, as if reading Jenny's thoughts, "It's no good placin' confidence in the religion Martin Harris promotes."

Tom got to his feet. "I'd not worry much. I hear Pa Smith is callin' the whole thing about the gold Bible a 'speculation.' That don't sound too serious to me. At least, it don't seem like it'll be a hellfire and damnation kind of religion." Chuckling, he left the house.

Martin Harris left for Harmony, Pennsylvania, without a promise of his return. As he packed his saddlebags, he said, "I'm just lucky the Lord will allow me to translate for Joseph again. This time I don't intend to let any trick of the evil one keep me from gettin' the task done." He threw a scowl at his wife and shouldered the bag. "I'll be back when the work's finished. The fellas here can tend to the plantin' if'n I'm not back before then."

Not withstanding the dismay Lucy Harris felt over her husband's departure, life without Martin Harris quickly slipped into an easy routine. Amos and Tom continued to handle the chores about the farm, leaving Mrs. Harris free to visit her friends or nod beside the fire with her knitting in her hands.

Jenny moved between farm and school in a bemused state, happy with the crisp autumn and her circumstances. She was keenly aware of bare fields and wind-lashed elm and birch shedding leaves in preparation for their ritual of rest. The backdrop of the dark fir forest seemed to cover the rolling hills of Manchester with mystery and solitude.

Each day Jenny followed a path to school which skirted the hills and the woods bordering the farm. Her walk was long, but Jenny didn't mind. Other students often slipped onto the path with her. First the Anderson twins joined her—Timothy and Angela were ten. At times, when Mr. Cowdery was busy with the little ones, Jenny had been called upon to help the twins with their sums and reading lesson.

Farther down the path Mary Beth and Cindy joined them.

But this school year, the two girls whispered just between themselves, and they seldom made a place for her. Jenny had noticed, but only Timothy dared explain it to her. "It's cause of Martin Harris being credulous."

"What do you mean?" She had kept her voice low, as the girls in front of them began to hurry. "It's all this about Joe Smith and the plates. Pa says people aren't taken in by it at all, leastwise no one much except Martin Harris."

"I suppose so," Jenny answered slowly, "but why does it make Mary Beth and Cindy shun me?"

"They think you are credulous too." Jenny had forgotten about the conversation with Timothy until late in October. Halloween was next week and the students were trying to outdo each other with stories of mystery and terror. Equally fantastic stories of bravery and daring surfaced. At noon Jenny joined the groups around the story-tellers and blended her screams of terror with others.

When there were no more stories to be told, Jeff Naylor began questioning Jenny. "I hear old Harris believes all those stories the Smiths have been circulating."

Jenny looked about the group, searching vainly for one of Joseph's brothers or sisters. Finally she straightened her back and met the curious eyes. "You'll have to be askin' him that. If you're tryin' to pin me with believing ghost stories told by the big people, I can't help you. I've never seen a ghost."

"And what would you do if you did?"

"Not believe it until I could walk right through him," she replied saucily.

Now Cindy, with her eyes wide, said, "I heard Samuel Smith say they were out digging over by the old schoolhouse one night and it all lit up. He said there was a fella at least nine feet tall sitting on the roof, yelling at them to clear out."

The group groaned their awe and dismay; Jenny thought about the story she'd heard Martin telling. Mary Beth was studying her intently. Jenny forced a smile and said, "Credulous they are. Now I don't believe—"

Nicholas interrupted, "Everybody that isn't credulous stick up your hand." And when all hands were quickly raised, he continued. "Okay, tomorrow's Halloween. I say you all be here at the schoolhouse just as soon as it's dark, and we'll all go over to the old school and prove there's no such thing as spooks." His eyes were on Jenny as he said, "And if you can get some doughnuts and apples, all the better; we'll make it a party. But you better all be here or we'll come after you."

The next evening Lucy Harris said, "I don't have any doughnuts, and that's the silliest thing I've heard of, going out there just to scare yourselves. You can take some apples."

As soon as the supper dishes were washed, Jenny wrapped Tom's old jacket around herself and stuffed the pockets with apples. Her excitement was almost as high as the time she had followed Tom and Martin to their meeting with Walters. But now as she scurried down the dark path, she felt her emotions flattening. "Silly baby stuff," she muttered, "pretendin' there's ghosts and goblins just to get scared."

Norton and Jeff and Nicholas had lanterns. Cindy and Mary Beth came with their pockets loaded with doughnuts. Norton was licking his lips with anticipation as he said, "Leave the goodies here. After we go and investigate the spooks, we'll all meet back here and eat the doughnuts. You fellas douse the lights when we get to the edge of the cornfield. We don't want anyone to see us and have a hysteria."

There were giggles, and a long line formed behind the lantern-bearers. "Quiet back there. Not a sound, now!"

A lonesome voice from the back of the line squeaked, "If the sheriff finds out, will he put us all in jail?" Hoots of laughter drowned the young boy's fears.

Only a sliver of moon hung in the sky, and even that disappeared as the path dipped into the trees. The group walked in silence except for an occasional gasp of dismay as someone bumped into his neighbor or a tree.

When they could hear the rustle of dry cornstalks, the warning hiss came to darken the lanterns. The wind was rising; Jenny could hear it keening through the fir trees. The sliver of moonlight appeared and disappeared as clouds blew by, and from behind Jenny came nervous whispers.

When they reached the far side of the cornfield, they could

see the shadowy bulk of the old schoolhouse. The rising wind slapped loose shutters, and the sudden banging brought out a nervous whimper. Quietly the group formed a semicircle on the edge of the deserted school yard.

The creaking old building was dark. Norton said bravely, "There's not even a ghost on the roof." They waited and the quietness of the night seemed to grow, broadcasting whispers of sound. The soft sighs of the students became eerie, and chattering teeth seemed to pound in Jenny's ears. When the clouds drifted away from the moon, Nicholas whispered, "Everybody satisfied?"

"We haven't even looked inside," voiced someone.

There was another whimper. "My ma said to hurry home."

Then out of the silence. "Seems a brave body oughta go inside and investigate."

"Without a light?"

After a pause. "There a volunteer?" Only the shuffle of feet in the dry grass broke the silence.

"Seems the one accused of being credulous would be the most eager."

The cornstalks rustled, the wind rose. Finally Jenny moved and swallowed hard. "You're meanin' me. So, we can't go have doughnuts 'til I do." She tried to make her voice brave, but it was thin, and the only response was silence.

Again feet shuffled and teeth chattered. The group melted back and Jenny faced the sagging door. "Oh, you babies," she hissed, moving quickly toward the door. In the sliver of moonlight, she could see the broken floor slanting inward. "How far do I go?" she whispered.

"To the far wall," a voice breathed in her ear. She shivered and stepped toward the slanting floor.

There was a hand in her back. She opened her mouth to protest, but her feet were on the slanting boards, and the boards were moving with a life of their own. Behind her the door crashed shut, and sealed Jenny in oppressive darkness.

When she slammed into the far wall, Jenny sat for a moment, stunned and trembling. Close to her head a rhythmic tapping began and a ghostly laugh rose. "Let me out!" she screamed. The laugh was drifting away.

Jenny jumped to her feet but the boards tilted, dumping her. She scrambled, scratching and clawing her way up the ruined floor. Now sobbing with terror, she discovered she was surrounded by boards that had a will of their own. They slanted and dumped her, pricked and stabbed. Some boards bound her feet and others slapped her face. In the deep darkness only silence answered her cries.

When she was nearly voiceless from screaming, she heard a sound. Rats. Rustles, scratching, a noise that must be gnawing; she gave one last feeble scream of terror.

A voice answered her. The schoolhouse door creaked outward and a dark shadow filled the doorway. Jenny flew toward it. Warm flesh, a beard and musty wool were against her face. It was a strange beard, but at least it wasn't rats.

"What happened?" The voice was strangely melodious, strangely familiar. He led her away from the building while she gasped out her story.

In the dim lantern light she could see the beard, the black cloak, and a shiny disk. The last time she had seen that disk it had been circling and glowing in the light of a lantern beside the diggings. She studied the man's face. "Are you Walters the Magician?"

"Of course. Who else would I be?" The remembered melody of his voice returned to her. Forgetting her terror and exhaustion, Jenny wanted only to hear him reading those singing words out of his book again.

CHAPTER 11

Did her encounter with Walters the Magician radically change Jenny, or was it the final disappointment of her friends' betrayal? Whatever the answer, Halloween night irreparably separated Jenny from her schoolmates. She felt the division strongly. Jenny stood alone, the one against the many.

Fortunately for Jenny, the Smith youngsters returned to school. They were immediately pushed to her side of the chasm. Now Jenny had friends, just as she also had a label she didn't understand.

She continued to skirt the hills going to and from school, lonely now in her solitary walk. As autumn passed, she began to experience the deepening calm of the trees—or so she thought it.

One afternoon as she stood beneath a fir tree, watching the wind lash its top branches, she felt as if her mind were unfurling and becoming one with the surging forces of nature. The sensation of sharpened awareness left her feeling as if she were mentally standing on tiptoe.

The silence surrounded her, sharpened and real. What was happening? Was this sensation rising only from the wellspring of loneliness in her life?

Waiting, wondering if it was all just chance, she reached out, wanting to touch that appealing sense of aliveness. She sat motionless, unmindful of the cold, searching for words that would link her with that sensation of mystery. Finally a scrap of rhyme popped into her mind.

"Luna, every woman's friend,
To me thy goodness condescend,
Let this night in visions see
Emblems of my destiny."

Jenny had started reading the green book again, and lately a strangeness surrounded her reading. She had been reaching out to the unknown and now the unknown was reaching out to her.

The penetrating cold through Jenny's thin shawl brought her back to reality. Shivering, she hurried down the path toward the farm. She thought of Lucy Harris nodding by the fire in the evening, while Jenny carried the green book downstairs to read. Although Lucy had made clear to Jenny her feelings about the book with the golden lady on the front, she had never forbidden Jenny to read it. For the first time since she had discovered Pa's strange book and been captivated by it, Jenny felt completely free of the fear of punishment.

As Jenny passed the wind-lashed firs each day, her thoughts always seemed to circle back to the book as if drawn into focus by the forest.

The forest attracted more than Jenny's thoughts. One evening, a sudden impulse sent her scurrying from the familiar path into the trees. Once she entered the shadowed depths, a new quietness surrounded her. She wandered deeper into the woods, and her mind wandered as well. Without willing it, pictures from the book leaped into her thoughts—some intriguing, some frightening. Immediately her mind was filled with alarm, as if a thousand warning bells hammered in her soul.

Shivering with fear, Jenny turned and ran back to the path, back to daylight and away from the eerie calmness. Did she fancy she heard her name called as she left the forest? She ran the rest of the way home. Not until she stood panting on the stoop outside Harris's kitchen did she dare to admit, "If I didn't believe in spooks before, I'm beginnin' to now."

The next time Jenny passed along the path, while the wind moaned and the trees lashed, she found herself hesitating, reaching out, wanting to know. Again, quickly before she could debate, she turned off the path and the lashing trees for the calm forest.

The mysterious stillness had begun to encircle her with a reality that tightened her throat and made her heart pound, when just ahead of her she saw a dark-clad figure moving slowly through the woods, poking at drifts of leaves with a long stick.

With relief Jenny ran toward the figure. "Hello there!" she called.

The woman turned and waited for her. "Are you lost?" she called. As she hurried toward the woman, Jenny studied her face, trying to identify the stranger. Surprisingly, the dark-cloaked woman was young and beautiful. In the shadows her face seemed a pale oval, but her eyes were large and dark. Her dark hair was swept back from her brow, and the widow's peak made her face heart-shaped.

Jenny was still studying the woman, wishing she could be just like her, slowly Jenny said, "I don't reckon I know you. I'm Jenny Timmons, the Harris's hired girl."

The woman nodded as if she knew. "You're very young to be working for your living." Without warning, tears stung Jenny's eyes. She rubbed at them, wondering why she was feeling the kindness so keenly. "Your parents have left you here. Do you miss them greatly?" Jenny shook her head, wondering how to answer such a question.

Slowly they walked together through the woods. Jenny responded to the gentle, probing questions as she still tried to identify the woman. Her face seemed familiar, but Jenny couldn't make her fit anywhere.

Suddenly the woman stopped. She pointed, saying, "There's Martin Harris's cornfield; you can cut through here."

"Oh my!" Jenny exclaimed. "We've circled the whole farm. I didn't mean for you to take me home." The woman was smiling, stepping backward down the trail. Jenny watched her curiously. "What's your name?"

She hesitated. "You may call me Adela."

"That's pretty. It sounds like bells." Now shy, Jenny dropped her head and scuffed her toe in the pine needles, wondering when she had ever before chattered on like this to a perfect stranger. She raised her head to speak, but the woman was gone.

Several times during the winter months, Jenny saw Adela when she ventured into the forest on her way home from school. Always she seemed to be poking, prodding with her stick, always alone. Jenny never felt free to ask about her activities nor to learn more about her.

One evening as Jenny left the forest after an encounter with the woman, she mused aloud, "Methinks, Adela the bella, you're as mysterious as—as a sylph." Her tongue slid over the unfamiliar word. Hadn't that word been in the book? She began to wonder why Adela made her think of the book. And more and more she realized that she didn't know the mysterious woman at all.

Finally, shyly, she described Adela to Lucy Harris and found her description as vaporous as her understanding of the woman. Lucy looked at her in confusion and Jenny ended her questions with a shrug.

So for a time, and for reasons Jenny couldn't explain, she avoided the forest path and the mysterious encounters.

As the winter waned, Mrs. Harris became an enthusiastic housekeeper, waging war against winter's accumulated dirt. She also took up the task of making a young lady out of Jenny, much to the distress of both.

As often as she dared, Jenny dallied in the afternoons instead of hurrying homeward. Still hesitant to go back into the forest, she frequently followed the Smith children home. Jenny enjoyed the chatter and laughter, the teasing and playful pranks. Aware of her loneliness, she was irresistibly drawn to the large family, despite Lucy Harris's disapproval.

Often the young schoolmaster, Oliver Cowdery, walked with them. In the past Jenny had found him morose and withdrawn, but on these walks he regaled the group with exciting stories of Vermont. Along with the stories he had to tell, he would demonstrate the art of using the rod.

The rod, delicately balanced on Oliver's fingers, would tilt as Oliver walked slowly down the path. "There!" he exclaimed. "That's signifying water's to be found here."

He was unabashed when Jenny exclaimed, "Who wants to dig a well in the middle of the woods?"

One afternoon in April Jenny followed the Smiths and their youthful schoolmaster home. It had been a beautiful day, full of the joy of spring and the excitement of a school term drawing to a close. But they met gloom as they stepped into the cabin crowded with people and piles of household belongings.

Lucy was talking rapidly, darting about the cabin gathering up bedding. Hyrum sat at the table watching his mother. His expression silenced the chattering brood.

Mrs. Smith clattered a load of kettles onto the middle of the table and turned to survey the silent group. "Well, 'tis the worst," she advised them. "We've lost the place. Get your things together; we're goin' home with Hyrum." The outcry began, but her raised hand cut through. "No fussin'. Don't give them the satisfaction of knowin'. 'Sides, we'll be back as soon as Joe starts a-sellin' the gold Bible and makin' a heap of money." She turned to Cowdery. "I 'spect the best you could do is go to Harmony and be helpin' with the translatin' to hurry things along a speck."

When Jenny carried the news home, Lucy Harris paused in her housecleaning long enough to think. She finally spoke, as if she were pulling out the thoughts like yarn from her knitting. "That'll mean Martin will be back soon." She eyed Jenny and sighed, "What's goin' to become of us all?"

"What are you meaning?" Jenny asked slowly.

"I expect more turmoil." She paused, then spoke briskly. "First things first," she instructed. She stepped down from the chair she was standing on and dusted her hands together. "Before I get the cleanin' done, there's something more important."

"What?" Jenny asked, mystified, as she looked at the litter of dishes and pans Lucy Harris had pulled from the shelf.

"I'm goin' to take the team and go into Palmyra and see the preacher at the church."

"Whatever for?"

"First off, I'm goin' to do something I promised I'd do long ago. I'm goin' to set up your baptism."

"What baptism?"

"Jenny"—Lucy leaned her face close to Jenny's—"we've talked before about the truth, remember? That real power, spiritual power, has the truth as its source. That truth—the only truth—is in Jesus, in His death and resurrection."

Jenny nodded, "But—"

"I know you've seen and heard—and read—a lot about other kinds of power. Even my husband Martin has shown you the other. And I let you go on and read your pa's book even though I didn't like it, and I let you run off to the Smiths and hear that Lucy's wild tales of gold plates and—"

Mrs. Harris paused, looking squarely at Jenny. "I don't claim to know all there is to know about the Bible," she sighed. "That's why I want to take you into Palmyra to talk to the parson. Everybody's got to make a choice, Jenny. If you don't make one—well, you make one anyway. And now's the time for you to think about yours."

Jenny thought about the church in Palmyra.

Every Sabbath day in that sanctuary, she had sat in cold, hard pews and listened to the organ draw threads of sound around her that amazed and awed her. She had looked at the small circle window of stained glass, showering arrows of brilliant color over the shoulders of worshipers, and had dreamed of them as mystical fingers bestowing blessing and fortune. Sometimes the parson's words dropped on Jenny with raw-nerve intensity, creating a moment of awareness. But for the most part, Jenny's Sabbaths were empty of the meaning of worship.

On this day, with Mrs. Harris, she reluctantly entered the cold building with solitary and lonely thoughts. In the gloom the round window was a beacon, throwing colorful shadows throughout the sanctuary and tipping the heavy wooden cross behind the pulpit with shades of light. Did it happen by chance that afternoon shadows funneled one beam of rich light into a pinpoint finger precisely at the center of that wooden cross?

Jenny's mind amplified the results. As she sat facing that cross, listening to that somber man spread heavy words she didn't understand, she felt the weight of light and form.

She watched him turn and lift the silver chalice from the sanctuary table. At the moment he poured the wine, purple light from the window caught the chalice, spinning webs of brilliance for Jenny's eyes. That moment of awe fell against her with greater weight than the words he spoke. The wonder of the total experience robbed words of meaning for her.

Jenny's mind reeled with the possibilities. In the cold church building, she had felt a sensation akin to what she had felt in the woods—with one exception. She was moved, but not frightened as she had been among the trees. The image of the chalice and the cross rose again and again to the surface of her thinking, until finally her question overcame her hesitancy, and she sought out Mrs. Harris.

"The cross?" Lucy Harris replied. "Why, Jesus died on the cross for our salvation. The silver cup holds the wine—representing His blood—that we drink at communion."

As Lucy tried patiently to answer the questions, Jenny's confusion grew. *Was the blood of Jesus in the chalice like the blood of the rooster sprinkled around the circle where Tom and Joe were digging? Was the cross like the sword Hyrum Smith carried—did it have power to break through the spells of spirits? Is this act of baptism the one event that will launch me into the world of true power?*

The next Sabbath day, in the shadow of the same cross, Jenny Timmons was duly baptized at Palmyra Presbyterian Church. But the finger of light at the center of the cross was gone; the web of color that haloed the chalice was gone. And Jenny wondered if this way of faith really was the way of power.

Just before she slipped under the water, her eyes met the eyes of that somber parson. For a moment his face brightened until he almost looked glad. She heard his words. "Jennifer Timmons, I baptize you in the name of our Lord Jesus Christ, the great God and Savior, who gave himself to redeem and to purify you. And just as He was buried to be lifted up, you shall be baptized to be lifted up for everlasting life."

"Child," said Lucy Harris at breakfast the next morning, "don't you just feel wonderful, now that you've chosen for the Lord?"

Jenny murmured a halfhearted agreement and went about her chores, while Lucy watched and waited for the significance of Jenny's decision to take effect. Jenny waited, too. She waited for the power to come, for the feelings she had known in the woods and in the church to return, for her mind to understand, for the vague thoughts that had haunted her to crystallize.

She was still waiting when Martin Harris returned to Manchester the following Wednesday. Subdued and tired, he was nevertheless full of talk of getting the gold Bible printed.

They were visiting Martin's brother Peter and his wife Abigail when Lucy Harris finally had heard enough about the gold Bible. "Martin!" she cried, exasperated. "This gold Bible business is no religious crusade! It's just a bunch of wild stories conjured up by those who'd take a gullible man for what he's worth. Like every other project you've been duped into—when you get a new idea into your head, you get shaken loose from your money. Please, Martin, can't you see—"

"Woman!" he roared, jumping to his feet and flinging his chair aside. "Will you leave me alone? What if it *is* a lie? If you'll just mind your business, I'll stand to make a pile of money out of it yet!" He stomped out of the house, leaving Jenny and Mrs. Harris to gather their belongings and follow.

During these turbulent days, Jenny noticed how often Lucy Harris bore bruises. Many mornings Jenny observed the woman's tear-reddened eyes and sensed her troubled spirit. As the summer drew to a close, Jenny's own tension mounted; then, abruptly, there was release.

Martin Harris turned jovial, kind—at least the few times he was at home. Most conspicuous was his absence.

One late summer evening Jenny watched the man don a clean shirt and leave the house. She turned to Mrs. Harris and said, "He's happy now. Where's he going?"

The woman's lips quivered. "He's happy because he's off chasin' after a woman." Jenny's fingers crept over her errant mouth, and Lucy Harris said, "You needn't be embarrassed. Everybody in town knows Martin's shenanigans. I can't change him—but I wish the Lord would."

Autumn crept up and Jenny was getting acquainted with another new schoolmaster. Rumor had it that her previous teacher, Oliver Cowdery, had finished the translating of Joseph's golden Bible—but not in Harmony, Pennsylvania. The whispers said that because Mr. Hale, Emma's father, had vowed to see the plates, a fellow by the name of David Whitmer had moved Joseph Smith, his wife, and the whole translation business to Fayette, New York. Now there was serious talk about having the manuscript printed.

One day, after Mrs. Harris had left to visit her sister for a week, Jenny discovered some additional information quite by accident. As she hurried about the kitchen preparing the noon meal, Martin strode into the kitchen ahead of Tom and Amos. He paced the floor with quick, excited steps.

"Mr. Harris," she apologized, "I'm hurrying. I just didn't figure on you coming so soon."

Unexpectedly he turned a sudden smile on her. "Jenny, lass," he chuckled, "don't give me no mind. I'm a-thinkin' about all that's goin' on with the gold Bible business and it excites me, my it does!" Tom came into the kitchen and began to wash up. With a note of apology in his voice, Martin said, "Tom, I'm about to run out on you again. I can't stand not knowin' what's goin' on in Fayette."

Tom slowly straightened from the washbasin and reached for the towel. "The writin' is all done; what's comin' up next?"

"I couldn't tell the old lady all this; she can only ridicule." He paused and shook his head piously. "I'm fearin' for her soul, makin' fun of the Lord's anointed like that. You see, Joe's had orders to be startin' a new church. All this translatin' is for a purpose. The Lord's given him a mission of goin' to the Lamanites with the story of their brothers and the early settlement of this country. He's appointed to take the news of the restored gospel to them, and we're all to help him."

"Where did you hear all this?" Tom asked as he took his place at the table.

"That's what the book is all about. The history of the lost tribes of Israel and how they settled in this country. Joe's responsible to get the story of Jesus Christ out to them. He's been gettin' revelations from the Lord right along, tellin' him what he's to be doin' for the Lord."

"Such as—" Tom said slowly.

"Well," Martin answered just as slowly, but with an edge of enthusiasm, "Joe had a revelation that there was a man in Toronto, Canada, eager to buy the history and be printin' it.

Cowdery and Hiram Page went up there."

"So they sold it?" Tom asked, and Jenny was surprised to hear the regret in his voice.

"Naw," Martin paced the room again. "They never could find the man."

"Why, that's surprising!" Tom exclaimed. "If the Lord sent them, you'd think—"

But Martin began to pace again. When he came back to the table, Jenny saw he was having a hard time controlling his excitement. "I'll tell you something else, if'n you can keep it under your hat. Me'n Oliver Cowdery and David Whitmer got the privilege of being witnesses to the book." His smile faded as he studied their blank faces. "You're not understandin' what that means, are you?" Slowly he sat down at the table and pulled his plate toward him.

"I don't rightly know how to explain it all so you'll see how important it was. See, Joe had a promise that some were to see the gold plates in order to bear witness. We went out prayin'. Now, I'll admit I don't convert easy—it took a lot of prayin' for me to get enough faith to see them, but when I did, I was convinced. Nobody can take that away from me. This angel from the Lord appeared. He was so bright it about put my eyes out to look at him, but he made himself known and then held out the plates so I could see them."

Tom and Jenny stared at him for a moment before Tom asked, "You really did, huh? How'd the angel look?"

Jenny heard the clatter of Amos's boots, and Martin whispered, "Hush about it. Joe doesn't want it nosed about for now."

During the winter of 1829 and into 1830, Martin Harris made several more trips to Fayette, New York, to see Joseph Smith. Just after he had returned in the early spring, Jenny came from school one day and accidentally interrupted something. She stepped inside the door and was halted by the sight of her mistress' flushed face. Although she knew she should leave, curiosity held her fast.

Lucy was standing in front of the rocking chair where Martin sat. "Martin! How could you promise to get that book printed even if you must sell your farm! Martin Harris, come to your senses! Because of that book, would you give up all we've struggled hard for? Has he *bewitched* you?"

He surged out of his chair, roaring, "You'll not be a-talkin' that way about the Lord's anointed!" Jenny scooted out the door. She dashed back down the trail, remembering her father's rage and desperately wishing for Tom.

As she ran, Mrs. Harris's words sank into her heart with undeniable impact. She slowed to a walk. "Jen, you could be without a home right soon," she murmured aloud. Thinking of Mrs. Harris, she winced, hearing again the dreadful sound of that whip snapping against her back. She fled into the sanctuary of the woods.

Jenny nearly tumbled over Adela before she saw her. Panting, she leaned against the nearest tree and watched the dark-cloaked woman on the fallen log. Snugly wrapped in the cloak, motionless, she could have been taken for a rock. Now her dark eyes glowed, blinked.

"You are a very disturbed young lady." The cadence in the woman's voice made Jenny think of music.

Jenny saw the stick beside her, took a deep breath, and asked, "Lookin' for treasure?"

Adela opened her eyes very wide and straightened up. "Oh," she murmured, "I've been sitting here for so long."

"You're waiting for someone?" Adela shook her head and smiled. "Someone to go digging with you? I'll go."

She laughed merrily, "Oh, Jenny, you are a funny child. You are thinking I'm like these silly little-boy treasure diggers. Who have you been talking to?"

Jenny felt her shame and was grateful for the deep shadows. "I'm sorry," she muttered. "But you were talking about the ancient religion, and how you are a nature worshiper."

"Now, Jenny," her voice was sharp, "that wasn't what I said. If you want to quote me, please get it right."

"Then please say it again so I'll understand."

"You're referring to what I said about my religion. Jenny, there's only one god; no matter how, or where, or when you choose to worship him, it's all right. I choose to worship him through nature. When I understand him and cooperate with him, I understand the mysteries of life and I am strong." Her voice dropped to a whisper. "He gives knowledge of the eternal, to know how god thinks. God-knowledge. Isn't that what mankind wants to know more than anything else?"

Jenny hesitated, thinking. Gnawing in the back of her mind was the half-formed belief that what Adela was saying was not quite right. Something was wrong—but what? Jenny grappled with the question for a moment or two; when she finally looked up, Adela was gazing at her with a strange, distant expression.

Although she was silent, her dark eyes shone, and Jenny felt as if Adela were peering deep into her, knowing all that Jenny felt and feared. But there was more. Even though Jenny didn't understand the strange woman, the words she uttered wrapped about the two of them, binding them together.

CHAPTER 12

Spring came to Manchester, New York, surging with life. The whole countryside seemed to move and stretch and come alive at the same moment. But feelings Jenny had experienced all winter—that discontent, the vague yearnings, the desire to split the narrow seams of her life—moved over her with an intensity she couldn't deny.

As if propelled by unseen forces, Jenny went into the forest nearly every afternoon carrying the green book. Part of her resolve this spring had been to question Adela about the book, but initially she was disappointed. Now that she had decided on action, she expected Adela to be there waiting, but it was many days before she saw the woman in black.

At the beginning of her wait for Adela she was filled with impatience. Forced into patience, she discovered the world about her and found that it all reminded her of Adela.

Often the still air of the fir forest seemed to blanket her away from thought and sound, releasing her to experience the quiet. On occasion, a lone shaft of sunlight would penetrate the darkness. That single ray reminded her of the light in the church, and she tried to reconcile that experience with what Adela had said about worship.

Under the intensity of that arrow of light, she discovered flowers blooming in miniature, with an extra wash of color. She found the herbs and mushrooms Adela had gathered so eagerly with her long stick. Jenny tried to recall the ways Adela had used them, and she remembered one occasion when Adela had dipped a jug full of the fetid swamp water, guarding it as if it were a treasure.

When Jenny's thoughts were spun out, when she was tired of sighing with loneliness, she opened the green book and studied the strange words and promises.

In April, before she had seen Adela again, Smith came back to Manchester. Coming in from school one day, Jenny heard his voice, and at the same time, she heard Martin. Every word the man uttered sounded like a prayer. Jenny crept through the hallway to the parlor, and peered through the draperies. She saw the difference; this Joseph stood tall and square-shouldered before the cold fireplace. His presence commanded attention, and Martin was most certainly giving it to him.

Joseph's arm rested on the mantle, nearly against Lucy's best lamp. Jenny was heedless of his words; she had eyes only for the arm that pushed against the lamp. Remembering Lucy's last encounter with Joe in her kitchen, Jenny was mesmerized by the lamp. If he were to knock it to the floor, would Lucy dare chastise him?

But then the words and Joe's solemn expression caught her attention. "Martin," he was saying, "I've long delayed coming, but the Lord reminds me I have a grave obligation. He's given me a message and a mission that I must not ignore—on pain of death."

Again Jenny marveled at the difference between this powerful presence and the bright-haired boy with the peepstone. "Bet Emma has been working on his talking," she muttered to herself. "He sounds like a gentleman."

Smith dropped his arms from the mantle and folded them across his chest. There was regret in his voice as he spoke slowly and softly. "Martin, are you man enough to hear what the Lord has commanded me to say to you?" Martin hesitated a moment, then nodded his head.

"He let me know that you were wicked when you wearied me for the manuscript. It is only because of his purposes which must stand that I'm forgiven and restored for letting you have the papers. But I told you this last year. I'm only reminding you now so you'll remember how fearful it is to neglect any word of the Lord."

Jenny watched him pace the room and then stop in front of Martin. "Now, Martin, here is a new message from the Lord. You are to repent. I have written out the revelation and I will let you read it for yourself, but I am to warn you to your face and then let you dwell upon it.

"Do you remember how in the revelation to Oliver, the Lord said that when man has truth given to him, he is to study it in his mind? If it is correct and from the Lord, he will have a burning in his bosom. This will let you know what is right. Don't forget, Martin, it's the burning in the bosom."

Joe paced the room again, and Martin pleaded, "Please tell me. I know it's bad, but I'd rather just hear it."

"For one thing," Joe's voice was gentle, kind, "He's said that if you don't repent, you must suffer. Martin, He's said you are not to covet your neighbor's wife, nor to seek the life of your neighbor. You are not to covet your own property, but to impart it freely for the publishing of the Book of Mormon, the word of God. He has commanded you to pay up the printer's debt and release yourself from bondage. Leave your house and home, except when you want to be here."

The import of the words struck Jenny and she shoved her knuckles against her teeth. She was trembling, but she willed herself to silence. There was a tumble of words from Martin and in the confusion, Jenny slipped from her hiding place and rushed through the kitchen and up to her room in the loft.

"What is *sabbat*?" Jenny sat on the log beside Adela. She clutched the green book tight and waited.

Slowly Adela moved, stirring as if just awakening. She looked at Jenny. "Where did you get the book?"

"It belonged to my pa."

"And he let you have it?"

Jenny hesitated only a second. Somehow she knew that Adela wouldn't disapprove. "I stole it from him. When they left for the West without me, I just took it."

Adela smiled gently, her voice dreamy and soft. "You really

want the knowledge, don't you? I think that back in the past there was someone in your family, someone who—"

She didn't finish her statement, but Jenny saw her eyes shine their approval. Adela stood, moving as if she were drifting to her feet. "Jenny, you are very young. There's much to learn. This is a start, reading the book, but now you must let me lead you step by step." As she spoke her hands moved as if drawing an arc in the air.

She whispered, "If you will learn the mysteries truly, if you allow them to sink into your mind, they will shape you into a person of power." Her hands reached toward Jenny and then abruptly she pulled back. She whispered, "It must be done in the right way." She pulled the cloak about her and started down the trail. "Come now, there are many things for you to see."

Jenny trotted to keep up, but her stomach knotted with an unknown apprehension. She watched Adela using the long-forked stick as a walking stick. Eyeing the stick she said, "Martin said Joe had a revelation from the Lord for Oliver Cowdery, and the Lord told Oliver that using the rod was a gift from the Lord and that he was to use the rod to hear messages from God."

"It's true. He has it right. There's only one god, just many different ways to know him." She turned to face Jenny again and said, "I am anxious to teach you this way. Jenny, you'll have power to help people, to heal them, to do good—or evil—in their lives. It is for you to decide how you'll use the power."

That night, long after the supper dishes had been cleared away and Jenny lay in her room under the eaves, Adela's words continued to ring through Jenny's thoughts.

Restlessly she tossed and turned, excited, troubled, questioning, uncertain. Images from the past danced through her mind. She could see Tom laughing, throwing back his head and shouting with glee when she had informed him that someday she would marry Joseph Smith.

Funny, the thought was still there—cold and lifeless, but still there. *Power.* Jenny was filled with uneasy desire. Adela had said, "There's just one god, and how you worship doesn't matter. But I can show you how to have power, power for all the things you desire. Jenny, what do you desire more than anything else in this world?"

Jenny hadn't answered. Adela's words hadn't seemed real at the time, but now with the full moon streaming its silver light into her room, Jenny realized that her old desire had not diminished but gained new strength.

She sat up in bed and hugged her knees against her chest. She could feel her breasts against her legs, and the soft fullness reminded her that her life was changing, moving forward.

"Jenny," she whispered to herself, "just like Adela said, you've lots to learn. If Joe Smith can change, so can you. If the moon is what you want, Adela can tell you how to get it. They say Joe's wife is sickly and can't give him young'uns. I'll be the second Mrs. Smith, and I won't share him with another woman on earth."

The next day Jenny eagerly sought out Adela. Once again she sat on the log beside her with the green book hugged tightly in her arms. Adela was talking but Jenny was only vaguely conscious of the rhythm of her words; instead, she was studying Adela, from her flawless ivory skin to the red chiffon that showed through the heavy folds of her cape. She murmured yes to questions that slid over her head. But mostly she wondered how she could become like Adela.

Abruptly she asked, "Where did you get your pretty red dress?"

Adela pulled away from her and for a moment her lips tightened with displeasure. "You have not been listening to me! Jenny, how do you expect to learn? You wouldn't treat your schoolteacher that way, would you?" Suddenly her face softened, "Jenny, I didn't mean to scold. You're young. I forget. At your age it is hard to take life seriously. Never you mind. I'll be patient till you see."

Abruptly she jumped to her feet and dropped the dark cloak. Before Jenny had time to blink her startled eyes, Adela spun away from her in a dance. Her red dress rose and fell like a flame as she danced through the trees, dipping, swirling. She retreated through the firs, then came flying back to Jenny.

When she finally stopped Jenny watched the flame red dress

slowly float downward, quiet again. Adela pulled the shrouding cape around her shoulders and dropped to the ground in front of Jenny.

"I feel part of the god of light when I dance," she murmured. "Only then do I transcend this place and reach the eternal and become one with him."

Jenny frowned trying to understand the concepts, and Adela patted her knee. "You need to read more. Here, I'll mark portions for you to read, just like your teacher at school!"

Jenny spoke slowly. "You asked what I desired in life, and I couldn't answer. Now I know. How do I get the power to have my desires?"

Adela studied Jenny and her pretty lips pulled down into a mocking pout. "You make a light thing of it all; what do you want, a new dress like mine?"

Jenny shook her head, "No, its—well it's personal and I just can't talk about it. But I want it very much."

Jenny saw Adela look down at her clenched hands as she said dryly, "I don't think you yet realize we are not trading for little favors. Serving the god of the universe for a new dress isn't done. Jenny, I've tried to tell you that this is serious business. True, there is great satisfaction and power, but more—there is great responsibility. You don't enter lightly into searching out the eternals. You don't learn the secrets and mysteries of life itself without a great deal of—of soul searching. This is a pathway; once you start there is no turning back. You yourself will become in tune with nature itself. Like a harp plucked by the hand of the master, you must respond.

"If you will use, you must be used. Taking vows is serious, embarking on the tunnel toward that light is a glorious journey, freeing the spirit to soar with others of our kind." Now she leaned close to Jenny and peered into her eyes. Jenny could only shiver, transfixed; she felt she had already started down the path.

But later, on another day, Jenny opened the book in Adela's presence and ran her fingers under horrifying words. "Adela, they don't mean this, do they, about drinking blood?"

Adela nodded in affirmation, and her face hardened in response to Jenny's whispered, "No!" But as soon as Jenny said it, she knew she had to decide. The thought of losing Adela—and Joe—was unbearable.

When the woman's face softened and she knelt before Jenny with that beautiful smile, Jenny knew she couldn't say no. Finally, when they both stood, Adela smiled gently, "Before the power begins, you must go to the sabbat with me and prove you are ready to start down the path of power."

Jenny started to ask her again about the word *sabbat*, but decided against it. If she went to one, she would learn what it was.

The time came, the eve of May Day. For weeks Jenny had trembled between wanting what Adela had promised, and fearing the coming unknown in a way she could neither identify nor understand.

Even now, on this chosen night, Jenny hesitated, filled with doubt. She slipped from the silent, sleeping house just before midnight. For a moment she was filled with a voiceless plea for Tom. Then she straightened her shoulders. Adela would be there; that was all she needed.

At the end of the path, at the edge of the dark forest, Adela met her. Without a word they moved swiftly through the woods toward a pale light shining through the trees. Jenny realized they stood on a moonlit path at the edge of town. She gave a gasp of relief as Adela motioned her on.

When they stopped in front of the church, Jenny's words burst out in astonishment. "I didn't know we were goin' to church! You said—"

"Where else would one go to worship the beautiful god of light?"

Jenny shrugged. Trying vainly to express her tumbled thoughts, she said, "I—I guess when you explained about renouncing all other covenants and talked about the new communion, I guess I just—" Other shadowy figures were joining them, and Jenny said no more.

The church was lighted only by a tiny cluster of candles. For a moment Jenny thought back to the afternoon she had come here with Lucy Harris. How brilliant the beautiful light had been! Now the dark-robed group moved slowly and silently toward the candles.

A sudden chill swept over Jenny. The cross which had hung on the wall was being lifted down. They dropped it in front of the candles, and one dark figure kicked it into position.

A black-robed man with a goat's head tied around his neck began to sing. And after a few minutes the singing gave way to chanting, a strange rhythmic chanting which surged and pulsed through Jenny's body. Their chant was strange and disturbing.

Abruptly the chanting ceased, and Jenny felt the strange, heavy silence settle over her spirit. A man moved slowly toward the priest. She watched him take a deep breath and lift his head. Clearly his voice rang out, "I beg you, honorable one, that you add my name to the Book of Death. It is only by moving beyond this life and into the next that I will enter the eternal progression."

For a moment Jenny lost the tread of thought as the man continued with his vows. She was frowning, trying to understand what he was saying. Suddenly new words grabbed her attention, spreading meaning over her with a chilling blast.

The priest was saying. "Do you deny the Christian faith, the creator of heaven and earth? Do you renounce your baptism and promise to give your allegiance only to the god of light?"

The words were still underlining themselves in her mind, spreading confusion and a fear that she didn't understand, but she pushed them away as the man squared his shoulders. She heard the first initiate echo a dark-sounding oath, and she felt an urge to run. She cringed as he stomped on the cross. Then they removed the chalice from the altar and poured a dark substance into it. This chalice she had drunk from on that day of glory and light, they were desecrating with animal's blood!

Clasping her hands against her throat, Jenny backed away, shuddering as horror coursed through her. Jenny felt hands pushing her forward, cold and insistent, for she was the next initiate. Adela's sharp voice reminded her, "You said you would do anything for power. Have you changed your mind?"

As Jenny hesitated, a clear picture of Joe's intense face

framed with bright hair rose in her mind. Still she pulled back as Adela's cold hand pushed. As she took a step, the group parted to accept her. The cross lay at her feet.

Suddenly she whirled and ran down the long aisle, past Adela and the motionless dark figures. Through the darkened streets Jenny ran, her mind filled with remembered glory— brilliant color broken by the window and thrown against the cross and the chalice.

All that night horror held her motionless, wide-eyed in the darkness of her room. As morning broke she watched for the sun with hungry eyes, wishing she could get enough of it to last her through the coming night and then the next.

But within the week a new horror came. Life with Martin Harris had been rising to a climax for a long time. Jenny had felt this, but even she was surprised that evening.

He came in for his supper, saying in a matter-of-fact tone of voice, "I've sold part of the farm."

Lucy was very quiet for a moment. Then she sighed and moved. "How much did you get?"

"Three thousand—and there's not a penny for you," he said stoutly. "It's all for the Lord's work. Joe's had a revelation sayin' I'm to pay the printer's debt."

He settled himself at the table and pulled the plate of bread toward him. "The printer's debt," Lucy repeated slowly. "You mean you're paying for printing Joe's gold Bible with the money from our farm?" She walked slowly toward him. "Martin, I can't hold my peace any longer. You've always been restless, seekin' after new religions, never satisfied with the truth. But to sell the farm for this heresy—"

"That's enough, woman!" Martin roared. "I'm leavin' you. You're rebelling against the Lord and I'll have nothin' more to do with you! You'll have this house, but you'll have to feed and clothe yourself. Maybe that Lord of yours will take care of you!" He jumped to his feet and headed for the door.

Lucy ran toward him, reaching for his arm. Jenny stood horrified, unable to move as the quick sweep of his arm threw off Lucy's clinging hands. Without thinking, Jenny rushed to-ward her as Lucy spun off balance.

"You leave her be!" Martin roared, and swung at Jenny. Again and again he struck her, then turned on Lucy. When Jenny returned to consciousness and looked around for Lucy, Martin was long gone.

They surveyed each other's wounds; then their eyes met. Heavily Lucy said, "You can't fight a revelation. He thinks it's God speakin' to him—but God don't make people mean."

During the following week, Jenny and Lucy did little more than nurse their battered bodies. But the memory of the terror returned when Tom came home and saw the results of Martin's fury. Anger and despair swept his face; he hugged Jenny and she cried with pain. During that week, he scarcely let Lucy and Jenny out of his sight.

One evening as Jenny limped into the kitchen, she heard Tom talking to Lucy. "Ma'am, there's no work here, and you don't need the worry of extra mouths to feed. Amos and the others have found a spot for themselves, and I mean to be off myself. A buddy's in town and he's talkin' me into movin' east with him. I—"

Jenny's cry broke through his words, and the two turned to her. "Oh, Tom, you can't leave me! Not now!" The arm she stretched toward him was still badly bruised and she saw him wince. "Take me with you, please."

While Tom hesitated, Lucy sighed, "Much as I hate to lose her, Tom, she's right to ask. You're her blood relation and that means much to a young'un. Take her away from this place and find her a position wherever you go."

Jenny's poor battered body robbed her of the sense to ask about their destination and with whom they would travel. When the day came and she stood in front of Mark Cartwright with her bundles of belongings at her feet, she realized that Tom hadn't mentioned her to Mark, either.

Tom stumbled over his explanations and Mark's frown changed to pity. While his eyes measured the bruises on her bare arms, Jenny realized that her ordeal had become an asset. It was winning her release from this place.

CHAPTER 13

The stagecoach was just beginning to roll, pulling out of Manchester for eastern New York. Mark Cartwright and Tom sat facing Jenny. At the crack of the driver's whip and his shout, "Move it out!" the horses responded with a surge of speed and the stage rocked around the corner. Jenny's knuckles were white as she gripped the handrail.

"Your first time on a stagecoach?" Mark observed and was given a tense nod. Cautiously she leaned against the doorframe to watch Manchester disappear from sight.

Tom lowered his voice. "We've just traveled in Pa's wagon. Mark, we're greenhorns, and mighty grateful we could travel with you. You've got kin in Cobleskill? I've never heard of Cobleskill."

Jenny leaned forward. "Your ma and pa there?"

Mark shook his head. He was studying Jenny, marveling at the difference four years had made. "My mother lives in Ohio, just inland from Cleveland. My father died three years ago. I'm headed for Albany, New York. An uncle on my mother's side has offered this fledgling attorney a spot in his law office until I get some experience." He watched curiosity flit across Jenny's face. "My mother has a sister in Cobleskill," he added. As Jenny's large gray eyes watched him intently, he lapsed into silence, remembering South Bainbridge. What a pathetic little tyke she had been in those days! Only her eyes still seemed the same—curious gray flecked with amber, just as steadfast and serious now as when they had caught his attention in the schoolroom at South Bainbridge.

Mark continued to watch Jenny as she shifted her attention to Tom. He found himself speaking just to recapture that play of expression on her face, to see the changing light in her eyes. When Tom was voicing his fears of the future again, the shadows in Jenny's eyes had Mark leaning forward, raising his voice against the clatter of the coach and the shout of the driver.

"Tom, I'll help you find a position. There are friends enough around Cobleskill who'll know of jobs for the two of you. You needn't settle for just anything; you've both worked, and you'll find good positions. Don't worry about a thing."

When they reached Cobleskill Mark was true to his word. He soon found work for Jenny, but things just weren't working out for Tom. Tom was figuring how to explain this to Jenny as he sat in the kitchen of the Hamilton Barton home. Watching his sister working in the kitchen, he couldn't help admire her easy manner.

"You're fittin' in well," he observed, nodding his head toward the hall. "I was sure flabbergasted when I saw the place. Mark did well for you."

"It was actually Mrs. Weber, his aunt Mabel. She knew the Bartons were needing a girl." She paused in her task of mixing bread and lifted doughy hands. "I've Lucy Harris to thank for showing me the way around a lady's kitchen. But I'm also thinking Mrs. Barton's mighty generous to take on such a raw one and train me up; no doubt Mark and his aunt had something to do with it all. Leastwise, the Bartons seem to think well of Mark." She covered the bread pans and turned to Tom. "You didn't come just for a chat, did you?"

Tom shrugged and then admitted, "Jen, I'm for goin' back."

"Back!" she echoed, whirling around. "You don't mean Manchester."

"I'm not sure where," he admitted miserably. He knew he was failing her. "I can't get myself settled to anything, and I thought if I were to just wander back for a time, it might settle my feelings."

She continued to watch him and he resisted the urge to squirm. Her eyes were too much like Ma's, guessing his thoughts. Slowly she said, "I think what you're feeling has something to do with Joe Smith. He was sure getting lots of sympathy from you."

"Jen, he's my friend. It hurts to remember how the people back there ain't givin' him a chance to prove himself. A crowd is followin' him now, and listenin' to him, everywhere except Palmyra and Manchester. There they wouldn't even let him have the town hall to have his say."

Jenny rubbed her chin with a floury hand, and Tom chuckled at the childish gesture. Gently he said, "Rub the flour off your chin. Jen, I'm not tryin' to lay my burdens on you; I only want you to understand why I'm leavin' now."

"Tom, I'll not hold you. I've this position here and I'll make it. Only—" her voice caught and she took a breath, "just come see me once in a while. You're all I have. Sometimes I pine for Ma and I think to look for her. I wish they'd be writing, so I'd know where to find them."

"You know Ma can't hardly put a pen to paper," Tom responded, getting to his feet. She only nodded as she followed him to the door.

Jenny's words and the memory of the one tear that had escaped down her cheek stayed with Tom as he packed his gear and headed back. As he trudged the roads and trails, passing through small towns and walking the country roads past prospering farms, he pondered and chided himself. "Tom, here you are, twenty-one years old and roamin' the country like a tad with nothin' to do. Seems you ought to be settlin' down."

But then he admitted it—he had unrest inside, and this was the only thing he knew to do to get rid of it. Abruptly his feet veered off the west-bound road and sought the southward cut toward Pennsylvania. Later, when he wondered why he had chosen that path just then, he concluded it must have been the Lord giving him one more chance to pay attention.

It was a late summer afternoon when he reached the main street of South Bainbridge, weary and foot-sore. Trudging into town, he could see the school through the trees; just ahead was the tavern, to his right the general store. Absorbed by memories, Tom nearly stumbled into a group of men standing on the corner.

"Tom Timmons, can I be dreamin'?" Tom stopped abruptly and his startled eyes met those of Martin Harris. Behind him stood Joe Smith and Oliver Cowdery. Joe grinned with delight as he clapped Tom on the shoulder.

"The Lord is good!" Joe exclaimed. "David Whitmer, this is Tom Timmons from up Manchester way." He turned his attention to Tom. With a broad grin he said, "You've come just in time to celebrate with us. How did the news travel so fast?"

"News?" Tom blinked, still not believing his eyes. "I'm just travelin' through—what news?"

For a moment Joe looked startled; then he threw back his head. "The Lord sent you! That's even better!"

Tom looked slowly around the group of sober men, "What's goin' on?"

Joe stepped closer and clapped Tom on the shoulder again, "Let me tell you. We've been bringing the gospel to the people of South Bainbridge and Colesville, and the Lord's blessing mightily. Everybody's buying the *Book of Mormon* and they're falling over themselves to join the church."

"So you really have started a church," Tom said slowly.

Joe nodded. "April 6, 1830, at Fayette, New York, the Church of Christ was organized with six people. Now there's so many converts we can hardly keep up with the baptizing. This will go down in history, mark my word. The Lord has revealed His restored gospel in these latter days, just before the end of all things as we know them. Tom, my lad, there's a new day dawning. The Lord's going to be returning to claim His own and set up His kingdom. It is our task to carry the news to everyone. Will you be joining us?"

"Joe," Tom said slowly, studying his face, "you're so changed I can't hardly believe it's you. I was wantin' to find you, to see if we could get the diggin' bunch together again. I'd heard you was serious about this church business, but I didn't reckon it had gone this far. Join, huh?" He scratched his forehead. "Mind if I hang around a while and see what's goin' on?"

"I'll bring you up-to-date," Martin said eagerly, not noticing how Tom pulled away from him. "Soon as we started havin' a little success convertin' folks here, the soreheads began makin' things hot. They brung up that old charge against Joe here."

He paused to snort his disgust. Tom thought incredulously, *This man beat up his wife and my sister, and he stands here talking to me like nothing's wrong!*

"Chawin' it like a dog with a bone," Martin continued. "I don't see the sense of it. They made a big fuss over Joe usin' the seer stone, like it was the worst thing that could happen. I set them straight. Leastwise, they shut up when I told them that Joe used the stone to find the gold plates. I think that pretty well convinced them the business couldn't be bad."

Tom recalled the battered faces of Jenny and Lucy Harris. Finally, he shook his head as if to clear it as Martin's excited words and joyful face pushed through that ugly picture. It was impossible to understand, to fit the two views of Martin together.

"It was the churches," Cowdery added. "They didn't like seeing their people so happy, seeing them pull out of the old dead places and go to the true church. That's why they brought up those old charges against Joe. Lo and behold, the statute of limitations had passed, so they had to let him off scot-free!"

David added enthusiastically, "Practically as soon as he stepped out of court, the law from Colesville slapped him with another warrant. But they couldn't stick him with anything there, either."

Martin Harris chuckled, "Court spent twenty-three hours listenin' to everybody in the country complain about the man. But they weren't able to make a thing stick. The feelin' is that Judge Noble wasn't a bit happy with his decision. He was sayin', aside like, that you cain't do much with a fella who's practicin' his religion, even if you don't like the way he's a-doin' it."

"Joe's lucky." Tom turned to see the stern-faced older man speaking. "The laws against digging for money and treasures been on the books since 1788, and I don't expect them to be dropped soon. I'm advising him to keep his nose clean."

Joe threw his head back and laughed joyously, "Ah, Thompson, the Lord's a step ahead of you. An angel's come and told me to give up the digging business." Tom began to chuckle and Joe linked his arm through Tom's. "Why don't you come along with us?" Tom nodded, and immediately Joe sobered. "Tom, this may just seem jolly, but it's a burden, and don't you ever forget it. The Lord's laid a mighty responsibility on me, and I need all the help I can get from my true friends."

Looking back on it all later, Tom continued to marvel at the tilting of events that had so quickly tumbled him back into Joe Smith's life again.

The easy camaraderie among these men made the whole situation nearly unbelievable to Tom. But life seemed to fluctuate incessantly. The group shifted from gaiety to desperate prayer and fasting until Joseph sent them two by two into the surrounding area with their bundles of books and the tale of the new church.

All the while, Tom stood by as a spectator, watching the events surrounding Joe. New converts continued to flock forward for baptism, and opposition continued, too. Just as quickly as Joe erected dams for his baptismal pools, townspeople tore them out.

Tom watched Joe struggle with the tension between his new converts and the need to support his wife. Joe finally went back to farming. On a day that Oliver Cowdery paid his visit, Tom was pitching hay while Joe drove the team of horses.

When Tom rammed his pitchfork into the ground and walked up to the wagon, he heard Oliver Cowdery chiding Joe about neglecting the church. Even Tom breathed a sigh of relief when Joe recited a new revelation from the Lord, telling him that the new church was to support him and his wife. But the hard words at the end of the revelation, stating the Lord would send curses instead of blessings if His people didn't follow this command, left Tom feeling uneasy.

The first leaves had donned autumn colors before Tom gave serious consideration to the winter ahead. He chewed a straw and pondered the end of the carefree summer. "Tom," he addressed himself, "it's time for funnin' to end. The winter will be hard and hungry if'n you don't get yourself a real job and snug in for the season."

He was still muttering to himself when Joe came out to lean on the fence rail beside him. "Tom," he said, facing him with that penetrating gaze which still made Tom squirm, "I've been meaning to have a talk with you. Seems you're still on the fence about your beliefs. Now, Tom, you know I'm not pushing a single person to accept what his mind refuses to entertain. But, my friend, I must caution you to not delay. If you are convinced that all this is from the Lord, then choose ye whom ye will serve."

"Joe, it isn't that. You're my good friend, and I'm happy bein' around you, but this is all like a box canyon. I gotta get out and be gettin' on with life. I've a livin' to earn, body and soul to keep together."

His lips twisted at his attempted humor, but Joe's steady gaze tore the grin away. "You're not facing the seriousness of it at all. Tom, if this is from the Lord, there's no way you can turn your back on it without losing your soul."

Tom chewed his straw and thought. Finally Joe said softly, "I'm not of a mind to persuade anybody. Tom, you must decide for yourself, but I can give you some help. The Lord gave some good advice to Oliver and I'm prone to use it to help you. He said to him that a body is to be studying out truth in his mind. Then he should ask the Lord if it is right. The Lord will cause his bosom to burn within as a testimony if it is."

"Joe, it isn't that I doubt. It's just that I don't care for religion. Seems to me there's enough trouble in life without gettin' connected with more. And I see you headed for opposition."

"So, other things are more important than following the Lord's commandments? You need to open your heart to what He's revealing. I'll be praying that the Lord will convince you otherwise." Joe paused for a moment and then added, "You're footloose now. How about coming to Fayette with us for the general conference of the church? Might help you to see how the Lord's operating now."

At the church conference Tom listened as Hiram Page stood to his feet and humbly confessed the sin of having used a seer stone. With a voice full of contrition, he admitted, "I was a-tryin' to elevate myself. I promise to give it up. I know now it is only the Prophet who has the gifts. I'll never use the stone again."

Tom met Newel Knight at the conference and heard his story. "The Prophet cast a devil out of me," he said soberly. His tiny wife nodded at his elbow, as he added, "If it hadn't happened, I'd be dead now. Satan had me by the throat squeezing the life outta me, and I was even unconscious for a time. When you have a testimony like this, you know this has gotta be the right church."

In October, Tom left Fayette with a group going on the first missionary journey to the Lamanites. When he returned, there was a new face among the converts—Sidney Rigdon. Rigdon was a preacher, formerly a member of the Cambellites.

It didn't take Tom long to see this new convert's impact on the scraggly bunch of farmers who comprised the new church. This dignified man had the voice and demeanor of a professional orator.

Standing in the shadows watching the two men together, Tom saw Joseph stumble in his youthful inexperience. He also saw the attention the new convert was attracting and began to wonder if Joe was losing out to the newcomer. But while pity was stirring in Tom's breast, the Lord spoke to Joseph again.

When Tom heard the revelation read, he breathed a sigh of relief for Joe. "That's right good," he muttered to Martin Harris standing beside him. "Now we all know for certain that the Lord sent Rigdon to Joseph just as He sent John the Baptist to Jesus. Rigdon's to be Joe's helper. It's good to know that the Lord approves of Joe just the way he is, and He isn't faultin' him 'cause he's not the smooth talker Rigdon is."

CHAPTER 14

"I tell you, these are the last days!" Tom was watching as Joe Smith leaned forward to rest his hand on Rigdon's knee. Joe's earnest gaze was fastened on the older man as he repeated, "The last days. It wouldn't surprise me none to see Jesus Christ return during my lifetime. Sidney, we've much to do before His return!"

It was the end of October 1830. Joe, his family, and some of his followers had taken up residence in Fayette, New York. They were on the Whitmer farm where the new church had been started the previous summer.

Tom looked around the tiny room where that event had taken place. Rigdon's voice was taut with excitement as he answered Joe, and Tom felt a shiver run up his back. "I know, I know. The whole country is feeling it, talking about it, and doing nothing at all." He paced the room, saying, "Every other soapbox has a prophet on it nowadays, proclaiming the return. But they will all fail."

Joe's voice overlapped Rigdon's, "We've a big mission for these few short years. With the Lord on our side, nothing on this earth will stand in our way. Priestcraft has corrupted the church Jesus started; no wonder He swept truth from the earth! But now the true church of Jesus Christ has been restored in these latter days." He stressed his next words, "In this dispensation God has prepared men's hearts to accept the truth."

Rigdon's eager hand reached out, but Joe shook it off. "That guarantees success," he continued. "But it isn't only telling about the true, restored church and bringing the lost tribes into

137

the fold." His voice deepened. "There's something else that must be done."

Rigdon shifted forward on his chair and waited. Tom's attention was caught by the older man's excitement before he heard Joe's words.

"Zion," he said. "We have been given the task of building Zion on this continent. Jesus Christ is going to return to this continent, not to Jerusalem. How do I know? He's told me so. Let me read to you from the latest revelation."

The sun of the late October day streamed through the window. Joe wiped perspiration from his face and picked up a sheaf of papers. Clearing his throat, Joe began, "Now this is just part of it: 'And Enoch and all his people walked with God, and he dwelt in the midst of Zion; and it came to pass that Zion was not, for God received it up into his own bosom; and from thence went forth the saying, *Zion is fled.*'

"Enoch built such a perfect city God removed it from earth." In the quiet Tom heard a fly buzz against the window. Joe sighed and leaned forward. "Sidney, my friend, we have been given the task of building the New Jerusalem. When Christ returns, the city of Enoch will descend out of heaven to that very spot."

Sidney Rigdon jumped to his feet and paced the room in quick, hard strides. He stopped in front of Joe, his eyes burning with excitement. Surprisingly his voice was low and controlled. "Smith, we've got a whole bunch of converts just sitting out there waiting for us."

Joe looked startled, and Sidney explained. "Kirtland, Ohio. These people are ready for the message right now, and we mustn't delay." He paused and then added, "You know, converting them will be easier if we're all there."

Astonished, Tom cut into the conversation. "We're to uproot the whole lot and move to Ohio? Get the people from Manchester and Palmyra, Colesville and Bainbridge all to move? Rigdon, that's asking too much." Tom looked at the man's square jaw and hastily added, "I guess I'd better get busy with my chores."

During the following weeks Tom held his tongue while the members of the new church argued with Joseph. Through it all ran Joseph's quiet persuasion as he reminded the people of the Lord's instruction. "Kirtland is the eastern boundary of the promised land. We must claim our inheritance."

When the next general conference of the church convened, winter was well upon New York State. Outside the crowded building snow was falling steadily. When Joe Smith arrived, the sixty members met him with worried gazes.

Moving purposefully, he turned the pages of the newest revelation he had received from the Lord. "My friends and fellow laborers together, I beg your attention while I instruct you with the Lord's wisdom." Tom was sitting where he could see the faces as Joe read the words. There were smiles of satisfaction at the description of Zion. ". . . a land flowing with milk and honey." But Tom saw their despair at the words, "And they that have farms that cannot be sold, let them be left or rented as seemeth good."

Later as the people pushed their way out of the hall, Tom listened to the comments. "Lucky for us he's appointed someone to take care of the poor; I'm feeling we're all going to fall in that category." "At least we know the riches of the earth are the Lord's to give; maybe we'll get some of that by and by." "Do we have to wait fer the Second Comin' to get 'em?"

One terse remark that reached Tom's ears troubled him for weeks. He had nearly reached the door when he heard, "I think Joe himself invented that revelation just so he can get a spot of cash from all these farms."

During January and February, the first line of wagons and carts headed for Ohio. Joseph Smith and his pregnant wife left by sleigh. Some of the more fortunate had shipped down Lake Erie to Cleveland, but Tom bartered a ride in a sleigh traveling along behind Joseph.

Nearly as quickly as the first body of believers descended on Kirtland, the eager and the curious began to pour into town to see this new prophet.

The story of the golden Bible attracted them, but they stayed when they saw the miracles and heard Joe's sermons, which kept the listeners in gales of laughter, or suddenly reduced them to tears.

While the growing community of New Yorkers settled in the town of Thompson, Joe Smith took up residence in the Whitney home and began his translation of the New Testament. Tom had found a position working in the livery stable. From there he watched and marveled.

The weather had just begun to soften with a hint of spring when Emma's second pregnancy ended in the loss of twins. Tom had known nothing of the event on the day he rode out to visit the Prophet. He had nearly reached the Smith farm when he spotted the lonely figure trudging toward him.

"Hello, Joe, my friend!" he hailed. As Joe drew near, Tom slipped from his horse. "What's wrong, Joe?" The Prophet's face was white and drawn, and his eyes were troubled.

"Why is it," he asked Tom, as if continuing a conversation, "I've the power to heal everyone except my wife? I can bless others with health, but I can't call down the power to deliver my wife of a live child."

Tom shook his head, startled.

"Twins this time; they both died. I was powerless. It was only the gift from heaven that kept Emma from following them."

"What do you mean?"

"God gave us twin girls. Their mother died in the birthing. Another man's loss, my gain." Joe seemed to brighten, to toss aside the dark questions. As they rode toward his farm, and Joe talked about the translating and the newest revelation, Tom remembered his mission.

He interrupted, "Joe, my friend, I feel I should report the gossip."

Joseph grinned wryly. "Let me guess. It's the revelation on the United Order, isn't it?"

"Well, every other religion's pullin' the same thing. Rigdon's fellow Campbellites had been practicin' communal living, sharin' everything. They said a body could expect to see his shirt goin' down the street on someone else's back. It's not settin' too good with people who've been right particular about their belongings. I'm reluctant, too, about sharing my money and horse."

"Don't fault me," Joe said defensively. "You know this isn't my idea; it's a revelation from the Lord. My only responsibility is to teach it."

"Part of the bad feelings have to do with Rigdon's flock bein' caught up in this before we came."

"Don't forget we got a church full of people along with Rigdon," Joe cautioned. "Count it wisdom of the Lord to show us how to live together."

Tom still hesitated, "Well, revelation about the Order was a mighty long one, and it just hit wrong."

"What was hitting wrong? The part about murder and there being no forgiveness, or was it about loving your wife with all your heart and not cleaving to anyone, not committing adultery? The people of God ought to be able to live with that instruction."

"No, 'twasn't that; it was the money thing. The part about writin' a deed, which can't be broken, givin' all a man's belongings to the church. That's pretty hard. What's a man to do if he decides he don't want to be a part of the church anymore?"

Impatiently Joe said, "Tom, are you suggesting that I change the revelation? Do you realize what you're saying? This is the Lord's command! Not a word is to be altered. Changing's saying God doesn't give perfect revelations."

Tom stuck his hands in his pockets and muttered, "Sorry, Joe. That wasn't what I had in mind. If you could just find a way to make it a little easier to swallow."

"Well, we've found it! You know the people from New York have all settled in Thompson. Thanks to their obeying the Lord, Leman Copley and Ezra Thayer have given generously of a big chunk of land to provide for the people."

"You don't say!" Tom exclaimed, slapping the reins of his horse across his hand, "That's Jim Dandy. Just the verification that everybody's been lookin' for."

"Verification?" Joseph stopped and turned a sorrowful look on Tom. "I'm surprised you even admitted it. Tom, that isn't faith!" He continued to study Tom with sad eyes.

In the silence Tom remembered another reason for his visit. "Joe, I wanted you to know I'm plannin' a trip to see my sister for a bit. She's hanging on me, since we're family, but I'll be back." But Joe Smith was lost in thought and he merely nodded.

In May, Tom once again sat in the Bartons' kitchen. He watched Jenny moving about her work, marveling at the stroke of luck that had provided this work for her. He also measured her size and the changes in her body.

"Jen, this place agrees with ya. I left a little 'un; now you're taller and fillin' out like a young lady should." Surprised to see her blush, he exclaimed, "Aw, Jen, I'm your brother."

She detoured from dashing about the kitchen, and pressed a kiss against his beard. "I'm not faulting you. It's just unexpected, having family. Do I look better?"

He studied the coil of dark hair on her neck and admired the way the smooth sweep of her hair emphasized the heart shape of her face. "That widow's peak, I guess they call it, makes your gray eyes twice the size they oughta be. I 'spect next time I see you, the fellas will be a-sparkin' ya." She threw him a startled glance, and he hooted, "So! They're startin' already."

"No—" She drew out the reply slowly, then quickly looked at him. "It's just Mark. He don't count, though."

Mrs. Barton swished through the door and said, "Jennifer, the word should be *doesn't*. Mark is coming to tea. I'm sure he'd like to see your brother." With a quick nod in Tom's direction, she left the kitchen.

At tea, sitting stiffly in the Bartons' sitting room while Jenny served them, Tom juggled his new images of his sister. *Which picture is the true Jenny?* he wondered. And when he saw Mark's attention wholly devoted to her, he added another picture of her, one colored with respect.

Curiously he studied the young man in the well-tailored suit, admiring the silk string tie and the polished boots. As Mark talked, Tom became sharply aware of the contrast between Mark and the fellows Tom had been listening to lately. *You just automatically hang a "gentleman" tag on him*, Tom mused.

Returning his attention to Jenny, Tom noticed the new neatness, the polish that hadn't been there a year ago. Jenny was becoming a lady. Glancing quickly back to Mark, he decided that anything was possible.

During the days Tom spent with Jenny, he followed her about the Barton household, talking about all that had happened to him since he had last seen her. He held the basket of laundry while she fastened the sheets to the lines. "I'd no intention of going Bainbridge way," he admitted, "but once there, it was like old times. There were new faces in the crowd, the Whitmers and an odd fellow named Thompson, but with Joe around, everybody was easy-like."

Jenny frowned and jerked the clothespin from her mouth. "I suppose you were all off digging."

Tom shook his head, "No, there wasn't time. The new church seems to keep him hoppin'. People are at him all the time. Seems he's preachin', or prayin', or doin' his paperwork constant like."

"Paperwork, what's that?"

"Well, he's getting plenty of revelations, and he's makin' a translation of the New Testament—you know, the Bible. The Lord's let him know that the present translation's been corrupted. But there's more. The Lord's revealed much about the Second Coming. He's tellin' Joe to get ready to build the city of Zion—but then He told Joe that He won't give him any further information about all this until he gets the New Testament translated."

"You don't say." Jenny turned to study Tom with those curious gray eyes, and he was caught by the play of expression in them. The questioning frown between her eyes smoothed out, but she still chewed at her lip.

"What is it, Jen?" he asked. "I'm your brother, remember?"

"I'm thinking about it all. The things you said about Joe. Tom, he used to be a friend; now you act like you really do believe he's a prophet from God."

Tom cleared his throat nervously. "Jen, I know this seems strange to you, that I could change and suddenly start believin'. But I'm findin' if you stick your neck out, lookin' for answers, you have to take them when they come."

"Meaning?"

"He said I was obligated to myself to investigate, that my

hereafter depended on it. He said to study out the truth and then ask God, and He'll make you have a burnin' in your bosom if it's right. Well, I asked about Joe and I had the burnin'. Even if it sometimes goes against my grain to say it, I gotta admit, I've had the witness."

He saw dark questions of disbelief appear in Jenny's face. "Jen," he went on slowly, "another revelation Joe had I think is for people like you. It says some are given by the Holy Ghost to know and have all these gifts from God, and others believe on their words. I think that means believe on their belief." There was a faraway expression in her eyes. He asked, "What ya thinkin'?"

"I was remembering South Bainbridge. He was tryin' to teach me some of the things he knew. There's not that much difference in it all—his beliefs before and after the book." After a moment she asked, "Did you join Joe's new church?"

"Well, not yet, but I figure I will."

A strange expression veiled her eyes now. "So Emma's lost twins. A man sets a store by a family, so I guess Joe's pretty unhappy. Is she well now?"

Tom nodded. "Adopting the little girl twins took care of their wanting a family. Least, Joe hasn't said more."

When it was time for Tom to return to Ohio, he sensed Jenny's restless spirit. "I've got to go," he apologized. "I promised Joe." Then he brightened, "Maybe you could come to Ohio for a visit, see it for yourself. From the sound of it all, it's goin' to be the new Zion. Joe's talkin' some about puttin' up a big meetin'house. I think he called it a temple, like in Jerusalem."

After Tom left, Jenny surveyed her domain, filled with a new discontent. "This was nearly heaven itself," she muttered gloomily as she surveyed the littered kitchen and piles of dirty dishes. "I'd thought everything in the past was gone, even that—" She sighed deeply, unable to speak of those past desires she had entertained for bright-haired Joseph.

During the following weeks, only half of Jenny's mind worked on the tasks in which she had once taken delight. One day while she slowly pushed a scrub brush across the floor, Mrs. Barton spoke from the doorway. "Jenny, what's wrong? I've been watching you drag about this house for weeks. Are you ill?"

Jenny rolled back on her heels and surveyed the messy puddle under her brush. "Ma'am, I don't know. The heart's gone from me. I miss Tom." She lifted her eyes to give the lie.

"Oh, Jenny!" Mrs. Barton knelt and squeezed Jenny against her. "I'm thoughtless, taking for granted that everyone on this earth has had a life as pleasant as mine.—I came to bring you a letter. Here, go to your room and rest while I finish. It's senseless to work hard in this heat, anyway."

Tucked in her room under the eaves, the fresh scent of growing things wafting through the window on the afternoon breeze, Jenny leaned against her pillows and studied the envelope. The return address indicated it was from Lucy Harris.

Slowly she pried open the envelope and pushed aside newspaper clippings to find the letter. There were two. Jenny sat up and stared in disbelief. The first was a letter from Nancy!

Dear Jenny, she read, *I've just moved back to Manchester and Lucy Harris has guilted me terribly for not having written to you. We did make an attempt to write, but the letter was returned. I have married and now am expecting a child.* Jenny stopped to check the name on the paper: Alexander MacAdams. It was unfamiliar and Jenny returned to the letter. *Ma and Pa have moved on west. Of course you would expect that. Even I have lost track of them. Mostly I wanted to write and tell you that Ma and the rest never ceased grieving about leaving you behind. Mostly because of your tender age. Please, if you can, come visit me in Manchester and meet your new brother-in-law and the little niece or nephew you will soon have. I would like to contact Tom, too. Mostly, Jenny, I am heavy over the way we left you. We all suffered thinking that Satan had his iron grip on your life. Mrs. Harris seems to think all things have worked out well for you. I am your affectionate sister, Nancy.*

Jenny frowned as she studied the brief letter. The words had stripped away the rosy glow around her memories of home and family. Jenny leaned against the pillows and whispered, "Satan."

How often, during those final months, Ma and Nancy had aligned against her with puzzled frowns. Search as she might,

Jenny couldn't recall a reason for the frowns.

With a sigh, Jenny dug into the envelope. She fingered the newspaper clippings, then rejected them in favor of the other letter.

Jenny read rapidly. Lucy seemed contented. She hadn't seen Martin since he had left Manchester for Fayette. Her life was narrowed by money worries, but pleasant. She recounted the events since Jenny and Tom had left, then said: *I've been nagged into writing to you since last February when these articles came out in the Palmyra* Reflector. *I'd intended writing before, but didn't. Jenny, I've done much thinking and praying since you've left. I'm still uneasy about your time here and thinking that I didn't do my duty by you. Somehow, despite the church meetings and the baptism, I don't think you understand all I wanted badly to teach you about being a Christian. In a short letter, there's little space to make up the lack. For most of us it takes a lifetime of living to come to an understanding that bears weight. But there must be a beginning. For some of us, going to church, being baptized and partaking of the elements is enough to want to love God. But I'm beginning to think that for some it isn't enough. It's like breaking a horse. For some it's easy, others it's nigh on a death struggle. Now, Jenny, I don't want you to think I'm calling you a rebel, for I'm not. You are a very dear girl. But your spirit runs deep and high. Most of us have gentle streams of a spirit, content with the low, easy path. My girl, I sense you may have to fight your spirit, maybe much harder than most, in order to hear what God is trying to say to you.*

Down at the end of the letter was a postscript. It said, *What I meant to say all along was, I think you should read your Bible.*

Jenny folded the letter and pushed it back into the envelope, still trying to understand why Lucy Harris cared enough to fuss over her.

Pulling the newspaper clippings out, Jenny saw immediately that they dealt with Joseph Smith. An amused smile touched her lips as she straightened the paper on her knees. Why would these clippings finally force Lucy to write her letter? Maybe the unsaid things in Lucy's letter were that she needed to be in church learning about God. No matter what church, any was better than none.

Lucy had underlined parts of the article and Jenny's amusement grew as she read. The first article, dated February 14, 1831, pointed out that prior to the discovery of the gold plates, a spirit in the form of a little old man had appeared to Joseph. He had promised great treasure and a book about ancient inhabitants. The article concluded by saying that at the time the event was said to have happened, no divine activity was claimed, although citizens of the area well recollected the incident. Jenny was genuinely puzzled as she thought back over the events of that time. There was that bunch of men calling themselves the Gold Bible Company. There was also the talk of spirits and that little old man. Was the article meaning the two views didn't add up to the divine? She frowned and shook her head, remembering those things Adela had said about worship.

The next article, dated February 28, 1831, started out by saying that Joe had never claimed communion with angels until a long time after the advent of the book. The article also mentioned his peep stone and Joseph's accounts of seeing wonders in it, as well as his interviews with the spirit who had custody of the hidden treasures. For a moment Jenny thought about the time Joe had offered to let her look in his stone. Now she was filled with regret for her timidity.

Reading on, she murmured, "So it was Cicero's *Orations* I heard Walters reading! Whatever he was reading, it was beautiful." She finished the article, amused by the report of the digging she had witnessed from the bushes on the night she had followed Tom and Martin Harris into the forest. "Little did I know that there was someone else hiding out in the bushes!" she chuckled. Slipping the articles back into the envelope, Jenny leaned against her pillows and stared out the window.

She let the words of the letters and the articles tumble through her thoughts in a haphazard manner. Slowly an uneasiness began to grow, and a few of the words kept circling back: *Satan, baptism, rebel.*

She turned away from the window and looked at the green book wedged in the shelf between her sewing basket and her hat. Deliberately she forced out of her mind all thoughts generated by the letters and articles and began thinking back to those long-ago days. Foremost was her childhood resolution regarding Joe which had fastened itself on her mind; then she recalled Tom's words. "So Emma is well and Joseph is happy," she murmured.

Like wings whisking her away, her thoughts transported her in time and place. The dark, mysterious forest of Manchester surrounded her, and out of the blackness danced a figure in red. "Ah—Adela," Jenny murmured with a smile. "I wish you were as easy to come by as thoughts. I'd like to talk to you. What would you have to say about my feelings? I know; I've listened to you often enough to know you'd ask what I really wanted from life, and then you'd tell me that I could have anything as long as I wanted it bad enough to—" Jenny stopped, shuddering at the memory of the last time she had seen Adela.

She recoiled from the memory of the horrible scene in the church. But in spite of herself she was murmuring, "Adela, I ruined forever my chances of truly being your friend, didn't I? I wish I could have another chance."

Jenny fell to musing about it all, weighing the significance of the step Adela had urged her to take. Once again she shivered; then, as if returning from a far country, quickly she sat up and smoothed her hair. Adela's suggestion was impossible, but there must be another way. Maybe Joseph and his new church held the answers.

Although the hot sunlight streamed in her bedroom window, Jenny smoothed her tumbled hair and murmured:

"Luna, every woman's friend
To me thy goodness condescend.
Let this night in visions see
Emblems of my destiny."

Jenny felt better after her rest and went downstairs to her tasks with a lighter heart.

As summer gained momentum, life pressed hard against her. Mrs. Barton wasn't a difficult person to please, but it was a busy household.

One day Mrs. Barton looked at Jenny's tired face and said, "I must find another girl. You're doing the work of two right now, and there's school soon."

So at harvest time Clara joined the household. Clara was short and plump, with a frizzle of light hair. Her blue eyes, Jenny immediately noticed, were prone to disappear completely when she laughed, and that was often. *Too often*, Jenny thought as she moved behind Clara, catching broken pieces, and rescuing abandoned tasks.

Soon Jenny was as frayed as Clara's hair. If it hadn't been for the book, Jenny realized later, her nerves would have been as fragmented as Mrs. Barton's berry bowl when Clara tried to wash it.

During the hot, heavy days of August, Mark came calling. Mrs. Barton called it "courting," and she said it with a gentle smile. But whatever it was, Jenny was glad to see him.

They sat on the side porch, shaded by vines that wandered up the lattice to the second story, and Mark filled her full of his tales of the law office. Later as she slowly climbed the stairs to her room, she mulled over the meaning of his visit, and frowned over the memory of the look in his eyes and the way he had pressed her hand.

She lingered on the stairs trying to understand her emotions. Were the mingled memories of the past responsible for the discontent she felt around him? Fleetingly, she wondered what he would think about the green book and the growing need she was feeling in her life.

The moment before she touched her door, she saw the slit of light. "Clara!" she exclaimed, then saw the book she held. "Oh!"

Closing the book, Clara laughed merrily. "Your face! Jenny, don't look so frightened. I won't tell our good Presbyterian lady, and I won't be corrupted. You see, I know all about it." Her voice dropped to a whisper. "Perhaps I'm sent to help you understand even better."

CHAPTER 15

When Tom returned to Kirtland after visiting Jenny, he had the sense of being dropped back to earth with a jolt. Going about his duties at the livery stable, he mulled over the feeling. Had he painted a rosy picture for Jenny that didn't exist? Did the complaints and gossip he had been hearing since his return reveal the true facts?

Just this morning, Knight had stepped into the stable. His usual good humor had been masked behind a perplexed frown. "What's your trouble?" Tom asked his employer as he stabled Knight's horse and tossed in hay.

"Just chewin' over events," he muttered, picking up the account books and heading for the office.

"Like what? You forget I've been gone."

He turned in the doorway. "I did forget you've not been hearing the rumbling. Right now seems everyone's out to prove he's special with the Lord. Joseph started it with his promise of blessings. My idea is that Rigdon's glory halo rankles Joe. He ought not feel that way. 'Tis obvious Joseph's the Lord's favorite."

He stopped to glance at Tom. "Then a new thing happened to shake people's faith. The Mortinsens over Thompson way had a sick baby. They were all set to take him to the doctor, and one of the brethren told them not to. Said the Lord had promised the child would be healed."

"So, isn't that the way we are supposed to be livin'?"

He looked at Tom. "So they say. The Mortinsens are having a hard time believing that. Their baby died. Now a faction's saying only false prophets have their prophecies fail. No matter. I experienced the Lord's healing at Joseph's hand." He turned and left the room.

The next day was the first day of the June church conference. Slicked up and wearing a new shirt, Tom walked toward the meetinghouse with Lyman Wight. The older man was bringing him up-to-date, detailing all that had happened while Tom had been in New York. "You should've heard Joe," Wight said, shaking his head. "There's sure been a high tide of feeling that the Lord's about to be blessin' us in an unusual way."

"What did he say?" Tom questioned as he followed Lyman to his seat in the assembly hall.

For a moment Lyman looked startled. "Oh, he said that not three days would pass before someone would see the Savior face to face." He continued, "This is like it was last year when we first came, the excitement."

While Tom looked around, greeting friends who had come to hear the Prophet, Joseph Smith got to his feet. From the podium his eyes swept the room as he spoke. "I've much to reveal to you of the Lord's wisdom and plans for these final days before the Second Coming. Now I want to give you the story of just what happened to the ten lost tribes of Israel. I will also be revealing to you God's plan for the priesthood in these latter days.

"In the past only Jesus Christ and Melchizedek held this priesthood, but now it is ours. We have been given the power to become high priests before Him. Now is the time to confer this order of priesthood on the righteous."

With beckoning hands, Joseph Smith called out names and began to ordain his men to the priesthood. Joseph's gaze swept toward Tom, hesitated, and moved on. Tom's pounding heart attested to the tension in the room, but he reminded himself, "Fella, there's no call to get excited. You had your chance when Joe pressed you to join up with him, and you put it off. Now stand back and watch the others get the blessin'." His disappointment was tempered as he began to realize the responsibility these men were taking upon themselves. "The true church," he whispered. " 'Tis a big task to take out the message to the world."

Beside him, Lyman Wight suddenly surged to his feet. With outstretched arms held rigid, he shouted, "You want to see a sign? Look at me. I see the heavens open and the Son of Man!"

In the confusion there came another cry, "Brother Joseph, Ben here's been struck deaf and dumb. Come heal him." While the Prophet crossed the room, Tom was wondering if the others remembered how Joseph's prayers for healing had failed in the past. The man sitting beside Tom whispered, "Just yesterday Joe said that now was the time for great miracles to break out upon the church."

As Joseph reached out to touch the man, Tom found he was holding his breath. Joseph turned to the congregation and said, "Remember, now's the time for the Lord to break out upon us. Pray, my friends, pray!" His voice was rising in intensity, and a surge of excitement filled the room. As people jumped to their feet, Tom could no longer see. He heard a sigh of relief, and then, "He's healed!" Tom saw the beaming face of the man.

With new confidence, Joseph whirled about and crossed the room. He stopped before a man with a crippled hand. Grasping the bent and tortured limb, he cried, "Brother, in the name of Jesus Christ I command you, straighten this hand." Grasping the crumpled hand he pulled it straight. But once released it returned to its tortured position.

The crowd waited and the silence stretched uneasily. Suddenly the door opened and a man and woman entered. Tom saw the bundle they carried, and with a sinking heart he recognized the Mortinsens.

"Prophet Smith," the man said, speaking softly and rapidly. "Our baby is dead, and I bring him here to you. Restore him to life." The man's voice broke. Together, he and his wife, clasping the gray form of their infant, dropped to their knees before Joseph.

Quietness held the room like a vise. Tom studied the patch of sunlight spreading across the floor. Feeling his unbelief poison the very air, he dared not lift his eyes to the group, although he could hear Joseph's prayer.

At last Joseph stepped back. With a face nearly as gray as the dead infant's, he whispered, "I cannot."

In the waiting moment, Tom was aware of the buzz of flies, the uneasy creak of chairs. When Mortinsen arose, still clutching the limp form, he turned to a bowed and sobbing man seated nearby. "Brother," he whispered, "you advised me that the Lord would heal, and that there was no need to go to the doctor." His voice was heavy. "In the name of God, I hold you responsible for destroying the life of my son."

A troubled Tom made his way back to his room over the livery stable. As he did his evening chores around the stable, Newel Knight entered.

"Tom," he asked soberly, "are you hearing rumbles about what happened today?"

"Yeah, there's a whole tide of bad feelin's adrift, what with Joe pullin' these healings and nothin' comin' of it."

"I urged caution, but a little success goes a long way."

"It's worse than just the failure," Tom said as he pitched hay to the horses. "It's what it's doin' to these here folks."

Knight sighed and nodded. He cinched the saddle tight and led his horse out the gate. "Well, tomorrow's another day; maybe Joseph will receive the words to undo the harm."

The second day of the conference the Sabbath services had only begun when Rigdon slowly got to his feet, lifted his hands, and pronounced the benediction. Tom sat in stunned disbelief.

On the way out Tom heard a man beside him mutter, "The spirit was tellin' me we needed a sermon; how come the spirit told him different?" Tom had reached the door, but on impulse he turned. Joseph and Sidney Rigdon were still facing each other at the front of the room.

A stranger, too, hesitated for one last look, and the eyes he turned toward Tom were scornful. Dryly he said, "I'm waitin' to hear how he explains this." Tom watched him walk away before he made his way toward Joseph.

"You realize what this can do to the church, don't you?" A sober Joseph nodded in reply to Rigdon and turned as Tom stopped beside him.

"You may as well hear it now," he said heavily to Tom. "Williams just brought word from the town of Thompson that Copley and Thayer have yanked their gift of land to the church."

"That isn't all," Rigdon said as he took quick, nervous steps across the room and back. "They're using the law to dump themselves of what they're calling New York trespassers. That means we've a bunch of people without a home."

Jenny and Clara were sitting in the middle of Jenny's bed, the green book open between them. Jenny ran her fingers under the words and lifted her face. "Clara, what can you tell me about charms?"

"How come you have the book and have been learnin' under Adela and yet you know so little?"

"If she told me about them, I've forgotten. Maybe I wasn't needing them."

"Charms. A love potion? I'm thinkin' you'll not need it for that young man."

"Mark? Oh, no—and not a *love* potion. Oh, dear," she murmured, suddenly visualizing how Mark's face would look if he were listening to the conversation.

Her horror must have shown on her face, because Clara laughed and said, "Don't give it a worry. I don't go spreading tales."

But the memory of Mark's face and his clear, steady eyes wouldn't leave Jenny. Quickly she led Clara away from the subject. "Tell me, Clara, how did you come to get into—this."

"You can't say it, can you? You needn't think it's all so awful. I'm a white witch."

"What's that?"

"That means that I don't do evil things to people. Except for callin' up storms, I try to do only good things for others."

"Some don't count the difference; to them a witch is a witch."

"That's 'cause they don't understand the craft. 'Tis the oldest, the most ancient religion. 'Tis nature's religion. All we do is worship the way we were intended to worship from the very beginning of time. I know you've been fed a different story. See, it's all twisted. The lie's been twisted and given as truth and the real truth is being lied about. You know how to tell the real truth, don't you?"

"Well, I'm beginning to wonder," Jenny faltered, remembering Lucy Harris's words about truth and power.

"It's the power. If you get power, then you know it's the truth."

"Do you?" Jenny whispered.

Clara nodded and patted the book. "I've never seen the book before, but I've been taught by my mother and grandma. What the book says is just what they say."

"Have you—" Jenny's voice dropped to a whisper, but she felt compelled to say it. "Do you go to sabbats?"

"Of course. It seems you've had a bad time. Granted, it takes some gettin' use to. But there's lots in life that takes bein' brave." Jenny saw the sly look creep across her face.

Hastily Jenny asked, "What power do you have?"

"I told you about the storms. That's the one that's most easy to see. Want me to demonstrate?" Jenny nodded and Clara continued, "I'm doing charms too, to keep off the bad spirits and to bring good luck, things like that."

"Tell me a charm to use."

"Well, you have one yourself—didn't you recognize it as such? You're prayin' to the moon goddess when you recite that Luna verse asking for emblems of destiny."

"It is!" Jenny exclaimed in surprise. "Then why don't I find out about my destiny?"

"You're just sayin' it; you're not bringing down the power. See, if you want to get the knowledge, you put a prayerbook under your pillow and place on it a key, a ring, flowers, a sprig of willow . . ." and Clara's voice continued the list of common enough items.

In silence Jenny pondered Clara's instructions, and deep within she found her spirit sinking. How could she possibly believe in Clara's charm? Finally she sighed and asked, "What did you have to promise to get the power?"

Clara looked at her quizzically. "Nothing. Just use the charms and follow the rituals."

"You didn't have to—to make a pact with the devil?"

Clara laughed merrily, "Oh, Jenny, your face! Your eyes are as big as saucers. It's hard to take you serious-like when you're so scared. Jenny, don't fuss so; relax and enjoy yourself. That's the whole meanin' behind life."

Her voice dropped to a gentle note as she studied Jenny's face. "If something big comes up and nothing else works, you may have to make a pact; it all depends how important it is to you. Some things mean more'n life."

After Clara left her room, Jenny picked up the book and slowly thumbed through it until she reached the section that talked about making a pact with Lucifer, god of light, god of good.

She closed her eyes, willing the memory of Joe's face to come before her. She studied the remembered features, that beak of a nose, those laughing eyes. How her hands ached to move through that shining bright hair! "Too bad just thinking isn't enough to put you here," she murmured.

As Jenny thought about what Clara said, she hesitated, shivering. What about that unknown cost? Was Joseph really worth it? The thought grew in her mind. But also there grew the feeling she must be certain before she took that step.

Jenny had just finished the noon dishes. Summer heat simmered in the air, sucking out moisture and giving dust in exchange. She trailed her finger across the dusty table just as Clara walked in.

The girl was grinning and beckoning, excitement sparkling in her eyes. Today was the day Clara had chosen. Clara's face wore a funny half-smile, like the Bartons' cat, just in from the pasture full of mice. "It's a good time to go. Let's be off." Her eyes narrowed to slits of ecstasy. "Perfect. Not a cloud in the sky, and hasn't been for days. And the hay's in, so we'll do no harm."

As soon as they stepped into the woods, Jenny was aware of the change coming over her companion. No longer playfully happy and carefree, she began to walk with slow, deliberate steps. The deeper they moved into the woods, the more oppressive her spirit became. Glancing at her face, Jenny was surprised to see the heavy frown.

For a moment she thought to tease Clara about looking like

the clouds of storm she hoped to conjure, but then she saw Clara's eyes. It would be impossible to get her attention.

When they reached the deepest gloom of the forest, Clara waved Jenny aside while she moved about her task. Now Jenny was aware of the low, guttural murmuring that Clara was making as she moved methodically, marking a circle, inscribing strange figures in the soil, and stacking sticks with crumbled dry herb over all.

When she finished, she sat down in the circle. Jenny settled down on a fallen log and fought the sleepiness that seemed to be washing over her in waves. She lost track of time and had nearly forgotten where she was. Abruptly Clara jumped to her feet. "We must hurry!" she gasped, and she turned and ran back down the trail.

When they reached the edge of the forest, Jenny understood why. The sky was a mass of dark, boiling clouds. As they ran across the pasture, the thunder grew louder and the lightning flashed. They reached the kitchen door just after the rain began.

Mrs. Barton was standing by the stove, and she turned to them with a worried frown. "Oh my, you're wet. But then, who would have guessed we'd have a storm like this!"

On the third day of the church conference, Tom sat on his bench and looked at Joseph Smith and Sidney Rigdon. They were on the platform, quietly facing the congregation. Rigdon's face was pale, and Joseph seemed subdued. Tom moved uneasily on his bench and wished that he'd had the gumption to stay home this meeting. Nat Johnson was sitting beside him. His smooth, expressionless face did nothing to calm Tom's churning insides.

When Joseph stood to talk, Tom breathed a sigh of relief. At least Joe was his usual jovial self. "My friends and fellow believers—" He paused, and his gaze swept about the room until every rustle stilled and all were hanging on his words. "I deeply regret all that happened on the first day of conference, and I've been rebuked by the Lord for failing to understand and accept. I have a revelation from the Lord which I will read to you, and then you will comprehend what the Lord is trying to do for us."

He lifted the paper and cleared his throat. "I the Lord will make known to you . . . the next conference, which shall be held in Missouri, on the land which I will consecrate unto my people." The revelation was long, and only a few words hit Tom with meaning. He heard that the land of Missouri was the inheritance, but it was also the land of their enemies.

There was a low growl beside Tom, and Johnson said, "Zion, Missouri. The Lord is givin' us a hard assignment. That means we'll be a-fightin' for it."

When Joe folded the papers and tucked them away, he said, "The Lord has very plainly told me there will be no miracles until we are settled in Zion. There we will erect a glorious temple. Now you men who have been commanded by the Lord, be part of this first group. Spy out the land and prepare a home for those who will be moving from Thompson to Missouri. I say, obey the Lord, and prepare to go."

CHAPTER 16

In June 1831, Joseph Smith and Sidney Rigdon, along with thirty others chosen by the Lord, left for Missouri. The men were instructed to go two by two, making their way to Missouri, preaching the gospel as they went. Joseph and Rigdon were to travel as far as St. Louis by steamship.

Though Tom was disappointed in not being included, he busied himself around the livery stable, while the men were gone. One day, soon after Joe's return, Tom was shoeing Knight's saddle horse when Joe came into the shop. "Looks like Knight's bound to make a smithy out of you."

Tom grunted and drove the last nail into the horse's hoof. "I'm hired jack-of-all-trades," he said shortly, "and I'm glad to be learnin' this. If I had stayed in Manchester, I *might* have worked up to this in another year." He released the horse and stood up. "I hear you've moved your family to Hiram."

"That's right. The Lord's been impressing me with the need to get at the translation of the New Testament." Tom wrapped the reins around his hand and Joseph fell in step with him. "You're heavy-hearted; what's troubling you? Is it the reports of the trip that have you down?"

Astonished and curious, Tom turned to look at Joseph. "I've not heard a thing. I'm heavy because I was thinkin' about losin' my job when Knight and the rest move to Zion."

"Well, you needn't be worrying yet," Joe said abruptly. "The Lord's instructed Knight and Whitney both to keep their businesses here until the last of the church has moved to Zion. From the looks of things, it'll be a while."

159

"Well, I'm glad," Tom answered. "But from the slant of the revelations, I figured we'd all be a-pullin' up stakes right away."

With a rueful sigh, Joe said, "Some of the Lord's anointed in Missouri would like to see that happen, but the Lord's revealed most of the elders are to return here and support their families while they get busy with spreading the gospel in the eastern part of the country. Anyone who wants to settle in Zion right now will do it only after his prayers assault heaven for the privilege."

"Why's that?" Tom asked.

" 'Tis a fair land," Joseph said slowly, "but it's costly. The price of moving to Missouri will only be met when every man here gives liberally to the Lord. But that isn't all. The Lord doesn't want His people complacent and mingling with the Gentiles. His revelation says God's people'll push the Gentiles off the ends of the earth."

They stopped at the hitching post in front of Whitney's general store. Tom looped the reins of the horse around it and turned to wave at Knight who was standing in the doorway. "Your filly's the proud owner of new shoes," he called.

"Well, maybe Missouri was a disappointment to some," Joe continued, "but at least things are moving in the right direction here."

"You sound satisfied," Tom said. "What's happened?"

"The United Order has received a loan of $10,000 from Charles Holmes. I've appointed Whitney bishop, and his store'll be the storehouse and commissary."

Tom pondered the information in silence, and then added, "So the translation business is back in full swing."

"Tom, the Lord's blessing us in these last days!" Joe exclaimed. "He's given me a special blessing. Translating in Genesis, I've discovered a prophecy concerning my coming."

"No foolin'!" Tom turned to look at his friend in awe. "Are you sure?"

"Well, what would you think if you read that the Lord will raise up a seer in the last days and give him the power to bring forth the word of the Lord? And his name will be Joseph just as his father's name is Joseph."

"Huh!" Tom grunted. "You sure can't argue that."

" 'Twas a great comfort to find He promised safety," Joseph added seriously. "I needed the assurance that the Lord was on my side."

"What did He say?"

"Those who seek to destroy the seer, Joseph, will be confounded."

At the livery stable the two of them perched on the fence rail while Joe continued. "Another thing, the Lord's made known the degrees of glory. There's three kingdoms in the eternities. All men will be assigned to one of them. The highest is celestial for the members of the true church, the terrestrial is the dwelling place of those who've never heard the gospel, and the third degree is called telestial, for those who've refused the law of the Lord. Liars, sorcerers, adulterers will be going there."

"You mean there's a heaven for everybody?" Tom said slowly. "Well, that takes a big load off my chest; I guess I just won't worry no more."

Joseph threw back his head and laughed. "Then you're not wanting to be part of Zion. You're throwing away the privilege of being with the people building the city of God. Tom, my lad, you're a gambler at heart. But I know you won't pass up that glory. When are you going to join up? I saw your face during conference. You were wanting to go to Zion so bad it hurt."

"You're right," Tom admitted, recalling that day. He raised his head and slapped Joe's leg. "Oh, all right. What do I need to do?"

Jenny pushed open the Bartons' kitchen door and a wintry blast followed her. She tumbled her books inside and turned out to the entry to shake her snow-laden shawl. Popping back into the kitchen, she shook her hair, exclaiming, "What a storm! It makes a body glad to be home and warm and dry." She tossed her hair back from her face, then stopped. Mark and Mrs. Barton were sitting at the kitchen table.

"Mark!" she exclaimed, as astonished at her glad rush of surprise as she was by his unexpected presence. "It's been so long!" She hurried forward. "Oh, you're already having tea,"

162

her voice flattened with disappointment.

Mrs. Barton laughed. "We couldn't wait; it *is* cold out. You might offer him some of the cookies you baked yesterday."

Mark was pulling a chair forward and grinning down at Jenny. "I've never before seen you with such rosy cheeks. That's nice. Shall I bring tea for you? From the looks of you, you intend to let snowflakes melt into your cup."

Mrs. Barton handed her a towel. "You'd better let me get the cookies." She disappeared into the pantry and Jenny dared look at Mark. Wordlessly he beamed at her until the cookies were placed between them.

Later Jenny wondered what Mrs. Barton had been saying before she came. But for now she watched Mark eating her spicy raisin cookies as if he were starved.

"I came intending to entice you into ice skating, but I *may* be snowed in for a week." He grinned happily.

"Ice skating?" Jenny whispered in panic. "I've never even touched a pair of ice skates."

"Well, you shall now, and I promise I won't let you fall."

Mark *was* snowed in, as was everyone else in town. Clara had gone visiting early in the day, and it was three days before she returned. Mark volunteered to fill in for her.

During the three days, as Mark carried in wood and dried dishes, Jenny's surprise grew. She was discovering a Mark totally different from her picture of the nice young schoolmaster with his spotless white shirt and shiny boots.

As she watched him roll up his sleeves and scrub pans, she listened to him talk. First law, then books; next he described a hunting trip into the mountains with his father.

Blue-misted mountains, crimson trees, and the mingled scent of woodsmoke and frying bacon lingered in his memories. What he described in detail wasn't the deer he shot, but the leggy fawn, faltering timid and curious on the edge of the clearing.

They discovered there were books they had both read, and they discussed them eagerly. They shared the poetry he could quote, and the plays he wanted her to see.

When the sky cleared, a dozen eager boys pushed snow from the lake and Mark and Jenny tried out the ice skates.

At first Jenny was shy with this new Mark, but she grad-
ually thawed beneath his genuine warmth. Before the week
was over, she knew that she was privy to a secret side of him.
She sensed it first when he quoted poetry to her; even more
clearly she recognized the difference when Clara walked into
the kitchen, and the contained shell of the old Mark settled
around him like a protective armor.

As Jenny said good-bye, Mark lifted her warm hand to his
cheek and then he was gone.

Jenny watched through the kitchen window as his horse
loped down the lane. Secret whispers moved through her heart,
reminding her that rich young men married proper girls from
proper families. The real Mark, those whispers nagged at her,
was the one she watched as he joked around and teased Clara.
The casual shell was real, the tenderness inside was a dream.

In Kirtland the new year slipped in on snowy feet, nearly
unheralded. At Hiram, Joseph Smith and Sidney Ridgon continued to work at the task of writing. But unsettling things
were going on. Often the rumbles started at the livery stable
in Kirtland, where winter-bound men gathered to talk. But
there were winter discontents in Hiram, too.

Ezra Booth, formerly a Methodist minister, then Mormon
convert, had turned apostate after the first trip to Zion. Now
he was exciting curiosity. Copies of letters written by him and
printed in *The Ohio Star* were read and passed around the stable. The first comment was, "Joe shouldn't have taken him in
to begin with. A preacher in the Methodist church is bound to
be a mighty poor follower. Has too many ideas of his own."
Another said, "Some of his complaints were right, like Partridge's quarrel with Smith."

A few nodded, and a voice spoke from the back of the group.
"Partridge didn't make no bones. Told Joseph he didn't like the
land and Joseph told him heaven chose it. So then Partridge
told him he wished he wouldn't say he knew things by the spirit
when he didn't, such as that Oliver had raised up a big church
when it was plain to see he hadn't. Joe said if he said it, then
it would be."

"What about Rigdon telling him the vision of Zion was a bad thing?"

There was silence when Tom replied, "Seems it falls in a category of faultin' the Lord." He went back to his workbench.

While Tom mended harnesses in front of the sheet iron stove at the rear of the stables, he listened to the talk going on around him. *Malcontents*, he decided. But some of the men had been on that journey to Missouri. They supported Ezra's statements in the newspaper.

One thing was certain, a storm of unrest was brewing among the men of the church. Later, when news from Missouri indicated that Zion was suffering the same kind of unrest, Tom decided it was time to visit his friend in Hiram.

It was late that March evening before Tom could leave the livery stable to go to Hiram. Even in the small town of Kirtland, Saturday night revelry added to the chores that must be done before the Sabbath.

Tom rode his horse toward Joseph's home, grateful for March's softening wind. He was nearly to the outskirts of Hiram when he met a group of riders coming toward him.

Thinking that he recognized one of them, he called, "Hello, is that you, Williams?" No answer came, but the riders veered away. Slowly he rode on, pondering the strange event.

As he reached the Johnson farm where Joseph Smith was living, Tom noticed light spilling out the open door; but until he stood in Joseph's parlor staring at the spectacle, he didn't understand. Slowly he walked across the room.

Emma was already digging at the mess of tar and feathers which covered her husband. "What happened?"

Joseph could only mutter, while Emma answered shortly, "Busted in here, the whole lot of them, and dragged him out into the night. This is the way he came back."

Throughout the night, Tom and Emma dug at the mess that covered Joseph's body. It was nearly morning when Joseph picked up a quilt and handed it to Tom. "Here, my friend and bodyguard, stretch out in front of the fire. You'll need a little sleep to stay awake during my sermon this morning."

"Joseph!" Emma exclaimed in horror. "Surely you don't intend to stand before the church and preach!"

But he did, and Tom was there to watch and listen and gain new admiration for his friend. The sermon, delivered in quiet dignity, made no reference to the incident of the previous evening. And if the culprits were in the crowd, they were wearing the robes of righteousness this Sabbath.

The Monday morning crowd at the livery stable seemed to know the details of Saturday night.

"They say he had it coming . . . Word's going round that Eli Johnson got the mob together . . . Said it was 'cause Joseph has been too intimate with his sister, Nancy Marinda . . . Eli wanted to castrate Joe, but the doc chickened out."

Five days after the tarring and feathering, one of the twins adopted by Joe and Emma died. Tom was there afterward to help move Emma back to Kirtland to live while Joseph and Rigdon journeyed to Missouri.

Mrs. Barton came into the kitchen as Jenny was finishing the dishes. She picked up the dish towel and a handful of spoons. Jenny shook off her dreamy mood and reached for another pot. When Mrs. Barton reached for the forks, she said, "Jenny, you've had your eighteenth birthday. Have you given any thought to your future? Young ladies your age have married. And as for school, you're educated enough to teach. I'm afraid there's little more they can offer you."

"Oh," Jenny sighed, abruptly realizing she hadn't given a thought to life as Mrs. Barton was seeing it. She shivered, thinking how horrified that good woman would be if she were to tell her what she had in mind for the future.

"Jenny, don't misunderstand," Mrs. Barton continued. "I'm not at all anxious to have you leave us; you'll have a position here as long as you wish."

"Thank you, ma'am," Jenny replied meekly, still wondering what she could say.

"Also," Mrs. Barton continued, wiping more slowly now, "I'm concerned about Clara. Not that I think you're easily led astray, but there's strange going's on in her life." She hung the towel on its rack. "If you're troubled and need to talk about it, please—"

Jenny widened her eyes. "Clara *is* strange, Mrs. Barton, but she doesn't trouble me."

"That's good. Now, Mark is coming tonight, isn't he?"

"Yes." Jenny looked at Mrs. Barton, wondering if she could sense the churning inside her.

"He's a fine young man. I've met his mother and think well of her."

Without planning, the words burst from Jenny, "Fine young men don't marry kitchen maids!"

"I have a feeling that young man is looking beyond the kitchen," Mrs. Barton responded gently. She watched Jenny carefully empty the dishwater into the pail beside the door, and just as carefully Jenny avoided Mrs. Barton's eyes. She didn't want to talk about Mark; she didn't even want to think about the confusion of her emotions every time he came to visit.

Jenny looked at the floor, fearful her eyes would reveal her thoughts, thoughts about what she and Clara had been studying together. They just didn't fit into the picture with Mark.

By the time Mark arrived, the evening was cooling and the primroses were slowly unfolding their tight buds. Jenny was sitting on the side porch, thinking of nothing except the evening calm spreading itself across the land.

Then Mark was there, offering her a yellow primrose. "Jenny," he whispered with a teasing grin, "tell me your secret. Does it take the mysterious night to bring you into full bloom? Most times I find you a tight little bud like an evening primrose at high noon."

"I think it takes the moonlight to bring me to life," she whispered back. "I need to follow the creek until it disappears into the moon. I need to walk the pasture fence until it falls off the earth."

"Walk the pasture fence!" he exclaimed, dropping down beside her. "That is a very different thing to do."

"See there—" She pointed to the line of fence that rose and fell with the contours of the earth. She knew that at the point of disappearance, it followed the slip of the hill.

"It does fall off the earth," he whispered. "But maybe it

tunnels under the haystack; then where would you be?"

"Why, I'd be obligated to tunnel, too."

"Then let's go!" He took her hand and pulled her to her feet, toward the pasture. When they reached the fence, he lifted her to the top rung. Gathering her skirt in a tight wad that threatened her knees with exposure, Jenny ran lightly along the rail, slowing only to step gingerly across the posts before she ran on again.

At the end of it, when the fence plunged down the hill, Jenny jumped lightly to the ground. With a thud, Mark landed beside her. "You did it, too!" she exclaimed in delight. "Mark, the lawyer! You must be good to me, or I will tell all your clients that you are addlepated. That I know, because you walk fence rails in the moonlight!"

"Oh, my dear Jenny!" In mock horror he threw himself to his knees beside her. "I implore you, marry me, marry me so that I can keep you silenced forever. With trinkets and baubles and all of my gold, I pledge my heart as long as I may have your vow of silence." And they both laughed in joyful merriment.

Much later Jenny ran lightly up the backstairs to her room, still chuckling her enjoyment over Mark's foolishness. Clara was sitting on Jenny's bed, in the center of the patch of bright moonlight. "I needed to do my thinking, and there wasn't moonlight in my room."

Silently Jenny took her place beside Clara. Crossing her legs, she folded her arms and waited. She heard the faint sound of a horse trotting down the lane—Mark's. In the renewed silence the crickets took up their chirping and from the creek the frogs answered. The heavy night air wrapped scent and sound about the two.

Finally, Jenny asked, "What are you thinking?"

"You were very joyful and happy, laughing your way up the stairs."

Jenny thought back and then whispered, "I was. I hadn't thought of it that way. It was the night, the moon, and—"

"Mark?" Clara whispered. "Jenny, where does he fit into all this?" Her gesture swept only the room, but Jenny knew what she was thinking.

"He doesn't." Slowly pulling the pins from her hair, Jenny began to put into words all that she had avoided thinking about before. "Mark wouldn't approve; I'm sure of that. He is my good friend, but he wouldn't be if he were to know. He mustn't find out."

Out of a long, dreamy silence, Clara finally spoke. "Jenny it's gettin' near the solstice. If you are serious about learning more, you'll need to go to the sabbat."

For a moment Jenny closed her eyes against the bright moonlight; almost against her will she whispered, "Power! If only I could have it all."

Clara was whispering too, "Mark or the craft, Jenny? You must choose. I'm feelin' there's much you are unwilling to tell me. So be it; decide alone then what's important. I'm feelin' he won't allow Mark in your life."

Although the night air was heavy and warm, Jenny shivered as if a winter wind had chilled her. Clara had just said "he," but the unnamed one struck terror in Jenny. How much longer could she avoid facing that *he*?

CHAPTER 17

In May of 1832 Kirtland seethed with excitement. Not for more than a moment could the young church forget these were the days of gathering. Very soon Jesus Christ would be returning to claim His own, and the Mormon people had been chosen to prepare Zion for His dwelling place.

Tom was well aware of the excitement as he walked into the assembly hall on that first Sabbath day following Joseph's return from Missouri. Beside him was his friend Aaron Seamond.

Aaron had been one of Sidney Rigdon's followers when Kirtland's people had belonged to the Campbellite group. At times Tom had been prone to charge Aaron with cynicism, but today his fervor was as high as Tom's as they listened eagerly. Joseph was giving the details of his trip.

"Brothers and sisters, I know the Lord has chosen you to bear the gospel in this generation. The Lord has blessed us mightily; He has let us know by revelation all He commands us to do. Brethren, we must be about the Lord's business.

"On every hand we see these are the last days. Very soon the Lord will be walking the earth, His footstool. This whole continent is sacred ground!

"Now, I will tell you what transpired on my journey. By the Lord's direction we have combined the United Order under one governing body. Presently we are negotiating for a $15,000 loan. This has been a glorious year in Jackson County, Missouri! The church has grown; we have a membership of three hundred. Many more will be coming.

"Now, let me tell you about the remnant of Jacob. Bless the

Lord! The federal government is cooperating with the Lord. Thousands of these people are being moved through Independence. Shawnees, Kickapoos, and Pattawattamies—all are being moved from lands in Ohio, Kentucky, and Illinois.

"Old Andrew Jackson doesn't know it, but he's a tool in the hands of the Almighty, helping Him prepare for the gathering of Israel!" Joseph leaned forward, his voice dropping nearly to a whisper. "I'm predicting the Second Coming is less than nine years away!"

The high tide of excitement which greeted Joseph Smith's prediction that Sabbath morning lingered with the people of Kirtland and colored their lives.

Tom didn't see much of Joe Smith that summer, but then, that was to be expected. Both arms of the church, as well as the heavy writing schedule, demanded most of his time. Tom was aware of the new mood of confidence in the people. In Kirtland the unrest of the winter was given a passing salute of apology by the church members as they began working doubly hard. With renewed enthusiasm they scurried about the country with the message of the church and the *Book of Mormon*.

It was nearly October when the Prophet came into the livery stable. "Let me guess!" Tom exclaimed. "You want shoes on that filly right this minute."

"Wrong. I'm taking the stage to New York City. I intend to negotiate loans in the name of the Kirtland United Order."

Tom thought he detected a slight swagger as Joe paced the room, saying, "The way we're growing, this church will stand with the best of them, and we might as well put ourselves on the map by growing as fast in our business dealings as the Lord indicates we should."

"We'll be anxious to hear what's goin' on."

Joseph's brilliant smile lighted his face. "You shall, my friend and bodyguard. When I get back, I'll take time to sit down with you and tell it all. I'm not forgetting your faithfulness to me, and the next trip I make to Missouri, you will be going too."

On November 6, 1832, Emma gave birth to a son, and to the relief of all, the child survived and was named Joseph after his father. The whole community rejoiced at the news, and Tom felt much like a proud uncle.

The child was two weeks old when Tom rode out to the farm for his first peek at little Joseph. He had his brief glimpse and heaped his awkward congratulations on Joe and Emma. Taking his arm, Joseph said, "I don't think we're wanted in here. I'm headed for the woods to split a couple of logs; want to give a hand?"

"You've grown pretty soft pushing that pen; guess I'd better," Tom joshed, following the Prophet out the door.

They worked most of the afternoon. When Tom paused to wipe the sweat from his face, he said, "My, the smell of that pine puts me in mind of splitting logs in Manchester. I like the feel of an axe in my hands."

"Hello there! Is Joseph with you?" The hail came faintly through the trees.

"Right here!" Joseph bellowed back, saying to Tom, "From the sound of the horses, it's a battalion. Did you bring your gun?" Tom looked at him in astonishment and Joe threw back his head and laughed.

The men burst through the trees and John Whitmer threw himself off his horse. "Have a fella here who wants to meet you. This here is Brigham Young."

Tom watched the stocky older man slowly dismount. There was an air about him that caught Tom's attention. Without a doubt, this was a man of action and authority. Joseph must have felt it, too. Tom watched the two men, now deep in conversation. Young was talking about reading the *Book of Mormon* as he and Joseph wandered toward the edge of the clearing.

Suddenly Joseph stopped and turned. "I clean forgot what I was doing. Tom, you're right about my being soft. Could you and John finish up the cutting and then come on back to the house for a bite of supper?"

That evening after they had eaten, the men continued to talk, and finally they prayed together. Tom wondered if the excitement he was feeling was evident to the others. He knelt beside his bench and listened. When it was Brigham's turn, Tom found himself straining his ears to understand the words. Suddenly it dawned on Tom that this new fellow was praying in tongues.

"Well, Brig," Tom muttered into his sleeve, "you just cooked your goose. Someone should a-warned you how Joe's dealt with this kind of thing in the past."

Tom felt the tension creeping over him. The others must have sensed it too; abruptly the prayer meeting was over. As the men got awkwardly to their feet, Joseph spoke. He was shaking Brigham Young's hand. "Fellas, I want you to remember this night. Our friend here has been speaking in the true Adamic language."

Later, as Tom prepared to leave, he bent over the cradle for another look at the baby and Joseph asked, "Tom, just when are you going to take up the yoke of matrimony?" Tom ruefully rubbed his jaw, and Joseph burst into laughter. "That expression! What's the problem? It wouldn't hurt to do something besides shoeing horses."

Indeed, Tom took up letter writing—to Jenny. Spurred by his guilty conscience, knowing he had neglected his sister, and driven by his memory of how hard she worked at the Bartons', he wrote. "Jen, I miss you sore. Why don't you take the stage and come visit me. I've already talked to old Mrs. Knight and she will be glad to put you up at her house." He paused to reflect on the implications, and a slow grin came across his face.

Although he did not say so in his letter, he realized having Jenny here would settle a problem he had been ignoring. Joe was always urging the missionary work on him. And he was convinced, too, that Jenny needed to do something about her salvation. Jenny's coming would take care of his brotherly responsibility and possibly also convert her.

"Wonderful!" he muttered; then he wrote, "I miss you, Jen. Since I can't come see you, well, it looks like you could see your duty clear to visit here." As a postscript, he added, "Emma Smith has finally gone and done it. She produced a little boy for them. His name is Joseph, after his father."

And Jenny received the letter. Sitting in the rocking chair in the Bartons' kitchen, she rocked lazily and read the letter with a gentle smile. Dear Tom! She chuckled over the scrawly words and wondered what could have spurred him to such an enormous endeavor. Shaking her head, she murmured, "Tom, knowing your love of the written word, I'd expect a journey to see me would have involved less pain and time."

Mrs. Barton came into the kitchen, saying, "That lazy Clara! It takes her twice as long to run an errand as it would the average person.—A letter?"

Jenny nodded. "From my brother. Oh, there's a postscript." She caught her breath and when her voice broke in mid-sentence, Mrs. Barton turned in surprise. "Joseph Smith and his wife have a little baby boy, named Joseph."

Mrs. Barton was frowning. "And that saddens you."

"Oh, it doesn't," Jenny gasped. "It's just unexpected." After a moment, she added, "Tom's wanting me to come visit."

Mrs. Barton, still studying her face, said slowly, "You could take the stage."

"I would like to see Tom," Jenny said wistfully, "and," she rushed on, "I've never been as far west as Ohio. Everyone's talking about going west; I'd like to at least see Ohio."

Jenny realized later that her reply to Mrs. Barton had been simply words—the kind of words she was prone to pick up and toss around, just because words were expected.

But those words had consequence, and almost before she knew it, she was on her way to Kirtland, Ohio.

Leaning out the window of the stagecoach as it swayed slowly through the streets of Kirtland, Jenny finally accepted it. This was Joseph's town. Seeing it was like tying two ends of a dream together, making reality.

Tom was there to lift her down from the stagecoach; his rough hug and whiskery kiss filled her eyes with tears. "Oh, Tom, I didn't realize I missed you so much!"

"Tom!" the booming voice came from just behind her. "I see you've taken my advice, but I meant for you to choose from among our own."

Tom squeezed Jenny again and whispered, "See, I told you that you're all grown up. Even Joe didn't recognize you."

"Oh." Slowly Jenny stepped out of Tom's arms, and just as slowly she turned. Blinking, she stared up at the man. Twice as tall and broad as she remembered, he was clad in dignified black, and for a moment she wished for the farmboy's shirt. She stepped backward to see his face. It was the same cheerful grin beneath the bright hair. The grin became puzzled and now Jenny could laugh. "You really don't remember me, do you? I'll give you a hint. The first time you saw me, you said I was the ugliest thing you'd ever seen."

"Ma'am, I'm humbly begging your pardon, but no lady as fair as you would merit such talk from me."

"Joe, you're puttin' on," Tom protested. "This is my sister, Jenny." And by his grin, she knew he did remember.

Jenny stayed three weeks in Kirtland, Ohio. As she rode the stage back to Cobleskill, her mind was a patchwork quilt of pictures and words, woven together with emotions as brittle as old thread.

Tom was heavier than she remembered, with bundles of knotted muscles from his work at the forge. She had watched him pounding the glowing iron against the anvil until she expected the two to merge. She walked to church on his arm, and quietly listened to his constant stream of talk.

He obviously felt compelled to convert her to the new church. And while her eyes were busy about the town, sorting and storing impressions, seeing faces that she would remember, she was amused by Tom's earnestness.

In three weeks' time, the shape of her thoughts and feelings were influenced not by the commitment of these people nor by the thrust of their creed, although they saw to it that she was bombarded with fearsome words about her fate; the real attraction of Kirtland was one dark-coated figure. All others became peripheral images, colored only to supply contrast to him.

She had witnessed a painful scene, too. From a distance she had seen Joe and the woman beside him bending over a bundle in her arms. At Jenny's whispered words, "Why, Emma is dark, too!" Tom looked at her in surprise.

"Too?" Tom questioned. Jenny bit her tongue.

Jenny had been astonished by another scene also. From the window at the Knights' home she had spotted a cloud of dust and heard cries. One of Newel's sisters joined Jenny in her dash from the house. They found the crowd and wormed their way toward the center.

Betsy backed off in disgust. "It's nothing but a bunch of grown men going at it again. One of these days the Prophet'll have someone catch him at these shenanigans, and he'll wish they didn't."

Beside her a man turned, saying, "Prophet! You mean that's the Prophet in there wrestlin' like a commoner? Lady, we've come from Pennsylvania hearin' about how this is God's people preparin' for the end times, with His word writ out on leaves of gold, and you're tellin' me this is the man who did it all?" He turned and grasped the arm of the dusty woman beside him. "Mattie, I can't follow a man who spends his time wrestlin' in a dust pile."

Jenny watched the couple leave and shrugged. A victory shout cut the air and the dust settled. Joseph Smith sat astraddle a panting young giant with a torn shirt.

She was smiling as she followed Betsy back to the house. Later she saw Joseph, properly free of dust and impropriety, standing behind the pulpit. His solemnity nearly dulled her resolve, but in the middle of his sermon a smile crossed his face, and he delivered an illustration wrapped in the homey scent of the farm.

On the way back to the Knights' home, Tom had anxiously asked, " 'Twas a good sermon, wasn't it?" She looked at him in amusement and nodded. She needn't tell him only one illustration lingered in her thoughts.

Once again in Cobleskill, Jenny discovered discontentment dogging her heels and coloring her days. When Clara confronted Jenny in her room under the eaves, Jenny was forced to admit all that she had been thrusting to the back of her mind. And yet she couldn't tell it all.

"There's a man there," Jenny admitted.

Clara's eyes were shrewd. "Being a good looker like you, you shouldn't have no problem." Jenny shrugged and Clara said, "Oh, one of those situations, huh? Well, get ye some dandelion root and some river water. I've the other charms. Want me to come while you make a circle and cast your spell?"

"Isn't that too easy? Is it fair?"

"It isn't easy. Fair? All's fair in love and war."

Clara went with Jenny, giving her instructions. Later, at home, Jenny was emotionally drained, despairing of success.

In the kitchen she said, "I'll write to Tom; he can keep me posted."

Once again Clara's shrewd eyes pierced her pretense. "If it's that bad, you can have some beeswax for a voodoo doll of the woman in your way." Jenny's heart chilled. "If that don't work, you may have to make a pact." Slowly Jenny turned and looked at her friend. For just a moment Jenny closed her eyes and saw that page in the book over which she had trembled in the past. She could only shake her head, and Clara's smile shamed her. "You don't want to admit you don't understand how it works, do you?"

"I've read a little bit about it," she answered in a low voice. "But if you were to tell me, it might help."

Later Jenny tossed on her bed and tried to forget what Clara had suggested. The questions tumbled through her mind, and finally she slipped from her bed, lighted a candle, and opened the book.

Carefully she avoided that section. Thumbing through the book, she muttered, "There's got to be another way."

The next morning, while she and Clara were preparing breakfast, Jenny asked, "Clara, do you know anything about talismans?"

"Of course—I have one. Wanna see it?" Jenny's hands trembled as she nodded.

It was late afternoon before the two of them could slip away to Clara's room. Kneeling beside her bed, Clara pulled out her satchel. "You're supposed to wear or carry this all the time for it to have the most good, but I paid a good sum for it, and I can't afford to lose it. 'Tisn't as important I carry it right now as it will be in the future when I really plan to use it."

"When are you going to use it?" Jenny watched the sly expression creep into Clara's eyes as she placed the strange object in Jenny's hands.

After a moment she replied, "When I find a man I really want. See, there's power here and I don't want it attractin' just anybody."

"Tell me what it means." Jenny turned the round object over in her hand. The heavy gray metal was marked with curious designs and unfamiliar letters.

"Well, in the first place, it's a table. The markings add up to meanin's that are related to the energy of the stars. The writin's different names for God, and blessings."

"What'll it do?"

"Well, for instance, see these little marks? They mean you can call upon the celestial powers that's been assigned to you. They can be invoked. That's where I get my power to make charms and cause storms."

"Is that all?"

"No, there's lots more. You can use it to get rich, have power and love, peace—oh, just lots of good things. But for some of them, it takes a bit of practice."

"How's that?"

"Well, I'm good at storms, but so far, I guess I haven't tried love too hard."

"Clara, will you sell this to me?" Clara drew back, and Jenny pressed. "You said you didn't even carry it yet. You can get another one. I need one now."

"These are hard to come by. A special man makes 'em, and he's got to do it at a special time and in a special frame of mind. Serene like, or there won't be the proper magnetism in it." She studied Jenny's face. "Why don't you tell me what's goin' on? If there's a person on this earth who can help you, it's me. I figured out that you were settin' your cap for Mark. But you've come back from your trip all like a thundercloud."

Jenny took a deep breath and slowly lifted her face. She was still clutching the talisman in her damp hand, desperately knowing she must have it. "If I do, will you promise to sell the talisman to me now?"

After studying her face for a moment, Clara nodded.

"It's Joseph Smith. I want him."

"The Mormon prophet," Clara said slowly. "I can't see any person in their right mind wantin' to be stuck with a preacher. And he's already married."

Jenny slowly shook her head. Miserably she whispered, "I

don't know why either, but ever since I was a little tyke I've loved him. He's never paid any attention to me. It hurt when he got married, but then she was sickly and losing her babies. I thought sure the heavens had willed me to have him. Now I see I need help."

"Maybe so, maybe so." Clara pursed her lips. "You're wantin' her to die, aren't you?" Jenny hid her face in her hands and nodded. "Well, I guess you've come to the right place, 'cause there's no way on this earth you'll get what you want except through the craft."

Clara watched Jenny make a tiny pouch of cotton to hold the talisman which she pinned inside her dress, just over her heart. Clara chuckled and said, "You're wantin' him bad, aren't you?" She nodded. "Well, I have a feelin' it's gonna take a lot of power. Better think about what else you're willin' to do to get him. Have you figgered out yet how you'll know when the talisman's workin'?"

Jenny caught her breath and for a moment stood very still, lost in thought. "This is real, isn't it? Well, I guess when I hear from Tom that—that she's dead."

CHAPTER 18

The sound of sawing and hammering was music in the streets of Kirtland. The Mormons were building a temple. On the construction site workmen swarmed, thick as ants. But twice as thick were the crowds who constantly walked the streets, keeping track of every nail and board and the scores of quarried stones piled high beside the excavation.

The spectators saw Joseph Smith working beside his men, cheerfully heaving the foundation stones into place. They also saw Sidney Rigdon, well known for his emotionalism, walking the masonry at night with tears raining down his cheeks as he petitioned heaven for the blessings of God upon the new temple.

When Tom joined the spectators, he frowned at it all. Sweating and panting, Joseph came to him, grinning.

"Joe, how can you call this a temple?" Tom challenged. "I recollect your sayin' this isn't consecrated ground and that we're to be a-movin' to Zion."

"Call it what you wish," Joe said shortly, his grin replaced with a frown. "Until we do move to Zion, we need a house of worship, and a place for learning. Remember, we are still waiting for the Lord to instruct us when to move." His brilliant smile again in place, he said, "I'll tell you another thing. The Lord himself has set the timing of all this. Now He has commanded that the building of the temple in Zion be commenced. There needs be a tithing collected from the people immediately. For now, how about giving us a hand on this job?"

Several days later, while Tom was on the construction site working beside Joseph, Oliver Cowdery appeared. He was striding through the piles of lumber when Tom spotted him. His face was lined with fatigue and his clothes still bore Missouri dust.

"Joe, look," Tom said slowly. Together they waited in silence as the man walked toward them.

With a terse nod, Oliver handed a folded paper to Joseph and then sat down on a quarry-stone to wait. It was a Missouri newspaper, *Western Monitor*, dated August 2, 1833. Slowly Joseph read aloud, "Number one says no Mormons are to settle in Jackson County in the future. Two, those settled are to sell out and leave." His startled eyes turned to Cowdery and then returned to the article. "Number three, the Mormon press, the storehouse, and the shops are to close immediately. Four, the leaders are to stop emigration from Ohio. Five, the brethren, referred to as those with the gift of divination, are to be informed of the fate that awaits if they fail to comply." Joe snorted and crumpled the paper.

"Cowdery, what happened?" Tom asked.

"They've smashed the press. Everything's gone. Took all the copies of the *Book of Commandments*; Partridge and Allen got tarred and feathered. Later the Gentiles threatened to burn the crops and houses if we didn't promise to clear out."

Tom turned to pace the construction site as Joseph continued to talk to Oliver. Miserably he studied the jumble in front of him and thought about the revelation which Joseph had just sent to Missouri, commanding them to gather tithes in order to start the temple in Zion. "Temple," he muttered. "Bet they wish they'd never heard of the place."

Oliver left and Tom went back to Joseph. "I've letters to write to send back with Oliver," Joseph said abruptly. "I'll walk down the street with you."

"What ya gonna say?" Tom asked.

"The Spirit tells me to instruct them to renounce war, work for peace, and put up with the fussing." After a moment he added. "I'll instruct the brethren there to petition the governor for justice. He will not fail to give ear to them."

Tom stopped by Joseph's office the next day. A still weary Oliver Cowdery was waiting for a final letter before starting his return journey.

Joseph finished writing, then lifted the paper. "You might as well hear the letter I've written. I'm not the least surprised at what's happened. I can't help thinking that Zion's brought the trouble on herself. Notwithstanding the articles written by Phelps in the *Star*, there's a deeper reason for the problems. It all goes back to men not being willing to obey counsel and take instruction from those the Lord puts over them." Silently he folded the letter and handed it to Oliver. With a sigh and shake of his head, Joe added, "All I can do is allow the Lord's wrath to be poured upon His people until they will confess their sins."

It was well into September 1833 before another communication was received from Jackson County, Missouri.

The day it came, Joseph stopped at the livery stable and waited until Tom finished shoeing Hyrum's horse before he showed the letter to him. "My friend," he said, "much of this matter with Zion can't be discussed with just anyone on the street. Bear with me while I tell you about this letter and air the problems. It relieves me to see they're handling the situation in a worthy manner, but still—" He unfolded the letter.

"Phelps, the writer of those articles, explains the explosion down there. Seems it started with his article in the *Star*; he was just trying to handle a sticky problem. Since Missouri is a slave state, they're mighty edgy over the issue, more so than ever since they know we prophesied that slavery will be abolished."

Tom added, "Cowdery admitted to me that part of the problem is our own people bein' too free with the prophecy that Jackson County is goin' to be cleared of the Gentiles and become the inheritance of the people of God."

Joseph moved his shoulders impatiently and continued, "They got wind that some free Negroes had converted to the church and were trying to emigrate to Independence. Phelps discovered a Missouri law that decreed they must have citizenship papers from another state before they could enter Missouri. After that came the article stating that the church had no policy regarding colored people. That blew the powder keg! Phelps says he tried to right things by admitting he wasn't only trying to stop them from coming, but to prevent them from joining the church."

"Doesn't seem enough to start those problems!"

"The Gentiles said it was an open invitation for the Negro to emigrate, and that it would stir up problems with the slaves in the state," Joseph sighed.

"Phelps said they've petitioned the governor for troops to keep order until their suit for damages is settled. Since that's under control now, Sidney and I can make our trip to Canada with an easy conscience."

"And since you're leavin', I think I'll be makin' my own missionary trip," Tom stated. Joe turned to look at him, and Tom added, "To see my sister Jenny."

"You bringing her back with you?"

Tom shook his head. "I've no ideas on that line. I just feel the spirit's urge to talk to her about her salvation."

Tom didn't bother to write to Jenny that he was coming. Reflecting on her teasing about his letter writing, he decided he could beat the letter there.

When he walked into the Bartons' kitchen that October evening, Jenny's surprise held her motionless, and then she threw herself into his arms, crying, "Tom! I am so glad to see you!"

As she continued to cling to him, hugging and patting, he said, "Well, Joe thinks I should bring you back with me."

She tipped her head and slowly said, "Whatever for?"

"He thinks you'd make a good Mormon." In a moment she began to laugh. "That surprises you?" he asked. "Well, Joe doesn't think of much else."

Later Tom met Clara, and then Mark Cartwright made an unexpected appearance. As Tom shook his hand, he said, "Jen didn't tell me she was expecting company."

"I'm not really company," Mark said with a glance at Jenny. "I'm over this way frequently since my Uncle Thomas is ailing. I offer only moral support, but Auntie seems to need it."

Clara was unable to take her eyes off Tom, saying, "So you're the Mormon." Jenny wished desperately that she hadn't shared her secrets with Clara.

During the following week Mark stayed in Cobleskill because of his uncle's health, and Tom lingered on at the Bartons'. In the evenings, after the Bartons and Clara had gone off to their bedrooms, Mark, Jenny, and Tom sat by the fire with apples and corn to pop.

Mark asked a flood of questions about Joseph and his new church. Jenny listened and watched his keen eyes probing her brother's as Tom talked.

Mark's voice was low. "I've not forgotten the things that happened in South Bainbridge. Tom, you and I both know that an awful lot of shady things came out at that trial, and there were many unanswered questions. Wouldn't the Lord demand a higher level of integrity in choosing a prophet?"

Tom's gaze was just as earnest. "Mark, Joseph was just a happy-go-lucky youngster back in those days. You have to know Joseph the Prophet. The mantle of authority and righteousness clearly rests upon him."

On subsequent evenings Mark asked about the *Book of Mormon*, and Tom could admit to knowing only what he had heard read aloud. Mark persisted, "Then what do some of these other men have to say about the book? What about Sidney Rigdon? I'm hearing he's a Campbellite preacher and well-educated. Has he investigated it all?"

"Well, in the beginnin' he wasn't sold on the idea, but after he took the occasion to ask the Lord for a sign, he could believe. He said that if we aren't familiar enough with our God to ask for a sign from Him, and if He weren't willin' to give us one, well—I think he said God was no better than a Juggernaut, whatever that is."

Mark slowly chewed his apple, swallowed, and said, "*Juggernaut* is the American title for the Hindu Vishnu; it means *lord of the world*. So Rigdon thinks a God that doesn't do what is demanded of him is really no god at all!"

And when Mark ceased asking his questions, Tom turned his earnest argument on Jenny. "You've heard Joseph and the others preach. You know yourself that we ought not neglect our salvation. Jen, I'm wantin' to see you join up. Joseph said that to turn our backs on the revealed truth in these last days means we won't make it. That's eternal damnation."

Jenny shivered and Mark laughed. "Tom, you take life and other men's thoughts too seriously." There was a touch of scorn in his voice as he leaned forward and added. "The plain, good, old-fashioned religion has been around long enough to convince me that the tried and true way can be depended on. But right now, religion doesn't interest me. I intend to leave it all until I'm so old I have nothing more important to think about."

His eyes danced toward Jenny, "And now I do have more important things to think about. I'd like to squeeze your pretty little hand before I say good night, and I'd also like to extract a promise that you'll accompany me to the Christmas festival the first week in December."

And so Mark departed and Tom prepared, rather gloomily, to leave Cobleskill for Kirtland in the morning. Jenny was left to muse over their conversations; her only reaction had been a hearty laugh over Mark's silly conclusion to the matter.

That night as she prepared for bed, she chanced to see a corner of the green book protruding from under a stack of schoolbooks; her heart grew heavy with its old burdens. *One thing is certain*, she decided as she pulled pins from her thick dark hair, *at times Mark nearly tears me away from that resolve.* She frowned. *I wonder*, she thought briefly, *whether that is good or bad.*

By the time Tom reached Kirtland, Joseph Smith and Sidney Rigdon had returned from their preaching mission in Canada. Within two days of his return, Tom heard rumbles in the community against Joseph for his lack of action in defense of Zion. But things settled down with time.

Soon Oliver Cowdery returned from New York with his new printing press. Joseph had promised him the position as editor of the *Star* if he would set up the press in Kirtland.

One crisp morning in early December when Tom walked into Whitney's store, he found Joseph Smith clutching a letter and Whitney stoking the potbellied stove.

Tom glanced at Joseph's sober face and then at the letter.

"Soon as I think things are runnin' smooth around here," Tom said, "you get another letter."

Joe lifted it. "It's from Missouri. On October 31, fifty men attacked us just west of the Big Blue River. They ruined ten cabins and whipped our people into the forest. Later they got into the storehouse and were caught redhanded. For the trouble of catching the culprits, our men were jailed." His voice dropped to a rumble as he studied the letter. "Next, David Whitmer banded together a bunch to protect their places. They tangled with the Gentiles, and in the scuffle two Gentiles and one of our men were killed.

"Whitmer says here the story got blown twice its size, and soon the Gentiles were threatening to kill those in jail. Well, the militia was sent out to meet our men, and old Boggs sweet-talked our men into laying down their arms."

"Who's Boggs?"

"The Lieutenant governor of Missouri." Joseph continued, "That night every Mormon community was attacked, and by morning all twelve hundred of our people were driven out of their homes. A few of them went to Clay County, he says, but the rest of them are shivering in the cottonwoods along the river. Everything's gone."

He continued reading. The Mormons' lawyers had won support from Governor Dunklin. Dunklin quickly gave the Mormons the promise of military escort to return to their homes. Dunklin also instructed them to raise a militia and granted them public arms.

On a happier note, the letter ended with the tale of a miraculous display of meteor showers. To the exiles, it was a glorious sign of the end of the world.

As soon as the news of the letter was out, the city of Kirtland rocked with confusion. These were kinfolk and neighbors; these were the children of Israel, and this was their Zion! Joseph sent a quick dispatch to the leaders in Missouri, ordering them to remain as near Jackson County as possible. He also ordered them to retain their lands.

The following Sabbath when Joseph stood before his people

and relayed the information to them, a mighty cheer went up. When he raised his hand for silence, he added, "I believe in law and justice. The Lord inspired noble men to write the Constitution of the United States. Justice will prevail."

As the crowd voiced their hearty approval again, Tom sat back and beamed with pride. Lately, Joseph had disappointed him; he had thought there should have been action and encouragement, and that Joe had a blind spot.

Now Joseph lifted another sheet of paper. "Brethren," he called, and there was instant silence. "I instructed Phelps to petition Washington for help. I have also prepared a letter to President Andrew Jackson, which I mailed along with a copy of the latest revelation given by the Lord. I will read to you only snatches of this December 16 revelation, because it is very long and I don't want any of you to go to sleep on me and fall off your benches, as Michael Williams did last week." The levity caught everyone by surprise, and Joseph waited for silence. Even Tom grinned, remembering the youth's embarrassment.

Joseph rattled the paper. "Oliver Cowdery has our new press set up, and he will be glad to sell you copies of the revelation for one dollar apiece.— Now, referring to the people in Kirtland: 'Verily . . . I the Lord have allowed the afflictions in consequence of their transgressions. . . .' " A sigh and murmur swept the room. " 'Zion shall not be moved; there is none other place appointed for the gathering of my saints. A commandment I give to all the churches: purchase all the land around Zion which can be had. There is already an abundance of money to redeem Zion.' "

Above the murmur sweeping the room, Joseph's voice rose: "Now regarding their present trouble: 'Let them importune the judge . . . the governor . . . the president. If he will not heed, I the Lord will arise . . . and vex the nation.' "

In April the Kirtland council dissolved the United Order. Tom heard about it at the livery stable, and he crossed the street to Whitney's store to confront Joseph.

"I hear the Order's finished," he said. "And I also am hearin' funny things about the revelation dealin' with it."

Joseph got to his feet and stared down at Tom. "They're

saying it's funny, huh? Well, the revelation isn't to be given out just yet. It's dealing with the distribution of property and it's the business of the council."

Tom returned his stare, unwavering. "Joseph, they are also sayin' you've had a letter from Phelps in Missouri, that the people are in desperate condition. Is it right that the innocent must suffer with the guilty? Surely all of those people there aren't sinnin'."

"You're suggesting that I step in and do something about it? Any such action before the Lord gives the command puts my soul in jeopardy. Let the Lord handle it. I understand most of the people have settled in Clay County. I've instructed them to hang on to their land." He paused a moment, then added, "About the revelation, the council is mindful of who's involved. No one else need know." Joe's level gaze quickly reminded Tom he had no business probing into the Prophet's affairs.

The silence stretched between them until suddenly Joe smiled. "Tom, looks like you might just get your wish to visit Missouri. Pratt and Wight are back in town and they have some pretty good ideas. They also brought the news that Governor Dunklin is working for us; among other things he's urging the church to apply for public arms, and go to work defending themselves. But, as the fellows pointed out, even with all our men holding guns, the old settlers still have us outnumbered."

"Now, who was it preachin' that in Bible times the children of Israel were outnumbered mighty often, and the Lord was pleased to do their fightin' for them?" Tom murmured.

Joseph ignored Tom and continued, "Well, here's the plan they proposed, and the revelation the Lord gave. They suggest we get us an army together, a well-trained one, but move into the area like a bunch of settlers. The army would just hang around until the church can buy up all the land of those Gentiles opposing us. The Lord's affirmed that we're to redeem Zion by power, and that He's already raised up a man to lead the army of the Lord, like Moses led his people. I've already got fellows out recruiting from all the churches. Tom, you can join up if you have five dollars and a good shooting iron."

Joseph's army didn't grow as quickly as Tom expected, but

he swallowed his disappointment and continued to work at settling his affairs.

Writing to Jenny, he informed her of his plans. "Right now, it looks like we'll be leaving this spring and won't be back until Zion is well-established and prospering. Hopefully, by then there won't be a Gentile in the state. You know the revelation from the Lord about the settling of Zion; He has said we are to inherit their land and their riches. I don't feel too sorry for them; they've been warned they'll either have to join us or forfeit it all. I'm led to believe that this very revelation has caused some hard feelings in Missouri. I suppose, if I were one of that bunch, I might have a hard time swallowin' it, too."

On May 4, 1834, the day before they were to leave for Missouri, the army gathered in Kirtland to hear an address by Sidney Rigdon. Looking about the packed hall, Tom whispered to James Taylor, "The church could use this kind of enthusiasm every Sunday!"

"Yeah," James returned, "but it would take a new army every week to see it done."

During the course of his address, he urged the church to change their name from Church of Christ to Church of Latter-day Saints. The crowd rustled with excitement, and James whispered, "I like the sound of that; it has a good ring to it."

Tom nodded. "Maybe he's got somethin' there. We'd be sheddin' the tag of Mormonites; nobody's heard of Latter-day Saints. That could be a real advantage when we run into any opposition."

The following day, as the army started marching across Ohio, Tom could see that more than just good sense dictated the name change. Looking around at the motley crew called Zion's Camp, Tom saw old muskets, ancient pistols, and rusty swords. Some of the men were armed with butcher knives. No wonder Joseph Smith wanted as little commotion possible as the army marched westward! It made good sense to divide the army into small groups and take different routes through larger communities along the way.

Joseph was at ease, even content, in his new role. During a three-day rest period at Salt Creek, Illinois, he took over the instruction and drilling practice the men sorely needed. Under his direction, within a short time the men mastered the simple maneuvers.

But not many days passed before Tom began to be puzzled about his colorful leader.

James brought up the subject. He and Tom sat together on the far side of the campfire, polishing their rifles. In a low voice James asked, "Does it strike you odd that the Prophet spends so much time hiding who he is? I heard him tellin' Wight to pass his name off as Captain Cook to strangers."

Tom drawled, "Well, it might just keep us all safe if there's questions asked."

James nodded and added, "But he keeps changin' his position in the company, even to ridin' in the supply wagons. And that dog—the nasty tempered thing—oughta be better'n the twenty men he's askin' for as bodyguards."

Tom tried to shrug off the questions, but in the following days he became aware of his own doubts. The feeling guilted him until he saw the measuring look Brigham Young turned on Joseph the day his anger lashed out at Sylvester over the bulldog.

Tom heard the tirade of abuse spilling from Sylvester and came running. He arrived just as the man screamed, "If that dog bites me, I'll kill him!"

And Joe roared back, "I'll whip you in the name of the Lord. If you don't repent, that dog will eat the flesh from your bones."

After a moment of stunned silence, Thompson exclaimed, "Aw, Joe, that dog is a blamed nuisance all around. There's not a fella here who can tolerate 'im."

Tucker, a quiet, serious-minded man, spoke thoughtfully, "Joseph, you ought not go around talking of whipping in the name of the Lord. It's unseemly for a prophet."

Joe took a quick step backward, and his words drew that look from Brigham. "You're seeing how this all looks. I did it on purpose to show you how base your attitudes are! Like animals. Men ought not to place themselves that low."

As Tom and his tentmate had bedded down a couple nights later, Matt commented on the large white dog, curled up in front of Joseph's tent. "Seems strange," he muttered, pulling off his boots. "The Prophet being on such good terms with the Almighty, getting revelations that the Lord will fight our battles for us, and yet he gets an old dog to stand guard."

During the second watch of the night, a single gunshot brought the men running from their tents. Joseph was kneeling in the dust before his tent, and the white bulldog was making his last convulsive movements. The apologetic guard stood hat in hand. "Forgot about the dog," he muttered. "Just saw a movement and shot quick."

When Tom and Matt crawled back into their tent, Matt yawned and said, "Well, guess now Joseph's going to *have* to rely on men and angels."

CHAPTER 19

The confrontation between Joseph and Sylvester soon was pushed into the background, forgotten in the light of a more compelling issue.

Orson Hyde and Parley Pratt rode into camp after their conference with Governor Dunklin. They had barely dismounted when the entire army surrounded to hear the news. Taking their cue from the men's grim faces, the foot soldiers waited quietly as Joseph and Lyman Wight joined them.

"It's not good news," Pratt said shortly. He wiped his hands wearily across his face before continuing. "Unbeknownst to us, Governor Dunklin has been working for our cause. He's been dickering with the War Office to secure a federal arsenal, with plans to build it in Jackson County." He paused and added, "Right in our own backyard, along with the federal army as a guard."

"Glory be!" Wight exclaimed. "There's not much chance of the Gentiles fightin' us under those circumstances."

"But wait," Pratt interrupted, "on top of that, Dunklin was considering dividing Jackson County so our people and the Gentiles would have equal shares. Later in our meeting he dropped the information that on May 2, he dispatched orders to Colonel Lucas to restore the arms they took from us. But before Lucas got the order, news of the coming of Zion's Camp leaked." He looked slowly around the assembled men. Deliberately he added, "Dunklin said the Missourians stormed the jail where our arms were stored and took every one of them."

With a muttered curse, Wight flung his battered old hat to

the ground and stalked away. Joseph watched him go, then turned back to Pratt. "Before any action could be taken they ravaged the rest of our property. Every last one of the hundred and fifty houses was destroyed."

Groans of dismay erupted in angry words, and finally Joseph lifted his hand. His face white and rigid, he said, "Let's hear the rest of it."

"Well, that cooked our goose with Dunklin. He was pretty frosty. Said the comin' of Zion's Camp plus the fact that all our houses were destroyed made it impossible at this time to restore our property to us." He paced the trampled ground in front of Joe.

Watching Pratt, Hyde added, "News about the army has traveled fast. We're findin' out it ran like wildfire ahead of us. Militias from four different counties have moved out to meet us. They had our number right off. They knew we were an army, not a bunch of farmers with a sack of grain to plant. The word was passin' ahead of us, with people yellin', 'The Mormons are comin'; they'll murder our women and children!' "

The group turned to Joseph and waited in stunned silence as he paced back and forth, head bowed, hands clasped behind him. Wight had crept back to the edge of the crowd, and Joseph stopped in front of him. "I tell you, it's best we don't make a wrong move; we're sitting ducks!"

Wight bristled, looking at the men clustered around them. "We can't go back, not after comin' this far!" A rumble of assent rose from the men, and Tom remembered the confident assertion that angels would fight for them.

Finally the army moved out, advancing cautiously, disheartened and confused. The men needn't be told that Joseph was as deeply disturbed as they. On the second day further bad news drifted back. An armed band was waiting across the Missouri with plans to attack.

Immediately Joseph Smith ordered the men to move out to the prairie.

"Smith!" Lyman Wight roared. "These men'll have neither decent water or wood for fire. I say let 'em all spend the night in the woods."

Joe turned back to argue the matter, and then impatiently wheeled about. Raising his voice, he shouted, "Thus saith the Lord God, march on!"

In disgust, Wight silently turned aside and waved his men to camp in the woods. Sylvester turned to shout at Joseph's men, "Who are you following? Wight's in charge of this army!"

That night, just as Wight predicted, Tom and the group who had followed Joseph were forced to drink bad water and eat raw pork.

The following day, Tom was surprised to hear Joseph defending his position before the men. Stepping close to Joseph, Tom growled from the side of his mouth, "Forget it, 'tis all come to naught."

But Joseph pressed his case. "By the Spirit of God I know when to sing, to pray, to talk, even to laugh."

Wight and some of the other men became apologetic, but Sylvester raged. "You want a man in bondage, without the freedom to speak! These prophecies, they're lies in the name of the Lord. You're as corrupt as the devil himself in your heart."

Joseph seized the horn used to call the men to prayer and threw it at Sylvester. Tom caught his breath, then gasped with relief as the horn missed the man and smashed into pieces.

Three days later, the Camp of Zion moved up the bank of Fishing River, just on the border of Clay County. But before Joseph could advance his troops, cholera struck.

One by one the ranks of Zion's Camp fell victim to the dread disease. Within two weeks sixty-eight of the army had succumbed.

Thus far Tom had been spared, but each day he counted his chances with a sinking heart as more of his comrades took to their pallets. Carrying water and the common remedy of whiskey mixed with flour, Tom made his rounds among the sick. At the same time, Joseph moved among his men, praying and laying hands upon the stricken.

Early one morning, Joseph approached as Tom filled his jugs. "You're looking mighty worried this morning," Tom said as he mixed the whiskey and flour together.

"Leave that mess for someone else," Joseph ordered in a low

voice. "I've another task for you." He led Tom away from the men. "I understand today's the day of the confab across the river in Clay County. You know we've promised to stay put until the business is settled, so I can't stick my nose over there. I hear a Judge Ryland is meeting with the Gentiles and the Mormons to read them all the governor wants done to settle this problem."

Tom looked at him for a moment and said slowly, "You want me to slip over easy-like, huh?"

Joseph nodded, "I want a quick report from someone I can trust to give me the truth."

"Still scratchin' for a fight?"

"Not me," Joseph said bitterly. "I want a peaceful settlement of all this. It's Wight who's itching to use that cannon."

Tom nodded slowly. "You're bein' cautious, but I heard the fellas talkin'; from something you've said, they're believin' that once they strike a sword, there's gonna be angels right there fightin' for them."

Joseph turned away. "Just get over there and find out what's going on. Keep your mouth shut as to who you are."

Tom cut downstream and found a youth idly fishing from the security of his crudely made raft. Pulling a packet of fishhooks from his pocket, Tom hailed the boy. "You headin' across the river?"

The boy poled closer to shore and blurted, "Them's hooks? I wasn't, but I would for hooks."

It was nearly noon when Tom sauntered into the clearing where the two groups belligerently faced each other. Another group of men approached, and Tom silently merged with them, resisting the urge to pull his hat down to his ears.

He was eyed suspiciously, but was momentarily forgotten as a gentleman entered the clearing. The drift of conversation about him stopped as he surveyed the two groups. "Come close, men; I've no intention of straining my voice. The original settlers of Jackson County have drawn up a list of proposals to present to the group of Mormon settlers. With no further ado, I intend to read them to you, and then, gentlemen, the mode of settlement is upon your shoulders.

"Be advised that Governor Dunklin insists that a settlement be agreed upon. Adherence to the settlement will be enforced by law. There are a number of points that need to be made before we read the proposals, points made by legal counsel which must be taken into advisement before a satisfactory solution to the problem can be reached. First of all, Governor Dunklin points out that the Constitution of the United States guarantees that the citizens of any state shall be entitled to privileges and considerations in all states; the state boundary is no license for discrimination regarding emigration. The constitution of this state allows men the right to bear arms in defense of themselves. Also, the Constitution of these United States guarantees freedom to worship according to the dictates of a man's conscience.

"I wish to point out that whereas the state allows arms for defense, it is strictly illegal for any group to promote the use of cannon. That is considered aggressive action, not defensive. It is rumored that both sides of this faction are preparing to use cannon." An angry growl swept through the crowd, and Tom noticed hostile looks turned his direction. He held his breath and returned the glances with a level stare.

"Now," continued the judge, "the proposals set out by the residents of Jackson County are as follows. With due appraisal by disinterested parties, the residents of Jackson County are prepared to buy the property of the resident Mormons of Jackson County at double the appraised value, to be paid within thirty days. If this proposal is not met with agreement by the Mormons, then the counter-proposal, the sale of the Missourians' land under the same agreement, is also made."

Silence held both groups. Tom was busy thinking of all the implications. The foremost memory he had was that revelation from the Lord. Briefly he closed his eyes and could clearly hear those words: "Zion shall not be moved out of her place. . . . There is no other place appointed."

When Tom opened his eyes, Phelps was walking toward the judge. His voice rang with confidence and conviction. "Sir, we cannot accept your proposals at this time, but I do promise you that until a settlement is reached, Zion's Camp will remain in their position on Fishing River."

Tom straightened his shoulders, and his heart soared. Phelp's statement brought to mind all those other revelations concerning Zion—surely not one of them would fail!

The Gentiles didn't look as if they were planning to give up any of their positions, either. So the two groups parted with the understanding that the governor would look further into the matter.

As he made his way back across the river, Tom thought about the revelation the Lord had given Joseph in 1831. Of all the promises, this one was the most vivid, telling Joseph that Satan was stirring the Missourians to anger, to the shedding of blood, and that the land of Zion couldn't be obtained except by purchase or the shedding of blood. Well, it didn't look like there would be a purchase.

In Zion's Camp, the cholera continued to claim its victims. The number of dead rose to fourteen before the disease abated.

Just two days after Tom's foray as spy, Gilliam, Clay County's sheriff, visited the camp. Handing Joseph Smith a copy of a letter written by the chairman of the Jackson County committee, he settled back and waited for him to read it.

When Joe folded the letter, he said, "I understand you want me to pay particular attention to the section underlined, in which it is noted that our communication is signed by persons not directly owning land in Jackson County, in other words, the heads of the church; and therefore we have no right to our claims. It's correct that we don't directly own land there, but we are spokesmen for the church."

The man spoke dryly, "We understand your church has given all the property into the hands of the leaders, but around here I don't think that'll work. It's each man for himself."

Joe chewed his lip. "You are also using a revelation from the Lord to prove we have come with the intent of shedding blood. The Lord was only alerting us to the character of the inhabitants of this county. You're trying to prove we have no intention to come by the land honorably. Seems you're using this means to force us to buy out the Gentiles. I refuse to be threatened."

The man pressed, "Dunklin's directive has also stated that

militia from outside the counties is unlawful. You've no legal right to enter the county with weapons unless you have permission from him. It is obvious you have come to Missouri with only one intention—to show force."

"That is not the truth." Joseph paced back and forth before the man. "We've come in peace!"

Tom listened as the men continued to argue; finally Joseph drew himself erect. "Gilliam, I have a plan to offer you." An expression of surprise and relief crossed the sheriff's face. While Joseph explained his plan, Tom watched Gilliam's jaw drop. Then he jumped to his feet as Joseph said, "We will purchase all the property of the settlers who've been the warmongers. Have twelve men set the price, to be paid in one year. Then from that price we shall deduct the amount of damages sustained by our people."

"Only if you throw in the moon to boot!" Gilliam exploded as he stomped out of the camp.

Tom watched Joseph turn away. Without another word, he entered his tent. Late in the afternoon, Joseph reappeared and called his men together to hear the latest revelation from the Lord.

Sitting on the edge of the crowd, Tom studied the men's faces. Some of them were recovering from cholera, others had watched their friends die. All of them, from the beginning, had fretted over the whole sad situation. All were listening intently. For the first time in days, Tom watched relief and hope flicker on their weary faces.

Tom turned his attention to the words Joseph was reading. "Wait for the redemption of Zion. I will fight your battles for you. I will send the destroyer in my time to lay waste mine enemies . . ."

Tom's relief and satisfaction were total—almost, until he heard the final words. As he walked back to his tent, the man in front of him limped along slowly, quoting the words bitterly. " 'It is expedient that they should be brought thus far for a trial of their faith.' " He turned and saw Tom. "I can't see a blessing in the temple helping out those lads who died. That was a sore trial for the Lord to put on us." He continued on his way, sadly shaking his head. At the sound of an angry voice rising beyond the circle of tents, Tom stopped and listened. With a sigh he turned back.

It was Wight. Standing in front of the Prophet's tent, he shouted. "If you choose to back out now, all right, but I'm going to fight! The Lord has promised to help, and I'll hold Him to it!"

As Tom reached the tent, Joe Smith stepped through the doorway, revelation in hand. Thrusting the papers at Wight, he spoke quietly, "Here, read it for yourself. I know you're disappointed, but thus saith the Lord. It may help you to know that in three years' time, we'll march against Jackson County, and there won't be a dog to open his mouth against us. The Lord revealed the date unto me. The day for the redemption of Zion has been set—September 11, 1836."

That night Tom accompanied the Prophet across the river to visit the Mormons in Clay County. Joe comforted the little band of discouraged settlers with his promise to return to Ohio and raise money to buy all of Jackson County.

Finally, Joe ordered the leaders of Zion to return with him to Kirtland, Ohio, to receive their special endowments in the temple. Before they left Missouri, Joe instructed the people remaining behind to hold no public meetings and to stay away from the upcoming elections. "Don't give them opportunity to quarrel with you," he concluded.

Zion's Camp tarried just long enough to hear that their settlement proposal had been rejected.

Phelps rode into camp with a copy of the *Liberty Enquirer*. There was a wry twist to Joseph's grin as he read the paper. Tossing it aside, he said, "The educated opinion of the editor is that the Mormons have scattered and that the war is over. Little do they know the Lord has promised to sweep away their pollution from the land."

CHAPTER 20

In May of 1834, Jenny received a letter from Tom which disrupted the peaceful procession of ordinary days on the farm. Suddenly her mind was filled with the romantic picture of Joe, astride his steed, commanding Zion's Camp as they marched into Missouri to claim their sacred possession.

Together with Clara in the kitchen, Jenny was preparing to feed haying crews. Caught up in her thoughts of Joseph and Missouri, Jenny stood at the kitchen window. The sun-baked fields of ripening grain and the mounding hay stacks retreated into a haze of sun-shot gold. Opening her eyes wide, she sighed and blinked.

"Jenny!" Clara waved a butcher knife at her. "You're goin' to blind yourself starin' into the sun. Give that chicken a turn and go to shuckin' that corn. Those fellas are going to be in here for their dinner. Mrs. Barton won't be a bit happy if we make 'em wait for it." She continued to study Jenny. "You haven't said much lately. What's the problem?"

Jenny walked to the stove and picked up the meat fork. "I've Tom on my mind a bit. He's gone out Missouri way with Joseph Smith's army to rescue their settlers there. I've been feeling lonesome, thinking how it would be if he were killed. Clara, you don't know what it's like, when you've got ten brothers and sisters. Tom's all I have."

"If you were being sensible, you could have Mark." Clara sighed, shook her head, and began to slice bread to stack on the platter. "Shall I do three loaves? There's all that corn and 'taters. I hope the rhubarb pie is sweet enough." She threw a quick glance toward the door. "With a fella as promisin' as Mark, with all that money he's bound to inherit from his mother, and bein' an attorney, I'll never understand how you got your stars crossed and ended up wantin' that preacher Smith."

Jenny was forking the sizzling chicken onto platters. As she lifted the first platter to carry out to the tables under the trees, she glared at Clara.

"All right," Clara muttered, "so you don't like hearin' about it. I guess I'll be settin' *my* cap for him."

She looked at Clara and then laughed. "I give you my permission. But you can't have your talisman back."

Mrs. Barton came into the kitchen and threw a startled glance at Jenny. Then she asked, "Where's the tomatoes and cukes?"

"Settin' under a damp cloth on the table," Clara said hastily, heading for the door with the bread. Jenny scooted for the backyard. "Are you fetchin' the milk?" Clara called.

Later, when Jenny was washing dishes, her thoughts returned to the subject that never released its grip on her restless heart. It was true that she had been thinking about that march to Missouri, feeling the sun smite her eyes just as it would those soldiers, but it hadn't been Tom who occupied her thoughts. As she moved the dishcloth slowly over the plates, she dreamed about the sun turning Joseph's hair as bright as his golden plates.

When Clara carried in the last dish, she whispered to Jenny, "In that letter, did Tom say anythin' about—about her?" Jenny shook her head without looking up. "Do you wanna try that other?"

Scratching at the crusty skillet, Jenny said slowly, "Clara, I can't even think that way."

"You don't even understand *why*, do you?" Clara whispered. "Can't you see we have the *right* to order the events of the universe? Life and death's all part of it. Because you don't like to see someone die, you think death is bad, but that is because you're lookin' at it from down here. People only progress to a better life by passin' through death."

Mrs. Barton spoke from the doorway. "Clara, it's mighty

hard to convince people of that when they've just seen someone die. Mark's Uncle Thomas has just passed away today. I don't recommend your philosophy for him."

Jenny turned quickly, "Oh, I'm sorry. Mark was very close to him. I suppose they will need help."

"Yes," Mrs. Barton said. "I was thinking of food, but with folks coming in from as far away as Albany, it will be good household help they'll need. Jenny, the menfolk won't be harvesting again until next week. Why don't you help me wrap up this ham and some preserves and we'll take them over. Take your bag. If need be, I'll leave you there for several days."

Mrs. Barton's offer of Jenny was gladly accepted by the Webers, and she was immediately settled in the garret with Phoebe, Weber's hired girl.

In the kitchen with Phoebe, listening to the sound of carriages arriving and the tide of voices rising in the parlor, Jenny soon discovered why Mark's Aunt Mabel had welcomed her with gratitude. Phoebe was frozen into mindlessness by the crisis. Jenny sorted the jumbled pantry, planned meals, and shoved teacups into Phoebe's limp hands. Late that night, with the windows open to catch the slightest breeze, Jenny stood at the kitchen table rolling out sugar cookies and sand tarts. A lone horse moved past the house, and the back door creaked, but she didn't look up from her task until the hesitant steps stopped.

"Jenny, is that really you?"

"Mark!" Jenny bit her lip, recalling the last time she had seen him. What a silly quarrel it had been! His last visit had come close on the heels of Tom's letter, and her mind had been filled with the vision of Joseph.

Now looking at his wretched face, her heart squeezed tight with pity. He was still wearing his dark suit. She watched him dab at the perspiration on his forehead and tug impatiently at his tight collar.

"I suppose they've all retired for the night."

She nodded. "I think so. Take off your coat and I'll bring you some cold buttermilk." He was staring down at the table when she returned from the springhouse.

"Do you always bake at midnight! And what are you doing here?"

"It's cooler at midnight, and I've just come today. Mark, have you had supper?"

He shook his head. "I'd be happy with a cookie to go with the milk."

He reached for a sand tart and Jenny said, "There's cold ham; wouldn't you like some?"

She was caught by the sadness in his eyes, the tired lines around his mouth. "Mark, I'm sorry."

Quickly he asked, "Then you'll forgive me?"

"What? Oh, that silly quarrel. I've forgotten why we even argued."

"It wasn't the argument," he said thoughtfully. "It was my pigheaded need to be right. Jenny, you've a fine mind, which shouldn't be put down. Be patient with me as I learn to deserve you."

He bit into the cookie and turned away. Jenny stared at him while all he had just said rolled around through her thoughts. How could a man like Mark talk to Jenny, the hired hand, like this?

He turned abruptly. "Are your cookies burning?"

In the days that followed, Jenny saw Mark infrequently as he took charge of the Weber family. Up until the funeral the stream of carriages seemed unending, and Jenny was always ready with tall glasses of lemonade and cups of tea.

Phoebe continued to move only as pushed—all thought had slipped from her mind except for the task before her.

When the day of the funeral finally came, the sound of carriage wheels and horses suddenly ceased. Phoebe signaled the change by collapsing. Mark took her home and returned to beg Jenny to stay on a few days longer. Aunt Mabel came to the kitchen to add her plea; then both she and Mark settled down at the table as if it were the most pleasant spot on earth.

The kitchen table conferences grew into midnight trysts for the threesome, with sandwiches and cookies served by pale lamplight. Jenny felt herself prodded and probed by Mark and Mabel, but she also knew their friendly jabs were without rancor.

One night after Mark had left the room, Mabel turned back to Jenny and said, "You know he loves you, don't you?" Jenny felt her back stiffen, and Mabel continued, "I'm not trying to give you that speech about how you are as good as any of us; I believe you know that. But I sense you're not taking him seriously, and I can't understand that. You see, Mark means a great deal to me. You seem so sensitive to our every need and emotion, yet—" She leaned forward to study Jenny's face. "Why do I feel you're set apart and divided from us? You know I welcome you with open arms. If you're worried about his mother, you can rest assured my sister will love you just as I do."

Jenny watched Mrs. Weber walk from the room. She was thinking about the talisman pinned inside her dress, and about the green book. Could those other thoughts make all this difference?

The following evening Jenny was a spectator as Mark and Mabel carried on a lively argument. She was thinking about Mark, and wondering for the first time how he really felt about her. There had been those times when she had felt as if unseen bonds were drawing them together in a way she neither understood nor really wanted.

She studied his face; he was the same Mark she remembered from the Bainbridge days; his youthful face was open, honest. His sandy hair and freckles, the square jaw and eyes—not quite green and not quite blue—seemed very ordinary. Yet—she frowned, wondering why there was that memory from the Bainbridge days. She recalled the day she had first seen Mark and that other young man. For a moment they had seemed wrapped in a splendor more brilliant than any dream she had known. Then unbidden, the vision of Joseph Smith appeared, and Jenny moved her shoulders uneasily.

Mark reached for Jenny's hand and lifted it. "I don't know anything about reading palms, but just guessing your past, I'd say, young lady, that one day you'll drop in your tracks if you don't start taking more rest." He turned to his aunt. "If Jenny's to be returned day after tomorrow when Phoebe comes back, please, Aunt Mabel, may I take this fair lady to the city tomorrow?" Mabel nodded with a pleased smile.

While Jenny waited for Mark the next morning, she contemplated their day in the city and wondered at her mounting excitement.

He had his aunt's carriage, and Aunt Mabel had lent Jenny her straw bonnet covered with silk blossoms. Mark was wearing a straw hat that made him look suddenly mature even as it heightened the effect of his boyish grin.

She settled herself primly, asking, "What goes on in the city on a common old workday?"

"The fair, with booths and displays and fireworks and a band in the park. When it gets dark I shall sneak you behind the bushes and teach you to dance."

"Oh, horrors!" The impulsive words leaped out before she could think to harness them. "I understand that Joseph Smith excommunicated members of his church for dancing. Do you think—"

He looked at her strangely. "I didn't know you were keeping score for the Mormons."

After a long moment, she could say, "But Tom—"

At the fair he held her hand while they petted little black lambs. They ate ice cream and watched fireworks. They sat in the park and listened to the band. There was dancing on a proper floor, and with a teasing grin, Mark led her through the steps.

And when the moon was cresting the trees, he put her in the buggy and held her hand. Beside Mabel Weber's barn, he lifted her down, even though she could have hopped from the carriage just as she had on other days. When he cupped her chin in his hands, Jenny couldn't remember why she shouldn't rest her hands on his shoulders and lift her face. But when he whispered, "Jenny, I'm falling in love with you," she shook her head. "Don't, Mark."

Phoebe came back the next day, and Mark returned Jenny to the Bartons. They rode in the same buggy, but now Jenny wore her faded calico bonnet, and there were unspoken questions in Mark's eyes.

When she stood in the Bartons' kitchen and watched Mark's square shoulders disappearing down the lane in a cloud of dust rising from the buggy wheels, Jenny touched the hard metal disk fastened in the folds of her dress.

Months rolled by, and although she heard of Mark's frequent visits with his aunt, he hadn't called. Jenny thought she had nearly forgotten him; certainly, he had forgotten her.

The autumn leaves were crisping underfoot and the aroma of the apples Jenny was picking filled her senses with an earthy impulse to dance through the orchard, hugging all its glory to herself. She had her eyes closed as she sat in the comfortable cradle of tree branches. Holding the apple against her nose, she breathed deeply and gloried in the gentle warmth of the sun and the touch of wind.

"Hello!" Her eyes popped open, and she saw Mark's eyes nearly on a level with her knee. "I see you've picked lots of apples today." He was peering into the basket which held three apples.

Jenny smiled, pulled off an apple bobbing at her elbow, scrubbed it against her sleeve, and offered it to Mark. She watched him sink his teeth into it; all the while her emotions skithered skyward and then settled down like milkweed.

"How's lawyering?" she began.

"Pretty fair." He was watching her from the corner of his eyes as he pitched the apple core through the trees. "I would ask you if you're still enjoying doing dishes, but I'm afraid you'll say no, and I've nothing better to offer."

In silence she sorted through his words, grabbing and then discarding meaning. In the open neck of his white shirt, she could see the heavy beat of his pulse, and her fingers wanted desperately to touch the pulse, to steady its throb.

"Jenny—" he paused, then with more control said, "I've missed you terribly. I've come to ask you to marry me."

Jenny bowed her head against the roughness of the tree and slowly shook her head. Her mind filled, not with Mark, but with that bright, arrogant head. The talisman cut into her shoulder as she pressed against the tree, but she kept her eyes shut to hide what she knew she would see in Mark's face. "Mark, please go."

The sun had ceased to warm her skin when she raised her head. Mark was gone. Quickly now, she stripped the apples from the branches, shivering in the hostile tree.

CHAPTER 21

Tom chewed the end of his pencil and stared at the blank sheet of paper in front of him. It was a cold January, and the stove in the tack-room of the livery stable glowed red-hot. The door behind him creaked open and slammed shut before he stirred himself enough to turn.

The Prophet was shaking snow from his coat and slapping his old hat against the horse collars lining the wall. "You're studying that paper like you expect it to bite." He sat down and lifted his icy boots toward the glow of the stove.

"Since gettin' back from Missouri last summer, I've been meanin' to write a letter to Jenny," Tom muttered, shoving the pencil into his pocket with a sigh of relief. "I left her with the information we'd be stayin' in Missouri a spell."

Joseph pondered Tom's statement in silence. With a rueful grimace he said, "Tom, maybe the sadness of the trip doesn't warrant writing about."

"I wasn't thinkin' to air grievances," he said shortly. "I just had in mind lettin' her know I'm still in the land of the living. In addition, I'm lonesome for family."

"If you're serious about her soul and getting her into the only means of salvation, why aren't you urging her to move to Kirtland?"

"I'd not given it much thought," Tom answered slowly. "She's happy where she is."

"I could ask around and find a position for her," Joseph said thoughtfully. "If this had come up sooner, Emma could have used her help. The little ones had her about worn down. We've

207

relief now, with hiring Fannie Alger."

"I've seen Fannie at meetings, a right comely gal," Tom observed. "The fellas around are wishin' Emma didn't keep her so busy. They'd all like to try their hand at sparkin'."

Joseph laughed. "My idea is that she's not interested in the ones presenting themselves at the door." He lowered his feet and leaned forward, "Seriously, why don't you speak to Jenny about coming? She's a comely lass, too. If we can't find a position for her, we'll be marrying her off shortly."

"Marryin'—" Tom hesitated. "I guess she's old enough. I still forget she's not a tyke. Matter of fact, she's had her twenty-first birthday this month."

Joseph stood up and reached for his coat. "I'm headed for the temple. We've good news. A fellow by the name of John Tanner heard about the money troubles and met the foreclosure notice on the temple mortgage. He'd sold his farms and timber acreage, getting set to move to Missouri, so once again the Lord's provided for us."

"And the temple will be finished on time and things will be movin' just like the Lord promised in the revelation," Tom said softly.

"That's right," Joseph agreed. "First the temple is to be completed, and then the elders will be endowed with power from on high. Brother Tom, this will be a time of the outpouring of the Lord on the whole church, but especially on the leaders. I'm expecting a manifestation of the Lord's blessing at the time the temple is dedicated, and then we will be released from this place to possess Zion.

"Soon 'twill be time for the gathering up of money to purchase Zion," Joseph continued. "The Lord has promised that He will fight our battles for us. He has also said the destroyer has been sent forth to destroy, and it will not be many years hence until the Gentiles won't be left to pollute and blaspheme the promised land of Zion."

"How will we know when that time will be?" Tom asked.

"When the other promise is fulfilled, when the army of Israel becomes very great." While Tom remembered the poor army which had marched into Missouri last May, Joseph's words cut through his thoughts again. "At that time, the Lord will not hold us guiltless if we don't possess the land and avenge Him of His enemies."

Jenny was bending over the pile of calico in her lap when Clara came into her room. "Ugh," she declared. "I've not seen the likes. Every time I look, you're sewin' another fancy dress for yourself. I 'spect every cent of your pay has gone that way. How many does this make?"

Jenny raised her head, "Counting the winter frocks and the cape, 'tis five. I've a new bonnet too, see?" she nodded toward the shelf.

Clara looked and said softly, "Jenny, we'll be missin' you. Does Mrs. Barton know?"

"No, I've not set a date in my mind yet and she's not asked, though she's seen the frocks."

"I'm not certain you're ready," Clara said slowly. "You're claimin' power, what with the talisman, but you've not heard from your brother. I can't get you to a sabbat, and another solstice has passed. I've told you about the wax, but ya won't do a thing except wear the talisman and work with the herbs and charms." She shook her head sadly.

"But I *feel* ready," Jenny insisted. "I've read; I'm gaining power. For nearly a year now, I've been practicing up, learning to use the herbs and charms for healing. Mrs. Barton doesn't know it, but I healed her of the ague. She thought the herbs I mixed and gave to her did the trick, but you and I know it was the charms. Where I'm going there'll be a need, and I want to use the power to heal."

Clara was shaking her head. "I'm still thinkin' you've no idea of the real power needed if you're goin' to be more'n a white witch. You're play actin', Jenny. When you're ready to make a pact, then the *real* power will be yours."

Jenny studied Clara's serious face, "But *you* haven't made a pact; why must I?"

"Our power is limited, but do you want to be a white witch all your life? That's all I intend for myself. Bein' a good witch, helpin' people. I've the idea you had something else in mind."

Jenny was silent, staring at the sewing in her lap. Finally she shrugged and stood up. "Anyway," she said lightly, "I'll have a chance to practice my power on Mark this evening. He's coming to take me to a concert at the town hall. I'm tempted to wear my new cape even though it's nearly too warm for a wrap."

Clara went to the window. "I can't believe winter's gone and spring is here." Abruptly she turned from the window and asked. "Are you certain you don't care if I use a talisman on Mark?"

Startled, Jenny raised her head to meet Clara's worried eyes. She visualized Clara's frizz of hair and pudgy figure in soiled calico alongside Mark in his dark suit and shiny boots. She kept her face averted as she said, "You were the one who told me everything was fair in love and war. Besides, there's still Joe Smith; and didn't you say that where there's life, there's hope?"

When Clara's eyes began to shine and she opened her mouth to speak, Jenny added hastily, "But tonight is mine; sometime I must tell him my intentions."

In the end it turned out to be easier than Jenny expected. Mr. Barton had carried in Tom's letter just minutes before Mark arrived. Jenny, wearing the new dark challis print, was still holding the unopened letter when she heard Mark's footsteps on the porch.

When she went to greet him she waved the letter and asked, "Do you mind?"

They sat together on the bench under the kitchen window and she pried open the envelope. "It's the first I've heard from him since the army went to Missouri. They were to stay until Zion's problems were solved, but—" She had the letter open and was scanning it. She sighed and frowned.

"It doesn't seem things worked out as they had expected," she said slowly, puzzling over Tom's fragmented letter that nearly ignored the Missouri trip. She slowly refolded the letter, saying, "Tom's urging me to join him. He says Joseph Smith has promised to find a position for me."

"Do you want to go?" Mark's voice was low, and Jenny was tensely aware of that distance between them. She studied his face half hidden by evening shadows, knowing again the misery she felt every time they were together. Since apple-picking time last autumn, the times they had been together could be counted on one hand; even then he had stayed away until nearly Christmastime.

As she studied him, she was aware of his restraint. The old happy, easy days were gone. This new Mark was serious, cordial, persistent. And Jenny felt uneasily helpless in the face of his determination. Each time she had seen him, she had vowed it would be the last, yet the resolve wasn't kept and the reason she had for not keeping it grew more troublingly vague each time.

She sighed and got to her feet. "Isn't it time to go?"

He stood. "It is. I've taken the liberty of promising us to Auntie Mabel for a reception after the concert. You must have at least a shawl; it will be cool later." When she handed him the new cape, she saw the approval in his eyes. "Is it new?" he inquired. At her nod, he said, "That's a becoming dress, too."

It was late when they departed from Mabel Weber's home, and Jenny left reluctantly. Walking out to the carriage with Mark, she admitted, "Those people made me forget I'm the Bartons' hired girl."

He turned to her with a puzzled frown. "Jenny, what difference does it make? You're well-read and intelligent; those are the qualities that endear you to others. I wish you would stop being sensitive about your position." He helped her into the carriage and took the seat beside her.

"Mark, I don't fit in, and I'll never forget my poor beginnings. I wish you would find company more suitable to—you are going to be an attorney!" She knew her voice was stilted; she gulped and added, "Besides—"

"Jenny!" Mark interrupted. He was dragging on the horses' reins, guiding them off the main road onto a bumpy trail. Under the trees, he pulled the team to a halt and wrapped the reins around the hand rail.

He took her hand and turned her toward him. "Jenny," he said again in a voice so firm, almost stern, that she moved away from him. "I'm trying patiently to get across to you that I love you for yourself. I want to marry you, and I'll not take no for an answer."

She shook her head slowly, studying his determined face and shrinking further back into the shadows. Now his voice was gentle and low. "I've tried to talk myself out of feeling this way, but I'm convinced that you love me despite your attempts to push me away—which, by the way, seem rather feeble. If you mean no, I'd expect a little greater force behind the word." He had clasped her shoulders in his two hands and was gently pulling her closer. The hands Jenny lifted were leaden, but she must plant them against his chest and push.

"Why?" he asked gently. "Don't I deserve knowing why?"

She turned away and after a moment found that she could answer in an emotionless, even manner. "Mark, I count you the dearest friend I have. Never will I forget you, and never do I expect you to understand, but I can't marry you. I'm leaving the Bartons very soon; I'll be joining Tom in Ohio."

At last he stirred and spoke. "I think I'm beginning to understand. It's the pull of Joseph's new religion, isn't it? It would be easier to let you go if you assure me that you don't love me."

Jenny was silent for a long time; when at last she answered him, she knew her confusion echoed through every word. "Mark, I—I honestly wonder what love is."

On the trip to Kirtland, as the stagecoach bounced through rutty roads and the mud clutched at the wheels and flew from the hoofs of the team, Jenny had plenty of time to think about that last conversation with Mark. Only her fellow passengers were aware of her sighs, but she did finish the trip with a conviction. If she loved Mark, then she loved two men. If the intense desire she felt for Joseph was love, then denial was surely impossible.

Partly out of curiosity and partly out of obligation, Jenny stayed over in Manchester a few days. Stepping into Lucy Harris's open arms was almost like sitting on her own mother's lap again. Nancy was thrilled to see her, and Nancy's lanky husband, Alexander, just about crushed her hand with his long, bony fingers. Baby Andrew, named after President Jackson, added a life to their home which Jenny had forgotten was possible.

Still, Jenny was glad to be back on the bumpy coach three days later. She was weary with Nancy's religious prying. And Tom and Joseph waited at the end of her journey.

Her previous visit with Tom had taught Jenny her way around Kirtland. She stepped from the stagecoach and headed for the livery stable. Tom was at the forge. Standing behind him, she said, "I'm here."

Tom turned, dropped the horseshoe back into the fire, and rubbed his arms across his sweaty face. "Jen!" he exclaimed, "I didn't know you were comin'."

"You invited me." She moved restlessly. "I had a little trouble making up my mind, but when I did, it seemed best to come immediately."

He studied her face for a moment. "Mark?" She nodded and turned away. "Well," he sighed, "Joseph has found you a place at Andy Morgan's home. He's married now and his wife needs help with the young'un she's just given him."

Tom loaded Jenny's trunk into a wagon and drove her across town to the Morgan home. As they rode, he announced, "That's the temple," and pointed his whip toward the quarried stone edifice on the hill. "There's three stories. The top one's to be the school for the prophets. The auditoriums aren't finished yet, but they'll be grand. Joseph's fixin' them up with pulpits for the apostles."

"What's an apostle?"

"Joe's had a revelation about the structure of the church— the governing body, I mean. Right tonight there's to be a council meeting with blessings on us all."

She studied his face. "Then you'll be part of it?"

"The governing body? Yes, many of the army will be members of the Seventy."

She nodded toward the building. "You'll meet here?"

"No, the temple isn't finished. Dedication's still a year off. 'Twill be a grand event." Suddenly he turned to her with a happy grin. "Jen, I'm right glad you're here. There's big things in store for the church, and you're gettin' in on it just at the right time. Things are lookin' up for us. The Lord's supplied the money for the temple, and soon as it's finished and the elders get their endowments, we'll be about buildin' Zion in Missouri."

"A temple here and then Zion?" Jenny questioned slowly. "Sounds like there'll be parts of Joe's church scattered all across the United States."

"Eventually. He's plannin' to keep headquarters here for a time until we're really settled in Missouri."

That evening Tom went to the assembly hall, knowing this was the final council meeting before the twelve apostles were to be sent on their missions around the country.

When he walked in, Joseph and Rigdon were standing at the entrance. As Tom approached, Joseph hailed him. "Well, my brother, the grapevine has it that you've had a blessed surprise this afternoon."

Tom nodded. "Jen finally made the break and moved out. She'll probably be comin' to see you shortly."

"She's settled at the Morgans' ?" Tom nodded, and Joseph turned to follow Rigdon to the podium.

After the twelve had been called forward for the laying on of hands, prayer was offered for power and blessing. Joseph returned to the podium to speak to the men.

The rustle and rumbles in the room subsided and Joseph spread his papers before him. "You men have been chosen by the Lord to be the governing body of the restored church of Jesus Christ. Tonight I want to instruct you about the Lord's revelation on the orders of the priesthood. In Old Testament times, this priesthood was passed down from father to son. But we lost knowledge; through sinning it passed from us.

"There are two divisions in the priesthood, the Melchizedek and the Aaronic. The Melchizedek is the highest order and holds the right of presidency. In other words, the church president will be taken from this priesthood. No one will be able to hold the office of the Aaronic priesthood unless he is a direct descendant of Aaron."

There was an uneasy flutter of movement throughout the room, and Joseph lifted his hand. "Now, don't you fret. The Lord has revealed to me just how many of you are in that lineage. Also, there is a provision through the power of the Lord, whereby those men becoming members of the church will literally have their blood replaced with new through the power of the Holy Ghost. Thus you will become the seed of Abraham.

"Now, three years before the death of Adam, he gathered together all who were high priests from his posterity, taking them to the valley of Adam-ondi-Ahman for a final blessing."

Joseph paused a moment. "Most of you had the privilege of being with me when we discovered the valley of Adam-ondi-Ahman in the promised land of Zion."

An excited rustle rose and subsided, then Joseph continued. "At this time of blessing, the Lord appeared to them, and they rose up to bless Adam, calling him Michael, the prince, the archangel. The Lord comforted Adam, telling him at that time that a multitude was to come from him and that he was to be a prince over them forever. He told him that he would sit on a throne of fiery flame, just as the prophet Daniel predicted. All of these things are written in the book of Enoch, and they will be given to you in due time."

Later Tom, thinking over what the Prophet had said, joined the hushed group of men making their way toward the door. From the quietness of the men surrounding him, Tom guessed the others felt the weight of blessing and the burden of responsibility just as he did.

When he stepped out into the starlit night, he lifted his face to the cool breeze and his heart responded with gladness. "Jen," he whispered, "oh, Jen, how good that you've come now before the fullness of time!"

CHAPTER 22

The Morgan home was a pleasant one, built of log like many others in Kirtland. Situated on the far edge of town, it provided ample room for a vegetable garden and corrals for the livestock.

Jenny gloried in the fresh, clear air and the view of the young town encircled by the forest of oak, hickory, ash, and maple. Trees towering beyond the town placed a hedge of solitude and separation around the Mormon community, separation which to Jenny seemed symbolic. The isolation of Kirtland made it hard for her to realize that Lake Erie, with its busy ports, lay just north.

Living with the Morgans was a new experience for Jenny. A young couple not much older than she, they were obviously deeply in love. Jenny blamed her uneasiness in the situation on her role as the outsider. She was needed, certainly; the new mother had her hands full caring for her baby. In truth, Sally Morgan didn't know her way around her own kitchen.

During her first weeks, Jenny aired her uneasiness about being the extra person in the household. Sally, sitting in the rocking chair holding her infant daughter, looked up at Jenny with blue eyes as wide and innocent as the baby Tamara's, and exclaimed, "Oh, Jenny, how can you possibly feel that? Haven't you noticed how many of the homes in Kirtland have boarders in them? Most aren't nearly as valuable as you. You know we need you terribly. We Mormons are getting accustomed to sharing our homes. Otherwise there just isn't enough room for everyone."

"I've heard even the Smiths have a girl living with them," Jenny said in a low voice.

"Yes, Emma's had her there quite some time. She calls her an adopted daughter, and right fond they are of each other. Poor soul, with the Prophet gone so much and the trouble she's had with babies, Fannie is a great help."

Although Sally's reassurance helped, Jenny could see there was scarcely enough work to occupy the two of them. She was glad to busy herself in the vegetable garden, but her free time increased as the summer wore on.

As Jenny became acquainted with Kirtland and her neighbors, she readily observed the truth in Sally's statement about the Prophet. He was gone much of the time. She heard he was busy with missionary journeys about the country.

She also discovered that Kirtland had grown into a bustling town. Since Jenny's last visit new buildings had been erected everywhere, and daily more structures were being planned. The early homes had been of log, garnered from the citizens' front yards. The newer ones were of planed lumber, stone, and brick.

When Tom was there to listen, she commented about the expansion. "Joseph's much aware of the need to expand and build up the Lord's country," he answered. "While we're here, Kirtland's the Lord's country and our responsibility."

It didn't take Jenny long to discover that what she had heard about Kirtland was true. Joseph and his people had one object in mind: to prepare for the second coming of Christ. All life was bent in that direction.

"See," Sally said, "Joseph's received it from the Lord that we're to build up a city for the Lord to come back to. That's why it's so important we possess Zion in Missouri. Much depends on us. It helps to know the Lord is going before us; He will conquer His enemies through us in order that His purposes will prevail. Nothing must stand in the way of doing what He's instructed through Joseph."

Jenny was silent as she thought about Sally's speech. It sounded memorized, rehearsed.

Sally's voice broke through Jenny's reverie. "First off, Joseph started excommunicating those who were insisting on

dancing. He's right determined to keep us serious and holy."
She slanted her blue eyes at Jenny. "There's a few jolly parties,
but you'd best be happiest with going to church. Joseph's strict
about keeping the church pure. It could be a bore, but we can
take it since Christ is returning very soon. You know, Jenny,"
she shivered fearfully, "it will be terrible for those not ready,
for those who've rejected the Prophet's teaching."

"Tom told me there was a school started for adults," Jenny
said. "I guess that's to help prepare people. He called it a school
for prophets."

"Oh, that's just for the menfolk." Sally lifted the baby to her
shoulder. "Only the men can have the priesthood. Besides, they
just study the revelations Joseph's had from the Lord."

"Well, do the women do anything?"

"Yes. Joseph's urging them to busy themselves. He's of the
opinion that the best way to be content is to work. There's
quilting bees and such all the time."

"After Tamara is older and you don't need me so much, I'm
of a mind to find a way to occupy myself." Jenny said. "I understand there's a newspaper here now. Do you suppose they'd
let a woman work there?"

"It's Cowdery's pet; I suppose the best he'd allow is for you
to sweep the floor."

"Oh, Oliver—I know him!" Jenny exclaimed. "But he was
in Missouri the last time I was here."

"The newspaper was destroyed there. Joseph promised Cowdery he could be editor here."

Kirtland was a town populated only by Mormons, and slowly
Jenny came to see just what that meant. Everywhere she heard,
*Joseph says. . . The Prophet tells us. . . The revelations say this
is the way we are to live. We must sacrifice for Zion.*

Just as Jenny began to chafe against the restricted life,
discontented and frustrated by a prophet who was either away
or writing scripture, summer burst upon Kirtland. Roses spilled
over fences and crowded ditch banks; daisies and bluebells filled
every nook; and Jenny discovered life in Kirtland was as unexpected as the bounty of nature.

She had been busy with her own thoughts, feeling the weight of summer on her restless soul. She imagined the horror on Sally's sweet, gentle face if she were to reveal her secret thoughts. While Sally trembled over being holy enough for Joseph's church, Jenny was studying, planning, plotting—but not how to possess a spot in the kingdom; Jenny's designs were for Joseph himself.

Guilt surged through her as she compared her seething spirit with Sally's sweet serenity.

And then Joseph Smith was striding toward her. His large figure was clad in his customary black broadcloth. She had barely seen him when he gave a curt nod and continued down the street. She hesitated on the sidewalk, stunned. Turning, she dashed across the street to the livery stable.

The tack-room was empty, but the blast of heat and the clang of metal led her on. "Tom!" she gasped, circling the anvil and facing him. "I've just seen Joseph Smith, and he's had a terrible accident. His face is all battered and swollen until I hardly recognized him."

Tom paused. "Well, did you ask him why?"

"He plowed on past me like he didn't know me."

Tom struck the cooling metal with his hammer. "He tangled with his brother William." Dropping the hammer and turning away from the fire, he said, "It's no wonder he didn't do no extra talkin'; the whole church is ashamed of the Prophet bein' whipped by his own brother. William accused him of bein' a false prophet. The fightin' is not something the lot of us can take easy-like."

Jenny was thinking aloud. "When I last visited, he was scrapping in the street. Then the people cheered him on."

"But now he's been whipped good. There's a difference. Then he was winnin'. You can overlook 'bout anythin' when a fella is winnin'. If he's losin', you question."

Jenny recalled Tom's words next when Joseph's excitement surfaced again. This time, when she joined the spectators and listened to him lecture, she realized he was on the winning side. The incident with William seemed forgiven and forgotten.

The new excitement that buzzed in Kirtland was about

mummies from Egypt. Jenny joined the crowd outside the office building which had been hastily renovated to hold the pine cases. When she joined the group, Joseph had just opened them and pointed to the withered human figures.

"What are those things?" Jenny asked.

Someone hissed for silence, but the woman beside Jenny whispered, "They're Egyptian mummies. 'Tis the finger of God sending that fella into Kirtland with those mummies. Joseph's found out there's important writings with them."

Standing on tiptoe, Jenny watched Joseph hold strange, stiff documents so everyone could see the markings. "This one," he pointed, "has the writings of Abraham, and another bears the writings of Joseph of Egypt. I will be formulating the Egyptian alphabet and grammar in order to complete the translation of these writings."

When he finished speaking, Joseph stepped aside and allowed the people of Kirtland to file past the pine cases.

During the remainder of the summer, all of Kirtland waited eagerly while Joseph struggled with the Egyptian writings. Even Jenny's discontent was swallowed up in the curiosity of the event. Some voiced their impatience as he painstakingly labored with the Egyptian alphabet and grammar. They suggested he return to writing by inspiration instead of trying to learn Egyptian. After all, inspiration had given them the *Book of Mormon.*

Some satisfaction did come, however. Joseph discovered enough about the papyrus containing the writings of Abraham to be able to reveal important teachings to the church.

One hot August afternoon, Jenny and Sally had been sharing the latest gossip about the mummies when Sally suddenly asked, "Jenny, are you for joining the church?"

Jenny hesitated for a moment. She recalled the many times she had intimated to others that she intended to join the church. She had even led Tom to believe she was seriously considering the step. She stared at Sally. *How can I say yes? But yes, if that's what it takes to get Joseph. You can't tell people you intend to run off with their prophet because you find him a very attractive man. How do you admit that your designs on a holy man are not holy at all?*

Jenny lifted innocent eyes. "Why do you think I left my job and moved to Ohio?"

Sally leaned forward and clasped Jenny's hands. "I know the feeling. It's an irresistible pulling of the Almighty. Jenny, do you know that some women here in town have left husbands and children to follow this man of God?"

"I haven't joined yet," Jenny said hastily, "but I'm considering."

"Well then, you need to be learning about the laws and ordinances of the gospel. Jenny, the church conference is in a couple of weeks. I believe this is important for you. I'm so convinced, I want you to take time off. Do nothing that week except attend the meetings."

Jenny was ready to protest. She wanted to do almost anything rather than sit in a boring meeting, listening to silly old farmers. Sally lifted her hand, "I know you don't want to be beholden, but your soul's welfare is more important."

So on August 17, 1835, Jenny found herself adorned in her most modest dress walking beside Sally's neighbor, old Mrs. Applewaite. The woman was heavy and walked slowly, but her mind and tongue were quick; she showered Jenny with a fine sprinkling of town talk that bordered on gossip.

"When you get to be my age, there's not much left to life except sittin' on your own front stoop and watchin' the world go by. But that's interestin'. Doesn't take long to begin puttin' two and two together. Like, do you know what's goin' to happen in the Baily-Knight situation? And who's goin' to win out with the Fannie Alger gal? Me, I'm a-keepin' my thoughts to myself on that one, but I don't see any of the young men scorin'.'"

Jenny slanted a glance at the perspiring, red-faced woman and said, " 'Tis such an effort for you to get to meeting, they'll be thinking you've earned those jewels for your crown, most certainly."

She chuckled, "It's worth the effort to hear what those stuffy men will find to talk about today. Some days it's right earticklin'. Won't be so good today; the Prophet's out of town and Rigdon's inclined to be a straight-laced one."

"Oh, my," Jenny sighed and her disappointment was genuine. Any further inclination to attend the meeting vanished, replaced by mounting frustration. She had failed again. The dream which had brought her to Kirtland contained only two people—Jenny and Joseph. It was up to Jenny to make the dream come true—but how could that happen?

They slid into their row and Mrs. Applewaite began fanning herself vigorously. "Whew, 'tis hot! I'm glad we didn't come this morning, too." A dark-suited man headed for the front. "That's Levi Hancock. I guess we'll be singing. There's some good hymns they're a-gettin' up."

When Oliver Cowdery got to his feet, Jenny recalled the Manchester school days and stifled her yawn. He was saying, "I'm before you this afternoon to introduce to you the *Book of Doctrine and Covenants*. Pursuant to this morning's activities, our task will be the endorsement of the book this afternoon."

Rigdon followed him to the podium and began to introduce those chosen to endorse the book. Mrs. Applewaite whispered the names of the men, as if Jenny hadn't already identified most of them on the platform. "That's Phelps. He's the one who got us into a peck of trouble in Missouri by what he wrote in the newspaper there."

Jenny nearly lost track of the day between the woman's whispers and the sameness of the dark-coated men who took their places and advised the congregation that they knew the revelations in the book were true, and that they had been given by the inspiration of the Lord.

In the midst of Mrs. Applewaite's whispered commentary, an idea took shape in Jenny's mind. It had come as Mrs. Applewaite said, "I'm of a mind that most of the people don't have an idea of what's in the revelations. Sure, we've heard snatches and we remember the scary parts, but other than that, we take our beliefs spoon-fed. Ten years from now, we'll have no idea what we believe, betcha. But I reckon it doesn't make much difference; we're followin' the man and a-trustin' him to give it to us straight."

Although Jenny seemed composed and attentive, her fluttering hands twisted the handkerchief into knots, her thoughts as busy as her fingers. In the months since arriving in Kirtland, she had not managed more than a word with Joseph Smith. Certainly not once had there been a chance to be alone with him. She hadn't even a hint of how to bring that about. Now Mrs. Applewaite had given her the solution, gift-wrapped in a clumsy book.

During the rest of the afternoon, Jenny's attention surfaced occasionally as she grasped at straws of information coming from the pulpit; then she succumbed to her private thoughts again. Near the end of the day, the entire congregation was given the opportunity to endorse the *Book of Doctrine and Covenants*. As Jenny's attention lagged, Phelps approached the podium to read an article on marriage. Immediately Jenny's mind was captured, and she strained to catch every word.

Phelps, in his sonorous voice, declared, "Inasmuch as this church has been accused of the crime of fornication and polygamy, we wish to advise the world that we believe one man should have one wife and one woman should have but one husband, except in the case of death, when either is at liberty to marry again. It is not lawful to influence a wife to leave her husband; it is not lawful to influence a child to embrace a religion other than the religion of his parents. It is not right to prevent members of the church from marrying outside of the church, and we believe marriage performed by other authorities than this church is valid. All marriages made before a person becomes a member of this church are to be held sacred." Jenny sat back, lost in thought . . . *except in the case of death, when either is at liberty to marry again.* Unbidden, the picture of the waxen figure came into her mind.

When Oliver Cowdery stood at the podium and opened his paper, Jenny's thoughts were still in turmoil, first attracted by the possibilities, then repelled.

When she finally pushed those dark thoughts aside and straightened, she heard Cowdery saying, "We believe it is right to preach the gospel to all of the earth, for this is the means of salvation. The righteous must be warned to save themselves from corruption. But we do not believe it is right to interfere with bondservants, and this means preaching the gospel to them and baptizing them contrary to the desires of their masters."

When Cowdery finished reading, the article was accepted and ordered to be printed into the *Book of Doctrine and Covenants* by a unanimous vote.

Jenny followed Mrs. Applewaite out of the meeting hall and they turned down the winding lane that led to the far edge of town. Mrs. Applewaite, uncharacteristically silent, was walking rapidly. Jenny studied her face as she trotted to keep up.

Finally Jenny asked, "What did you think of it all?"

"I'm still wonderin' about that last article," she puffed. "I can't decide whether it's sayin' the bondservant's soul isn't all that important or if it's sayin' you keep peace with his masters regardless. Right now, I'm guessin' the writin' came at a pretty important time, considerin' the trouble Joseph and his men had in Missouri. Missouri is a slave state, you know."

When Jenny's path separated from Mrs. Applewaite's, she dropped the good woman's argument just as quickly. As she walked slowly back to the Morgan home, she wondered what polygamy was and why William Phelps was called upon to denounce it.

CHAPTER 23

"I'm starting to feel like a library book!" Jenny exclaimed. Sally laughed as she held the soft blue shawl against her face before folding it. Jenny commented, "That blue matches your eyes—nearly makes me think it's Tamara peeking over at me."

"Oh, do you think we look alike?" Sally asked, pleased. "Her papa thinks so, but I believe he's partial."

"To what?" They turned as Andy Morgan entered the kitchen and Sally crossed the room to her husband. Jenny watched her smile up at him while she stroked his arm. Picking up the laundry, Jenny started up the stairs to her room. As she glanced back, Andy was pulling Sally close.

Unbidden, Mark's face interrupted her thoughts. Jenny recalled the curious blue-green of his eyes, the glint of red the sun coaxed into his sandy hair.

Now Sally was climbing the stairs behind her. "And why do you feel like a library book?"

"Because I keep being checked out."

"Oh, you mean the nursing, the way we pass you around. 'Tis your fault; you proved capable when we had the ague. I still don't know whether it was the nursing or those funny things you mixed together and burned while you were mumbling to yourself. Or perhaps it was the little packet of herbs you made us wear in our clothes." Her eyes reflected curiosity as she studied Jenny. "At times I think I don't know you at all—but, whatever, we need you, Jenny—all of us."

"So you check me out and pass me around."

"Well, you're the most popular book in Kirtland. But you'd

better come back to this library when you've served your purpose."

Jenny finished packing her bag. "I hope I'm as good at the lying-in as I was at the ague. I've never been at a birthing, though my mother often was." Jenny sighed, and for a moment was silent, missing her mother and remembering the hard times.

"No matter, you've a knack. Did you learn from your mother how to use the charms and herbs?" Jenny winced and shook her head. How horrified her mother would have been to hear Sally's question! But for a moment she was caught up, seeing a similarity she hadn't considered before. As far back as she remembered, Ma had been busy nursing the sick back to health and sitting with new mothers.

Jenny turned to Sally. "You've made me think about my mother, and I'm seeing ways we are alike. I'd never thought of it before. Seems when I was at home, I considered Ma's nursing people just a way to earn a penny, but now I see it different."

She noticed the curiosity in Sally's eyes and hastily answered the unspoken question. "I've been living out as a hired girl in Manchester and Cobleskill since my folks moved west."

"Why did they go west?"

Jenny shrugged. "Same as everyone. Hard times and expensive land. They were saying the good land was all west; eastern land was worked out. Must've been true; folks all around us were moving west."

Both women were silent, busy with their thoughts until Jenny recalled her unfinished story. "Anyway, now I'm remembering how Ma would act about her nursing. She had an excitement we young'uns couldn't understand. All we knew was we were being left again. Now I see that the nursing made her feel important, as if she had found a place where she was terribly needed. That's sort of the way I feel. They need me and I feel good when I see people on the mend. I guess Ma and I aren't so different after all."

After Sally walked down the stairs, Jenny amended her statement, but she didn't say the words aloud. They would have shocked gentle Sally. *One difference between Ma and me,* Jenny thought. *Ma was just being a good Christian lady; I'm working with the power. They call me a white witch. And Christian ladies don't like white witches because they can never get past the word witch. They haven't discovered there's no difference in the work we're all doing, but there is a difference in the power to do it. Poor Ma, she could have been a really successful nurse. See, Ma, it isn't the herbs, it's the words you say over them and the power that you bring down that does the healing.*

Two weeks later, Jenny was walking through the streets of Kirtland, headed for a meeting with Joseph Smith—in his office, alone. Tom had passed the information on, and there had been a speculative glint in his eyes. Jenny asked, "Why does he want to see me?"

"Joseph's been hearin' about your nursin' duties and wants to ask a few questions."

While crossing Kirtland, Jenny resolved to question Joseph Smith about his book, the *Doctrine and Covenants*. With the press of nursing duties this autumn, she had been forced to abandon her attempt to confront Joseph. Now she rehearsed the questions she would ask. Surely he would find time to instruct a convert!

"Perhaps, Joseph," she murmured, "we will have many of these meetings." She pressed her hand against that sudden heavy pulse in her throat.

Jenny stopped in front of the print shop. Lingering on the stoop she wiped her sweaty palms with her handkerchief and tried to quiet her racing heart. The door stood open, and she could hear the clatter and thump of the press coming from behind closed doors inside. The aroma of printer's ink was heavy in the air. She sniffed and tried to recapture the excitement and curiosity print shops had inspired in her in the past. But today only one thought occupied her mind, and it had nothing to do with printing.

She bit her trembling lip and took a deep breath. "You silly baby!" she muttered. Over the rumble of the press, she heard the clatter of footsteps and raised her head. Joseph was lumbering down the stairs, two at a time. Abruptly that emotion-charged vision of Joseph and Jenny vanished and she was grinning up at her remembered friend.

Leading the way up the stairs, he opened the door of the room over the print shop, apologizing, "I'm sorry for the poor office, but I seem to be having a time settling down to one spot for more than a season. Next year, when the temple is completed, Rigdon and I will have offices there. Did they tell you the top floor is to be the School of the Prophets?"

She nodded and looked around the shabby room. The whole building was vibrating with the thump of the press at the foot of the stairs. Was it only fancy that the wooden floor moved beneath her feet as she walked? The plain room disappointed her. It was sparsely furnished with a row of narrow wooden chairs facing a table covered with books and papers. Across the room was a couch. And the single window was heavily curtained.

As she sat on one of the chairs, she murmured, "My, it's close in here. Can't we have that window open, Joseph? 'Tis only September; cherish the warm air later."

He laughed. "To tell the truth, that window's been nailed shut. It kept falling out of its casing."

She leaned forward to study the papers littering the table. "Is that part of your translation?" He nodded. "The New Testament? I heard the men talking at the store last week, they were wondering if you'll have to go back and rewrite the *Book of Mormon* now that you've done the translating on the Bible. They're saying the Bible parts in it are all the old—now how do you say it?" She paused, and when he didn't help, she struggled on, "Well, there's not been a Christian church on earth for 1400 years, so the King James Bible was not done by the power of God. This means the *Book of Mormon* needs to be changed where it's quoting the King James Bible, doesn't it?"

Joseph studied her for a long time before he answered. His voice was gentle when he spoke. "Jenny, I didn't bring you here to discuss my translating work. I'm afraid you'll have to leave those things to the presidency for their handling.—I understand that you've been passed around the town as a healer. Is that so?"

Jenny gasped. "Healer! That's the way they see my herbs and such?" She thought about it for a time. Slowly but with growing excitement, she said, "They really believe I can heal them. That's important. They don't think it's just chance. Maybe the power really is starting up!" She sighed a gusty sigh of relief and leaned back in the chair.

Joseph was pacing the room in slow, thoughtful steps. When he stopped he spoke again, "Jenny, you are a beautiful woman, but don't believe your beauty will win you favors."

"What do you mean?" she asked, searching his face and eyes for the kind of gentle charm she had seen at church. "I'm afraid I don't understand."

"You really don't?" He pulled one of the wooden chairs close and sat down facing her. His bright blue eyes seemed curiously light, and in an effort to steady herself, she forced her gaze down to the splintered wooden floor. "Jenny," he commanded her attention again. "You haven't been listening to the right gossip. Haven't they told you about the power struggle? Haven't they talked about Hiram Page using the seer stone, about the others faking the gifts of the Lord? Haven't they told you how the Lord dealt with them severely 'til they admitted they were trying to steal power and gifts that weren't rightly theirs?"

Jenny stared at him. She had heard the stories, but never once did she dream Joseph would see *her* in this light. She chewed at the corner of her mouth, ashamed and contrite. He was saying she was no better than the others. Now she straightened in her chair, realizing the implication of his words. Joseph was angry and jealous because she had power! He was saying she was a threat.

She looked up into that cold, troubled face and an idea surfaced in her thoughts. "I'm sorry," she whispered. "Tell me what I should do."

A smile swept his face with relief, and she closed her eyes against the sight, not knowing why she must, but feeling for a moment as if everything were out of control. He had taken her hands and was tugging her closer. "Jenny, my dear, does that mean that you are ready to let the Lord instruct you? Does that mean you are determined to become one of His chosen?"

She fought a dizzy sensation, like a whirlpool sweeping over her.

Now she remembered why she was here. Pulling her hands free, she opened her eyes, saying, "Joseph, if you've had your say, then I'll have mine. I think you need all the help you can get with these people, and I intend to continue using the power I have to help them."

He was still studying her warily. "Jenny, I've renounced the old ways."

"You mean you've given up using the seer stone and hunting for treasure? Joseph, why?"

"The Lord is helping me see there is a better way. The taint of the seer stone and all the rest will harm the church. I intend to stamp out the credulous and teach these people to rely on the Lord."

She looked at him curiously. "You're acting like you think the stone is bad."

"It's fakery."

The words burst from her before she could measure them. "All those other things, do you really believe them? That the Lord will fight your battles, give you Zion and the wealth of the land? Do you really believe that those who reject your new word from the Lord and the church you have started will be damned to hell?"

Again he captured her hands. "Does that last statement make any difference to you?" Unexpectedly she shivered. Leaning forward he forced her eyes to meet his, saying, "Jenny, I do believe it. All this is truth, and I will prevail as the Lord's chosen until His return to this earth."

With a gasp, Jenny pulled her hands free and jumped to her feet. "Joseph, I—I just can't think anymore today." She turned toward the door, and his hand was on her shoulder.

"Already I sense you are an unusual one. Little Jenny, who would have guessed you would grow into a beautiful—and powerful—woman." His fingers slipped under her chin and forced her to meet his eyes again. "I have a strong feeling that you can help me in the Lord's work." She closed her eyes against the intensity of that expression, but his hands drew her still closer.

For a moment the dizziness touched her again. "Joseph!" she gasped, stepping backward.

"Don't, sister," he warned, holding her firmly. "Jenny, my dear sister in the Lord. You have no idea of the great things that are in store for this church. The Lord himself is just now beginning to tell me His will concerning us."

"Us?" she echoed. "You mean me?" As he nodded and turned back to the table, her thoughts tumbled ahead. Was there a message behind his words? Power, a position close to Joseph, eventually Emma's place. The waxen figure loomed in her mind again—but he didn't know that part. She hesitated before turning back to the table.

Joseph was sitting quietly, barricaded by his books and papers. She rested her palms lightly in the litter and leaned forward. "You asked if I was ready to become one of the chosen—you call them the children of Israel, don't you? And the Indians—are they the lost tribes of Israel? Joseph, there is much I don't know about your church. You've already credited me with intelligence; I demand the satisfaction of knowing what I'm getting into before I join anything."

His lips twisted with amusement. "That's an unusual conversion. Aren't you afraid to risk hellfire and damnation while you are doing your questioning? Methinks you've decided on a better way than faith."

"I've never heard of being asked to believe something I know nothing about."

"Then ask your questions. I prefer that to having you charge out of here saying Joseph Smith demands blind obedience."

She stared at him for a moment, then leaned closer. "Joseph, you are a powerful man; I feel it. But you aren't so powerful that you can elicit cow-like devotion from me."

"And you are so proud that you can't imagine being humbled! Jenny, my dear, that is a challenge."

Now she sat down and smiled, confident that he didn't know how she trembled inside. Folding her hands in her lap, she met his gaze. "Joseph, I attended your church conference meetings. It was nothing more than a bunch of addlepated men who stood up, saying they believe the *Doctrine and Covenants* book is true and from God. I would like to read it for myself and decide whether or not I agree."

"How do you, a credulous child, expect to decide this? I suggest you take their testimony and start believing."

"And I don't get to read it? I haven't read the *Book of Mormon* either. Is that the way you treat all of your converts?"

"On your way out, stop in the print shop and Cowdery will sell you a copy."

She studied his hard jaw and couldn't resist spilling the gossip. "They say you are soft over women, and that Emma only needs to shake her finger to keep you in line. I may cry in order to get my book for nothing."

He bowed. "Go ahead, if you desire to be seen walking down the street with red eyes and the *Book of Mormon*. You may win more converts for me."

Laughing, she jumped to her feet. "Oh, Joseph, I think I shall enjoy taking religious instruction from you! Please sign me up for your classes."

His face froze. "You don't understand. There are no women in any classes I teach. If you need to learn, go to any of the godly women in the church, and they'll teach you."

"Their teaching falls in the category of sewing a quilt or diapering an infant."

His face admitted the truth. "You are right, Jenny. I'll give you books and you bring me your questions."

She got to her feet and leaned across the table. "Thank you, sir; I value your proposal. Now, I'll take the *Book of Mormon*, the *Doctrine and Covenants* and—" She spied the tattered book just under his elbow. "What is that? It looks interesting."

"You can't have that. It's called *Sacred Geography*."

"They say you're still struggling with the Book of Abraham." Instantly she saw the change in him and pressed, "Have you finished it?"

"No, but I've discovered many important things. How good the Lord was to use this method of bringing the books to us! He's given me understanding of the mathematics of heaven. I've learned more now about the star Kolob and how God measures time. He's revealed that the stars are inhabited by eternal spirits.

"—But back to more earthly things. The papyrus of Abraham reveals how the Negro came into being. When Noah cursed his son Canaan, his posterity was marked by black skin, signifying the continuing curse. Old Pharaoh of Egypt was the son of Ham's daughter. Through her line all the Egyptians inherit dark skin."

Jenny interrupted, "And the Negro slaves are part of the cursed ones? What is that supposed to mean to us? At the meetings I heard they weren't to be given the gospel if their owners object."

"That's right. Furthermore, because of their curse, no Negro will ever reach the exalted state. It is impossible to offer the priesthood to a man who wears the curse of Canaan." He sighed heavily but as he stood up, his smile washed over Jenny, lifting the dismal mood of his words.

Touching her shoulder, he said, "But don't let that trouble your pretty head. Just go home and read your books and pass it all around Kirtland that you bested the Prophet and seer by obtaining books for nothing. But be advised, I may have you scrub my floors yet."

Jenny went on her way laughing, but before the books were opened there was yet another call for nursing. It was old granny Lewis filling Jenny's time with the last of her tyrannical demands.

When autumn's browns rimmed with frost, the church took a new step forward. Since Tom's boss, Newel Knight, was involved, Jenny heard about it nearly as soon as the word was released.

For some time Jenny had known that Sarah, young Knight's wife, had died. In fact, until the arrival of Lydia Baily, Tom had tried to push Newel and Jenny together.

One November day Jenny went into the livery stable and found Tom looking as if he had adopted a permanent grin. "Give," she demanded and waited until he put down the harness he held.

"Well, it's this way, my sister, you've forfeited your chance, and Newel has won out doubly."

"Aw, Lydia's husband has consented to divorce."

For a moment his smile wavered. "No." He frowned, hesitated and said, "I'm supposing the world will fuss, but right now I'm too glad. I'll give it no thought."

"Well, what has happened?"

"You know already that Joseph doesn't have a legal state right to perform a marriage ceremony, because he isn't a regular ordained minister like Rigdon. Even a ninny knows that's ridiculous. Seein' he's subject to a higher power and with all the authority of the heavens behind him, well, he took it upon himself to do the marriage anyway."

Slowly Jenny said, "You mean she didn't get divorced, and Joseph married them without having the authority to do so?"

Tom scratched his head as if her words shed new light on the situation. "Jen, I can't understand it all, but I do have faith in Joseph's judgment. You know he has been given the keys of the kingdom. What he binds on earth will be bound in heaven; what he loosens on earth will be loosened in heaven. Matter of fact, Newel said Joseph implied that the church has been given other revelations to the ancient order of marriage that are yet to be dispersed."

Jennie frowned at Tom, watching his face. His smile was uneasy now, and she guessed it was the time to ask the question. "Tom, I heard whispers that Joseph had instructed some of the men going to Missouri to take Indian wives. I also heard Joseph promised that a man would be blessed of the Lord if he were to do so."

Tom moved uneasily. "Yeah, I heard likewise. It hasn't been put to me personally, so I conclude it's rumor." He turned to pick up another harness and Jenny went on her way, puzzling over it all. In the end she shrugged off the questions, laughing at the strange twist of events. She also reminded herself that it was time to forget about all the church structure and rules she had known in the past. This new dispensation had rules of its own, and they must be her rules if she hoped to gain her heart's desire.

CHAPTER 24

"Jen, you're lookin' mighty puny these days," Tom said as he stopped on the snowy streets of Kirtland and waited for Jenny to catch up with him. He took the valise she carried and asked, "Where you headed?"

"Back to the Morgans. Mrs. Lewis finally died," she said with a sigh. "Poor soul, I can't wish her dead, but she was a trial to us all. Angela and Cassy helped me, but she kept us all hoppin'. No doubt she was in pain, but the pain her tongue gave out balanced it all."

"And your herbs and amulets did no good?"

"Nor the charms," she said shortly. "This is likely to ruin my nursing."

"Oh, I don't doubt that you'll have the business."

" 'Tisn't the business!" she snapped. "I'm worried about believing when everything works against the power."

"You think there's a greater power to be had?"

"Could be. It is a lack in me, most certain." Abruptly Jenny lifted her head to look at Tom. "Why the questions? Have you been hearing things?"

"There's talk. People admire the things they can't understand. Where there's indications of the mysterious at work, they're right there lookin'." Tom continued to study the thin little figure at his side. Her shoulders drooped wearily and her head was bowed against the icy pricking of snow filling the air. "Why don't you come to the stable for some hot tea?"

She nodded and silently followed him across the street, through the building, and up the stairs to his room.

The heat of the forge provided warmth for the shabby room Tom called home. Gratefully Jenny sat down on his one straight chair and watched as he stirred up the embers in his stove and pulled the kettle of water over the heat.

After he put the mugs on the table, Tom placed a stool close to the stove and said, "You're pulled a mite too thin. Do you good to get off that horse you're ridin' and walk a spell."

"Meaning?" Jenny pulled the mittens from her hands and unwound her muffler. When Tom didn't answer, she continued, "I've a notion to look for something to do besides nursing. It gets me down at times. Especially when you're expecting results and there's nothing." Abruptly she shivered.

"What's wrong, Jen?"

She looked up. "Oh, I'm remembering the way Mrs. Lewis died. It was like all the spirits on earth congregated. Tom, I don't understand, but she died screaming and pointing. She had been muttering something for days that none of us could understand, talking about turning back. A foul old woman, no doubt, but she frightened us all to the bottom of our shoes." Jenny shivered again and was silent.

At last she roused herself. "I'm pricked with a desire to know the workings of the printing office. Tom, is there a chance Oliver Cowdery would have a little work for me in there? I know women don't normally do such things unless they are married to the fellow running the place, and that's out of the question, since Cowdery's married.—I wouldn't have him anyway. But I would like to look into the business."

"There's little chance. I 'spect the Missus would have your neck if you even went into the place. There's been some talk around about him not minding his manners around the females." Tom got up from his stool to pour the boiling water into his teapot. He was mulling over the problems that had been filling him with unrest for the past month. He glanced at Jenny, studied her innocent, girlish face, and felt again the stab of remorse. *What if she were to become another Fannie Alger?*

He watched her sip tea and then lift her face to smile at him. "Ah, Tom, you were right. I am pressing life too close, and I've a mind to take it easy for a few weeks. Could be I'll feel different about the healing then." The tender, nearly childish smile made him decide.

Taking a deep breath, Tom hunched his stool closer to Jenny and quickly, before he could change his mind, he said, "Jen, there's a few things I need to say to you. First off, Joseph sent a message. I don't know why you've come up with this thing about the healing with the charms and herbs, but for some reason Joe's bothered by it all. Could be it's related to the trouble we had in the beginning.

"See, Rigdon's followers, those that were in Kirtland when we arrived, were into some funny things. Come meeting times, they would work themselves into a real frenzy a-talkin' in a queer language and a-rollin' around on the ground and pretendin' to be convertin' the Indians, such stuff. Anyways, Joe cracked down on it and said it was all from Satan and that people had better be a-drawin' up tight and listenin' to him, since he was the prophet, seer, and revelator.

"Now, your healin's making him a bit uneasy. So I don't blame him. He called me in with a message. He didn't say 'thus saith the Lord,' like he does sometimes, but from the way he said it, I felt it anyway. Jen, he said if you're goin' to be actin' so saintly and do the healin' and all, that you'd better be bringin' forth the fruits of repentance."

Jenny frowned, "Now what on earth does he mean by that?"

"Simple. Joinin' the church and gettin' to services regular. You know Joseph won't abide people a-claimin' a religion they don't follow right."

"I've heard that," Jenny said dryly. "The Morgans let me know right off that I was expected to shun evil, such as dancing and fancy frocks and too much fun instead of work." She waved her mug, "But this latest about not drinking tea and such, I don't understand, especially in the cold of winter. What difference does it make whether we eat meat all year round or just in the winter?"

Tom didn't answer; he was busy thinking about the other things and wondering how he could warn Jenny. He took a deep breath. "First off, I want to remind you that I believe Joseph is called of God. I believe his book is from God, and that's because

I asked God and He gave me the burnin' in the bosom to verify the truth of it all. This keeps me faithful and trustin', even when I don't understand. Jen, I know I'm not too smart and book learnin' just didn't take with me. You'll never know how much I appreciate havin' a prophet and knowin' that I can trust him."

He was silent, staring into the growing dusk. "You were at the last church meeting when President Phelps read the article on marriage. What did you think of it?"

"Think?" Jenny echoed. "Why, nothing. Seems it's not a bit different than what we've always been told."

"Well," Tom said slowly, "I mostly wondered if you'd been hearin' rumors about some of the men misbehavin'. There's rumors circulatin' 'bout the Mormons practicing polygamy." At her blank look, he added, "Havin' more'n one wife. Jen, don't you believe it, and don't you let any fella persuade you different."

Jen laughed. "Oh, Tom," she said, "I'm not newborn. I know there's fellows who'll pass off any story, and I'm not swayed by their talk." She got to her feet and pressed her face against his for a moment. "You are the dearest brother a person could have. I love you for caring for your silly little sister. Now I'll be going before the snow's too heavy for walking."

Tom watched her walk down the street, relieved that he had said part of it, but still troubled by the serious-faced men he had confronted that morning.

"Our prophet," he addressed the line of harnesses hanging in the deserted tack-room, "is too good-lookin' for his own welfare. I hope his good looks don't do him in." He sighed heavily.

The words Warren Parrish and Oliver Cowdery had said followed Tom as he went about his work. *We know for a fact that Joseph has Fannie as wife; we've spied on them and found them together.*

As he sorted harnesses he muttered, "Joe, you told me those fellas were lyin'. I've got to believe you, no matter what. There's nothin' else I know, and there's Jenny; I'm responsible for her."

Jenny went home to Sally and Andy Morgan and baby Tamara. Her dismal failure at the Lewis home was soon forgotten, and January slipped into February.

Sally had assured Jenny that anyone would have failed with old Mrs. Lewis. But Jenny's thoughts whispered back, *Not a white witch. And not someone who's looking for even more power.*

On the days Sally and Jenny weren't busy, Jenny slipped away to her room to read deeply in the green book. After one frustrating session, she closed it, saying, "Oh, how I long to see Clara; if only Adela were here!" Even as she whispered the words, she admitted that the reason for her unhappiness was not her failure with Mrs. Lewis, but the feeling of powerlessness. Staring at the book, she whispered, "If I couldn't succeed with her, how do I get what I want?"

Crossing the room, she pulled out the hunk of wax Clara had given her. "Emma," she whispered. But immediately she pushed it away, shivering at the horrible images it conjured.

Later she pulled out the *Book of Mormon* and the *Doctrine and Covenants* and tried to read them, but within minutes she yawned and exclaimed, "Brother Joseph, we must have a conference!"

When she started down the street that February day, with blessings and admonition from Sally, she whispered to herself, "I've never seen a bunch of people so eager to convert me to the church as these Mormons. Even Lucy Harris wasn't this eager about her church. I can wrap anything up as a desire to know more about Mormonism, and I shall immediately have what I want."

But Jenny changed her mind as soon as she stepped into the print shop. The press was clanging and clattering and the building was vibrating. First she needed to find Cowdery to make her presence known.

When she stepped into the press room, she saw a strange look cross his face. Clasping the book tight, she bravely marched toward him, pushed on by her desire to learn printing. Oliver shut down the press. Giving a quick glance toward the stairs leading to Joseph's office, he closed the door to the street, "Jenny, he doesn't like young ladies in the print shop."

"Even those who would like to learn a little about the business?" she pleaded. "I'd sweep the floor for you if you'd only let me look on, Oliver Cowdery."

His inky hand tugged at his shirt collar and he tried to smile, but she was aware of his uneasiness. "Jenny, you were a good scholar back in the Manchester days, but a good scholar doesn't necessarily make a printer, especially a female."

"I've really come to see Joseph today," she admitted.

He hesitated, glancing upward. As he turned and marched across the press room, he spoke over his shoulder. "He's busy right this minute. This bundle of papers goes down to Whitney. If you'll deliver them for me, so's they can get in the afternoon mail, I'll put you next in line to see the Prophet."

When Jenny returned from Whitney's store, she was licking a peppermint stick. She was nearly to the print shop when the door opened and a young woman stepped out. Glancing at Jenny with a pleasant smile, she murmured, "Good afternoon. We haven't met, but I know you are Jenny. I'm Fannie." She glanced down at the candy.

On impulse Jenny broke the stick and handed Fannie a piece. "Fannie Alger. Sally's mentioned you, said you're the Smiths' adopted daughter." A shadow crossed Fannie's face as she accepted the candy and licked it.

"Oh, thank you, Jenny. It makes today a holiday!" With another pleasant smile she continued down the street, and Jenny entered the shop.

Oliver, now free of printer's ink, was standing at the foot of the stairs. Quickly he said, "Miss Jenny, do go up."

Jenny licked the peppermint and noted his nervousness. "I'd stay here with you if you'd let me help," she bargained, then nearly dropped her candy as a red flush washed across Oliver's face. Muttering, he turned and entered the press room, firmly closing the door.

Jenny was still shaking her head in bewilderment as she climbed the stairs and reached for the door. With her hand on the knob, she saw the sign on the door: *Positively No Admittance*. She was still hesitating when the door was snatched open. "Jenny, come in."

"That sign," she murmured. "I nearly left."

"You've a book." He walked to his chair and sat down. Indicating the chair across from him, he said, "I take it you've read it."

She shook her head. "No. As a matter of fact, I found it boring, and I decided to come ask questions instead."

"I told you it was too much for women to handle. Are you now willing to let the men wrestle with the doctrine and just be a good little lady like the others?"

She grinned up at him. "How do you expect me to be a good little lady when I haven't been told *how*?"

"That is another challenge," he replied softly.

In the silence of the room, she was becoming very aware of Joseph. Slumped and at ease across from her, he smiled and waited. She studied his fair hair and light blue eyes, wondering why sitting in the same room with him caused all her carefully prepared questions to flee her mind.

Not one question concerning the doctrine of his church presented itself, but other thoughts arose, the gossip. She wanted to ask him if it were true that he and Emma were having problems. What had Tom meant when he referred to the whisper of polygamy?

Jenny's mind floundered. Under the steady eyes, she struggled and brought up the only thing she could remember. "Your mother went to the Manchester church we attended. She was saying in front of us all that when the translating of the gold plates was done, she intended to show them. Now I'm hearing rumbles because you didn't. Why?"

Slowly Joseph sat up and leaned forward. He had discarded his jacket and loosened his tie. Watching him pick up a slender letter opener and flex the blade, she studied him. The muscles in his shoulders rippled as he played with the letter opener. For a time he bent the shiny blade back and forth. When he looked up the serenity was gone; a restlessness in his eyes caught her attention. The troubled frown darkened his face, making her forget her vision of the bright young giant.

"There's too many of these rumbles. Sometimes I hear about them. Sometimes I don't." He paused to pass his hand across his face in a weary gesture. Jenny was filled with an overwhelming desire to go to him, to touch away the weariness. She recoiled in horror when she realized the direction her thoughts were taking her.

As he got up and paced the room, Jenny bit her lip and clasped her hands together. One thing was certain: if just once she gave into those strange impulses, all hope of winning Joseph would be gone. She would be only a woman of the street. "Easy come, easy go," she whispered, grateful that somehow her mother had impressed her with that message.

He turned, "What did you say?"

"Nothing." She nearly stuttered the word. He crossed the room and sat beside her.

"Jenny—" His forced smile was twisted and miserable, his eyes troubled. "This being a prophet isn't easy street. It's a mighty lonely business. No matter how straight I walk the line, there's those who gossip and pick fault. My own close followers undermine me and try to ruin me. They don't understand. I didn't dream up the teachings and the revelations. I'm following God. Jenny, do you see? I need a friend. I need someone who will keep me informed of the whispers. I need to know how to answer these people. Will you be that person, to stand by me and be willing to tell me my faults, to help me in this business?"

"But I thought Rigdon was supposed to be that person. In the revelations the Lord said Sidney was to be your John the Baptist. I read that far."

Joseph shook his head. "He's too close. I suppose he has stars in his eyes. But I sense in you a willingness to tell me the worst and demand an answer. Help me, Jenny." For a moment he dropped his head and that bright hair was only inches from her face. She caught her breath and pushed back against the chair. When he raised his head his eyes searched her face.

"Of course, Joseph," she whispered. "You know I would do anything to help you."

And when she was at the door, ready to walk downstairs, she turned. There was a question in his eyes as he waited. She said, "You didn't answer me." She saw he didn't remember, and prodded. "I asked why you didn't show the plates like Lucy said you would."

He came and bent close so she could see the torment in his eyes. Slowly he said, "Jenny, I was deceived. Do you hear me, do you understand? Ask no more."

As she walked back to the Morgans', her thoughts were full of Joseph; particularly she was thinking of that last statement. *Who had deceived Joseph? Did this have something to do with his failure with the seer stone and his reluctance to use it now?*

The next Sabbath Jenny came down to breakfast wearing her dark challis print. Sally's eyes widened and Jenny nodded. "Your guess is right. I'm going to church with you today." The questions still filled Sally's eyes as Jenny sliced bread and carried dishes to the table.

"See, I've decided, just like Tom told me, that if I intend to join the church I'd better be finding out what's being preached on the Sabbath. Also, I've shunned church so I scarcely know my neighbors. Do you know, I met Fannie Alger coming out of Joseph's office the other day, and I didn't know who she was until—" Jenny stopped and watched Andy Morgan sputtering over his breakfast. Sally was thumping him on the back. "Whatever is wrong?" Jenny asked.

"I don't know." Sally's face tilted toward Jenny. "Get some water. Oh my, I hope it isn't his heart."

He pushed back from her restraining hands. "I'm all right, wife." His voice still sounded strangled as he said, "You are right, Jenny. It is proper that you go to church. What were you doing at the printing office?"

"Why, Joseph gave me books to read."

Walking to church, Jenny wondered about that strange expression on Andy's face. But she shed her thoughts at the door, uncomfortably aware that since last August's church meeting, she had filled every Sabbath with activity rather than face the restraint of the weekly meetings.

"Jenny Timmons—I do declare." The voice gasped close to Jenny's elbow, and she turned to see Lucy Smith, the Prophet's mother.

"Oh, Mrs. Smith!" she gave the little woman a quick hug. "And Mr. Smith," she added as she saw the tall, lanky man beside Lucy.

"It's been so long," Lucy continued, "since the Manchester days. I wouldn't have known you except that Tom told me you are livin' here now. You must come and visit."

When the couple sat down on the bench in front of her, Jenny realized, with a pang of regret, that she had missed them. The sermon droned around her head, but Jenny's thoughts were full of memories of the Smith home, and she quickly grew eager to take up the friendship again.

On Tuesday of the same week with directions from Sally, Jenny went to call on the Smiths.

Jenny had Lucy all to herself. With cups of the forbidden tea, the two spent the morning talking about all they remembered of Manchester.

At noon Mr. Smith returned with Oliver Cowdery in tow. Jenny was surprised at Oliver's discomfort. Excusing herself, she went to help Lucy prepare a meal for the men.

When she carried the bowl of stew to the table, she found the men reminiscing. They were crowded together on the bench, and Mr. Smith reached for her arm, saying, "We were a-talkin' about the things that transpired when Joe found the gold Bible. My, those were the days!"

"Fearful, wonderful days," Lucy said comfortably as she took her place at the table. "I was just thinkin' the other day of the findin' of it."

Oliver helped himself to the stew. "Willard Chase was telling me what you'd related to him, about dressing Joe up in his black suit of clothes and finding a black horse for him to ride. He also told me how when Joe got out the book of gold, he made the mistake of placing it back, and it disappeared. He explained that Joe found the book back in the box where it had been in the first place. He tried to take it out and was hindered by something in the box that looked like a toad; then, before his eyes the toad changed into the appearance of a man and struck him." Shaking his head, Oliver paused in his story and picked up his spoon.

Mr. Smith wiped his mouth and said, "Well, I'll tell you, those devils sure made a commotion."

"Devils!" Jenny exclaimed. "I didn't know about them."

"Yessir," he nodded. "Joe took a pillowcase to put the plates in and a bunch of devils followed him. See, they were trying to keep him from gettin' the plates. One kicked him a good one. Joe had black and blue marks for days."

Oliver nodded, saying, "Joe himself told me that when he first went to the Hill Cumorah, he saw the prince of darkness surrounded by his cohorts."

It was late when Jenny left the Smith home, much later than she had intended. As she walked through the shadowy streets of Kirtland, she realized she was the only person out.

The evening mists were drifting through the empty streets. The soft glow of lamplight filled the windows of the small log houses, streaking the street with pale light. She quickened her steps and heard the echo rebounding from the brick of the printing office and Whitney's store.

Now she caught the sound of footsteps ahead. With her mind full of the tales she had heard at the Smith home, she began to hurry, running to catch up with those other lonesome feet. Rounding a corner, she saw the dark-cloaked figure ahead. Jenny called, "Hello!"

Jenny saw a brief flash of red as the woman turned and the light from a supper lamp momentarily illuminated her. Jenny ran toward her, but the woman disappeared around the corner.

CHAPTER 25

Halfway through February, Jenny stood at the kitchen window in the Morgans' snug log house. Behind her the sun had painted bright strips across the whitewashed walls and the teakettle was shooting steam into the air. But Jenny was heedless of the pleasant picture Sally's kitchen presented; she was studying the landscape still painted in snowy outlines. A rustle behind her, followed by a coo and a gurgle announced Sally and Tamara's presence.

"I'm trying to list the changes in the neighborhood that indicate spring's on the way," she explained without turning. "Just moments ago I saw a cardinal—but that doesn't mean spring. The snow is starting to shrink in upon itself like old Mrs. Lewis did before she died."

Sally's skirts rustled again and Jenny turned. "You want gruel for Tamara?" As she passed the pair she fingered the baby's soft curls. "Oh, that's a pretty baby today." Tamara rewarded her with a gurgle while Sally nodded and smiled. Jenny poured the boiling water over cornmeal and stirred it as the thin mixture bubbled on the stove.

Sally sat down and tucked a bib under Tamara's chin. "Andy tells me that Joseph's talking hard about sending him to Missouri with the others in two weeks' time. I hope you won't be called to nursing. I'm so lonesome when he's gone I nearly perish."

Andy Morgan walked into the room in time to hear her lament. He bent over his wife and daughter and kissed them both. "I'm flattered," he murmured; "also relieved that you prefer Jenny's company."

Sally tipped her head back and looked at her husband. "Andy, what can you possibly mean by that?"

"Only that you are a beautiful woman and I don't want to share you."

Sally's voice was dry as she answered, "I'm also married." The silence in the room was broken only by Tamara's contented sounds and the clink of the spoon against the dish. Sally lifted her head again and watched her husband struggling with the buttons on his collar. "You are a very dignified attorney, and I am proud of you."

"I only wish there were a few more dignified attorneys in town; then I'd spend some time at home." His voice was grim, and Jenny turned from her spot at the window to study his face. He saw her and smiled, but she still noticed the tired lines on his face.

As Jenny checked the biscuits in the oven and turned the bacon in the skillet, she pondered the troubled air that had followed Andy into the room.

Breakfast ended and the outer door had closed behind Andy. Jenny, her hands moving among the dishes, gently asked, "Why is Andy going to Missouri, and why is he so disturbed?" When there was no answer, she turned to look at Sally. The blonde head was bent close to Tamara's as she wiped at the baby's face, but Jenny could see she was chewing her lip. Jenny waited until Sally lifted her head.

"You might as well know." Her voice was throaty with tears. "There's gossip among some of the apostles and the seventy that Joseph's been making indecent proposals to some of the married women in Kirtland. Every good-looking woman in town is suspect, particularly by her husband." She gasped and continued, "Oh, Jenny, don't look at me in that manner! I'm not making this up. I didn't know about it at all until Andy began questioning me as if I were on trial in court."

Sally's tears won out, and Jenny went to take the baby. As she cuddled the soft, milk-scented body against her face, she watched Sally struggle for control. Finally she knelt beside

Sally and said, "Andy can't believe those things about you."

"You don't know. He was so jealous before we were married that I dared not smile at anything in trousers."

"I'll have to go see Joseph today," Jenny declared. "I'll see that he reassures Andy."

Sally mopped tears from her eyes and soberly studied Jenny, "I wish that, but I wonder how much effect it will have. I understand the men are trying to quiet the rumors before they reach the church's enemies."

As Jenny walked toward the print shop, she was thinking of her first visit. Abruptly she realized she was giving Joseph the assistance he requested.

But at the office, Oliver's sweating face came between her and the stairs that led up to the little room. "Miss Jenny, I've told you before you must have an appointment. The Prophet is a busy man."

"Then announce me; I know he'll see me." Oliver's face flushed and the look he turned on her was perplexing. She frowned and waited.

His face cleared abruptly and he said, "You've been wanting to see the workings of the press—come ahead. I was just starting it up."

As they were bending over the neat rows of lead type and Jenny was trying to read the reversed words, a whisper of sound and creaking boards made her look up. Joseph was closing the street door after a dark-cloaked woman. Jenny's pounding heart gave weight to her guesses.

"Who was that woman?" Her voice came in a whisper as she moved toward Joseph, and the Prophet studied her with a frown before he answered. "She is Mrs. Martindale; her first name is Adela and her husband is William."

Now her voice squeaked, "They live in Kirtland?"

"Yes. They've just converted to the church and I expect we will benefit greatly. Martindale is an exporter worth a great deal of money."

Jenny followed him up the stairs. After his enigmatic look at her question, she dared not ask where the couple lived. He settled behind the desk and waited with a quizzical expression in his eyes. Jenny still hesitated over her mission; she was fighting the impact of his presence.

He broke the silence, "Did you read the books?"

She shook her head. "I haven't had time. Since last autumn I've had one round of nursing care after another."

"I've heard," he answered shortly. "And what is your rate of cure?"

"All of them." But she had to admit, "Likely they'd all have recovered without the charms and amulets."

"But you did a great deal of chanting and fussing and everybody treated you like God himself."

She sat on her hands to keep from squirming and retorted, "But isn't that the way they treat *you*?"

"Yes, but I am the Prophet and I deserve the recognition."

"Because you hear from God. More than I? Joseph, why is—" Abruptly and impatiently he got to his feet and stomped around the desk to her.

"Jenny Timmons, I will broach no sass from the baby sister of one of my men. Neither will you draw people to yourself. The Lord has commanded against such as this. If you had been reading the *Book of Commandments* you would know this." He pointed toward the door, "Now go and don't return until you've read them all."

"I didn't come to —"

"Go." His jaw tightened, and the color fled from his face. Jenny bit her lip and turned away.

"Joseph," she whispered, freely allowing the disappointment to well up in her voice. Her frustration was augmented by the memory of what she had heard—they said tears melted Joseph. "You've asked me to—to tell you, and now you won't listen." She touched her eyes and moved toward the door.

"Wait!" As she heard the command, she also heard the clink of metal striking the floor. She turned and saw a silvery disk spinning on the floor between them.

While Joseph fumbled with his handkerchief, she snatched up the talisman and held it in her hand. The strange markings were familiar, but where her own talisman had a woman's figure, his carried only strange letters inscribed within squares.

She was still busy comparing it with her own when the import of it all struck her. She raised her face to meet his eyes. "What does it all mean?"

"The letters? Jenny, it isn't important to you." He held out his hand for the talisman, and she quickly stepped away. He was perspiring.

"Not important? Then I'd like to keep it. I'll show it to my grandchildren to prove I've known the man from God, the Prophet Joseph Smith."

"Jenny!" he spoke sharply, moving toward her. She slipped the shiny metal down the front of her dress and hurried around the table.

"Joseph," she said, "what about Abbah and El Ob and Josiphiel?"

"Why, they are the names of God. How did you know?"

She patted the front of the frock. "And what are the powers at your disposal?"

He hesitated a moment before answering, but when he spoke, the words lay lightly on his tongue. "The celestial intelligences assigned to this metal will help me in all my endeavors."

She repeated slowly, "Abbah, El Ob, and Josiphiel—I know the last means Jehovah speaks for God. But the other two I don't understand."

Leaning forward he whispered earnestly, excitement mounting in his voice, "When these intelligences are invoked properly with all of the power of ancient magic, I am guaranteed riches, power, honor. Do you know, Jenny, when I control these forces properly, no one can resist my love, neither friend nor foe, man nor woman." He still held her with that penetrating gaze, and she felt the pulse in her throat mount in tempo.

She whispered, "But now the talisman is in my hands. Does that mean all the powers are for me?"

"You will give it back right now, or I will take it!" Turning, Jenny fled to the door. She had nearly reached it when she stumbled, and he was there with his arms tightening around her. He turned her, holding her motionless. "This is what you wanted all along. Yes, Jenny, the power is mine." He bent over her and his lips were hard and then gentle against hers. When he raised his head, he said simply, "It does work, doesn't it?"

She was trembling, and she took a moment to be certain her voice was firm before saying, "Yes, it works, but are you certain it is working for you? Remember, I hold it now." She laughed merrily at the startled expression on his face.

Now out of his arms, she moved to the door just as a pounding began on the other side. "Joseph!" came the low urgent voice, "Michael says Emma is coming to the print shop."

Joseph stared at her in dismay. "Quick, give it to me." She shook her head. "I will shake it out."

"Then you will be shaking it out when Emma comes."

Disbelief and distaste swept his face. He yanked at the door. "Jenny, you are a witch. I'll have you yet."

As he shoved her through the door, she hissed, "Andy Morgan will have your hide if you don't explain the gossip before nightfall. How is that for seeing the future?" She flew down the stairs.

The talisman bit into Jenny's flesh, but she hugged her shawl tight, put on a sweet smile, and walked serenely down the street.

A few weeks later Tom had left the stable and was turning his horse toward Thompson. Now, full of troubled thoughts about Jenny, he felt a compulsion. Abruptly he turned his horse off Kirtland's well-traveled main street and headed down the lane that led to the Morgans'.

The early March day had been balmy and sweet, and the evening sky was filled with color. Tom noted with pleasure that the few clouds visible were puffy and pale like mounds of whipped cream. Jenny was crossing the Morgans' yard.

"Sis, hold it!" When he reached her side, he said, "I'm thinkin' the Lord's promptin' me to go to Hyrum tonight. How would you like to ride with me? Joseph told me he would be leadin' a cottage meeting there this evenin'." While she hesitated, he added, "You made a good start with your church attendance until lately. Maybe the Lord's wantin' me to prod you on by takin' you to meetin' with me."

Jenny stood on the step with the warm eggs clasped in her apron and cocked her head to study Tom's earnest face. "I wouldn't mind going, but horseback doesn't appeal."

Sally stuck her head out the door. "I heard you, Tom. If your horse is willing, the horsecart's in the barn, you're welcome to it."

So Tom and Jenny set off for Hyrum in the Morgans' cart, with Jenny asking, "Why is Joseph in Hyrum?"

"I don't know his exact business, but I do know he was goin' to the Johnson farm where he lived some time back. He told me earlier he intends stoppin' by the Rollins farm, too. Sometime back they'd extracted a promise from him to hold a meetin' there."

"Cottage meeting," Jenny mused. "I've never heard of such a thing."

"Some mighty good meetin's we've had, when the Prophet's right down among us. You'll see."

By the time Jenny and Tom reached Hyrum, dusk had brought a chill with the drifting mists. Jenny snuggled gratefully into her shawl. "There's several wagons and carts here. How did the word pass so quickly?"

Tom shrugged. "I don't know. These folks work hard to get the Prophet to themselves for an evenin'."

Inside the tiny cottage Jenny and Tom found seats on the planks supported by boxes. The room was crowded, and the kerosene lamps were turned nearly to the smoking point. Jenny folded her shawl away from her shoulders and tried to make herself inconspicuous. She hadn't seen Joe since that day, two weeks past, when she had confronted him in his office. Now his talisman was pinned next to her own, and her lips tingled again with the remembered pressure of his kiss. She glanced about, wondering whether Emma Smith was in the room. Jenny was still darting quick glances about when Joseph entered. In the dimness his white collar above the dark coat framed his face with light, and Jenny felt her pulse quicken.

Even after the meeting started, people continued to arrive. Jenny and Tom squeezed close together along with everyone else. During prayer and singing, Jenny stumbled over the unfamiliar words. Finally Joseph stood to speak, but she was oblivious to his message as she studied his face.

Suddenly he stopped mid-sentence and stared out over the heads of his rapt audience. The moment of silence stretched, and Jenny felt tension mount; not a whisper of sound stirred the air. She watched Joseph's face pale and his eyes glow; their brilliance seemed to spread and infuse every pore of his face with light.

The silence held, but now Jenny was aware of a strange movement through her body, as if unseen forces were propelling her closer to the Prophet. His whole being filled her vision, and nothing else existed.

When his voice broke through, Jenny sighed deeply, hearing him say, "My brothers and sisters in the Lord, do you know who has been in our midst tonight?"

A breathy sigh echoed the answer, "An angel of the Lord."

Suddenly a man sitting on a box facing the Prophet dropped to his knees and wrapped his arms around Joseph's legs. Jenny watched his head tilt backward in adoration and the murmur of his voice held the room. "It was our Lord and Savior, Jesus Christ."

With a gentle smile, Joseph looked down at the man. As he placed his hand upon his head, he said, "Martin Harris, God revealed this to you. My brothers and sisters, I want you always to remember this. The Savior has been in your midst.

"Because you are weak in the Lord, He must cast a veil over you. You cannot endure the splendor of His presence. I want you to remember this. He has given you to me, commanding me to seal you up for everlasting life."

As Jenny and Tom rode back to Kirtland, he said, "Jen, you're awfully quiet. Did it affect you that way too?"

She stirred and sighed, trying to sort through the jumble of feelings, especially that most troubling one. "Martin Harris. I didn't realize he was in Kirtland." She shuddered, remembering the horror of the day in Manchester when he had beaten her and his wife.

Tom's arm wrapped about Jenny, and she knew he felt the trembling. He cleared his throat. "Tyke, Martin Harris is no angel, but if gettin' religion changes a man, you better believe Martin'll never be beatin' another woman."

CHAPTER 26

The temple was complete. The last stone and shingle had been placed, the final brush of paint had dried, and the last canvas veil had been hung. Only a few days remained before the dedication, and excitement in Kirtland was mounting.

The temple was situated on a slight rise, away from the congestion of the main section of town. Already the three-story stone building with its square steeple had attracted people from miles around.

These days Tom often found himself standing in the doorway of the blacksmith shop watching the people on the street. Like an indulgent uncle, he listened to their comments and noted their obvious pride as they detoured from their accustomed routes in order to pass by the temple.

"It's sure been a grand undertakin'," Tom said to Newel. "From the hole in the ground to the pile of stone and wood shapin' up, it belongs to everybody in town."

Newel matter-of-factly said, "It is. It's our money and sweat and even a little blood that's built it."

"Make you wonder what's goin' to happen at the dedication?"

Newel nodded, flipping away the twig he had been chewing. "Particularly after Zion's Camp." They fell silent, both remembering the pain and failure of that time in Missouri. Then Newel roused himself. "Prophet Joseph said the Lord promised a great blessing to the elders when the temple was completed."

"Even if it doesn't live up to what we're hopin' for," Tom continued soberly, "there's still the promise that just gettin' it

254

built and dedicated releases us to go and redeem Zion."

"Thus saith the Lord," Newel said softly, turning away.

Later that day, while Tom was sweating at the forge, Newel came in. "The Prophet has called a special meeting in the temple."

Tom shoved the sheet metal back into the forge to heat. "What's goin' on?"

"The apostles and the seventy as well as the councils are going to be given the rites for the temple ceremonials." He touched his forehead. "See you tonight. I've got to spread the word."

That evening when Tom walked into the temple with the other men, he was struck by the quiet dignity of the place. The group assembled in the lower auditorium. Tom knew from his work on the building that the floor above them held another auditorium with the same unusual feature—twelve pulpits to accommodate the twelve apostles.

Walking to the front of the auditorium, Tom stood looking up at the window arching behind the pulpits constructed for the members of the Melchizedek priesthood. Above the window, stretching like a banner, were the words, *HOLINESS UNTO THE LORD.* Soberly Tom took his place. The words ushered him into a solemn mood that made it easy to enter into the service.

When Joseph walked into the auditorium carrying the bottle of oil, the men were hushed and waiting. The lanky, graying father of the Prophet was called forward, placed on a stool, and surrounded by elders. Joseph raised his right hand and bade the men do likewise.

After Joseph had blessed the oil and poured some upon the head of his father, he motioned his men to come together. Gathering as close as they could, the men in the center placed their hands upon the gray hair of the man before them.

In the candlelight Joseph's face became transfixed and pale. Looking upward, he softly intoned, "The heavens are open before me. I am seeing the celestial kingdom of God with all attending glory. Whether in the body or out, I do not know. I see glorious beauty . . ." His words moved on, sweeping around Tom.

"The gate, like circling flames of fire, the blazing throne of God, and seated thereon, the Father and the Son."

Each of the elders in turn took his place to receive his blessing. With a shout, one lifted his arms and exclaimed, "I see the heavens opening before me!" Later another acknowledged, "The angels are ministering to us."

On successive nights the rest of the elders received their blessings. In culmination, Joseph sealed all of the blessings, instructing the men in this final ceremony that all which had transpired had been sealed in heaven.

At home Andy Morgan talked about these events. "He called this the patriarchal blessings," Andy said. "These days have yielded wonderful visions and promises given to the men called out to do the work of the Lord. Some of the patriarchal blessings were particularly noteworthy." He was silent for a moment and Jenny continued her work about the kitchen.

While Morgan talked about the meeting, a troubled frown kept appearing on his face. Now, as if suddenly recalling that he had stopped mid-tale, he raised his head and continued. "When James Brewster was receiving his blessing, it was revealed that he was to be a prophet, seer, revelator and translator. Power is to be given from God to enable him to discover and obtain treasures that are hidden in the earth." Jenny dropped the pan she was wiping and Andy jerked upright in his chair. "What's—"

"Oh, nothing," she broke in hastily. Biting her lip, she added, "But I understood that treasure digging was all in the past, that it was to be forgotten now."

Andy shook his head slowly. "I'd heard that too," Andy agreed. "I can't understand. But then, who knows the mind of the Lord except the Prophet?" He sighed and continued. "There was another one that was truly amazing. Joseph's father gave this blessing. He told a youth that before he reaches the age of twenty-one, he will preach the gospel to the inhabitants of the islands of the sea and even to the inhabitants of the moon."

Finally, hands on hips, Jenny demanded, "You're telling of the most wonderful things. Yet at the same time I see you frowning over it all. Why?"

He stared at her in astonishment. Slowly he said, "I can't forget the beginning days of the Mormons in Kirtland. You see, Jenny, I was one of Rigdon's original followers. At the time it rubbed us wrong to have this young man, Joseph Smith, claiming to be a prophet from the Lord, spouting the language of an uncouth farm boy while he was telling our silver-tongued Rigdon what to do. One of the first things he undertook was to call all the spirit outpouring the devil's work and demand that we forget it all." He stopped suddenly and flushed.

Jenny nodded, "And now the same thing is going on in the temple. The town's rocking with it. No wonder you frown."

His face cleared, and with a relieved smile he said, "I don't mean to complain; it's just a hard thing to swallow. Jenny, I do believe he's a prophet from the Lord; don't doubt my loyalty. Any common plowboy who can convince this lawyer he's from God, well—it's truth."

Sally had been nodding her head at every word her husband spoke. But Jenny was surprised at the wistful note in her voice as she added, "It is true, he is a prophet from God, and we must believe everything he says or we'll be damned for all eternity. It is impossible to reject truth and still make it to heaven."

The dedication took place on March 27, 1836. As Jenny walked through the streets of Kirtland to the temple, she was still mulling over Sally Morgan's statement. There had been something strange about her declaration, something that had tugged at Jenny and left her feeling uneasy. How deeply Sally feared for her soul's salvation!

Although Jenny had purposely left the Morgan home early in order to have a choice seat, the streets were already filled with people heading toward the temple. As she quickened her steps, the air of excitement engulfing the people grabbed her, too.

A reverent hush touched all who entered the auditorium. She recognized it as she took her seat beside her fellow worshipers.

Later, Joseph Smith, with the presidency and the twelve, filed into the building. How solemn their faces were! Their expressions reflected the awe she was feeling. The songs they sang, the music they heard seemed to echo about as if wafted on angels' wings. Later in the muted silence, even the smallest infant was quiet.

When the Prophet stood to speak, Jenny studied his broad, tall figure suitably clothed in black. The black heightened the pallor of his face as he shook back his bright hair and lifted his face heavenward. The words of his prayer fell like jewels on his eager followers.

Jenny forgot to bow her head. Caught by the mysterious air that filled the temple, she was momentarily transfixed. But suddenly her mood was shattered by a clear memory of the last time she had been with Joseph. He had been in shirtsleeves, with his collar loosened, kissing her freely, even passionately.

Jenny's eyes drifted toward the corner where she knew Emma was sitting with her children. The dark head was modestly bent. Jenny wondered at the astonishment and uneasiness that suddenly possessed her. Restlessly she moved, gripped by emotion. Was it because she was in the temple and under the mysterious influence called God? She studied the solemn face of the prophet and suddenly laughter formed deep within her. *If I am uneasy,* she thought, *what must HE feel?*

When Jenny walked home, the conversation around her reflected the grandeur and awe. A thousand believers had crowded the temple auditorium, and another thousand had lingered outside. But there was one note of disappointment. As old Mrs. Bolton said, "We didn't hear none of those grand things like those who got their patriarchal blessings saw and heard. I'm right disappointed about that. And seems on this day they'd let the womenfolk worship in there with the men come evening."

She paused for a moment and then added. "Those that got their blessings said that in the midst of the Prophet's praying, he stopped death-still and the men saw a white dove fly through the window and light on the Prophet's shoulder. He told them later it was the Holy Spirit."

That dedication evening the men began two days and two nights of worshiping and fasting in the temple. The women grumbled, but their curiosity remained unsatisfied except for occasional reports drifting out to them. The first report told of the Savior appearing to some, while others said angels ministered to them.

According to Tom, the Prophet had urged the men to prophesy, saying that the first to open his mouth would receive the gift of prophecy, and that whatsoever he prophesied would come to pass. At one point a sound like a rushing mighty wind filled the temple, and men jumped to their feet, speaking in tongues and seeing visions. As the stories spread, townspeople rushed to the temple to stand outside and stare in awe at the bright light coming from within. Angels had filled the temple, Joseph reported.

The final hours were recounted by Andy Morgan. Joseph and Oliver Cowdery climbed into their pulpits and lowered the canvas veils around them. He and his friends, Morgan said, had sat in the audience, hardly daring to breathe in the silence.

When the curtains were rolled back, the watching men gasped. Deathly pale, Oliver sat looking heavenward. Joseph stood to his feet and, lifting his arm heavenward, declared softly, "We have seen the Lord. He stood on the breastwork of the pulpit before us. Underneath His feet lay a path of pure gold, and His entire countenance gleamed. His message was that our sins are forgiven us. We are to lift up our heads and rejoice because the Lord has accepted this house and His name shall be here. Then Moses appeared and he committed to us the keys for the gathering up of the children of Israel from the farthest parts of the earth, beginning with the tribes in the northernmost regions of the world, the Eskimos.

"Then Elias and Elijah told us that we have the keys for this dispensation committed to us. By this we are to know that the Great Day of the Lord is close at hand."

"Oh my!" Sally gasped on hearing the report. Relief flooded her face with color and brightness, and she touched a finger to the corner of her eye. Reports continued to circulate and magnify. Jenny was aware that she was not untouched by it all, but Sally's later question made her face the issue squarely.

Jenny and Sally were working in the spring-warmed garden, and Jenny was particularly aware of the texture and odor of the soil. Sally broke the calm, "Jen, not once have you commented on the dedication of the temple. I know you have a seeking mind. What did you think of it all? Do you believe it was a manifestation of God?"

In the moment of waiting, Jenny realized that this was the question that had burdened her since the event. Examining the evidence, she realized there was only one answer. Rocking back on her heels, she looked up at Sally. "Of course. How could I possibly think otherwise?" But the answer left her feeling empty.

During the following two months, Jenny was surprised to find that no one in Kirtland needed her services as a nurse. Sally advised her to not fret about it; possibly the Lord realized she needed a rest and was keeping the Saints well. Then with a stern eye lifted from her sewing she said, "I'd spend the time reading up in those books you told the Prophet you must read before joining the church. Jenny, I must warn you; the Lord won't be patient forever—especially since you have the witness."

Thus on a bright day in May, Jenny tucked the *Book of Mormon* and the *Book of Commandments* under her arm and set out for the woods. She carried several small muslin bags in the pocket of her apron, knowing she would spend most of the time enjoying the sunshine and searching for those special plants to dry and grind into powder for potions.

With her nose bent earthward, muttering the names of the plants she should seek, Jenny was mostly oblivious to the day and the beauty that surrounded her.

Her restless feet roamed back and forth across the trail which cut through the woods. The various paths joined the settled areas around Kirtland.

"Salsify, cinquefoil, bluebonnet, vitch," she was murmuring when a voice broke in upon her reverie.

"It's Jenny. I do declare." Jenny heard the melodious voice and raised her head to blink into the shadows, searching for the speaker. "From the looks of things I do believe you are searching for the secret ingredients. That means only one thing."

Jenny gasped. "Adela! It has been years since I've seen you, but I'd know you anywhere. You haven't changed."

"You've grown," the silky voice continued. Jenny sat down on the log beside the woman and studied her carefully. From the glossy hair streaming down her back to the smooth ivory of her skin, she was indeed, the same. But there was one difference: Adela was now wearing the modest dress and apron of a common housewife.

"You aren't wearing your beautiful red chiffon!" Jenny exclaimed. "What a disappointment!"

"You nearly surprised me once in my red chiffon."

Jenny studied the woman, "So that *was* you. I dared not hope. I tried to hail you." Jenny was silent a moment thinking of the cloaked woman coming out of Joseph's office.

Adela folded her arms. "So you weren't ready for the sabbat. You ran like a silly baby, leaving us all to think you a waste. You nearly ruined the whole evening. Only after a great deal of effort were we able to salvage the ceremony. We had to coax before the spirits would come back."

Speaking as if in a dream, Jenny murmured, "The townsmen were angry the next day when they found what you had done to the church."

"But you didn't tell." Adela was whispering, leaning close to scrutinize Jenny's face. Jenny was certain she read her inmost secrets, but perhaps Adela had known them all along.

"For a while I was afraid we had lost you to Mark. Jenny, you will be successful, and you can have anything or anyone except Mark. If you are determined to follow through now, determined to work for the power, I will help you. This time you must not fail. They will not take lightly any more of your broken promises. Do you have any idea what angry spirits do to faithless followers?"

She settled back on her log and waited for Jenny to speak. The horror of the sabbat was still vivid in Jenny's mind. Now her thoughts were flitting back and forth between the memory of that night and Adela's words. Despair filled Jenny, and only then did she realize she was still fighting that final step.

As if guessing, Adela spoke again. "We have been very patient. You know we have the right to demand your cooperation. You used us to your purposes, tampered with our power. Now you think you can claim power with Joseph's talisman as well as your own. Jenny, have all of your lessons been for nothing? You know the spirits respond only as you approach them in the proper way. You cannot demand power; you are a weakling.

"Only those who have worked hard will be granted the powers of the universe to command as they wish. Jenny, even I have not earned that right yet. You are only a poor little sorcerer, not even a real witch. We have been patient with your silly charms and pallid potions. Jenny, it's the sabbat or nothing."

Adela stood and paced with impatient quick steps before saying, "You began all this when you chose to read your father's book. Jenny, the next step is a pact with his Highness. When the new moon comes, I will see you right here."

Jenny covered her face with her hands. *Only two weeks are left before the new moon,* she thought. Jenny was flooded with the memories—wishing for another chance with Adela. Then she saw a picture of the silver chalice, surrounded by the heavy scent of fresh blood. Jenny slipped from the log. Only when her face felt the freshness of forest fern did she realize she had fainted.

The afternoon was far spent now, but Jenny continued to sit numbly until the cool breeze and the musty dampness forced her to her feet. With a sigh she stooped to pick up the Mormon books she had brought to read. Then suddenly caught by a new thought, she stared at them.

Both Tom and Andy had been filling her with glorious reports of power and mystery. Even before the dedication, there had been stories of visions and prophecies. Maybe the church was the way to gain the power she needed without going through the sabbat! Maybe Joseph knew the secrets, after all!

Carefully she knelt beside the log and tipped open the first book. Before she began to read, she recalled her past amusement and disbelief. But that was in the past. Trembling, eager now, her eyes skimmed the pages, searching for the secret of power, the kind of power Joseph had. And Adela. Surely that had been Adela in the office. She must be searching for power in the church, too.

When it was dark and she could no longer see the page

before her, she sighed, stood up, and gathered her books.

Sally met her at the Morgans' back door. "Where have you been?" she cried. "We've been frantic."

Strangely detached, as if she no longer lived in her own body, Jenny eyed Sally's perturbed face. "Why do you carry on so? You act as fearful as if ghosts and goblins inhabited the woods." Sally's concern faded and questions grew in her eyes.

Feeling as dry and lifeless as Joseph's mummies, she prepared for bed. Only briefly did she wonder how Adela knew about everything, including Mark.

A week passed and a second was rapidly drawing to a close. One night Jenny stood at her window, looking down over the pale gleam of Kirtland, deeply conscious of the energy forces moving toward that time of the new moon. All nature seemed astir with the power. Night creatures rustled in the grasses. Far in the distance a wolf lifted his voice in a howl of desperation.

A brooding melancholy wrapped about Jenny. In one clear moment of illumination she saw her world's true state—without hope or comfort. "Powerless," she murmured into the night.

The moon was rising, and its heavy form seemed liquid and full of energy. Her eyes widened as she watched it; pulsing energy seemed to emanate from it. With a shiver she moved restlessly, but found herself unable to leave the window. Was moon energy surrounding her, holding her fast, striking off the minutes that remained? Had it staked a claim on her that she couldn't deny?

"Luna," she whispered, "every woman's friend—" Suddenly Adela's dark face and penetrating eyes seemed to sweep between Jenny and the moon.

The horror of the sabbat rose to overwhelm her. She pressed her hands over her eyes. "I can't, I just can't face that again." Even as she murmured the words, she shivered and wrapped her arms about herself, pressing Joseph's talisman between her breasts.

Slowly she dropped her arms and stared out into the night, now silent, cold, and powerless, as clouds slid over the moon. "It's an omen," she whispered. Her fingers reached to touch the metal disk, warm with the heat of her body. "It is an omen. God is telling me to escape Adela's terrible plan to force me to sell myself to Satan. Only with Joseph is there hope. Just like those men in the temple, I will have power. But there's another confirmation—Adela's secret. She's searching for more power, too, and she's doing it through joining Joseph's church."

CHAPTER 27

The door to Joseph's office stood open. Jenny, standing at the foot of the stairs, cocked her head and listened. The press was still and Oliver didn't seem to be around. Quickly and lightly she ran up the stairs.

Joseph's chair was tipped against the wall, his feet cushioned on the books and papers spread across his desk. His eyes were closed, and a wide grin covered his face. For a moment Jenny froze, unable to move. Unexpectedly her heart was pounding painfully hard, and it wasn't from the run up the stairs.

Dismayed, she recognized herself a captive of her own emotions. She trembled with the need to rush into his arms, to press her lips against that silly grin and bright hair.

Chewing her lip, she waited for her heart to slow. Once again she must face the questions that had been tearing her apart. Was there power to be had in the church, or was the idea a trick to force her to surrender that dearest dream?

She studied the face that was becoming as familiar as her own. For a fleeting moment, she wondered if the desire she possessed in reality possessed her. But she shrugged off the idea and clenched her fists. Power—it must be hers! Still she hesitated, poised to fly away from the resolution which had brought her here.

Could she trust this new promise of power through the church? The echo of Tom's entreaty to join the church thrust her into the room. She took one step, determining that if he did not hear her, it was to be an omen against joining the church.

Joseph's eyes popped open while chair and feet struck the floor. He recovered his composure, but papers and books slid to the floor at Jenny's feet.

She dropped to her knees to pick them up and he was beside her, his face nearly touching hers. His blue eyes were teasing, tempting. She rocked back on her heels and picked up a black leather book. "Holy Bible," she read, and looking up said, "My mother had one of these."

"Did you read it?"

"No. I was too busy sneaking my father's grimoire." She saw instantly that she needn't explain that a grimoire was a book of magic. He was grinning and shaking his head.

"And now you have so much power you are bringing my talisman back?"

"No, I've come to join the church." She watched the grin disappear. "You don't act too eager to have me."

He stood and walked back to his chair. "Tell me, Jenny, why do you wish to join?"

"Does it matter?" His eyes seemed to bore into hers, measuring, weighing. She knew hers were answering, but she didn't know what their promise was. Now his expression brightened, and she guessed he was pleased about something.

He chuckled. "So Jenny wants to be part of Zion's children. Tell me, was it the promises and the glory of the temple, or is it the enticement of some young man?"

"Of course it was the temple dedication," she answered lightly. From his expression she decided that he was encouraged. But she also knew there was an element in his expression that she couldn't fathom.

"Very well," he said, getting to his feet. "I'll put you on the roll right away."

"What do I have to do?" she asked in a playfully mocking tone. She saw the Bible. "Do you expect me to read that since I've not yet made it through the *Book of Mormon*?"

"No, that won't be necessary. You've only to be baptized at the first suitable time."

"Oh, don't trouble yourself," she said hastily. "I was baptized when I joined the Presbyterian church."

He shook his head, still slightly smiling. "Jenny, you don't understand. If you had bothered to read the *Book of Commandments*, you would have discovered the Lord's instruction."

"What do you mean?"

Picking up a book he began reading to her. "Revelation number twenty-three. The Lord has caused all past covenants to be done away, and even though you've been baptized a hundred times, it's worthless in this dispensation. Because of man's dead works, God needed to perform this new work. There's no other way, Jenny. This is the new and everlasting covenant. You must be baptized in the Church of the Latter-day Saints."

"Oh, all right; I suppose I'll survive another dipping." She turned impatiently toward the door.

"That isn't all, Jenny—" She turned back and saw his outstretched hand. "The talisman, Jenny. Give me the talisman."

She nearly walked out, but at that dark moment, the horror of the sabbat swept over her again and she felt those cold fingers clutching, demanding satisfaction. Still, she hesitated a long moment.

Slowly the rigid expression on Joseph's face gave way to a smile of satisfaction. With a sigh of resignation she said, "You must turn your back."

When she handed him the talisman, still warm from her body, he smiled. "Warm and sweet, like Jenny. That is a promise, isn't it?"

"I don't know what you mean," she said coolly. "I intend to be a good church member. I want all the—" She caught herself before she said *power*.

"My dear, I promise you, the women in my church will reap all the benefits of eternity, providing they are willing to follow the ordinances of the gospel."

Jenny walked slowly home, full of misgivings. She had gone expecting to come away victor, triumphant with the step which would release her into the realm of new power. Now she was feeling very much like the loser. The expression on Joseph's face stayed with her.

Briefly she thought of Emma and wondered how she was going to fit this new situation into her resolve to be the only

Mrs. Smith. Would that most desperate measure, the waxen image, have to be utilized?

Jenny went out to tell her friends that she had joined the church. With the handshakes, hugs, and kisses, she was immediately drawn into an inner circle she didn't dream existed. Within a few weeks she discovered another benefit: once again she was being deluged with requests for her nursing services.

After one such week spent taking care of a newborn and his mother, Jenny returned to the Morgans' to find Andy at the kitchen table poring over his account ledgers.

"Jenny," he said, "I'm just sitting here seeing in these figures the picture of all that lies ahead of us. I can't get over it. The Lord is preparing to bless the Saints just as He has promised. Look, last year, just over here in Buffalo, people were spending $500 for an acre of land. This year the same acre is worth $10,000."

Jenny dropped her valise on the floor and gasped. "That much! How can people possibly buy?"

"They aren't. Right here in Kirtland the price of a lot has risen from $50 to $2,000. Even the farms next to us have gone from $10 or $15 an acre to $150. Joseph thinks it behooves us to hang on to the land with all our strength. Right now, if there's buying and selling, it's done in shares and with securities or notes."

She frowned at him. "Then we actually don't have money to buy and sell."

"No, we don't. That's why I say the Lord is *preparing* to bless us. This is just the leading edge of the blessings. We must be very wise and cautious right now."

He was silent and Jenny could see his agitation. "What is it, Andy?"

Andy looked up from the ledger. "Jenny, you are one of us now. Also, you are a very intelligent woman." For a moment Jenny nearly lost his words as she considered his description of her; then she heard, "It is no secret; our Prophet doesn't manage money well. He is impulsive and good-hearted. That kind of handling the finances will get us in a fix sooner or later.

So I've been trying to get council to suggest we put Brigham Young in charge of the financial affairs, but not a man is willing to push the idea." He sighed heavily and stroked his beard. "We need to get a financial advisor or an attorney to come in and work with him."

He moved restlessly. "Trouble is, Joseph doesn't take kindly to the men under him lifting reins of responsibility. I guess I'll continue to search for a lawyer to come give me advice and work himself into Joseph's good graces."

A vision of Mark burst into Jenny's thoughts. Even as she recognized his suitability, she was recalling those last painful scenes with him. She winced and Andy saw it. "You don't agree?"

"I was thinking of a young man who seems ideal, but I was also wondering how I could avoid being involved in the situation."

Andy studied her thoughtfully, saying, "I wondered why an attractive young woman like you ignored the local swains. I understand. I'd be willing to give him a chance just for your sake, Jenny." She stared back at him, realizing explanations would only complicate matters.

He pulled a blank sheet of paper and picked up his pen. Lifting his head, he said, "Now, name and address, please."

Once alerted to the changing financial picture, Jenny began to see the events taking place in Kirtland with new eyes. Obviously the Saints were astir with the same money excitement that infused all the western United States.

Even Joseph Smith reacted to the excitement. He took to the auctioneer's block, and the Saints responded with enthusiasm. Under his hand, town lots were going from a hundred dollars to three and four thousand.

Some days Jenny joined the crowd just to feel the excitement and hear people's comments.

Emotions were riding high, and cautious ones said, "Doesn't seem proper for the Prophet to be buying and selling." The answer came back: "The prosperity of the Lord is His blessing for being a good Mormon and keeping the ordinances of the

Lord. What's more fittin' than for Joseph to help the Lord dish it out."

Jenny spent June with the Walker family. Matilda Walker had been ill with the summer fever, and it had taken all Jenny's skill with the charms and potions to nurse her back to health.

She left the Walkers with their praises ringing in her ears, but she also left exhausted, feeling as if life had been abandoned for the month's time.

As she often did after a nursing job, she stopped on her way through town to see Tom at the stables. She found him agitated and angry. "What's upsetting you?" she asked, settling herself beside the cold forge to watch him sort and clean his tools. When he raised his head she saw the tight, white line of anger around his mouth.

He continued to rattle his tools before replying. When he lifted his head again, he caught her gaze and held it. "How would you like an Indian for a sister-in-law?" She gasped and he added, "That's right. A plain old uncivilized squaw who can't even speak English."

"Tom, you're trying to shock me. If you choose to love an Indian, why, I'll accept her."

His face softened and he managed a crooked grin. "Sorry. I suppose the Lord is just trying my patience and willingness to obey the Prophet. Joseph's goin' to be sending me to Missouri right soon. And he's told me, since I'm not married, that I'm to marry an Indian when I get there. The Lord commanded that this be done. It's pleasin' to Him."

"I can't believe he intends you to just marry the first Indian you meet," Jenny soothed.

Tom snorted and flung a file to the trash heap. Looking at Jenny with a sheepish grin, Tom apologized, "I didn't mean to unload on you. It's just that some of these revelations try body and soul together. Jen, things are goin' bad in Missouri. I know Joseph is waitin' for direction before we all head west, but we can't go there until some of these troubles get solved."

"What's going on?" Jenny asked slowly.

"When the Saints were run out of Jackson County, most of them settled in Clay County, with the blessing of the residents.

But now the same tide of feelin' is sweepin' Clay County; in short, we're not welcome there anymore.

"Joseph is aware of this. Just in March, he sent men to Missouri with fourteen hundred and fifty dollars to buy land up in the northern part.

"They say the land isn't as fair as the southern part of the state, but it must do, and it's cheaper. Jenny, the people are sufferin' for want of food and clothin' as well as freedom. I fear that any day now we're goin' to hear that the Missourians have run our people out of Clay."

Jenny listened and studied Tom's face. Puzzled by his rambling explanation, she began to realize he was talking over the whole situation in an effort to understand why Joseph was pressuring him.

Tom paused in his work. "There's that revelation sayin' the Indians will be white and delightsome when they accept the gospel. Joseph's obviously tryin' to hurry things along by havin' his men marry the natives."

"But you said the Lord promised blessing if you were to do so." Jenny watched his face twist. As she pondered that expression, she realized that for the first time, Tom's whole manner revealed a skepticism he wouldn't yet admit.

When she arrived home, Sally met her. "Oh my, does Andy ever have a surprise for you!"

Jenny frowned. "I can't even begin to guess."

"Is there anyone on earth you are terribly lonesome for?"

Jenny's mind immediately flooded with thoughts of Mark Cartwright, but she restrained herself. "I wasn't aware of being lonesome, but you've made me think. Does it have to do with the name I gave Andy?"

"Oh, shy one you are! Just for that, you'll wait." She gave Jenny a quick squeeze and went to rescue her crying child.

Jenny carried her valise upstairs to her room. After settling her clothes in their proper place, she opened the window and leaned far out. Soft breezes wafted woody perfume from the trees pressing the fringes of the Morgans' property. The late June air bore the scent of every growing thing imaginable, and Jenny was overwhelmed with the need to be out of the house and among the trees.

For one moment, as she started for the stairs, she hesitated. Not since her last encounter with Adela, just before she joined the church, had she walked in the woods, nor had she again met Adela. Jenny shivered. Despite her best resolve, the memory of that one sabbat still invaded her dreams.

But the call of the woods won out and Jenny fled toward their serenity, wandering carefree and nearly happy. As the afternoon wore on, Jenny gathered mint and wildflowers as an excuse to barter time alone.

Jenny relaxed, forgetting her initial reluctance to enter the woods and the afternoon passed. In a dreamy mood she circled deeper into the trees. The sun-warmed air softened and sweetened with new smells as she walked around the moist swamplands.

Jenny didn't realize she was lost until she spied the little log cabin just beyond the marshy meadow. Stopping to study the building, she tried to guess where she was. As she peered at the cabin, the outline of a tall man was visible in the doorway. "Well, at least it is inhabited," she murmured, looking around to get her bearings.

Jenny tried to retrace her steps, but discovered the lush undergrowth hid the trail and familiar landmarks.

When frogs began their evening chorus, she turned and fled toward the cabin. She was muttering to herself, "Be grateful that Adela can't see you now. Fine witch you are! You can't even find your way home, let alone call down the powers."

The cabin was just across a marshy section, and she had to plunge through ankle-deep water to reach it. When she was nearly to the door, Joseph stepped out onto the stoop. He was pulling on his coat, and he stiffened when he saw her.

"Jenny Timmons, what are you doing here?" For a moment Jenny was surprised and distracted by the hard expression in his eyes. As she searched for words, the conviction that he suspected her of spying swept across her.

"I—I—" she stuttered and then laughed, "Oh, Joseph. I'm not trying to discover all those secret things you men are supposed to talk about when the women aren't around. I'm lost." She pointed to muddy boots. He studied her for a moment, then swung the door open.

"Come in. You'll find nothing more interesting than a quiet spot where we men have our prayer meetings." The one room was plainly furnished with a cot, a table, and a scattering of chairs. "I would offer you tea, but I have none," he said. "There's not even a fire, but you could rest for a moment before I send you on your way.

"Jenny, I have meant to talk to you. It has been a month since you joined the church. We need to have you baptized, and I haven't seen you in meeting."

"I've been nursing again," she explained, and saw his quick frown.

"That also merits some discussion," he added with a nod. "I've been hearing more about your charms and amulets and all the potions you use."

Jenny sat down on the chair Joseph indicated, accepted the towel he offered, and wiped her feet.

"It smacks a little of witchcraft," he said slowly as he continued to watch her. "But anything that keeps down the fever will be demanded by the people. I can't complain unless you go into competition with me."

She stared at him hard, trying to understand what he meant. He was beginning to relax, and the grin on his face became friendly. Abruptly he crossed the room to her chair and squatted close to her. "Jenny, tell me the real reason you wanted to join the church."

Shaking her head and looking away from him, all those visions of the sabbat filled her mind. She put the towel aside and looked up. The expression on his face was changing and his eyes glowed with a sweetness she didn't understand.

"Dear Jenny," he said. He took her hands and lifted her up. With his hands on her shoulders, he held her only inches away from him. The unexpected touch left her nearly swooning, unable to think of anything except his closeness.

Now he was saying, "You don't have to explain. I know. Jenny, I want you to realize that I understand you better than you do yourself. Do you trust me enough to follow all the directions from the Lord without question? During the next few years, the Lord will reveal many marvelous things to us." His voice dropped to a whisper as he said, "Trust me. I'll have you yet."

She was wondering whether she had heard correctly. But just as her foolish heart began its hurried, hopeful beat, his words snapped her to attention. "Jenny, one of the first responsibilities you have in your new church is to get married."

The room spun; she couldn't believe her ears. Woodenly she said, "Married? I don't want to marry, I—" She shut her hasty lips before they betrayed her. Disappointment flooded through her. His new command made her realize that his past caresses meant nothing. Her back stiffened and her chin lifted. Plainly, he was saying that those kisses had been an impulsive liberty; this was his signal that they had best be forgotten. "Joseph, church is one thing and a person's love life is another," she said frostily.

"You don't understand, Jenny. All the revelations haven't yet been written down and presented to the people, but God is making it very clear to me that it is His will for marriage to be the basis for a new and everlasting covenant in the hereafter. You see, we are not to be just human. Through His provision of exaltation, we shall become as He is right now. With kingdoms and powers, we shall possess more earths than you've ever dreamed about."

His voice deepened. "There are spirits already waiting in the spirit world. We need to provide bodies for them. That's part of our mission here and now. Together with them, we'll inhabit new worlds. Later, one of the most important teachings in the church will be about marriage. For now, the only thing you need know is that God wills you to be married."

Jenny was filled with the shock of Joseph's proclamation as he guided her to the right path and walked through the woods with her. Only when Jenny saw the lights of the Morgans' kitchen was she able to salvage her composure.

As she hurried toward the house, one word Joseph had said rang through her mind. *Power*—that word made all the difference in the world.

She forced a cheerful smile and opened the back door into the house. Mark was there. Slowly the events of the afternoon receded, like a dark stormcloud pushed by the wind. Against that backdrop, Mark was an oasis. She found herself clinging to his hand as she studied every familiar feature of his face.

It was easy to say, "Mark, it is good to see you. I'd not realized just how good it possibly could be." When she saw the flush of pleasure on his face, the wounds inflicted by the afternoon began to heal.

CHAPTER 28

During July, Sally determined to further the courtship of Mark and Jenny. At the same time Andy set out to make Mark into a financial advisor acceptable to Joseph and the first presidency. Jenny watched with amusement as the tug-of-war for Mark's attention lurched back and forth.

But Jenny had to admit, even secretly, that she had expected Mark to press his suit immediately, since it was obvious she was responsible for his being in Kirtland. To Jenny's confusion and even dismay, Mark was seldom at the Morgan residence except to consult with Andy. Even Sally's frequent dinner invitations didn't cause him to linger long in the soft summer evenings.

While Jenny was secretly troubled, Sally's annoyance boiled over one evening. After Mark and Andy escaped the house immediately after dinner, Sally shook the butcher knife she had been drying and exclaimed, "Do you have any idea of what you are getting yourself into? That Mark is not good husband material. Why I picked someone like Andy, who loves work more than wife, I'll never know. Haven't you taken lessons from the Morgan household?"

Suddenly she burst into tears, and Jenny's indulgent chuckle died away. "Oh, Sally! I'm sorry to take your problem so lightly. I didn't realize you felt this way about Andy being gone so much."

Sally blew her nose and wiped at her eyes. "It's all right," she muttered, shamefaced. "I'm angry because he carried off Mark right after dinner again."

276

Try as she might to forget the problem, Sally's words had an effect. As the days passed, Jenny's irritation over Mark's neglect developed into full-blown hurt. Jenny knew of no way around the problem, and the matter might have hung there in limbo if it hadn't been for another meeting with Joseph.

The day Tom was to leave for Missouri, Jenny had gone to the stables to bid him good-bye. Watching his gloomy face as he tightened the last pack on his horse, she said, "You know, you don't have to go. You are free to do as you wish about this whole affair, including marrying an Indian woman."

He looked at her, and she noticed the thinness of his features. "You are mistaken," he said shortly. "Joseph holds the keys of the kingdom. He is to be as God to us. Not one of us will reach heaven in the hereafter without his approval."

"Maybe heaven isn't that important," Jenny said slowly.

His hands stilled on the straps, and he looked at her in surprise. "Jenny, I don't think you have any understanding of hell. It's—"

With a half-laugh, she interrupted him, "I only fear things that go bump in the night. Besides, a good God wouldn't send people to hell."

Soberly he said, "I heard someone say God doesn't send us to hell; we send ourselves."

Later Jenny walked down the street, thinking about Tom's statement. Old Mr. Lewis was sitting in front of Whitney's store, whittling, and she stopped to watch. After more strokes with the knife, a whistle emerged from the wood. He brushed the last shaving of wood from it, put it to his lips and blew. The sound was surprisingly shrill. She watched him hand the toy to the little boy at his elbow.

Jenny thought, *It would be nice to whittle like that on my mind. I've a feeling that after stripping away the wood there'd be something completely different than I guessed.*

She continued on her way, her thoughts drifting to Mark and how she had responded to his presence in Kirtland. How strange, after months of being aware only of Joseph, she felt pulled asunder by Mark's neglect!

Suddenly Joseph was in front of her and he took her arm.

"*Miss* Jenny Timmons, still, I presume. I will have a word with you in my office." She followed him meekly and stood beside his desk as he took his place.

"I understand that you knew Mark Cartwright before he came to Kirtland. Is that true?" She nodded. "I like the man; he's honest and I think he'll make a good Mormon."

"Mark has a mind of his own; he will be hard to win to your church. You've forgotten that he was in South Bainbridge."

He ignored her statement and promptly continued. "Jenny, since you seem unable to settle on any of the lads in Kirtland, I suggest you marry young Cartwright and bring him into the church. It will be a good union, and we'll be pleased to have him as a member."

"Just like that," she snapped bitterly. "Joseph Smith, you can't order people around in this fashion!"

He was still smiling pleasantly. "Oh yes, I can. You are forgetting who you are talking to." He paused and then, holding her eyes with his own, he added slowly and deliberately, "Jenny, I am the greatest prophet ever arisen. I am as good as Jesus Christ. Don't ever forget that again. When I speak, I speak by the power of the Holy Ghost. Your place is to obey." He got to his feet.

"Remember, Jenny, joining the church was your idea, not mine. Now you are expected to obey—unless you have apostasy in mind." He remained silent for moment, waiting for her response.

Apostasy. The ultimate sin. She looked up at him, stunned by his statement. Images and word fragments piled up in her mind: the sun throwing blinding purple spears against the silver chalice filled with wine. *Jesus, the light of the world. He who has the Son has life. Baptized in death, raised to life.* But those words out of the past didn't spark her to life, not the way Joseph did. Now caught, looking deep into his eyes, she was conscious that she must please this man if she were to have faith. Faith, not power? Faith was the route to power that Lucy Harris offered her so long ago. Now Joseph, too, was speaking of faith, but the word seemed dry and dusty. Must power always give way to faith?

Now his voice was gentle. "I don't think Mark will refuse you. How could any man?" She started to leave. "Remember, urge him to join the church."

That word *apostasy* still vibrated through Jenny, and she found herself wondering why suddenly she was filled with the same dread she had seen in others at the mention of the word.

Within twenty-four hours, Mark appeared for dinner again. This time Sally waved the butcher knife at her husband, and with a laugh he tucked her hand under his arm, saying, "I shall lose my scalp if I fail to walk Sally and Tamara to the river."

When the door closed, Mark was silent. Jenny stood watching him, aware of the gulf that separated them. Now he was only a quiet, distant friend. How could she admit to him the strange yearnings she was having? How could she have taken the sweet things that had budded between them, stifle the life out of them, and then hope for a word to change it all?

Jenny moved, putting the kitchen back into order while she searched for words. Each time she passed Mark, she dropped pleasant words and received back his monosyllables.

Suddenly she circled the table and sat across from Mark. Smiling at him, she said, "Do you remember what it was like when we were snowed in?" He looked squarely at her and for just a moment, she saw the pain in his eyes before he readied the smile and opened his mouth to give a teasing reply.

Shaking her head she put out her hand to stop him. "Don't, Mark." He waited and she sighed, hunting for words. Her impatience broke through and she leaned toward him. "Mark, will you marry me?" The slender wooden spoon he held snapped and he looked at it in amazement.

She couldn't leave false impressions. "I've become a member of the church and Joseph Smith says I must marry. He says the new dispensation requires marriage to be an important part of the church."

"And you can find no other to marry you?"

She shook her head vigorously. "I *want* no other."

"What must I do?"

Of course Mark would ask that. His attorney's mind was always searching for facts. "Join the church."

"Joseph must want my services badly if he's reduced to bribing me. But I find it nearly impossible to resist the bribe."

"Nearly?" Jenny's hands were trembling and she didn't know whether she felt anger or some other emotion. She got to her feet and turned away from the table. "Sally won't be happy about the broken spoon. It was her favorite."

"Jenny, come here." When she turned he was standing and all that teasing laughter had disappeared from his eyes. She came, shyly. His strong warm hand lifted her chin and caressed it as he looked into her eyes. Gently his lips touched hers, he waited for her response before wrapping his arms about her.

When he raised his head, he clasped her face between his two warm hands. "I knew it; I was so sure," he murmured, kissing her again. She was reaching too, straining toward his lips, his arms.

Finally she remembered to ask. Loathe to leave his arms, she leaned back to see his face. "What did you know?"

"That you love me." His fingers explored the contour of her face. Just before he kissed her eyelids, she saw the expression in his eyes.

She was trembling as she pressed her face against his shoulder. *This was Mark revealed, not minding that she saw the tears. This was her Mark, that splendid gentleman acting as if she had just crowned him king.*

His voice was husky. "I'd join every church in America if it would bring me you."

He held her close. In the moment of silence Jenny began to feel the impact of her hasty proposal. He raised his face and said, "There's one thing. My mother lives only a day's journey from here, but she is unable to travel. I want her to meet you now and witness our marriage. Will you come home with me to the family farm to be married? And soon?"

Startled, Jenny leaned back to study his face. Was he fearful even now? There was a shadow in his eyes, dark but quickly fleeing. Was he remembering her long-ago statement, the time just before she left Cobleskill when she had told Mark she didn't know what love was?

He stirred uncomfortably and quickly Jenny replied, "Yes,

of course I'll come." The dark shadow was gone as tenderness and joy lighted his face. Hot tears burned Jenny's eyes. Even as his hand touched hers again and she was filled with the desire to run into his arms, she began to tremble over the irrevocable step she had taken.

Jenny was painfully conscious that the old dream still existed, the one that had sent her fleeing from Mark. "Mark," she whispered, "what am I doing to you? You are the best friend I've ever had. You deserve so much more than—than *Jenny, the kit*—"

His hand covered her mouth. "You'll not say that again." She could see his command was delivered with love, and fresh guilt swept over her. She sighed, recalling the conclusion she had reached as the stagecoach had sped down the road toward Kirtland, Ohio: If she loved Mark, then she loved two men.

Briefly she closed her eyes against the pain, and then she remembered Joseph's statement. She was marrying Mark because Joseph commanded it. The cold facts surrounding that final scene in the cabin with Joseph had stripped away any possibility of that old dream coming true. That dream was in ashes. Once again she was filled with the sure knowledge that she must do as Joseph commanded.

Jenny felt Mark's hand against her face, and once again she opened her eyes to see the love in his eyes. She reminded herself of how much this was meaning to Mark. She was *his* dream come true.

She brushed away the guilty knowledge that she was cheating him, offering only a fragmented love. As she hesitated before lifting her face for his kisses, once again she wondered why his touch left her trembling and yearning.

In the short week before Jenny and Mark left for Cleveland, they searched for a house for just the two of them and made arrangement to have furniture delivered. There were still times when Jenny felt as if she were walking in an impossible dream world. But their whispered plans became reality when she stepped into the house in which *she* was to be mistress. When she handled the new flower-sprigged china and smoothed the linens; when she shifted Mark's new chair nearer the kitchen stove, she reminded herself she soon would be this man's wife.

Then there came the day when the guilt dissolved. It happened unexpectedly when Mark pressed her hand against his face and kissed the palm of her hand. Those dark, shadowy dreams of Joseph had not become reality, and she was grateful.

Book Two in THE STARLIGHT TRILOGY, *Star Light, Star Bright,* continues Jenny's search for truth.

BIBLIOGRAPHIC NOTE

For the serious student of history, several books merits consideration for their value in providing a more complete historical picture of Joseph Smith's life. Fawn M. Brodie's book, *No Man Knows My History*, an Alfred A. Knopf publication, is an important biography. Jerald and Sandra Tanner of the Utah Lighthouse Ministry, P.O. Box 1884, Salt Lake City, Utah, 84110 have a large number of publications which are photocopies of original Mormon books, ranging from those written by Joseph Smith and his family to books written by his contemporaries. The Tanner's book, *The Changing World of Mormonism*, Moody Press, gives a broad overview of Mormonism. Early Mormon sermons can be found in *The Journal of Discourses*, a twenty-six volume work found in large university and college libraries. A two-volume set, *Joseph Smith Begins His Work*, is available through the Deseret Book Stores. These books contain the 1830 editions of the *Book of Mormon*, the *Book of Commandments*, *Doctrine and Covenants*, as well as other writings by Joseph Smith. These original works are particularly valuable because of changes made in later editions.